Something
in the
Water

BEN STARLING

EDINGTON
PRESS

Edington Press

ISBN: 978-0-9565812-2-8

www.ben-starling.com

For Melisa

1966 ~ 2012

CHAPTER ONE

New York, September, 2013

He didn't look like the hotel guests, the business people, or the tourists. He didn't move like them either.

He brushed past me as I climbed off my Vespa, stilettos in hand, outside the entrance of the Waldorf Astoria. Had he smiled at the radiance of my scarlet ball gown? Or was he amused by my battered Converse sneakers?

As a valet approached to take my scooter and helmet, I spotted my boss, Malcolm, waving hello from the lobby. He was approaching the glass doors that separated us when I noticed a small wooden box on the ground. Two steps later, I had picked it up. Who could have dropped it?

No one was close by, so I turned. The only man who'd passed me was already a half block away, gliding beside the cars that waited for the lights to change at the end of the block. Was it his?

What I knew for sure was that now wasn't the time to be tracking down the little box's owner. I should hand it in to reception and concentrate on the evening ahead. For a few seconds I relaxed as I studied the hotel's confident, soaring opulence—a world unknown to me before my arrival from Nantucket four years ago. The smooth texture of the box, however, drew my thoughts back to it. Was there something valuable inside? What if it *did* belong to that man, and he never returned to collect it? I turned the box over—and caught my breath.

"How on earth…?"

Malcolm emerged in front of me. "Hello, darling, you look absolutely—are you okay?"

I thrust my sparkly evening shoes into his hands and hitched up my shawl. I was about to give chase when a convertible Ferrari lurched to a stop beside me.

"Going my way, babe?" its driver shouted, over the thrum of the engine.

But my dress was redder and I got the better start.

The Ferrari leapt forward and the driver middle-fingered a BMW, triggering a duel of blasting horns that ricocheted around the street. I was sprinting now, with Grandma's trusty evening bag bouncing under my shoulder. I weaved between the oncoming gowns and dark tuxedos that ambled toward the hotel's art deco entrance, a stride…two strides…three strides ahead of the Ferrari, with my scarlet shawl streaming behind. Surprised glances. Someone called, "Teal Douglas?"

"Sorry—can't stop!" I answered, without turning.

The man I was chasing didn't seem to be hurrying; *preoccupied* was the word that sprung to mind. But he certainly covered the ground quickly, without apparent effort.

He slipped around the corner onto East 50th Street. The traffic was building and I could see the evening throng thickening, bolstered by more guests heading my way.

Out of sight now, there was a real danger I'd lose him. Then I realized what a fool I'd look if I caught him and the box wasn't his! So I glanced at it again, at the scratched writing on its underside. Yes. I hadn't imagined it.

Turning the corner, I side-stepped an old lady and without slowing, scanned the street. Ahead, a taxi door slammed. Was that him—in tan chinos, navy dock shoes? Or had he crossed the road and disappeared? Instinct told me he was in the cab, and I went with instinct. But I mistimed a dodge and the shriek of rending fabric brought me to a sudden stop.

A blushing jogger stepped off the hem of my dress.

"Hey, Lady! Where's the fire?"

I didn't dare look—I knew the tear was bad. Then seeing the taxi ahead, I called out, "Wait! You dropped this!" with the box held high.

I looped the torn tails of my gown over my arm and rushed on. For twenty strides, the gap closed. Then a delivery van changed lanes and the cab pulled out.

Another shout and the passenger turned. Yes, it *was* him! Strange…he heard me over the roar of the traffic? Though low in the sky, the sun threw a band of light across a face with an expression that blended surprise with humor. A face I'd rather like opposite me tonight, at the Annual Musculus Media Awards dinner. But now my dress was torn, my hair messed up. I felt hot too. I mouthed *Please stop!* but, as if in slow motion, the taxi and its passenger were swept away.

Catching my breath on the street corner, I ignored the staring passersby and fiddled with the torn ends of my once beautiful dress. A window reflection confirmed the bow I'd tied wasn't bad, in fact it wasn't bad at all. Giovanni's salon masterpiece though—my plaited bun—was a disaster. By jettisoning a few hair pins, I was able to restore some symmetry.

Walking back to collect my heels from a bemused Malcolm (and my thoughts), I noticed the box fitted snugly in my palm. As my finger stroked the well-sanded surface, I ran a nail along its snug join lines. When I shook the box, something rattled; despite pulling and twisting, it refused to open. Obviously made with skill, it offered little compensation for my disheveled appearance.

Why—tonight of all nights—had I been so impulsive? But deep down I knew the answer: I was a sucker for a mystery, and this strange box with the carved writing was right up there with UFOs, the Loch Ness Monster, and relationships that actually worked.

I stopped under the iconic entrance awning beneath the gleaming sign that announced the hotel's name. I dropped the box in my bag to be inspected later, when I wasn't in such a rush. Maybe then I'd discover a pressure point, and it would spring open. Mystery solved. I'd have time to fiddle with it over dinner or after the result was announced. *The result!* I caught my breath as I wondered what awaited me in the hotel ballroom where my colleagues would be collecting, laughing, drinking and discussing...*me*.

Then I froze as people turned and stared. A Rolls Phantom had sighed up to the curb. I backed against a wall to avoid the surge of the crowd. The praying mantis concierge oozed forward, and the chauffeur skipped around to open the passenger door.

"The media magician's here," a man in a tan raincoat beside me said.

"I heard Ronny's onto the old fox—expect a bloodbath," his friend answered.

They dropped their cigarettes and stepped forward. Two dozen more paparazzi jumped to camera-flashing attention. They focused on the older man in the immaculate white tux who slid from the car. Overhead lighting gleamed on patent leather shoes as he applied a three degree correction to his buttonhole rose.

"Basil, look here!"

"Give us a smile!"

"Yo, over *here*, guy!"

He continued to adjust his cuffs and smile until the camera motor drives fell silent.

He delivered a courteous, "Good evening, gentlemen." Spotting my buddy Natalie with her Nikon, he arched an eyebrow and added, "Excuse me. *Lady* and gentlemen."

A voice carried from the thicket of lenses. "Sir Basil, there's a story on the grapevine that all's not quite as it seems at Musculus. Would you care to comment?"

Sir Basil's eyes leveled on the journalist. "Ronny, isn't it? My dear fellow, my interest in grapes and, for that matter, vines is limited to First Growth Bordeaux recommendations from my wine merchants."

"But—"

"Oh, he's good!" The man beside me said.

Had I detected a quiver in Sir Basil's voice? If I had, it was gone when he added, "I'm here for an important annual event, not to give interviews. Now, if you'll excuse me...." He stepped purposefully towards the hotel's main doors.

Taking a deep breath, I darted past the pressing crowd and headed inside.

Let the fun begin.

CHAPTER TWO

If the rumors could be trusted, I was minutes away from the best moment of my life. Words like *redemption, validation* and *recognition* jostled for first place in my mind as they had most days since my story broke. But I wasn't celebrating just yet, because I always remembered what Grandma said about rumors: *Only believe the ones you start.*

I studied my champagne-fueled colleagues in the splendor of the hotel's Grand Ballroom. Two tiers of gilded balconies wrapped around the room above a stage big enough to handle a Broadway show. Four stories above the main floor's circular dinner tables, a massive cut crystal chandelier prismed light across the women's evening gowns that glowed with midnight blues, emeralds and golds. The men's somber dinner jackets countered the glinting eyes and sparkling jewels, as their bald pates shone.

A bow-wave of crisp linen preceded my untouched three chocolate soufflé (with wild strawberry drizzle) as I pushed it across the tablecloth. The chefs' lofty accomplishments were wasted on me tonight, thanks to my knotted stomach. *Relax, Teal. Our charismatic founder and chairman lives and breathes meritocracy, and he holds the deciding vote. Keep the faith. Surely, they wouldn't overlook you...*

For weeks, colleagues had been congratulating me—as if this year's Musculus Investigative Journalism award had already been announced. But with each hearty compliment, another wave of uncertainty crashed through me.

The past year had been a little crazy since I'd jumped at the chance to join the investigative team, following Greg's sudden departure on compassionate leave. As soon as I heard about the vacancy, I knew I had to apply. Some colleagues laughed, others shook their heads or even offered gloomy predictions, but the way I saw it, at long last I was going to be in a position to make a difference. And making a difference was what I'd always wanted to do.

Up until that point, my work at Musculus Media had involved profiling minor celebrities and socialites—not exactly the reason I had gone into debt to attend journalism school, done extra credit in investigative techniques and spent five years toiling for a small town Massachusetts newspaper. But the lure of The Big Apple's lights and a tip-off from a friend about a job opening had persuaded me to take the plunge for the chance to finally use my skills. A chance that somehow never quite seemed to materialize until Malcolm had volunteered me (*insisted* actually, to *his* boss in quite un-Malcolm-like tones) for the post. Malcolm the Marvelous, who had always championed me at every turn. And it came just as I was contemplating not only the next steps in my journalism career, but in my personal life as well.

This new rung in my career ladder had not been without setbacks, but I'd reappraised, regrouped and replanned, using every resource at my disposal (and a couple which, strictly speaking, weren't), to get the story. But I'd done it. And here I was in a city I'd always dreamed about, in one of the most beautiful hotels on earth, waiting to find out if all that persistence, sweat and lost sleep would be recognized.

I let the air escape gently through clenched teeth as I remembered the investment banker who'd been feeding price sensitive information to a hedge fund boss. Both had presented themselves as pillars of society. I wrote about the charities they supported (hosting fundraising events, but never putting their hands in their own pockets), and their generous donations to the same political party. It took me months to identify a link between the men, but hard work led me to an interesting discovery: They were both members of the same shady "tax efficient" investment scheme. Worth half a billion between them, how much money did these people need?

I looked around the room. Twelve hundred happy, excited, drunk colleagues, many of whom had flown in from all over the Musculus empire. The ethereal waitresses cleared the gold filigree plates and coffee (with cholesterol powdered truffles) was served. I scribbled an extra joke on the eleventh final draft of my acceptance speech that was balanced on my knees beneath the table.

I wondered if (despite what my colleagues had insisted) my story really was *that* good. Important enough to unseat last year's winner, the unctuous Simon? Well-crafted enough to prevent Deadline Donald from trumping us both on his way to a promotion and office of his own?

A lavender woman from the ninth floor walked over and dropped her hands on the back of the empty chair beside me.

"Edward's working late," I explained. "Financing deadline, contracts to sign, you know how it is..."

"Is he the boyfriend from Boston I met last year?"

I nodded.

"Sorry, dear," she said, before moving on.

"Thanks, Edward," I said under my breath. The most important event of my year, probably of my career, and I was rolling out the excuses for my partner. Again.

Next to me, Malcolm tilted the Moët, his thumb buried in the champagne bottle's concave base. He refilled my glass with a musical *May I, darling?* and a flourish. His efforts to play the sommelier may have gone unnoticed, but the unraveling of his rebellious bowtie was drawing increasingly amused glances.

"Only one glass, I think Teal, if you're planning to ride that death-trap home."

I sipped from my glass. "You're right. I'd better leave Audrey here overnight."

"How are my protégé's nerves?" he asked.

"Let me," I volunteered, as I manipulated the tie's yellow silk. "Despite having the best boss in the world, I'm not getting my hopes up, so I'm not too—"

"Nonsense, Teal, darling. It's a two horse race this year. The Star-Spangled Banner versus the Dis-united Kingdom. *Isn't it, Rob?*"

"What?" Rob asked, as the woman beside him shrieked. His hand reappeared above the table, curled around an ice cube. Pink cheeked, her cumulonimbus of curls trembled with her giggles.

"Next year you'll be up for a Pulitzer!" rasped Sammie on my left, her sixty-a-day baritone as unexpected as the first time I heard it. "As for *that* dress—hoping some flashed leg might swing it this time?"

I explained how I'd torn it chasing a guy in a taxi. I fished in my handbag.

"Well, that's one way to catch a man."

"He dropped this," I said, wooden box in hand.

"Whatever's that, darling?" Malcolm asked.

I passed it over. "There's something in it, but there must be a trick to opening it…"

Malcolm winced. "Damn! Thumb nail," he yelped. "Teal, darling, emery board? What do you make of it, Theo?" he asked.

"Locked shut. As mysterious as the Bermuda Triangle," Theo, who sat next to Sammie, observed. "Wait a minute—there's some writing. Left my glasses behind."

Sammie reached for the box. "Good lord! Why's your name carved on the bottom, Teal?"

"I was trying to find out—that's why I chased the guy."

She tried to twist off the lid.

"Darn thing!" Handing it back, she asked, "What do you think's inside? I say a gold ring."

"More likely a bullet," Theo offered. "The clue to an unsolved murder."

Malcolm was sawing away with the emery board. "That's what I adore about my team. You're all so *dramatic!* It's something a woodwork student knocked together in evening class. Too much glue. Probably his wisdom tooth."

"Anyway, I approve of showing a bit of thigh, especially at a stuffy event like this," Rob said, pulling his chair tight against his date's.

The box circled the table. Now that it was back with me, I dropped it in my evening bag.

"So, what lucky man had *you* chasing him?" Sammie asked huskily as her cheeks champagne-flushed.

"Only saw him for a second. I got the taxi number but that won't help track him down."

"Amaze me," Sammie said.

"5728 T1."

"Notice she didn't write it down. Darling, you're simply wonderful! Notice anything else?" Malcolm asked.

"Only the personalized license plate of a Ferrari. GREED E1."

"Ha! Well, if anyone can track him down, you can, Teal. God, I got hammered last year! D'you remember?" Sammie asked me, her voice infused with pride. "Keep an eye on me tonight?"

After last year's event Sammie and I'd shared a cab back to her fluffy apartment. Staggering in, I'd used her momentum to tumble her upstairs and roll her onto her bed, scattering her over-nourished cats. We'd discussed boyfriend problems until the early hours, and not for the first time she'd suggested that if things didn't improve, I should give up on men and surround myself with felines. A year later and nothing had changed. Well, I had visited the cat rescue website and found their phone number. But I hadn't dialed it yet.

"I remember losing my raffle ticket last year. Only time I've ever won anything!" I groaned. "It must have fallen out at your place, Sammie. Maybe Simba or Garfield ate it?"

"You never told me you won the company raffle!" Malcolm said.

"I came third."

"What was the prize?" asked Sammie, leaning forward.

"No idea. I guess it wasn't meant to be. But—"

"Ladies and gentleman...silence please."

With a jolt, I returned to the present. My knuckles gripped white on the bag. *Breathe, Teal. Breathe!* I glanced around at the expectant faces focused on the dais. Quiet rippled across forty tables, as indiscretions and flirtations were extinguished in its advance. I double swigged my champagne (and as no one saw—I did it again).

Above the raised podium, a vast screen flickered to life. The year's highlights scrolled past in a stream of award-winning photos. A banner proclaimed *Musculus Media* while pulsing speakers boomed Queen's *We Are The Champions*.

Our illuminated founder rose from his chair and negotiated the maze of tables, nodding here, shaking hands there, smiling everywhere. His magnified, digitally softened image followed him on screen, together with the legend's legend: *Your founder and Chairman, Sir Basil Thane.*

The room rose as one, cheering and clapping. Rob hurled his napkin in the air, and Sammie whooped. A radiant Sir Basil accepted the applause in his gleaming tux; both his hair and teeth looked two shades whiter than last year. His jacket hugged a physique that had claimed an Olympic rowing medal before flowing effortlessly over a claret cummerbund. I had to admit that the Errol Flynn mustache worked alarmingly well too.

Palms raised, I could see few signs of aging in the taut, tanned face— what was his secret—plastic surgeon or Faustian pact? This corporate icon, philanthropist and devoted family man was rumored to number world leaders and Nobel Laureates amongst his closest friends; some even claimed he was godfather to a royal prince. As winner of numerous business awards, he continued to wrong-foot the naysayers, the jealous and the merely average in an increasingly cutthroat industry and a decreasingly certain world.

"Friends…" he began and silence fell. "This has been—despite the turmoil in our sector—a memorable year for us. To each and every one of you, I humbly say…" He paused to lower his head and pyramid his hands in a silent *namaste*. "…thank you. Thank you for increasing turnover eighteen percent and profit seven. Every division's performance has improved over last year's, we now have a presence in twenty-two overseas territories, and our digital business has grown fourfold in three years. Your company, my friends, sets a standard the rest of the industry can only dream of. Please, feel free to applaud yourselves. Because you deserve it!"

Sir Basil joined in, eye-balling, pointing and thumbs-upping his section leaders. When his gaze fell upon our table, a chuckling Malcolm waved back.

"Some call me old-fashioned, but as a committed champion of ethics, I am horrified that our competitors' efforts remain mired in controversy and criminality." A sip of water and silk handkerchief dab later, he asked, "What's our motto?"

"*Instinct—Intellect—Integrity*," came the chant.

"I can't hear you!" he said, cupping his hand to his ear.

Theo sighed. "Citizen Thane can't resist showing off, can he?"

We repeated the battle cry three times, each time louder than the last, before he motioned silence. "And friends, I have exciting news. After nearly four decades as a private company, I have taken the decision to sell some Musculus equity. As seventy percent of profits are now US-generated, this will be via a New York Initial Public Offering. Our IPO is in the hands of bankers, lawyers, accountants, PR experts. What this means is that a year from now we'll be a publicly traded company. If we continue on this path of excellence, investors will be clamoring for our shares. Naturally, I will be making a suitable percentage of equity available to you, my friends, in an employee share scheme."

Cheering engulfed the room as Sir Basil solemnly bowed. When he straightened up, he was beaming again.

"It's essential we continue to garner our customers' trust. Without it, we are just another also-ran. Remember that image is everything, which is why I insist on absolute integrity from every single Musculus employee..."

His speeches were usually short, always rousing. My spy in Corporate Social Responsibility had told me to expect something new in his patter this year, right before he announced the winners.

"Helen from CSR has been brow-beating me about our employee-chosen charity scheme. Last year, of course, we supported *Action on Addiction* whose patron is The Duchess of Cambridge—or Kate Middleton, as she is known here. And I must say, that when I met her at Ascot last season, she was a perfectly lovely young—"

Lady T glared from her table by the stage. Sir Basil hurriedly shuffled his papers.

"But as many of you know, Lady T has a thing about wildlife in general and cetaceans—that's dolphins and whales—in particular. You should have seen how steamed up she was when she read that some Icelandic individual was granted permission to kill a hundred and eighty-four fin whales. And he intends selling them for luxury dog snacks in Japan! Never one so foolish as to thwart the wishes of two formidable ladies, I confirm that in a few weeks you'll all be in-boxed, inviting you to choose from a short list of wildlife charities."

Polite clapping.

The award ceremony would be next, and I gulped from my wine glass. With trembling fingers I lifted my acceptance speech, catching Sammie's eye. *Good luck,* she mouthed.

"Which brings me to the most exciting part of the evening—our annual awards—and this year we have six categories. We will begin the ceremony with Sports Journalist of the Year."

I watched in silence, feeding off the room's heady electricity. When the winner was announced, cheering erupted from a distant table. But my thoughts unwillingly wandered to my mother—and how often she'd told me my sporting successes had counted for nothing.

Rob drifted a question across the table. "Who do you think will win Foreign Affairs this year?"

I missed my colleagues' answers as I scanned my speech one last time. Now Sir Basil was announcing the *New Journalist of the Year* award. With a shriek, its leonine winner leapt up. Sammie waved and shouted. "You rock, Kenny!"

"Now we come to my personal favorite, as I began my career in this field: the Investigative Journalism award. Remember, this carries with it a $10,000 prize, which I will personally match with a donation to our first employee-chosen charity."

When the applause had abated, Devonte, the Will Smith clone from HR, stepped forward and handed Sir Basil a gold envelope. I swallowed my way through a wave of nausea. Everywhere I looked, people caught my eye and whispered, *Good luck*. Malcolm squeezed my arm. What started as a smile ended in a lip bite. Real recognition for my investigative exposé— without doubt, the most difficult and rewarding job of my career—rested on the contents of that envelope.

"And this year's runner up, with a superb report on patent-busting in the pharmaceutical industry, is Jason Walters. Jason, where are you?"

A roar of applause as an auburn-headed man with matching vest ricocheted towards the podium.

"It's yours, Teal!" Malcolm said.

"Gottabe!" Sammie slurred.

I wiped my damp hands on my napkin. Sir Basil was speaking again, teasing the audience with each precisely enunciated word.

"Choosing this year's winner was terribly difficult. After much deliberation and a dozen recounts..." Everyone laughed. "...ladies and gentlemen, the winner of the Musculus Media Investigative Journalist of the Year Award, for the second year running, is..."

The gasp that burst from my table stopped me hearing the winner's name.

"What, *him?*"

"Simon? Again?"

"With *that* story?"

Malcolm, eyes wide, turned to face me. "Darling. This is appalling. I'm utterly disgusted. I was sure—"

I nodded quickly and forced a smile. The walls were closing in, my vision had become misty. I waited until the music started. "Will you excuse me? Er—some fresh air."

I stood up in what I hoped was an elegant way, then walked with my head held high, ignoring the stares and comments. What did I expect? A fair shot? Life wasn't like that. Not in Massachusetts. Not in New York.

Not anywhere. Tears stung my eyes but by concentrating on a fixed point ahead, I made it back to the lobby, past the nine foot tall bronze clock there and finally, outside.

Sipping cool air, my pulse pounded in my ears. Was it time to move on? Perhaps I wasn't cut out for this after all. Maybe my story hadn't been so great. *But that's not what the whole office had said over and over*, insisted a clear voice inside my head.

Go back in there, Teal. March up to the head table, look Thane in the eye and tell him that his directors are a bunch of yes-men, and management nothing but two-faced puff-egos, that the spoon-fed Simon couldn't find a story if he typed "fiction" into Amazon...

"Teal? Teal Douglas?"

"Yes?" I said, jumping.

"I'm Sigvard. Sir Basil's executive assistant. He'd like you to join him at his table."

I should have told him exactly what I thought of his boss. Walked off into the night. Found a job in which—

"Ms. Douglas? Sir Basil doesn't like to be kept waiting."

CHAPTER THREE

"Champagne?" Sir Basil Thane said, indicating a perspiring green bottle poking from the ice bucket at his elbow. "This is a Californian Domaine Chandon Etoile Tête de Cuvée 2003. A wonderful wine. Only a pretentious fool would buy French champagne in America."

Sympathetic creases framed alert eyes. Was this an apology? I hated to admit it, but he was even better looking, more telegenic, more distinguished, close up.

"Um, no. Thank you."

"Dance, then?" Sir Basil was already standing, his hand out.

There was no polite way to refuse. I glanced nervously at Lady T, but she was too busy sloshing bubbly into Sigvard's champagne glass to notice, so I let Sir Basil lead me onto the dance floor. The crowd parted to make space and he signaled to the string quartet. I don't know whether he'd spent hours perfecting his waltz or was a natural, but Sir Basil danced like an eel in olive oil. Others slowed to admire, which made me even more conscious of my leaden footwork. I tried to remember how to box step and quarter turn as I breathed in his pepper and citrus cologne.

"So you wrote that excellent insider-dealing story?"

"I'm glad you liked it, Sir Basil."

"Didn't read it. Sigvard handles my inbox. But I'm told you're a talented journalist and that the story was excellent. Crooked financiers, tax avoidance, dodgy political donations. Our readers lap that stuff up." His right hand windmilled in emphasis while he steered me around the dance floor with his left.

But clearly it hadn't been good enough to win his award. So why did he summon me? Why was I dancing with him? And in a ballroom stacked with staring, fawning employees?

"I hope it made a difference—"

"Of course, stories like that anger and appall us. But when we turn off the TV or computer, fold the newspaper, after the tut-tutting's stopped, we return to our unshakeable conviction in our individual moral superiority. Remember, that despite our educations, our mortgages, our two point four children, so-called civilization is little more than a veneer—"

"You're saying we're only ever three missed meals from revolution?"

"Exactly."

Surely he didn't summon me to discuss societal fragility. His views on Armageddon. Did he expect me to ask why I didn't win? Or was he gloating? One minute more and I would make my excuses.

"Look, I imagine you're a bit cheesed off about not winning. Fact of the matter is—"

"Not at all," I said calmly.

"I've got a job that needs doing and Malcolm tells me you're the right person."

"Malcolm? What did—"

My question went unfinished because something had happened to the music. It started as secondary pulses and built towards a different, more insistent tempo. There weren't really any notes, just random harmonics that thrust and dissolved. I lost my rhythm. Sir Basil attempted to guide me, but with two competing tunes, I soon found myself hopelessly confused.

"What *are* they playing?" I laughed, making light of my bafflement.

"Perhaps we'd better sit."

Back at his table he ordered me a double espresso and iced water. Then he said something I didn't quite hear as the second tune faded.

Why was he staring at me like that?

"I asked if you'd ever been to the South Pacific."

Swaying palms, turquoise lagoons, golden beaches. Travel brochures and TV shows scrolled though my mind. "Well...no."

"I want you to go there, interview an old friend, Thurston Morfil. We were at Cambridge University together. Impressive guy, local Mr. Big, thoroughly good egg. In my opinion, his knighthood's well overdue. Anyway, he moved there in the eighties, set up a string of businesses around Oceania—New Zealand, Australia. I want a glowing report on him as he sits on our International Advisory Board. Positive media before the IPO. For obvious reasons. Take three weeks, all expenses paid. I'm sure you'll have a great time."

Nothing was adding up. Thane had dozens of experienced journalists at his disposal. So why put me back in the same old niche? One I'd never wanted to be in, in the first place. Right after I'd written a piece that Malcolm had gushed *redefined the investigative genre* and which should have launched my career. Sir Basil had also complimented me on my story. Sort of. It didn't make sense.

"Um—when would I go?"

"Don't know yet. He's devilish difficult to pin down, always traveling. If he's not involved in some tourist development, he's off sharing his environmental expertise with this or that UN committee. So Sigvard needs to keep on top of the situation with Thurston's PA, and you need to be ready to travel at short notice."

"Thing is," I said, building my excuse, "I'm onto a Mexican immigration scam. You won't believe what—"

"Nonsense. Do a good job and I've got a couple of other people I want you to write up. A French marquis, and a Brazilian soybean baron. Point is, I'm offering you a promotion and a generous pay rise."

Soybean baron? A guy who hacks down rainforest? "I'm very grateful. Really. But I don't get it."

"Get what?"

"I was hoping I'd proved myself capable of serious investigative journalism. But you're asking for a basic report. With respect, why *me*?"

"I thought a paid break would be welcome. I expect you're disappointed, and I like to look after my people. Impress me with this job and we'll take it from there."

"Thank you, Sir Basil. But it's not really my—"

"Let me put it another way. Life is all about choices. Sooner or later, we must all decide who we are and what we stand for. Turn my offer down and *I'll* be disappointed. Let Sigvard know. I trust I've made myself clear."

"Of course. I'll get back to you by Thursday, Sir Basil."

"Tuesday."

The almond eyes held mine. Would I be demoted, or worse, fired, if I refused? Clearly, yes. And what would Edward think? Would he come? Not unless he could combine it with some business deal—but what opportunities were there in the South Pacific? And how could doing something old prove I could really do something new?

"So, feeling any better? On the dance floor, you looked like you'd seen a ghost. Perhaps you should be heading home."

There was a finality to his words, so I agreed I felt a little drained and thanked him, before returning to my table to say my goodnights.

Malcolm intercepted me, gripping my arm and pulling me onto the chair beside him. "Do tell all, darling," he demanded.

"Not really sure—he offered me an assignment in the South Pacific."

"Smuggle me in your suitcase?" asked Sammie.

"And of course, you jumped at it?"

"Not exactly, Malcolm."

His chin settled in his palm. "Tell me you're *joking*."

When I didn't answer, he continued. "Listen, Teal. Everyone wants to work for Musculus. Like it or not, Thane's a living legend. Upset him, get fired...you'll spend the rest of your life writing parrot obituaries in Smallsville."

"Malcolm, Sir Basil said you recommended me. What's going on?"

"Dunno. Cross my heart and hope to die. He asked me last week who my best journalist was. I thought it was to do with the award."

"Well, thanks for saying me...but I still don't—"

"You *must* go, darling."

"I have till Tuesday to—"

"March right back there and accept. Before he changes his mind," said Sammie.

"She's right, darling. I've worked here long enough to know there are things going on that are beyond the comprehension of us mere mortals. If Basil wants you to climb Everest, you get Sherpa Tenzing on Skype."

I ate the last truffle slowly, employing my *Don't disturb, I'm thinking* expression as I wondered if I was over-reacting. It didn't work.

"By the way—your dancing, darling. What was *that* all about?" asked Malcolm.

"I couldn't help it. Why was the band playing two tunes at once?"

"I didn't hear—" Sammie began.

"Yes, the waltz and..."

A look passed between them.

"Didn't you hear it? It was loud!" I insisted.

"Teal," Malcolm said. "I think you glugged a little too much shampoo! I'll get you a cab."

Alone in the taxi, I went over it all again. I hadn't won the award. When I was about to tell our chairman (well, thinking about telling our chairman) what I thought of his company, he had offered me a raise and an assignment that made no sense. And why had the band played a second tune that everyone pretended not to hear?

I pulled out my compact and checked my face in the mirror. A little anxious perhaps, but nothing new there. I gazed at the roof of the taxi, imagining the vastness of the night sky. For a moment, I was holding my grandmother's hand as we scuffed the sand and brushed through the long grass on the Sconset dunes, while the surf gushed back and forth. Dear Lizzie. Who I'd never see again. My fingers stroked the beading on the evening bag.

I've never asked before but...please help, Grandma. I don't know what to do.

I replaced the compact and was closing the bag when something caught my eye. Neatly folded on top of the wooden box lay a piece of yellow paper. I lifted it, though I already knew what it was.

So how on earth did *this* get here? I'd emptied the bag twice, checked every pocket. Not trapped in a crease in the lining or buried under something but *on top of that strange box?*

I unfolded it. The words were printed in bold. "Musculus Media Raffle." Beneath, it stated that first prize was a mixed case of Chilean wine. Second prize, six month's super-fast Musculus broadband.

After reading the third prize, I looked out of the window. The city's urgent nightlife slid by as clusters of revelers rolled to the next bar. I found myself staring at a couple melded in a kiss, her long legs perched atop improbable heels, his fingers caressing. The hollow pang I felt was interrupted by a man beside them barking into a phone, who was oblivious to the upturned hat in front of a crumpled doorway figure.

I sighed. After a pause I read my prize again.

"Are you serious, Grandma? You want me to do a *tarot* reading?"

CHAPTER FOUR

Tomorrow was the Tuesday deadline to decide on the South Pacific assignment and, apart from the jaw-dropping surprise that my almost-but-not-quite fiancé Edward had shown some interest, I was no nearer a decision. I had consulted friends about tarot (mixed feedback), the trip (unanimous approval) and I'd reserved a table for tonight at a promising restaurant where I could discuss the proposed assignment with Edward.

He had asked a few questions about the wildlife, local politics, who I would be interviewing, and said he'd let me know his decision over dinner. He'd also said he would research some of the local resorts, which probably meant he'd pick ritzy ones that would cost a bundle. I checked my watch. Edward—*Bear*—was late again, no doubt chasing another deal.

I leaned back against the headboard of our bed, my mind wandering to the last real conversation I'd had with Grandma. Staring over my shoulder at the frothing surf, she'd described how, in unguarded moments, the ocean had "sung" to her. I fingered the ripples of my bedspread, remembering her description of erratic harmonies that drifted in on a flood tide. Sometimes she'd heard it in her seafront cottage, above the cry of the gulls on those condensingly hot nights. When I'd asked her who the singer was, she'd said perhaps "singing" wasn't quite the right word and had fallen silent.

Last night I'd woken with a jolt and sat up in bed, scanning the inky room. I'd dreamed I was at a classical concert in a huge auditorium that contained only a handful of people. The music was unfamiliar, haunting...erratic.

The strange thing was, as I rubbed my eyes, the music had continued for another half minute before fading into the background hum of the city. And this time it hadn't been distorted by champagne, Strauss, or a hundred conversations.

"Grandma, what does it all mean?" I asked.

Now I was pushing thirty and seven hour drive from home. On my last visit in January, I'd watched them bury Grandma in the iron ground of Nantucket's Prospect Hill cemetery.

Three numbered envelopes now lay on my lap addressed to me in her distinctive writing. They had arrived from the family lawyer this morning and were bound with a powder blue ribbon. Her lucky ring and a battered wallet still lay in the bottom of the packet. The lawyer's covering letter explained they'd all been found in a padded envelope, on the writing desk in her cottage.

It also explained she'd left me an oil painting—a seascape—which they were arranging to have shipped.

On a seaside postcard tucked inside the package, in her Copperplate hand was written:

Dearest, open the first letter when you hear the ocean music we listened for and please remember, you can never unread a letter.

Love you always, Grandma xox

The old wallet looked ordinary enough, though the curiously-textured leather felt unusually soft. The note inside the wallet read:

This was handed down through several generations and ended up with my beloved Bernard. Half a mind to throw it out as I always found it a bit creepy, but you may find a use for this strange family heirloom.

The ring was rather more appealing, with *To E with love & luck,* B engraved inside the gold band. "The ring you never took off Lizzie," I whispered, slipping it on to find it fitted perfectly. "I need some of that luck now, Grandma."

Thinking of Lizzie always lifted my spirits and I smiled, remembering the cooking lessons (flour in hair, food on floor), hikes (backpacks and blisters) and giggling when we taught her Great Dane, Dooby Scoo, to balance doggy treats on his nose. Then off to bed for stories with plots that unraveled in emerald studded palaces, Renaissance art galleries, or aboard steam-puff ocean liners. But they always began the same way: *Once there was a beautiful, dark-haired princess called Teal...*

I untied the ribbon and lifted the first letter, a tear plipping on the envelope. A waft of rose water brushed past me, taking me back to the funeral, to a day of blown snow and of whispered, cracked voices. There were hugs from strangers, uncertain handshakes from frail, bow-legged men and kisses from veiled old ladies. I smiled as relatives I'd never met, described cousins I'd never meet—then Uncle Felix got drunk, and his nurse gave him a shot.

One of my earliest memories was Grandma inventing a game that involved burying signs in her stories. A treasure map might be hidden in a cat's fur or a symbol reversed in a mirror. Everything, she explained, had meaning and I must learn to notice the important signs—and those were the ones which could be the best hidden. My challenge was to spot the sign and shout, "There it is, Grandma!" At first, I'd see unintended significance in open windows, boiling kettles and men's tilted hats. But eventually, Lizzie would smile and tell me I was improving.

There were so many stories, but today I couldn't recall how a single one ended because they had meandered on until I fell asleep. Looking back, I wondered whether that was the point: Maybe when you noticed things and acted on them, the endings would take care of themselves. *Is that how life works, Lizzie?*

But all I'd noticed this evening was my Bear-sized headache. I took two Tylenol and could almost feel Grandma's arms encircling me again, the warmth of her love. The phone broke the spell.

"You don't have to tell me…you're working late."

"Another half hour at the most."

"I'm sure The Blue Beluga will keep the table. I'll phone…could you bring the hotel info so we can—"

"Teal, I haven't decided your answer yet."

"But couldn't—" But the line had already gone dead.

On the plus side, he hadn't closed the door yet on coming with me to the South Pacific. If we went, would he remember why we'd started dating three years ago? I'd do my report on Thurston Morfil and between times, we could try to save our relationship. Not a great plan, but it was the only one I had.

I opened my trusty evening bag and lifted the yellow paper from the zipped compartment.

Curly gold script informed me that the tarot reading was by someone called *The Amazing Anastasia*. I read aloud, half hoping the prize would change into a box of chocolates. Grandma used to say that life could turn on a chance encounter, on a casual remark, even on a phone call. And right now, I wouldn't mind a little turning in my life. Or even a chance encounter.

But seriously, who calls herself 'The Amazing Anastasia'? Oh well. Here goes nothing. I took a deep breath and punched in the phone number.

The "Hello?" arrived a second before the coughing.

A husky voice shouted, "That you, Ron? Where the hell—"

"Anastasia?"

There was a pause. "Yes. Can I help?"

"I've got an old raffle prize—something called a *Telephone Tarot Reading*. Will you still accept it?"

"What's the reference number? I'll need to look it up in the green book." A drawer slammed, pages turned, more coughing.

I felt a little ashamed, disappointed even, that it wasn't an impressive, multi-digit number prefixed with a letter or two. "It's...four."

"That's a pre-paid, and it's expired."

"Well, don't worry I'll—"

"You're not from Brooklyn, are you?"

"No, Nantucket."

"Wherever that is. What's your name, sweetheart?"

"Teal."

"Never heard that one before. Some kind of flower, is it?"

"No, it's a type of bird."

When she didn't reply, I asked if she was still there.

"Sorry. I just had a queer turn.... You said a bird? A big bird was flying back and forth past my window yesterday. Ron said it was a falcon."

"A teal's a kind of duck."

"Your parents named you after a *duck?*"

"It's a color too," I said defensively. "A sort of green-blue. Same color as my—"

Coarse laughter, more coughing. "Excuse me."

I looked out the window at the sun fading in the windows of the apartment building across from me. This was taking too long. Bear liked to take all the time in the world, but if *I* was late, it was a whole different story.

She was speaking again. "Listen dear, I'm gonna do you a two card reading, okay? No charge because anyone who goes through life named after a duck needs all the help they can get."

I laughed weakly.

"Ever had a reading before?"

"No."

"Here's how it works." Pages turned. Words came with breathless, unnatural phrasing. "Tarot cards don't predict the future.... What they do is capture the subtle qualities...of the moment..."

I haven't even showered yet! What will I wear?

"...Everything you are experiencing now has been experienced by thousands...of people before you.... And all that feeling is stored in...a vast ocean...which some call the collective...unconscious. This making sense?"

With this time I could have triple-checked my interview to-do list and rung two private detectives for my new immigrant story. "Yes, a vast ocean, you said?" I tucked the phone under my ear and dragged my MacBook onto my lap.

"A two card reading helps you decide what to concentrate on now in

21

your life, and what can wait." Silence.

"Hello?" I asked. "Are you there?"

"I'm back. Just slipped into the ether to consult Spirit."

My doubts began growing about the legality of the contents of her cigarettes. Was she drinking too? Background noises, more coughing as my finger hovered over the red disconnect button, but she was back.

"The Moon and the Sun!" she announced with enthusiasm. "Those are your cards. Both are *Major Arcana*."

"Is that good?" I asked, as my mind wandered to the mouth-watering online description of The Blue Beluga's seafood platter.

"The Moon card is about confusion, change and doubt. You are a prisoner of your unconscious, and you feel helpless. But you mustn't let go of your dreams. Does that make sense?"

A crisp Californian Sauvignon Blanc would make a lot more sense right now...and complement the mussels, crab, smoked fish....

"What? Oh yes, I understand."

"And the Sun...now that's a nice card. Things are going to get clearer. You'll be able to plan for the future, because the light of the sun will dispel the darkness of the moon. What did you say your name was?"

"Teal," I said, louder than I meant to. I highlighted a sentence in my notes and added three exclamation marks.

"Things will start changing soon, Teal. But you mustn't fight it. Does that make sense?"

"I think so," I lied.

"I'll be.... There it is again!"

"What?"

"That brown bird. Flew past, it did. Do big birds mean anything to you?"

"In what way? I don't know anything about birds."

"Right by the window it was. Well, keep your eyes open."

"Um, right. So, thank you very much…. I must go."

"Wait! Someone's coming through."

"Coming through?"

A door slammed. Then shouting. "Ron, how many times have I.... You still there, Teal? Someone came through, but they're gone now. All I got was a name and something about travel."

"I'm sorry, I don't follow."

"Came through the ether. From the other side. And she said you *must* take that trip."

Then The Amazing Anastasia asked in a clear steady voice, "Teal...who is Lizzie?"

My voice caught as I said goodbye. The room felt tight, warm.

The bird—that meant nothing, of course. And the travel—I bet she used that line on everyone. *But how on earth...?*

"Grandma, you're scaring me," I said.

The instructions said to read the letter when I'd heard the music. I ran my finger back and forth along the flap. In my mind, the letter had become a Pandora's Box, crammed with a million secrets. What would escape when I opened it?

Had I really heard the music? As I hesitated, I felt like every single thing Grandma Lizzie had taught me was about to be put to the test.

I took a deep breath and worked the knife inside the envelope marked *Letter One*.

My very dearest Teal,

    Just back from my ladies' doubles game—would you believe I haven't missed one in forty-two years? But my neck is sore and I think this gal's getting a bit old to be chasing balls all over the court. There's a hot new coach called Anton and you know what he said? There are two shots I play as well as anyone he's ever seen: the double fault and the unforced error! Isn't that fabulous? The others have all booked private lessons with him, but I think it's time to hang up my racket and find something a little gentler to do, even though seventy-six isn't much of an age. I'll come back to that because I can't wait to tell you about my cute chocolate pug rescue called Titan and a chinchilla with a missing foot that Sally B dropped off (that brings my furry guest total to fourteen!). Any idea what I should call him? He's gray and film star handsome!

    Remember the rainy afternoons we'd sit eating popcorn in Silent Henry's movie theater, laughing at a Hepburn film—how many times did we see Roman Holiday*? Well, after he closed it because of that bat problem, his daughter Carmilla—who wants to be a vet (!)—now comes in every morning to help. She's full of energy and wonder (though she won't go near Monty's cage). In fact, she reminds me of you when you were sixteen!*

    Re-reading those two paragraphs reminds me why I'm writing. See how easy it is to get wrapped up in one's own thoughts? That's no excuse for forgetting to say things to those we really love, because suddenly it might be too late. So I'm writing you one of my world famous 'Lizzie's Letters to Live by'!

    The important thing, dear, is you heard the music too. I was certain that one day you would, and in my own way, I've tried to prepare you for this moment. A moment that's both exciting and a little scary.

    Your mother never shared our wonderful bond, God rest her soul. Heaven knows I've cried myself to sleep wondering why that was, as I *brought her up the very best way I could. The truth is, you always had the most beautiful smile and enchanting laugh. What happened to dear, dear Carly wasn't your fault and you must <u>never</u> blame yourself. Ever. I know you loved your sister deeply. I pray soon all this will make sense and you'll be able to forgive your mother for blaming you and one day, whether I'm still in the land of the living, teaching Judo on a fluffy cloud or in a bubbling cauldron, I'll hear you laugh again!*

I've always tried to live my life by the "Do unto others as you would have them do unto you" maxim. But when I think about the ocean music, it fills me with melancholy and I'm left thinking I've offended and/or harmed someone, but I just can't figure out who it is. About the only other clue I have happened that weekend you stayed with me after your twenty-first. You'd gone to bed and I was doing a little beach yoga. Don't think me mad, but the feeling I got that time was about love—love being close by—so I sat on the sand every evening till winter, feeling sure Bernard was trying to contact me. But now I'm not so sure. It was months before I heard it again.

Maybe you have a couple of weeks you can spare and you can come visit me in Scrimshaw Cottage? Then we can put your great brain to work—get to the bottom of this mystery. No pressure dearest—just an idea.

When I told Doctor Cold-Finger about the music, he wanted to put me on something with a difficult name and long list of side effects. Time for a new doctor, I decided. Never told anyone about it again. No one, that is, except you.

Another thing, dearest: I worry that you never really speak about Edward in your letters. Well, men can be tricky and I spent years learning to live with your grandfather, but deep down he was a good man and easy to love. If only they'd monitored his blood pressure, like they do these days. His smoking didn't help either.

Anyway, as I'm sure you've figured out, my storytelling was to teach you to watch for signs. Please keep these letters close by. Here's what I want you to do: Read Letter Two as soon as you see a <u>new</u> sign. Not just any sign—but an important one. By now, you should be able to tell the difference. I think things will start to move quickly soon How do I know this? Well, it's just an inkling. But I've noticed over the years that for me these little inklings usually pan out. So please be watchful.

And always remember this, dearest: You are special and unique. They say animals can tell if a person's good—well, I haven't forgotten how Dooby would only sleep on your bed when you came to stay. I want you to know how much you enrich my life. I admit I was a little heart-broken when you moved to New York—you can probably tell from all my letters! Whatever life throws at you, don't let anyone or anything stop you believing in yourself. And dear, do wear my ring. I hope it will bring you luck—the same good luck I had with your grandfather.

Your (always) loving grandmother,

Lizzie xox

P.S. You should also know that once, in a dream, I may have seen who made the music. It's all so fantastical that I feel foolish writing about it. But I do feel that the energy that comes with the music is numinous or phantasmic...or something. Do you feel that too? Maybe Grandma's getting silly. Or she could be a genius—it's got to be one or the other!!

P.P.S. I nearly forgot—guess what? The insurance came through and I bought another kayak!! I found one on eBay for $25 and like the old one, it's a two-person kayak so there's room for both of us. What fun it will be to paddle off the beach again! Charlie Hopkins saw some abandoned seal pups around the point. Maybe I can rescue them? Do seals like cat food?

"Oh, Lizzie," I said. I could almost taste the salt on my lips, feel the heft of paddle in hand as I leaned into a stroke while she steered the kayak behind me. One more magical adventure with my grandmother that could now only exist in my mind.

The next sign? Finding the raffle prize could have been a sign. But that was in the past and she had underlined *new*. Finding a box with my name on it struck me as an obvious sign, but that was also something that happened before I had read this letter.

I replaced the letter, rebinding the envelopes with the ribbon—her favorite blue—teasing the ends and working the loops until they were perfectly symmetrical. *I wish you'd given me a specific clue, Lizzie...because I have no idea what to do next.*

Then I closed my eyes. "Grandma, forgive me for not making that last visit in time. I promise I will come and figure out the music mystery one day. But I can't come right now because I may be traveling to the other side of the planet soon. Anyway, journalist or not, I don't have the faintest idea where I'd start. Will you forgive me, please, if I leave this for now? I promise I'll get to it one day soon."

I held the letters gently, sure I could feel Grandma's energy radiating from them. I pictured her, magnifying glass in hand, her old fountain pen sweeping back and forth in the magnolia glow of her table lamp. I imagined her gazing through the window at the vastness of the ocean. Then, as if returning from a long journey, she'd sigh, and resume writing, turning every now and then to study the oil painting that hung beside her. I could see every detail of the painting now: a pair of silvery gulls, wing tips touching, gliding low above a barren seascape.

Once, when I was six or seven, I asked what she thought about when she wrote. Staring at the advancing rollers, she said she felt the ocean was staring back at her, that it was a living thing. Then she used a word I never forgot. She said the ocean was a *gestalt*—something in which the whole was greater than the sum of its parts. Seeing the confused look on my face, she hugged me and said, "I'm sure that when the time is right, you'll get the same feeling." I'd wondered then: *How could a hole be greater than anything?*

The letter was undated. I lifted it to smell her faint fragrance again. I could feel myself wrapped in her hug. I knew that in time the perfume must fade, like the sepia photo of her as a girl, which I kept by the bed. The one she said looked like me.

Thank you, Grandma. I looked at the ring. Slim, elegant; a shiny circle of eternity. And Grandfather's wallet? Old and battered, with the strangest texture I'd ever seen.

Lucky in love? *You win Lizzie—but please don't blame me for choosing Edward. I'm doing the best I can, and I know he can be difficult. With all the pressures of work, I don't have time to be working on us like I should. Given time, I'm sure we can work it out. I'm trying.*

Then I wondered where I could hide the letters. Somewhere *he'd* never look.

I jumped when the phone rang.

"I'm sorry, Bear. I'll be there soon. I—"

"Hello? This is The Blue Beluga. Is Mr. Hamilton available, please?"

"Oh, he's not here right now. Can I take a message?"

"Please would you let him know we managed to get the vintage French champagne he ordered. Combined effort between the CIA and FBI. Probably the last bottle in North America."

"Excuse me? Oh, thank you. I'll tell him." I ended the call and replaced the receiver.

"Why on earth are you ordering expensive champagne, Bear?"

CHAPTER FIVE

The *Blue Beluga*, a faux-Victorian styled pub, nestled a Tiger Woods' drive away from Washington Square Park in Greenwich Village. Renamed and remodeled six months ago, it had phoenixed into a trendy gastro eatery-drinkery after a failed insurance scam earned its former proprietor four burnt fingers and five years. As I entered, I wondered if anything would emerge from the embers of my relationship.

The cavernous ground-floor split into two rooms: one for dining, one for drinking. I sat alone on the restaurant side listening to the uproar of the jovial crowd at the bar.

Mondays were devoted to *Quiz Night*. The shouts and laughs from the contestants didn't just spill into the dining area—the noise had a malignant purpose to invade, conquer and subjugate all conversation. Its WMD was the staccato laugh of a toothpick blonde that pin-balled from wall to brain.

Local artists had populated the walls of the restaurant with erotic offerings, and the one I now felt brave enough to study (by Cindy, dog walker and babysitter—except weekends) demonstrated impressive optimism in flexibility and pricing.

The menu lay closed at my elbow because Bear had confirmed his choice earlier by phone when he'd called to say he'd be there in ten minutes. Meanwhile, I continued to nurse my glass of house white, served by the long eye-lashed, delicate-fingered Russ (saving for a ticket to visit his girlfriend in Hawaii), who was refilling my water glass.

"Everything alright, ma'am?"

"Yes," I said, meaning *no*. Bear was late. Again.

An old guide book on the Pacific islands lay open before me, and I pored over the 'nesias of Poly, Mela and Micro. The pencil, which had performed only two circles and a single underline, lay on the table. Despite the aching beauty in every photo, nothing felt...*magical*. I recalled what Grandma Lizzie used to say: A vacation isn't about where you go, but who you go with.

A shadow fell across my page and I looked up.

"I hope you don't mind, but I see you're studying the Pacific."

He wasn't from around here. Then I noticed that he smiled with his eyes—and how well that shade of blue worked with his suntan. The watch, beside an elephant hair bracelet, looked chunky—like the ones divers wear. Who was he? What was he doing in the nearly empty dining area?

"Pear Whelm's *Essential Guide to the Pacific Islands*," he said thoughtfully.

"Oh, I'm thinking of a working vacation, not sure where to stay," I fumbled.

"Been there before?"

Did he work here? "Only in my dreams."

"May I?"

A waft of gin-lemon aftershave reminded me men didn't have to smell of sweat and stale cigars. He flipped a dozen pages in contemplative deceleration. "Here we are. This little island's way off the beaten track—the last in a chain—but there's a charming resort on it. I think it's...magical."

I took the guide and saw his underline. After reading the short entry, I said, "*Horseshoe Island.* Hmm, fascinating—apparently there's a spooky legend about the place. Well, it looks remote enough. Is there internet access there?"

"Not the best, but adequate."

"Thank you, I—" But he was backing away.

"I've got to get back to my hopeless team. I'm meant to be their wildlife expert." He walked to the doorway. *Please turn!* He did, and we smiled. Then he was gone.

From the bar side of the pub, the MC's voice reached me.

"Ladies and gentlemen, if I could have your attention. Silence please! Question seven!"

Shhh-ing, laughter.

"Most of us have heard of a CDO—as created by the financial services industry. But what does it stand for? Answers on pads please. Table Two, no peeking at Table Three's answers! And...get ready for the next question."

An appalling roar silenced both rooms. "Collateralized Debt Obligation, haw, haw!"

I choked on my wine. *Oh...my...god!*

"Excuse me, sir. Are you part of the quiz? If you wouldn't mind..."

My partner's silhouette flooded the doorway. "Evening, Teal!" he bellowed. I blushed behind the menu. Bear glared at Russ. "Large gin and tonic—pronto! And tortilla chips." The floorboards flexed beneath his lumbering advance. *If I was two feet taller everyone would be happy. What I have is a height problem, haw, haw!* he said without fail every evening out with his banking buddies. *That would make you eight foot five, Bear,* I had learned to chime on cue, to foot-stomping approval.

As usual, he wore his Ivy League school tie. The full brogues had been polished to a mirrored gloss. The Tartan socks no doubt matched his boxer shorts, because they always did.

He lunged forward, dropping his briefcase beside me, planting an air kiss sort of near my ear.

"What a day! The Dragon invited me for a drink that morphed into dinner—a *tiny* dinner, Teal, *tiny*—on my way here. He's talking deals, *big* time. Carlos is onto an asset strip, and the Wharton whiz kid's developed a debt instrument we've named the *Foreclosure*, haw, haw!"

"You're an hour late," I said softly. "And who on earth is the Dragon?"

"He's got an important birthday coming up. We threw some ideas around about that too."

"Why would a man you've never met before discuss his birthday with *you?*"

"And I've booked you into a bridge class. I want you to—"

"Did you hear me?"

"Apologies, my beloved. You look nice. New dress?"

"No."

"Let's choose food. I'm famished. Waiter!"

"I thought we'd agreed on the seafood platter?"

Russ wandered back. Had his eyelashes grown even longer?

"Evening sir," he said, with a cautious flutter.

"Ms. Douglas won't have a starter. Bring me the grilled lamb chops and—"

"As an appetizer, sir?"

"Of course. And Beluga caviar with the seafood platter."

"Erm…sorry, sir, but—"

"You serve caviar, I take it?"

"We might, sir. I'm not—"

"Well, don't just stand there. Find out!"

"Right. Sure." Russ slid away to the far side of the restaurant and whispered to the man who'd spoken to me earlier, who now approached, his smooth stride a dramatic contrast to Bear's brontosaural entry. The quiz sheet was tucked under his arm, and he smiled the same crinkle-around-the-eyes smile.

"May I help, sir? I understand you'd like—"

"The kid couldn't tell me if you serve Beluga caviar."

"I'm afraid we don't."

You get to know someone pretty well after three years, and the two most alarming Bear warning signs were: the long pause and the lowered voice. Now he combined them. Which wasn't good.

"I see. So you call this place *The Blue Beluga*...but you don't serve Beluga. What about Ossetra or Sevruga?"

"There seems to be a misunderstanding—"

"Correct me if I'm wrong, but Beluga's a kind of caviar which comes from a great big fishy called a sturgeon that swims around the Black Sea avoiding nets and hooks because it doesn't want nice people like me eating its babies."

"It's fine Bear, I'm sure it will still be excellent," I said hopefully.

"Yes sir, but—"

"But *what?*" Bear growled.

"I didn't name the pub after a fish. Belugas are also a species of—"

"You *own* this place?"

The man nodded. "*Delphinapterus leucas*. They're white whales. Live in the—"

"Lamb chops to start with. T-bone steak to follow. Both rare. I take it you *have* steak?"

"Of course."

"The seafood platter for me, please," I said, in my most summery voice.

"I'm sorry madam, the seafood platter's for two."

I looked at Bear who was smirking at an email. "Bear?"

"Rare."

"I'll see what I can do about a seafood platter for one, madam."

"Oh, thank you."

"Incidentally, all our seafood is from accredited, sustainable sources. The tiger prawns—"

"Did I hear her ask for their life history?"

"Bear, you sure you don't want the seafood? I've heard it's to die for—"

"You got the 2002 French champagne?"

"The Dom Perignon's chilling, sir. I'll bring it right away."

As the man walked away, I studied Bear's face searching for a clue as to why he had ordered, not just champagne, but an expensive one.

"Special occasion?" I probed.

"Did you see the way that guy with the phony accent dressed? *Linen* jacket and *open-necked* shirt! A classy guy wears a suit and tie at all times. What? Oh. Those of us with proper careers enjoy celebrating when important doors open."

"Journalism happens to fascinate me," I said, tracing patterns with my finger in the condensation on my glass. "I'm told I'm good at it."

"There's no money in it. And it looks like you'll never win that precious award. If you were due to win, you would have by now. That's the feedback I'm getting."

"And who exactly have you been getting feedback from?"

"Sir's appetizer," Russ said, leaning over.

Bear tucked his napkin into his shirt collar. "Got any mint sauce?" he shouted to the departing Russ, as he lifted a chop.

"That's the word on the street."

"Feedback? And what street have you been walking on?"

Instead of answering, he grunted.

"Bear?"

He pushed his plate away and lifted his phone. He sent some emails and made a call, ending it with, "You won't regret it, sir. I pride myself on being a great facilitator. May I call you 'Dan'?" He frowned. "I'm sorry Mr. Dragan. Enjoy your evening." He lowered the phone and looked at me. "You know who that was?"

"Let me take a wild guess. Dan Dragan? The Dragon, no doubt, to his friends."

"Indeed it was! The Dragon of Wall Street."

"Never heard of him."

"You serious? He's the twelfth richest man in the world."

"Please turn off your phone."

"Can you guess what his hobby is?"

"He collects impressionist art?"

"Apart from that."

"Races yellow submarines."

"Now you're being childish. He's a big game hunter. Flies to Africa, India, wherever, several times a year in his Boeing 757. Shoots gorillas, rhinos, lions, elephants—"

"Aren't they protected?"

"They're stuffed—he calls his Texas ranch his *trophy cabinet!* Complains he's running out of space there. Haw, haw, isn't that wonderful?"

I glared at the iPhone by his elbow.

"When you own a hotel chain, an airline, chunks of Vegas and Manhattan, three steel works, the largest waste disposal company in the world and a weapons company, you don't expect to go to voicemail."

"Your hero's an arms dealer? Seriously?"

"Pay attention, Teal. He's an arms *manufacturer.* He's developing something special for Shayetet 13—the Israeli equivalent of our Navy Seals. Their super-elite commando unit. Revolutionary diver's multi-barreled speargun with exploding shells. All super hush-hush. Sounds like a lot more fun than the weapons I used in my army days."

"The frying pan and chopping board?"

"Hardy har. I was in logistics, not catering."

"I bet you told him you were a weapons expert who could—"

"Knowing him, he's probably developing body armor to sell to the Palestinians, haw, haw!"

"If it's so secret, why's he telling *you*? And why are you telling me?"

"Explaining why I was late, that's all."

"So you're working with him on this?"

"No, of course not. Just keeping him sweet. But you never know…"

Then he smiled, though it wasn't the same smile he had aimed at me from forty feet away in a sleek Soho bar in 2010, two days after Super Bowl.

Looking back, it must have been a meticulously planned campaign. And it ended that brumous day with my hesitant capitulation in his penthouse apartment. "Trust me, I know this city's weather and it won't rain!" he'd promised as we set off without umbrellas. Surrounded by dripping clothes, the squall had looked almost friendly through the smoked glass bedroom window. After three dry martinis, he had too.

And Mom had been unexpectedly enthusiastic when I'd phoned to say I'd met someone promising. When she'd learned he was a financier from Boston who drank Manhattans in Manhattan, she'd even chuckled. She'd reminded me that due to my career ambitions, there were no other takers, and she'd run up my phone bill with a lecture about an older man being exactly what I needed. The ten year gap did make him seem sophisticated at the time. But deep down, I'd had the awful feeling she approved because she wanted me to stay out of the way. And New York to Nantucket can be a long, long way away.

When Edward Hamilton first smiled at me, it was like being hugged by a teddy bear. Now I felt I was being sized up by a bellicose hyena.

"Bear," I said, leaning forward, smiling back.

"What?"

"My assignment—what do you think?"

"I like the idea. Triple-F Fiona's found all the best places and stored them on my iPad." He reached for his briefcase. "And…Dr. Rosenberg wants me to take a rest."

"But don't you think it's a step backwards for me? I'm investigative now, it's all I've ever wanted to do. This is basic research…"

"Teal, listen. You, me. Tropical paradise. Some R and R. What d'you say?"

"Since when have you been so keen on the South Pacific? And since when have you taken *rests?*"

We avoided eye contact, and the silence stretched until he said, "1931."

"Excuse me?"

"That quiz question. The year Porsche was founded."

"I heard it's the regional final," I said, trying to restart the conversation. *That you nearly ruined.*

"Look, we agree I've been under a lot of pressure. Let's go. I'm sure they've offered you the assignment because they know you'll do a good job."

The returning owner broke another long silence. "Did madam enjoy the seafood?"

"Very much. What was the sashimi?"

"Line-caught yellowfin tuna."

"It was perfect."

"And did you enjoy the champagne?"

Bear grunted it was fine before dismissing the owner with a flick of the head. Then he rummaged in his pocket and with a grin, produced a small, robin's egg blue box.

"Tiffany," I said, my pulse quickening. *French champagne. Tiffany. My god, he's about to ask me to—*

"Open it, open it!" he said, before glugging from his glass.

I indicated that mine was empty.

"Don't mind if I do," he said refilling his. "Open it!"

Holding my breath, I flipped the lid. I wish I hadn't gasped. The pear diamonds, flashing an intense blue-green, floated inside a rim of white pavé clusters.

"A beautiful woman can't have too much jewelry," he said, teeth bared in a predatory grin.

I lifted the earrings. "They're exquisite. But..." *But they're earrings. And why is he spending all this money on me? He's never given me anything valuable before...*

"Try them on!"

I'm not for sale, a little voice inside me said. A voice that sounded a lot like Grandma's.

"Bear, what's going on?"

I replaced them in the box and put it on the table.

"Listen, I know we've been through a rough patch—*mea culpa* and all that. It's just that I think a break's a great idea and the earrings are this romantic fool's way of saying sorry. Let's take that vacation and give this thing another chance."

"I don't know, Bear. This is all very nice, but if I take the assignment..."

"If you don't, it could cost you your job and then how will you pay your half of the rent?"

I began carefully, "Grandma Lizzie used to say—"

"Do spare me Lizzie's pearls of wisdom!"

"...if something's broken, you try fixing it before throwing it away." This would be his last chance. If things didn't improve, I could look myself in the mirror knowing I'd given it my best shot.

I pulled the iPad closer. Fiona's links took me to thatched huts perched on stilts, aquamarine lagoons, and beach bungalows snuggling under jungle dreadlocks. The sand looked honey-sweet, the skies piercingly blue. "It's very beautiful."

"You'll come then? Nothing but the best for my Teal."

"Will you thank Fiona? They all look nice..."

"I sense a 'but' coming."

"It's just that..." I opened the guidebook. "If I said yes, what about somewhere like this? Less fancy. It's one of the outlying islands."

After a glance, he boomed, "Looks like a—"

"It's *not* a dump. I think it's got character." I started reading aloud, "*...Somewhat undeveloped...Kiwi proprietors Kris and Emma Davies have lovingly combined old world charm with an authentic South Pacific experience—*"

"Means the plumbing won't work."

"*The local seafood is superb, and braver guests have been known to try Kris's homebrewed 'wine'.* Don't be difficult, Bear. I think I like it. You know, the simple life doesn't hurt once in a while."

"I don't trust Antipodeans. Or natives."

"Oh come on, Bear! Meeting new people, experiencing new cultures is half the reason to travel! But you'll be glad to hear it says there aren't any islanders living on this island now. Something to do with a legend—"

"What's it called?"

"Horseshoe Island. And you know what? It speaks to me." I noticed the pub owner standing at the door. He mouthed *Good luck* before rejoining the quiz.

"In what language, pray tell? And what's the name of the hotel? I'll google it."

"It's called..." When I turned back to the guidebook I noticed something I hadn't seen before. A tingle ran up my spine. The hotel's called *that*? My mind raced back a few hours to when I was lying on the bed reading Grandma's letter. For the second time that evening, I gasped. *Is that it, Lizzie? Is that the sign I'm looking for?*

"If we go all that way, I want comfort. I want the Epsteins and the Mellons dying of envy. They'll laugh at this place." He thrust the iPad at me. "But look at this one—it has twenty-four hour restaurant and bar facilities, a casino, even a masseuse and personal trainer allocated to each room—"

"I'd like to stay somewhere simple...authentic," I said firmly.

"In which case we appear to have reached an *impasse*."

"Ladies and gentlemen, we now come to the final question of the evening. Pens poised, brains engaged."

"Bear, tell you what: If you know the answer, you choose the hotel. If you don't, I'll choose. Deal?"

"But I—"

"Quick!"

"Oh, alright."

"Who do scholars believe wrote the Book of Ecclesiastes?"

Blankness, sulkiness, then fury crawled across his reddening face. "Dammit, I don't do religion."

I clapped my hands with delight. "Yessss!"

He muttered, "What did you say this dump's called?"

"I didn't. But it's called The Sun and Moon."

CHAPTER SIX

The South Pacific, October, 2013

The twin-engine island hopper climbed between the puffs of cloud as it swung back towards the main island. It had left us, a dispersing group of vacationers, a thousand feet below beside the grass airstrip edged with rust-flaking oil drums. A pair of doves pecked at the weeds that sprouted from the broken tarmac we stood on. Vivid colors and bright, unfamiliar flowering bushes were attended by darting bees. Heat radiated through the soles of my shoes. Everything smelled exotic, wonderful and new, but I hadn't forgotten why I was here—the Thurston Morfil interview.

I would begin by gathering local information, build the background to my report and then start planning the interview. I was intrigued by the idea of a local legend—if things proved slow, I could always investigate that too. I knew that Thane could have sent anyone, but I'd put in that extra mile to show him just how good—

"Where's the damn bus?" demanded Bear.

"We go by boat," said the islander standing beside our luggage. "Horseshoe's out there." He indicated with a sweep of his arm.

"First my luggage is searched at your main island. Then I'm squeezed into some Mickey Mouse plane that lands on a lump of rock with a name I can't pronounce—"

"This island's called Tofua'a," I said, half to him, half to a stripy gecko that was eyeing me from a rock.

"Now I have to take a boat to get to this place? It had better be—"

"Boat coming soon."

"When is *soon?*"

"Boss is bringing *Coconut* when he's done fishing."

Bear's eyes narrowed. "I don't want a damn coconut. I want a cold beer and a room with air con."

"Wait for us!"

The elderly couple who had been passing around photos of their latest grandchild on our flight were dragging their suitcases towards us. Matching sneakers, khaki shorts, Hawaiian shirts. Gray, shiny, smiling. An impressive camera hung from his neck. "Hi," she said, extending a hand. "Frank and Nancy Butler from Florida."

Frank fanned his face with a copy of Time magazine. "This Sun and Moon place sure is remote!"

I nodded. "Remote suits me fine!"

Nancy said, "We've still got a bit of a journey ahead of us! Tell me about you, dear."

"Oh, just a journalist. On a working vacation. And you guys?"

"We're retired. He was in *everything* and I was in flowers and cement," she said.

"Cement?"

"Very set in her ways," Frank said.

I laughed as she poked him playfully.

Bear shook his head. "What I object to is being asked to confirm my weight three times and then ordered to stand on inaccurate scales before I was allowed to board. That mouse dropping of an airline will be hearing from my lawyers...if two battered planes constitutes an airline!" He marched off towards the dock that lay partly hidden by a clump of palms.

"Isn't this divine!" said Nancy.

Frank thumbed the pages of an insect guide. He pointed. "Pumpkin, some of the moths here sure look like butterflies. Think I'll set up a moth trap one night and see what—"

"Boss coming now," said the islander, with a nod of his head towards the water.

A yellow-hulled boat churned towards us, the rooster-tail wake comically disproportionate to its modest progress.

"Looks like someone stuck a helm station atop an old crabber," Frank said with a laugh.

Another islander in denim shorts gently stepped from the shadows of the airport terminal. He held a battered clipboard in one hand, a young girl's hand in the other. She was cute as a picture in her tie-died dress and carried a basket of flowers which were as white as the man's hair and as his T-shirt had once been. Why hadn't I noticed them before? They walked forward; the tilt of the man's head suggested scrutiny. When the sun lit his face, I saw deep creases.

The man stopped and the child ran forward, offering us each a white flower. Bear, who had wandered back complaining about the heat, mumbled something. Frank asked if it was okay to take the girl's picture.

When she came to me, the islander whistled. She ran back to him and I watched him reach into his pocket. He then leaned down and whispered in her ear. She ran back to me with a purple flower.

"Thank you, honey, but why do I get *this* one?" I asked.

The child looked at the islander who nodded encouragement and she motioned for me to lean down. "Special flower for special lady," she whispered in my ear.

The old man came forward. "Please would you sign my petition," he said quietly, clipping his words in an islander accent.

"Oh...what's it for?" I asked.

"Stop them building the Coral Palm Resort."

Frank looked up. "Why?" he asked.

"It's on a turtle nesting beach."

"Leatherbacks?" Frank asked.

"Hawksbills."

"Sure, I'll sign," Nancy said and Frank followed suit. After I'd added my name, I turned to Bear who crossed his arms and looked away.

The islander took the girl's hand and they shuffled off.

"I thought he wanted to sell us those flowers," Frank said, "but the sign says market days are Mondays and Thursdays."

"In Hawaii, a sexy babe greets you with a whole garland. Here it's an old perv and a child with a limp," Bear said.

"I just love morning glories," said Nancy.

Even from where we stood on the tarmac, I heard the boat thump the dock. A middle-aged blond man jumped off the side, tied up and jogged to the scrub thicket beside it. Then a vintage tractor, dragging a trailer (complete with sun canopy), lurched into view. It bounced towards us, halting with a crunch of gears. The man jumped down and wiped a glob of grease on his denim shirt. Smiles (nearly) all around as he offered us a tanned hand at the end of his tattooed, Māori-themed arm. "If you'll pardon the cliché, welcome to paradise! Kris Davies, co-owner of the Sun and Moon, at your service," he said in a gentle New Zealand drawl. "Beer and sodas in the cooler," he shouted over the coughing engine. "Help yourselves."

Despite a flat tire, we jerked our way towards the jetty.

"Hold on tight," said Frank.

"Isn't this fun?" trilled Nancy as we clipped a pothole and ducked under a branch.

"Beer's warm," said Bear.

We clattered to a halt beyond the trees beside a sparkling bay. The land met ocean in a sensorium of blues and greens, tans and gold.

"Oh my!" said Nancy, squeezing her husband's hand. There was a mesmeric *shush* from the surf as two butterflies pole-danced in a beam of sunlight.

"I bribed the tourist board to lay this on, Pumpkin," whispered Frank.

I turned to Bear, hoping he was also in the moment. If he was, it was an entirely different one...probably imagining an oil terminal out there. Complete with oil spill. *That was uncharitable, Teal—I'll never save our relationship with thoughts like that!*

Coconut's lines were decades old, drawn by a hand which had yet to discover the relationship between form and function. The closer we got, the more eccentric its proportions appeared—I half expected to see a giant rotating key poking from the cockpit. Bear demanded to know where the lifejackets were.

"Welcome aboard," said Kris from atop the raised helm. "Thirty-eight feet of local, err...craftsmanship. Coconut's tough—survived a cyclone. And a few brushes with the reef."

The diesel engines crouped to life, setting off a buzzing that radiated through the deck. The boat's stubby bow swung towards the distant islands and a back-draft of fumes flooded the cockpit. Bear clamped a handkerchief over his nose as the stern clumped a dock post.

"Man and machine in perfect harmony," Frank said, beaming.

Finally underway, the sun and sea air felt good. *Time for some Hawaiian Tropic for this pale girl.* The breeze threw a warm spray over the cockpit and I let it splash me, licking the salt from my lips.

I offered the factor thirty-five to Bear, who rolled his eyes. He pointed at the Time magazine beside Frank. "May I?"

Frank held it out but a gust of wind had other ideas.

"Darn," said Frank, as it fluttered into the swirling wake.

"We're hoping the sea air will help his arthritis," Nancy explained.

"No problem," Bear said, and turned to sulk on the gunnel.

Nancy walked over to me. "Why do you think he gave you a purple flower?"

"No idea." *Nice to be called special though.*

"Me neither. But they're interesting flowers. Morning glories only bloom for a day and represent love or mortality."

"Love or mortality?" I repeated, and smiled. "How do you know about flowers?"

"I owned a garden center when I met Frank—don't you just love flowers?"

Kris was pointing out and naming the distant islands. The wind carried much of what he said away or his words were drowned by the throb of the engines but I heard snippets like *turtle beach* and *pristine reef*. I didn't mind. I felt excited that after three weeks of doubts and anticipation, and twenty-something hours of travel, we were nearly at our final destination.

I spotted a white boat some way off. "Who's that?" I asked.

Kris shouted, "Local police."

"They patrol here?" Frank asked.

"They come through a couple of times a week. They like to keep an eye on the islanders' nefarious activities."

"Which include?" I asked.

"Smuggling coral and shells to sell to tourists. Some dope. Nothing too dramatic. I think it's more about putting in an appearance because tourism's growing in importance here."

A few minutes passed before I heard Kris answer a question from Frank with: *Pretty safe inside the reef but open water's a different story. Most dangerous time is dusk. Sharks feed then.*

A low island, fronted by a golden beach, lay maybe two miles ahead. Kris passed me the binoculars and I studied the broken skyline that was decorated with leaning palm trees, and terminated in bare rock. A set of squat buildings blended with the shadows. Either side of them, where the sand met the vegetation, stood regularly spaced dark triangles—from here they reminded me of large wigwams. A tall red and white striped mast topped with an aerial sprouted from a clump of trees.

"Broadband?" Bear shouted.

"That's a radio. We have a link to the hub on the main island. Reasonable internet service. Telephone and VHF backup, in case of emergencies."

"Computer, printer for guest use?"

"A couple of computers in the business center. There's a printer there too—on its last legs but it gets the job done."

"And tortilla chips? You got tortilla chips in the hotel?"

"I can probably get them."

"Emergencies?" I asked.

"Haven't had one yet." Kris smiled and I glanced at Bear, wondering if he'd heard the warning about swimming at dusk.

"Got a fish finder up there, Skipper Kris?"

"Sure do, Mr. Butler. It's—"

"Call me Frank, son."

"...Showing seventy meters—that's over two hundred feet—under the hull, Frank."

Ahead, the ocean sucked and filled around a small, flat rock topped with a knuckle of stone. Drawing closer, I could see dark shapes perched on its glistening surface.

Kris eased the throttle, though we were still some way off.

"Local shipping hazard as it's just about submerged at high tide. Called *Whaling Rock*. Apparently it was used as a lookout by the whalers. Good vantage point."

Frank raised his camera, "*Phalacrocorax carbo*, Skipper?"

"I see we have an expert onboard and you're correct, the great cormorant. Not too common around here. Must've flown in to greet our new arrivals."

"Can you get closer? I'd like to get a shot."

"Sorry, no can do, Frank."

"Why? What's the depth?"

"Oh, it's plenty deep. The strange thing is that rock sticks up from the bottom like a finger, with only the top showing. My guess is it's volcanic but I don't like to get too close, out of respect...local legend."

Nancy said, "I love legends! Tell me more."

"Me too!" I added.

"Afraid I don't know much except it was some sort of tragedy."

"What about the indigenous skink? Where would I get a photo of one?" Frank asked.

"Never seen one myself. Habitat destruction and the pet trade have decimated the population."

Our host swung the boat away from the rock. I climbed up to stand next to him to get a better view of the line of A-frame huts ahead. Offshore, the puffball clouds swelled against a backdrop of piercing indigo. Inshore, a line of foam marked the reef. The scarlet triangle of a windsurfer skipped across the surface.

"Looks perfect," I said to Kris.

"Half a mile of curved sand in the middle of nowhere. Electricity and plumbing problems, fresh water has to be brought by tanker. The restaurant's reliant on an old freighter for supplies. But you know what? I can't think of a single place I'd rather live," Kris said.

I laughed. "You sure know how to sell a place!"

A few small boats lined the jetty; at the far end of the beach, a solitary sailboat rested in the shallows.

"That white one with the awning looks fast. I've never seen a speed boat with three outboards," Bear said, pointing. "Can we use it?"

"Afraid not, *Spada* belongs to an Italian regular, he uses it to break every fishing record he can. It's mothballed until his next visit." He smiled. "The guy clogs my freezer with his catch."

"Fishing any good here?" Bear asked.

"Can be. This year I launched our billfish—that's marlin and sailfish—catch and release tournament. Sixteen fish in two days to five boats and that was in awful weather. We already have nine confirmed entries for next year."

The place looked...charming. Just what I needed. And I was here for three whole weeks because a stranger in a pub had recommended a resort which happened to share the same name as my tarot cards. An interview with Thurston Morfil, a couple of days writing it up and the rest of the time was mine to do with as I pleased.

Grandma wanted me to notice things—and *act* on them. Well, I might as well start now. I'd taken a chance, rolled the dice and stepped into the unknown. But one thing was scratched indelibly on my mental to-do list: Somehow, some way, this Teal was going to get a life. I'd never really had one before and everyone deserves one...right?

"What's that large tent used for, Kris?" I asked.

"Oh, I thought I'd be clever. You didn't used to have to pay room tax for canvas, so I added some cheap backpacker accommodation. But the authorities have spies—and they changed the rules. I ended up using it to store the boating and fishing gear."

"Spies? *Here?*"

"And when your lease is up for renewal, you try not to rock the boat," he added quietly.

"I didn't mean to pry."

"No worries," he said, but his frown lingered.

I studied Frank and Nancy as we closed on Kris's tropical kingdom. They looked so contented, happy with each other—for them, things looked like they'd fallen into place.

"What's that cordoned off piece of water, son?" Frank shouted.

"Emma—my wife—is farming seaweed."

"Why?" Nancy asked.

"She says the sea goddess *Nāmaka* has *impregnated* it with vitamins, iodine, selenium, calcium, iron, amino acids—you name it, apparently seaweed's got it. Knowing Emma, she'll try smoking it too...." Kris finished under his breath, but still loud enough for me to hear.

"You got my email about gluten-free?" Nancy asked.

"All taken care of," Kris said.

I gazed at the tropical panorama unfolding before me as Coconut chugged through the gap in the reef and the water paled to crystal. Beside us, the sepia coral clumped in organized chaos; below, our shadow glided over a rippling carpet of magnolia sand. I didn't care who heard me as I spoke quietly to the ocean.

"Lizzie, I've traveled nine thousand miles. Please help me find my magic."

CHAPTER SEVEN

The bamboo-walled A-frame was simple and spacious with rattan furniture and sun-bleached cushions. The walls were hung with cheerful island-themed paintings, in a pseudo-homage to Gauguin. Frayed matting softened the concrete floor. Despite rinsing my feet in the water-filled giant clam shell outside our door, a sprinkling of sand had found its way into our bed. Not difficult to work out how, with Bear hauled out beside me, his sandals still on his feet. I lay half naked, tickled by the breeze of a rusting ceiling fan.

"Unpacked my suitcase yet?"

"Yes."

The swell of his belly obscured my view but I knew what he was doing.

"Up periscope," he announced with pride.

"Must you do that in front of me?"

"I'm thinking of Triple-F Fiona."

"That's not funny. Can't you go into the shower-room—"

"Well, if you'd grant my little request, I wouldn't have to think of her. Your problem is you're selfish."

"Couldn't we snuggle instead? I'm exhausted."

"You know Dr. Mortimer's two for one offer's been extended."

I didn't answer.

"Think what it would do for your self-confidence."

I turned away, shutting my eyes. His breathing deepened. I felt the tears welling and bit my lip. "Anyway, I like it here," I said, pulling the cowrie at the end of the cord that hung down beside the bed. The ticking fan picked up speed, groaned, stopped.

"Now look what you've done."

I pulled the cord again. Nothing.

"Congratulations. You've broken it."

I propped myself on an elbow to face him and inhaled the warm air. I needed to appear strong, as nothing else would work.

"Look Edward, if every single thing you say is going to be unpleasant, then this is a waste of time. Let's try and make the most of it, okay?" I kept eye contact, my heart pounding in my chest.

"Whatever," he sighed. Then he looked at me. "That old guy..."

"Frank?"

"He dropped the magazine overboard deliberately."

"Edward, wait till you're—"

"By the way, did you boil-wash my chinos?"

"Of course not."

"How else could they have shrunk? Think I'll have a look 'round." He rolled off the mattress, which refilled with an asthmatic wheeze, and slouched towards the front door. "And I need to send an email."

"Who to?"

But he was gone.

I walked into the shower-room, which was festooned with cheerful signs including *Solar Powered!* and *Please don't waste the precious water!* I lifted out Grandma's letters from my toiletry bag. Brushing off a few muesli flakes still clinging to the envelopes (I knew he would never have looked in *that* container back home), I fiddled with the bow, remembering the blue of Lizzie's favorite dress. I felt an urge to open the second letter but Lizzie had asked me to wait for another sign, and so wait I would. Grandma always had a good reason for everything she did or asked.

Returning to the bedroom, I wondered if there would in fact be another sign. I wedged the letters behind a picture, called *Dugong and Calf* ($50) and picked up the hotel's leatherette information folder on the desk below it. Outside, I settled onto a deckchair in the shaded part of the veranda with the folder on my lap. I adjusted my turquoise bikini, and alternated between learning about the resort's facilities and enjoying the view.

Ours was the last A-frame. A short distance away, the beach broke up into a weathered stone and knotted scrub. Beyond the reef, I could see the black slip of rock the cormorants had been sitting on.

I put down the folder and walked around our hut. Behind it, I found a table and two varnished logs, acting as benches. Bear's XL flip-flops had plowed tracks in the sandy path leading to the main building—which meant I'd find him at the bar.

A few months ago I'd never have guessed I'd soon be half a world away, mulling over my past and praying that it might shed light on my future. Or that in her own Lizzie way, my grandmother would be here, helping me. I looked down at her lucky ring and drew the first really relaxed breath I'd had in, well, I couldn't remember how long.

Bear was the only son of a now semi-impoverished umpteenth-generation Boston family with Scottish roots, for whom history and tradition meant everything. He kept his family contacts alive via annual fishing trips to a Lowland salmon river at which a handful of clan members gathered. I was regularly reminded of the family motto *Sans Tache*—French for *Without Stain*. In hindsight, I probably shouldn't have asked his mother, Patience, why Bear's ancestors had banned mustaches and followed up with a question about the family's history of close shaves. In strangled tones, she had enlightened me about the centuries of tradition underpinning the Hamiltons' status in society which weighed in at somewhat heavier than the gravitational constant of the universe. Or something like that.

Over the time I'd known him, an endearing desire to rebuild the family fortune and a derelict Scottish castle had evolved into a single-minded obsession. One day a bank statement revealed he'd canceled our charitable giving. On another, a party invite list was amended to exclude anyone of no use to his network—which in practice meant all *my* friends.

I flicked through the hotel guide, reading a section on biting insects (the sandflies sounded worse than the mosquitoes) and a list of other warnings to guests who might wish to venture on day trips to any of the distant islands that surrounded Horseshoe:

1. *Many islanders remain fiercely independent. Permission should be obtained before taking photos of them or their homes.*
2. *Never walk into a village—wait to be invited by an islander.*
3. *If invited, it's a good idea to take small gifts such as drawing books and colored pencils for the children.*
4. *The ocean's bounty is the property of the local chief.*

I skimmed numbers five to ten, then came to a section on local religion:

Traditionally, islanders believed that all living creatures have a spiritual essence. Known as animism, this belief system was largely displaced following the arrival of Christian missionaries in the nineteenth century though isolated pockets of animism remained until the 1940s.

The author of the hotel guide had even included the cliché: *Leave nothing but footprints—take nothing but pictures—kill nothing but time.* Well, it was mostly common sense and easy to live by. Since Kris had said no islanders lived on Horseshoe, I knew it would be safe to explore without breaching local etiquette.

I picked up my mask and fins and shielding my eyes, stepped onto the beach, flexing my toes in the warm sand. Then I walked into the ocean until I was waist deep in the surf. As it sploshed over me, dragging me back and forth, I pulled on my fins. Mask cleaned, I bit down on the snorkel mouth-piece and dived in. The waves butted gently against my head. I crawled hard into deeper water, keeping my form until my limbs cried out. As high school freestyle champion, I'd qualified for the state finals and I still never felt completely at ease when I wasn't around water. Swimming had always been my escape, the one place where people always smiled when I showed up. I don't know how I would have survived my parents' divorce without it.

I stopped swimming in the deeper water a hundred yards off the beach where the chalky sand surrendered to a coral garden, to drift spellbound as the scene beneath me exploded in a patchwork of confused patterns.

Sun bursts dragged across the greens, yellows, browns and reds in cadence with the passing waves. Clumps of coral bulged like giant brains; elsewhere, the light flickered on antler-shaped points or warmed funneled sponges. Sea fans swayed to a silent orchestra whose audience comprised surreal fish, decorated by a master's brush: I admired darting Chagalls, pouting Cezannes, circling Van Goghs. A troupe of nickel dinner plates glided past mid-water, their goggle eyes tracking me when I swam too close. My shadow fell on a brown eel that coiled back into its lair. I dived to admire a slender trumpet-faced fish which hung head down, as a school of fingerlings spun above me in a swirling ball. So much life, variety, color.

Surely, this was about as unlike the cool waters of Nantucket as it was possible to be. I swam deeper but soon my bursting lungs reminded me of my land-based origins. If only it could be like those dreams when you can breathe underwater.

I turned, swam back over the reef and wished its inhabitants goodbye, then kicked for the beach.

Treading water above the sand, I paused to let my breathing return to normal. A large seabird swooped, hovering above me, so close that I felt the draft from its beating wings. With a cry it turned and flapped along the surf line. *That funny looking bird had bright blue feet! I bet Frank will know what type it is.* I rolled over and backstroked for shore.

Standing in the shallows, a tiny silver fish darted in and out of the puffs of sand at my feet. Braver now, it began to nibble. *Don't women pay $100 an hour for this in Manhattan?* I felt the tightness of my muscles and the crispy salt in my hair. With an invigorated step and newly exfoliated toe, I climbed from the water and started walking along the beach towards the hotel bar to find Bear. A short distance later, I stopped dead. "That bird's feet…were the *exact* same color as Lizzie's ribbon." Was that a sign? Should

I open the second letter? Or was I so curious I was seeing signs everywhere? I slowed. Okay, I decided: After dinner—when he starts snoring.

"Tannhauser. Of course, Wagner really surpassed—"

"Hello, Bear. That drink looks good, what is it?"

"I was telling...oh!" A dark-haired mother and daughter hurried away, "A little culture never hurt the French," he boomed after them.

Bear motioned to the aproned bartender who advanced, cocktail shaker in hand. He said hello to me with a smiley mouth and sad eyes. His name tag read *Toka*.

"We've been inventing a cocktail. Can't think of a name for it. We came up with—what was that fellow's name?" he asked the bartender.

"His name was *Fonu*, boss."

"That's it. I think *Fonu's Curse* has a nice ring to it."

"Toka, who is Fonu?" I asked.

"Young man who was born here a long time ago, lady. When his mother went into the birthing hut, a young whale swam onto the beach and died right then and there. That was very bad luck. Everything went wrong after that and his older brother died a few years later."

"That sounds tragic. What happened to Fonu?" I asked.

"Drowned when he was sixteen, haw, haw."

"What was the curse about?" I asked Toka.

"That's all I know, lady."

"Let me ask you...have you heard of someone called Thurston Morfil?"

"Not now Teal—can't you see the man's making my drink—"

"Everybody heard of *him*, lady."

"What do they say about him?"

But Toka was distracted by some limes that urgently required segmenting. I lifted my glass and pushed the parasol aside, sipping the foam-topped liquid.

He turned. "Careful lady, never made one so strong!"

My taste buds moon-walked across my tongue.

"You could name it *Cry Baby*," I spluttered, wiping my eyes.

"Haw, haw!" Bear pointed at Toka's necklace. "This fellow tells me there's one tooth from each shark he's caught. Some of them were man-eaters."

"Some real big ones out there, boss."

"What types?" I asked.

"I don't know their English names but a shark's a shark. The ones in deep water are the meanest. Plenty been caught by the longliners."

"The fewer sharks the better," said Bear. "What about deep sea

47

fishing? I want to catch a marlin and it would be a good experience for Ms. Douglas to watch me. Maybe she could try too."

"Bear, I'm not sure I—"

"Make a change from flogging over to Scotland every year to a fishless salmon river."

I certainly didn't want to kill anything but how could I expect to improve our relationship if I didn't involve myself in what Bear enjoyed?

"You speak to Mr. Davies. He can organize fishing."

"Trust me on this, Teal. You'll love it."

"The brochure mentioned whales," I said.

"Catching *whales*? Brilliant, Teal! Even I didn't think of that."

"You here at the right time of year, lady. Humpback, a few sperm whales too. Some beaked whales and always dolphins and pilot whales. Mr. Davies has license to watch them from his boat. And if there are no whales around, you can always ask old Bob to call them up." He laughed. Toka leaned closer to me. "Some say he still has the magic."

"Welcome to the twenty-first century!" Bear said, slurping his drink.

I stifled a yawn. The jet lag was catching up with me.

"If you wake up early, go to the end of the dock at eight and watch the fish feeding. A lot of big ones come in. And bring a camera—*Black Jack* will be there for his breakfast. Goliath grouper, big as a car. They come from all over the world to take his photo."

Walking back, I asked Bear if he thought the bartender had seemed reluctant to talk about Fonu and Thurston Morfil. He didn't reply. Instead Bear insisted we detour via the dock as I counted the minutes till I could open Lizzie's next letter. A large sign read *No Fishing. Ever!* Was there a subtle change in him? The fishing seemed to interest him and he'd enjoyed the bar.

"I like it here," I said, soothing my way into a friendly conversation.

"It's crap. If I can't find something fun to do pronto, I'll go stark raving mad."

*   *   *

Despite my best efforts, dinner was an ordeal of stifled conversation, though Bear did ask the waiter a string of questions about his Spanish mackerel. The firm white steak occupied much of his plate and all of his attention, before he curled his lip and pushed his salad away.

"A local vegetable?" I volunteered.

"If we'd stayed in a proper hotel…"

"Oh, Bear, I know this isn't the Ritz Carlton but for once—"

"No, I damn well can't. Waiter!" he shouted, waving his arm. "Bring me something familiar to my delicate Caledonian palate and make it pronto!"

After the surprised islander had removed his salad and the other guests had stopped staring, I looked around and recognized the French mother and daughter from the bar. Talk about *haute couture*, the mother's strappy, silk chemise made a statement that would have looked at home on the cover of French Vogue! Her Gallic profile inspired me to play a game of *Guess the Guest* with myself. I identified an Australian politician with her toy boy (newspaper setup), a honeymoon couple (yawning), a father and son (minor lottery winners from Belgium), a tour group (matching T-shirts) and a Ray-Ban wearing weightlifter (anabolic steroid smuggler).

Kris came over with a rakishly thin woman he introduced as his wife, Emma, who sported parrot earrings and tangerine braids. She explained she'd come here to research her PhD—was *soul-kissed* by Kris and side-tracked by a *divine benefaction* (ten-month old, *Luna Solstice Diadem*). She described how she "interrogated herself every single day regarding her confusion about island existentialism". Or by then, she may have been explaining the menu.

"What's your thesis about?" I asked, distracted by a metallic green beetle climbing her grass skirt.

With a swish of her bangles, she answered, "I studied theology and social anthropology. But the islanders are so *recalcitrant* with their conversation. One old dude promised to tell me a local myth about someone called 'Fonu' but he changed his mind because apparently I hadn't journeyed far enough along the path."

"The bartender mentioned someone called Fonu. And a curse. A whale died when he was born."

"I've always wondered if Toka's got an over-active imagination. Now you know as much about Fonu as I do. For some reason the locals claim ignorance if you ask for more."

We discussed their international clientele, and I learned there was an English guy who occasionally dined here as well. Emma pointed at an empty table. "We save that one for the 'Pacific Pacifist' but I think he's hiding from Lorraine, *ooh-la-la!*"

"The Gauloise-smoker with the teenage daughter?" I asked.

"God knows why that daughter sulked so much when I informed her I had ancestors in the Ninety-Second Gordon Highlanders, who helped thrash that snail-munching Napoleon fellow at the Battle of Waterloo," Bear added.

"Lorraine started glamming up right after she'd spotted the English guy. Dude's a marine biologist. Probably getting high counting starfish right now. Hey, whatever runs his bath."

"So you can squeeze a few more people into the restaurant, if need be?" asked Bear.

"No problemo."

"I'll let you know how many. Or they may make other arrangements." He caught my eye. "Don't worry about it, honey."

We finished dinner, and headed back as the tide pulled away beneath a building moon. I padded behind Bear trying to step in the divots his sandals carved in the sand. I kicked a tar-covered plastic dish, then a bundle of fishing line. "Look at all that junk. Where's it come from?"

"On the plus side, it provides work for the beach cleaners, haw, haw."

* * *

I stood in front of the shower-room mirror, poised between flossing and brushing.

I'd seen a strange bird with feet the same shade of blue as Lizzie's ribbon. Did that qualify as a sign? It would be nice just to hold her letters, to check they were safe, even if I didn't open one now. But that had to wait. I didn't want Edward making fun of me.

"Bear, who've you invited?" I called to Edward who was lying on the bed.

"Me and my big mouth. It was meant to be a surprise. Okay, the McDonalds may drop by."

"They're *your* friends. You might have asked me."

"You like Alice—"

"That's not the point."

Perhaps it *would* be nice to have Alice here though, as a girlfriend. A chance to get to know her better. And Hugo could be amusing, in his schoolboy way. *I'll email her and find out more.*

From the bedroom, I could hear the sinusoidal snoring had already begun.

I found my earplugs in the bottom of my cosmetics bag, slipped out of the shower-room and tiptoed around the bed. The picture glowed in a shaft of moonlight above the little desk, with the dugong suspended like an airship, dwarfing the calf beside it. A bit like us, I thought, then quickly pushed the unkind thought away.

"What are you doing?"

I jumped. "Oh, chasing a mosquito."

"Come to bed."

With a sigh, I let my hand fall from the picture frame and walked back to him.

CHAPTER EIGHT

"Just look at *that* one!" Bear said, as a great silver fish glided under the jetty. "They must know it's feeding time."

The water was so clear I could count the undulations inscribed on the sandy bottom. Sharks, three or four feet long, with black tipped fins, snaked past. Great blunt-headed fish, with large eyes and twitching mouths bossed the others about. They twisted, circling this way, turning that, their speed building. I sensed the growing anticipation as more fish arrived.

"That one must weigh forty pounds," said Bear.

"Giant trevally, more like seventy, mate," said a glowing Australian in a bandana. "Top game fish around here. Second only to marlin."

A clatter behind us announced the arrival of two islanders—I recognized Toka—who pushed a wheeled bin heaped with restaurant scraps. At the end of the jetty they began ladling the contents into the water. The fish moved faster now, darting and diving. A school of what looked like snappers charged in and a trevally burst through a group of minnows to inhale a sinking chunk. A pod of fish streaked past, flashing red, blue, silver while the water boiled with each splash of food until the surface foamed.

"My god!" said Bear.

"Wait for us!"

Frank hurried along the jetty, camera in hand. Nancy, all smiles, followed at a more leisurely pace a few yards behind.

"Wow! Look at them go!" Frank shouted, clicking away.

A dark lump I had thought was a boulder began slowly turning on the bottom. It rose on fanning fins, hovering at the side of the feeding frenzy, watching, waiting. With a gaping lunge, its mouth flashed white and a trevally was seized. The other fish scattered like a bursting firework, the food settling unmolested on the sand. As the goliath grouper hovered, the

51

twitching tail that protruded from its jaws disappeared in a grotesque convulsion of head and gills.

"That one bad fish!" Toka said, shaking his head as Black Jack cruised off.

Bear laughed too, delivering his haw, haw in a higher register. "I need to organize something," he said, rubbing his hands. Spinning on his heel, he stomped off towards reception.

"Think I'll go for a walk," I called after him. "Meet you for breakfast in twenty?"

"Care for some company?" Frank asked, Nancy at his elbow.

"We saw a quite lovely sailboat from our room. Frank wants photos for his grandkids."

"I'd like that," I said.

Nancy unfolded a garbage bag she pulled from her pocket. "One for you, Teal?"

"Err...?"

She pointed at a plastic bottle on the sand. "Whole world's drowning under plastic."

We strolled past the bar and restaurant. The deck chairs and umbrellas were arranged along the beach in untidy rows. Soon we'd left the last A-frame behind.

For the first time since we'd arrived, I could feel the tension and bustle of the city wafting away, a little more each time I exhaled.

At the end of the beach, a kaleidoscope of windsurfers and jet skis lined the sand. "Motorized beach toys should be banned," said Frank, his face pensive for the first time since we'd met.

Nancy pointed out to sea. "I asked the waiter last night about Whaling Rock. Some sort of tragedy involving a father and son."

"Anything more?" I asked.

"The kid was nothing but trouble. But the islander wouldn't go into detail. He seemed to think even talking about it would bring bad luck."

The sailboat presented stern to, its slim form reflected in the ripples like a flickering mosaic. Closer now, I admired the timeless elegance of a hull of polished ochre. The off-white cabin shone and bronze hardware lit a curved deck that swept sensually to a compact cockpit.

"They don't make them like that any more. Not a right angle or parallel line to be seen on that old lady," mused Frank.

"A bit like me!" Nancy said.

"That's why I love you, Pumpkin," said Frank, absently draping an arm around his wife and pulling her against him, his eyes still mesmerized by the lines of the wooden sailboat.

"You know about boats," I said.

"Frank used to own a small marina."

"Do you know whose boat that is?" I asked.

"An English guy's," Frank said, now moving to full controls-adjusting and camera-clicking mode. "You see the tender tied up to the stern? Means the owner's probably aboard."

"The marine biologist?"

A man climbed from the cabin. From here I could make out his black hair and the contrast between his suntan and bathing suit. He rolled his arms and shoulders and scrambled his hair in a no-one's-watching, wake-up ritual.

Nancy's nudged my ribs. "I hope Frank gets a picture of *him*!" she whispered.

The man threw something and a large seabird swooped to catch it.

"I'll be darned...that looks like *Sula nebouxii*," said Frank. "Shouldn't occur in these waters."

"I think it dive-bombed me yesterday," I said.

"What's the boat called, dear?" asked Nancy.

Frank adjusted the lens. "F—A—"

"Falcon," I said quietly.

"My, you have strong eyes, dear," said Nancy.

Frank lowered his camera and turned to look at me too.

"I didn't read it...the name just popped into my head."

CHAPTER NINE

Bear's cheeks chipmunked with semi-masticated bacon, tomato, ham and eggs. Without swallowing, smoked sausage was crammed in. The good news was I wouldn't have to make conversation until his plate, and mouth, were empty. Miscalculation.

"Something amusing you?" he mumbled.

Instead of answering, I frowned and returned to my thoughts.

I wished I'd paid more attention now, when the Amazing Anastasia had mentioned a falcon. Because I'd guessed, no I'd *known* the name of the sailboat. Maybe, just maybe, she *was* a little amazing.

I also found myself wanting to find out more about the man who lived aboard. Not because he'd looked good. It wasn't that—up close he'd almost certainly be just a regular guy. It was because he'd turned to face us. For a second I'd felt a flash of interest in him as I tried to make out his features, because I was sure he was trying to see who *we* were too. But from that distance, he could have been anyone. No doubt he thought the same about us. That was when Frank had claimed he was only six gym visits away from a body like that.

The mystery marine biologist's table remained empty in the restaurant. One thing was clear though: The sailboat's name *must* be a sign and that meant it was time to open the second letter!

But with Bear hovering around, I hadn't been able to read them in peace. I resented this cloak and dagger stuff but I didn't want him knowing about them. Why? Because they were personal, because they were from Lizzie. And because he wouldn't have understood. But sooner or later I'd be alone, I could sit down, adjust my mood and savor the last thoughts Grandma would ever share with me.

Kris approached our table. "All organized, Mr. Hamilton. *Tango* will be at the dock at seven tomorrow morning. The captain knows these waters like the back of his hand. Best boat around, as you requested. I'll have picnics outside your room for 6.30. Wake-up call?"

"I didn't know you'd booked—" I started.

"Tell me about the captain."

"Australian guy, fished all over the world. I should say..." Kris hesitated.

"What?"

"...One in ten chance he won't be able to make it but he's lined up a great back up. His wife's expecting their second child. Their first was early...it's possible—"

"I don't fish with understudies."

"Perry's very good. Our inaugural catch and release tournament champion. Beat all comers including Americans, a French team, our own mad keen Italian—"

"Wake us at six." Bear stood, dropping his napkin on the table. "And whoever shows up better be good. Computer in the business center free?"

"This way, sir."

"I'll be in the room, Bear," I called to his retreating back.

I lifted *Teal and Edward* (the picture formerly known as Dugong and Calf) and removed the envelopes. How long did I have? I fiddled with the knot. *Come on!* But it wouldn't give.

I pushed and prodded. Finally, just as the knot was loosening it came to me. *Why was it so tight?* I certainly hadn't left it like this.

Which meant one thing: Someone had been looking at them. The letter inside the first envelope had been refolded clumsily. I was sure of it. The others were still unopened. *What the heck's going on?* I felt a surge of disgust...someone had touched my last link with Lizzie. My cheeks burned.

"Hun?"

I replaced the letters and faced him as he strode in, struggling to control my breathing. "Someone's been reading my letters," I said, glaring at him.

"No idea the fishing was so expensive—it better be worth it."

"They're *very* private!"

"Kris recommends seasick pills."

Finally he noticed the fury in my face, my knotted fists.

"Must have been the maid, snooping around. You know what these people are like, unless, of course, you made a mistake."

He dumped his sandy flip-flops on the matting and stomped past, humming what may have started life as Wagner. Was it him? The cleaner? Or someone else?

"Let's get some sun," he suggested on his return from the shower-room.

I picked up my beach bag, confirming my MacBook was in it. Bear stopped in front of the mirror.

"Everything okay, Teal?" he asked, without facing me.

"No." *No, it certainly is not.*

"I'll mention it to what's-his-name, the Kiwi guy."

He flexed his arm and ran a finger over his soft bicep, smiling at his refection. Then he prodded his stomach before stretching the elastic at the top of his swimming trunks. He loosened the cord there. "You boil-washed these too?"

I went over it again: Of course it was him. He saw me with the letters last night and anyway, the cleaner hadn't been yet. Of what possible interest could they be to him? This man really had absolutely no respect for my boundaries.

CHAPTER TEN

About the only things today's boat, Tango, shared with the hotel ferry, Coconut, were blunt and sharp ends. Tango looked half as big again and it crouched like a hunting cougar. A large chair faced backwards in the fishing cockpit, stubby rods with golden reels bristled from the gunnels, along with gaffs, lures, nets, and lots of equipment I didn't recognize. A pair of long poles reached skyward, braced with wire on X-shaped supports, which were taller even than the aerials that topped the fish-spotting tower. Everywhere, I saw electronics, dials, screens that glowed green and orange and technology. It didn't seem fair to the fish.

I hadn't complained when Bear announced the fishing trip—though it had never featured on my to-do list. I could shout encouragement while he grappled with his catch, or do a little research on my own if the action was slow. Maybe a good day's fishing would get him to relax a little.

The captain approached. "Good morning, welcome aboard—"

"That's not an Australian accent. You're the understudy, aren't you?" Bear asked, eyes narrowing.

"The name's Perry. Suzi went into labor at 3am."

"How exciting!" I said.

"You any good at this?"

"Some people think so."

"License? Insurance?"

"Black folder in the cabin. Feel free to take a look."

"I certainly will." Bear stomped off.

"I'm Teal. And that's Edward, he's doing the fishing today. I'm just along for the ride," I said, extending my hand.

He stood frozen, staring at me. He blinked, the smile returned and he shook my hand.

"Is everything alright?" I asked.

"I'm sorry. Yes, absolutely. Perfect."

A young islander, all shoulders and sinewy arms, put down the huge fish hook he was sharpening and introduced himself as "Lotu".

As if weightless, Perry bounded up the flybridge ladder, where he began checking the instruments.

His polo shirt matched the blue of the sky. I noticed the way his biceps filled the cut-off sleeves, how his black hair had that rebellious curl-thing going on behind the ears.

He lifted the radio handset and listened, tapping it in the palm of his hand, a puzzled look spreading across his face. He sighed and began fiddling with switches.

"Everything okay?" I asked. Why didn't he answer?

Bear stood in the cockpit, inspecting the fishing gear. A warmth crept up the back of my neck—I had a strange feeling Perry was watching me from the corner of his eye.

"Can never remember which lever makes this boat go forwards," he said, just loud enough for me to hear. I stiffened.

He turned, grinning.

"You got me!" I said, laughing. Then I had a thought: Was that the first time I'd laughed since we arrived?

"English?" I asked.

"Guilty as charged."

"What are you doing so far from home?"

"Have you read War and Peace?" he asked.

"Sometimes, I think I wrote it."

For a second he held my gaze, then he pushed some buttons and turned the keys. The engines burbled. Perry checked his watch and studied the sky in a series of ninety degree chunks. He donned headphones, listened, then jotted something on a pad. Finally he checked the dials and turned to face us.

"Let's catch some fish!"

Lotu was talking to Bear. "For real big fish, we use the chair, boss. Otherwise, when a fish is on, you brace yourself here and give him line like this—"

"Listen son, you're talking to a man who's caught the king of fish—that's salmon—in Scotland. If you know how to play *them*, well obviously, you can handle anything that swims around here."

I gestured to Lotu to please continue as Bear advanced on the cooler and his first beer of the day.

The engines throbbed as the boat left the dock and swung towards the gap in the reef. I saw our A-frame, the empty bar. Falcon rested at anchor at the far end of the beach.

"So what would you like to catch?" Perry shouted.

"We have a choice?" I asked.

"Anything, as long as it's not endangered."

"What about one of those giant groupers, haw, haw?"

"You saw Black Jack?"

"Why's he called that?" I asked Perry.

"Named after the first owner of the place who built a remote fishing camp here back in the day. Because of the island's shape, he renamed it *Horseshoe* and told everyone it was lucky."

"And is it lucky?" I asked.

"Not for him. He ate the wrong fish and was poisoned."

"Salmonella?" Bear asked.

"Ciguatera. Caused by a number of toxins in a group of marine planktons known as dinoflagellates that coat parts of the reef. Herbivorous fish eat it, then predatory fish eat them and the toxin increases up the food chain. Most poisonings aren't fatal but the story goes he got drunk and took a bet. Ate a moray eel—they're full of the stuff."

I think you can relax Bear: This guy knows what he's talking about.

"What do you think that grouper weighs?" asked Bear.

"Seven, eight hundred pounds."

"He could feed a village," Bear said.

"He'd poison them too. No point killing him. I can show you where he lives."

Perry slowed the engines as we closed on the reef. "You see that red buoy, there's a coral overhang down there. He sits under it all day. Divers like to take photos of him. He's a local celebrity and he's used to people—well, he hasn't eaten anyone yet!"

"How deep is it there?" Bear asked.

"Twenty-five feet at low tide."

"Too deep for me."

"All you have to do is bang the end of the dock loud enough and he swims over like a faithful dog. Okay, time to get serious. The rods are numbered 'one to four'." Perry pointed at the left rod. "That's 'one'. So if I shout a number, you'll know which one to grab."

I don't think Bear was listening. He was still staring at the red buoy. I could tell he was thinking as he looked back at the dock. *Why's he so interested in an inedible fish?*

With the reef behind us, Perry pushed the throttles forward and the boat was soon flying, the morning haze swallowing our spreading wake. We headed around the island into the chop of the open ocean and slowed in the fathomless blue.

"There's a current here, we'll troll along it and see what's hungry," said Perry. "Birds working the end of it...worth checking it out with the sun at this angle."

"That makes sense," Bear said, rubbing his hands. "I use that trick with salmon."

Really, Bear? "Have you always fished?" I asked Perry.

"Yes, but very little these days except for the odd catch and release tournament if it's properly organized. I do take guests out if no one else is available."

"Does fishing worry you? I mean…"

"It's important people know what's involved in putting fish on the table. Then they can make their own choices. Anyway, I'm aware of the fragility of the local economy and I'm doing my bit to help. I try to fish responsibly and educate our guests, but I don't pretend it isn't a delicate balancing act."

To me the water had an endless uniformity to it. A vast shifting ultramarine desert which sparkled like a living thing. *Maybe people who live on boats aren't crazy after all.*

Two baits skipped and splashed on the surface behind us, the others worked below it.

"You think we're going too fast, Skipper?" shouted Bear.

Lotu came over and smiled. "Baits working real good, ma'am," he said softly.

"Perry said something about not catching endangered fish."

"He's careful what he catches, puts many fish back. Only keeps a few for the restaurant. If we're lucky, I get one too."

An hour later the sun had dissolved the last of the haze and the heat was building. The baits had been changed and the island had flattened to a strip of green that came and went as we rode the swell.

Lifting my beach bag, I pulled out a battered paperback entitled *Nomad Joe's South Pacific Wanderings*, and smiled at finding a section on Horseshoe Island. I flipped the pages but found nothing on local legends.

"Strike—line three!" Perry called, pointing.

Bear lurched towards a bucking rod. "Wind, boss, keep the line tight," Lotu said as he brought in the other lines.

"Smooth action, pump the fish," Perry added, slipping the boat in neutral. "Pump and wind. If he runs, let him go. Always keep the line taut. Not like that—smooth pumps…"

Bear wound in sharp bursts, jerking the rod with the same violence as his grunts. He swore and stood still.

Lotu shrugged and I noticed Perry raise his eyebrows. Then Perry said, "Bad luck. Wind in and we'll try again. Let's hope there are more yellowfin tuna around."

Bear thrust the rod at Lotu. "You wind it in. I need a beer."

My mind wandered back to the Blue Beluga with my seafood platter and delicious yellowfin sashimi. Who would have guessed a few weeks later

I'd be fishing for them?

"The day's still young," Perry said, as he rechecked the instruments and swung Tango onto a new heading.

I sat on the gunnel, enjoying the breeze and Nomad Joe's wanderings.

"Soda, ma'am?"

Popping the can, I asked him, "Are you from round here, Lotu?"

"Sure am."

"I heard there's a story about someone called Fonu. I assumed it was a local name."

"It was but that name's not used now because—"

"Strike! Line four!" shouted Perry.

Bear leapt across the cockpit and lifted the bent rod. Way out, a green and gold fish erupted in a cascade of spray. The flexing bar of energy twisted, sun flashing on its streaming flanks. It fell back with a splash to jump again, head shaking, as its tail threw an arc of droplets across the surface.

"Mahi-mahi!" Lotu said.

"A big one!" added Perry. Then, "Line two! Quick, Teal!"

"I'm not sure I want—" but Lotu thrust the rod in my hands and I tried to remember what I'd heard Perry tell Bear.

A voice was close behind me, "That's it, nice and smooth," Perry was leaning over me. "Follow my instructions and we'll boat this one for sure," he said.

I felt the weight of the fish and watched mesmerized as line blurred from the reel. When it stopped, I pumped and wound the reel handle, drawing the fish closer. I looked at Bear who was brutalizing his fish, sweating like a window in a car wash.

"What is it?" I asked Perry, as I paused to get the strength back in my arms.

"Another mahi-mahi. Take your time, you can't rush them."

Bear's fish was rolling on the surface. His breathing rasped as his sodden shirt stuck to his back and his neck glowed purple.

"Keep him coming, that's a good fish," Perry said to me. "We'll boat Mr. H's first."

"When I take the leader, reduce the drag, boss," Lotu told Bear.

He slipped on a glove and grasped Bear's line. He was leaning forward, gaff in hand, when the fish jumped. There was a crack like a pistol shot. Bear lurched back, swearing. He thrust the rod into Lotu's hand. He looked at Perry. "Anyone check this line recently. Obviously faulty."

"It's brand new, premium quality," Perry answered.

"I need a piss," said Bear. He headed for the cabin.

My fish was closer now and I marveled at the turquoise and golds that flashed from the water. Its strength surprised me. As it shook its head, I whispered, "I'm sorry, beautiful fish…"

"It's all about anticipating your opponent's next move," Perry said, as he leaned forward and pulled back a lever on the reel. "If he jumps now, he won't break the line."

The fish darted and kicked. When it swam broadside, Perry explained it was using its body like a keel to resist my pulling. Even as, little by little, it came closer, I wondered how the fight would end. In its death? Did I want to be a part of that? Then Lotu lunged with the gaff and lifted the gasping fish into the boat. It was huge, with a blunt head and scimitar tail. He raised a club. A hollow feeling flooded my stomach as he took aim. "Poor thing, do we have to—"

Bear was back, pounding across the deck. "I'll do that!" he shouted, grabbing the club.

He cracked the fish on the head, which shuddered into stillness. "Haw, haw!"

A wave of dizziness hit me as blood oozed from the creature's shattered eye.

Bear disappeared back into the cabin.

Perry spoke softly. "Jesus ate fish, his disciples were fishermen and mahi-mahi aren't endangered. Well, not around here. Yet."

"Still, it's…"

"I know what you're thinking. Some people give up meat. Others, like me, go the sustainable route. Plenty don't give a damn. It's one of those things we all have to make a choice about." He was looking at Bear when he added, "I've learned many people give up meat and fish when they see the killing."

"If you don't mind, I won't catch another."

Two hours later, the cloud had whisped to filamentous strands. Where the boat's wake quarreled with the freshening breeze, baby rainbows hung in the drifting spray. Bear was back, his eyes locked on the baits.

"Don't like that Perry guy," he said in a stage whisper. "I hope he isn't expecting a tip."

I resumed reading about the South Pacific and learned of the migration from Asia five thousand years ago of the people who first populated the islands. There were chapters on Magellan, Cook and Darwin, the impact of the Second World War and the region's economic prospects. But it was the local history that interested me most—and on that, Nomad Joe was disappointingly silent.

I looked at Lotu. "Can you tell me about the Whaling Rock?"

"That was bad business, ma'am. Long time ago."

"What happened?"

"Fonu was the son of the chief. They say he was a strange boy."

"In what way?"

"He was afraid of the ocean and disobeyed his father. A shark ate him."

"I thought he drowned," I said.

"Lots of stories about his death. They say he was born with a scar on his arm and that was why he was cursed."

"What else do you know?"

"Foreigners came to hunt the whales here. He got into trouble with them too."

"Oh, I don't know why that reminds me—" I called up to Perry: "Any news on the baby?"

Perry tapped the side of his head in an apology for forgetting; he lifted the radio handset. A minute later he jumped up and threw a barrage of punches in the air. "It's a girl!" he shouted, arms raised in victory.

Lotu laughed. "Normally he saves his *Rocky Dance* for when we catch a marlin."

"That's wonderful news!" I said, observing my emotionally inert partner from the corner of my eye. What was it Lizzie used to say? That other people's happiness could be shared or envied.

"Is there somewhere I can find out more about this Fonu story?" I asked Lotu.

"Library in town's got books.

"You're kidding, right? Haw, haw!"

"You mean all the way back at the main island? There's nothing closer?"

He shook his head.

"One more question, if you don't mind. Have you heard of someone called Thurston Morfil?"

"Do you see that?" Perry nodded at a rust-brown ship which dipped and rolled on the horizon. "It's disgusting."

"What is it?" asked Bear.

"Longliner. Taiwanese or Korean. They set a sixty-mile long line. Thousands of baited hooks. Totally unsustainable, and they know it."

"Sixty miles?" I repeated, trying to picture a fishing line stretching four times the length of Nantucket Island.

"When they've cleared out one part of the ocean, they move on to the next."

"Can't something be done about it?" I asked.

"Zero policing, greedy, crooked politicians, a lack of political will and turning a blind eye make a deadly combination. And it's not just the game fish they catch—the tuna, swordfish, marlin, sharks—but the by-catch, like turtles and seabirds."

"What nonsense, haw, haw. I read that the scientists were wrong about the rate the atmosphere would warm. Why should I believe the doom-mongering about over-fishing?"

I saw Perry's eyes flash but his voice remained level. "They've refined their models and established that the extra heat's been absorbed by the oceans. And the increased CO2 is causing acidification which has dire consequences for coral, the food chain, in fact—"

"Will the acid burn my delicate Hamilton skin?"

"No, but—"

"So what's the problem?"

"One problem is that a Hawaiian professor reckons longlines kill a hundred thousand albatrosses a year. These islands used to be important nesting sites for turtles. Only a few colonies left now. Doesn't help that the locals still eat them. And dolphins."

"They *eat* dolphins?"

"Hundreds, maybe thousands a year. And they also export them to Dubai and China for the aquarium trade. When they can make up to $150,000 for a single dolphin, you can understand why. I could go on and on about the ocean's problems…"

"Please don't, haw, haw!"

"Please *do*," I said quietly.

"The purse seiner trawlers are really bad news. The Spanish have a giant which can take three thousand tons of tuna in a single trip. *Three thousand tons!* That's more fish than some Pacific nations catch in a year!"

"How do they fish?" I asked.

"They encircle the tuna with a huge net, draw in the bottom and the fish are trapped. The ships have electronics, storage and refrigeration on board, spotting towers, some carry helicopters. Look at the mighty bluefin—the population's dropped by ninety-six per cent. Now they've added FADs to their toolbox. I wake up in a cold sweat thinking about it."

He noticed my puzzled look.

"Fish Aggregating Devices. Any sizable object floating out here causes fish to congregate around it. FADs are buoys equipped with GPS and sonar, so the fishermen know exactly when to come back. The by-catch problems are massive too—pilot whales, dolphins, rays, sharks, you name it, they're all dumped back in the ocean…dead."

"What about the government? Isn't there local pressure to keep these people out?" I asked.

"The Minister for Fisheries is a disgrace. He answers to the local Mr. Big who's untouchable. A few weeks ago I found a FAD, dragged it aboard and disposed of it on land."

"So they're here already?"

"Yes. But it's not all bad news. Marine charities have campaigned hard and brought purse seining with FADs to the attention of the public and some supermarket chains now ban tuna caught this way. There are other ways to fish, just less effective. With a pole and barbless hook, for example. A bunch of guys line the back of the boat. They spray the water which makes the tuna think there are baitfish around. They still take plenty of fish but at least there's no by-catch." He paused. "It just shows what can be achieved when the public learn about something and get behind it. I complained to the Ministry of Fisheries once and guess what? The local police now conduct random searches if they think I'm captaining a boat. It's a thinly veiled threat. So I keep my head down and my mouth shut. Well, for now anyway."

Perry eyes shifted and he stared over my shoulder at the ocean.

"Now they've built a cannery and processing plant on the main island. God knows what will happen to local fish stocks. Strange thing is, I tried to take a look at it a few weeks ago but they chased me away."

"I love your...passion."

"I've got passion too," Bear said with a meaningful look at my chest. "And if you'd only take up Dr. Mortimer's offer, I'd have a whole lot *more* passion, haw, haw!"

"I'm sorry—once I get started..." Perry said to me.

"Have you met the guy who lives on the sailboat?"

"You mean Falcon?"

"Yes."

Perry smiled. "You could say so."

"Why are you smiling?" Then I got it. "Oh, *you're* the marine biologist!"

CHAPTER ELEVEN

Why was I blushing? *Anyone could have made that mistake.*

"The fishing industry has a lot to answer for. They make me feel like crying," I said to cover my embarrassment.

"*I'm* crying out for another beer. Let's catch a marlin," shouted Bear, who thudded over to the far side of the boat.

"Right. Break out the heavy tackle," Perry said.

Lotu reappeared from the cabin with two rods as thick as snooker cues. The reels had doubled in size. He rigged them with great multi-colored lures; soon they were popping and plunging, streaming bubble trails in the wake.

"I call it 'all or nothing fishing'. You'll see why," Perry called.

We dragged the lures beneath a brutal sun, the boat rolling when we cut across the waves. Downwind the cockpit filled with nauseous diesel fumes. I tried to read but finally gave up. Bear paced the deck, finished another beer and retired to the cabin with a curt *Wake me if anything happens.* Today it looked like marlin fishing was going to be a nothing. Which was fine by me.

Lotu retrieved a line and was removing a clump of weed from the hook.

"I was asking before whether you'd heard of a man called Thurston Morfil," I said to him quietly.

"Everybody knows Mr. Morfil," he said without facing me.

"Can you give me some background? Like…what do people think of him?"

Lotu turned. "Fine man. We are lucky to have him here."

"Can you be more specific?"

"Whales…three o'clock!" Perry shouted.

The cabin door exploded open. "Which rod?"

"Look Bear, over there, whales!" I said, pointing at a cluster of dark shapes on the surface.

"A pod of sperm whales," said Perry. "Bring the lines in. We can get closer."

I counted six whales. They moved slowly, their black backs glistening like a huddle of submarines. Despite the distance and distortion of the water, I could see their enormous bulk. Though I held my camera ready, for now I just wanted to watch them, to be a part of their magical presence.

How strange that I'd shared a planet with creatures so vast and magnificent my whole life...yet had never really thought about them. As they nudged each other, I felt the bond between them. Then the smallest whale left the pod and swam towards us.

"Shhhh! Keep still. Here comes a calf," Perry said, cutting the engines.

The boat rocked gently as the creature, all head, tail and legend, approached. I sensed the inquisitive child in our trusting visitor. The little whale rolled to raise one eye out of the water...and in that moment I was *sure* she looked right at me. I held my breath as alien studied alien in the ocean-sky infinity of no man's land.

"Anyone got a harpoon? Haw, haw!"

A larger whale left the pod, blocked the calf's path and shepherded it back to the pod. Instinctively, I knew it was the mother. Something profound stirred within me: a sudden awareness of their intelligence, a recognition of the forces that bound their relationships, just as those forces bound ours. *How could anyone think of harming these gentle leviathans?*

"You're not really crying now, are you Teal?" Bear asked with a snort.

I wiped my eyes. "Something in my eye."

"Plenty people cry when they see whales, ma'am."

Finally, with unsteady hands, I remembered to take my first photo. I glanced at Perry. Was he wiping his eyes too? The whales slipped beneath the surface, their black tones fracking the cobalt, until the swirls and chop settled and they were gone.

Perry waited before restarting the engines. "We're lucky to see sperm whales. They're rare in these waters," he said.

"They were incredible. So...gentle and...huge," I said, embarrassed by the chasm between my words and what I'd seen.

"And mysterious," said Perry. "Scientists say they can hold their breath for ninety minutes. They can dive thousands of feet to catch giant squid..."

"I think...they're the most amazing things I've ever seen."

"Someone tell David Attenborough this is costing me money. We've got marlin to catch," called Bear.

"To think, we used to reduce such mighty, sentient creatures to candles and lamp oil," said Perry.

"And dog food," I added, remembering what Basil Thane had said about Icelandic whaling.

We dragged the lures back and forth. When a breeze picked up, I noticed how Perry ran at different angles to the waves and at different speeds too. He changed to larger lures then smaller ones, and he tried different color combinations. We worked them in the paling water close to the reefs, and far off in the deep where shifting obelisks of light broke and reformed beneath the swell. But the lures remained untouched. I found myself wondering if Perry was failing to catch a marlin on purpose, or if he ever found fishing boring. Then he surprised me.

"Some people find fishing boring. But there's always something to see, something to learn. I'm always trying to read the water. For me...it's about more than being here. I love the ocean's hidden language. The currents, the light, depth...the clarity, the time of day. Your world makes sense to you with dozens of things you respond to without thinking." He pointed at the on-screen chart. "Look at this trench in the ocean floor, we're right above it. Two thousand feet below us there's a crack a mile long. The US navy may know how deep it is. Don't think anyone else does. This place always makes me feel a bit strange."

"What caused it? Earthquake? Landslip?"

"No one knows. Maybe it's a relic of sea floor spreading—you know, plates moving apart. What I *do* know is you get weird currents around it and the fishing can be good here. That's my approach to fishing: I try to decode the water like a fish would."

Bear wandered over. "Listen, if you'd spend more time decoding the ocean and less time decoding my girlfriend, we might actually catch something."

Perry didn't respond immediately. When he did, it was as if he hadn't heard, or chose to ignore him. "It would be easy to blame the longliners and purse seiners. Or come up with some reason why the fish aren't hungry right now. All I can say is if I could guarantee fish, I'd call it 'catching' and not 'fishing'." He faced Bear. "And I'd lose interest in five minutes."

Bear didn't reply.

When Bear was back at the stern, Perry said, "If you can handle more ocean facts, I'm usually at the bar mid-morning. That is, if Violet isn't giving me flying lessons."

"You're learning to fly?" I asked, but I didn't hear his answer because Lotu called him over with a query, which he answered while I wondered who Violet might be.

A blow of spray on the horizon brought my thoughts back to the whales. The mother, when she'd approached, before she nudged her calf away, had passed us side-on. It was then, with her vastness suspended in the ocean that I'd looked into her eye too, right after the little calf's. Though she wasn't too close, I'd *known* she'd not only looked right back into mine, but she'd held my gaze for some of the most intense seconds of my life.

Perry was standing behind me. "That was magical," I whispered to myself, half hoping he'd hear.

"I told you this place was."

I wasn't sure I'd heard him correctly. Turning, I looked into his eyes. It was the first time I'd noticed their mischievous sparkle and how the sunlight that danced on the wave tops, danced there too. Suddenly I was back in The Blue Beluga, as a suntanned man recommended a remote island in the South Pacific.

"Oh," I whispered, as a wave of dizziness washed through me. "It's *you*!"

CHAPTER TWELVE

"I'm off for a walk. I need some photos of the sunset, Musculus's travel section might use them," I called to Bear who was exuberantly ignoring the sign asking guests to conserve water when showering.

"Meet you at the bar," came the muffled reply. "If not there, in that sweat hole they call the business center."

The sky softened as heat abandoned the day, but the sand still held its warmth. I photographed our A-frame before setting off along the beach. Bear seemed to have no interest in a tour of the island with me. Or a swim. Or anything else for that matter. He was spending a lot of time in the business center. When I had asked what he was working on, he'd grunted. And with me catching the only fish today, his mood had plummeted.

I scrolled through the photos in my camera's LCD panel and came to one of me on the dock. Lotu, all teeth and wiry muscles, held my fish out in front of us. On the blackboard below my name was *mahi-mahi 38 lbs*. Perry probably shouldn't have asked Bear what the largest salmon he'd ever caught weighed...

Passing the hotel computer room, I found myself wondering whether Alice had answered my email yet and decided to look in.

A frozen screen and two reboots later I read:

Hi Teal, glad the place is fab. I asked Warren, but you got your wires crossed because we're visiting my family in San Francisco—he told Edward way back, so if Edward's expecting someone, it's not us. Can't wait to catch up when you get back! Love, Axx

That was odd. Why would Bear make that mistake? He wouldn't. Which meant someone else was coming. But who? Should I ask him straight out or play it cool?

I clicked next on an email from Malcolm.

Ran into Sir B—you need to do a really good job on Thurston Morfil, darling. And don't take forever getting something to me, even if it's routine background stuff at this stage—I need to show him you're on the case. M

Malcolm had always impressed on me the need to read between the lines of what people said and wrote. Was there anything I'd missed in his message? Or was the ramping up of pressure just standard Musculus tactics?

I tapped an email back informing Malcolm that Thurston Morfil's office hadn't confirmed a date yet, but initial indications suggested some of my piece would indeed be routine, banal, even. I giggled at what I'd written because the *b* key hadn't worked. Two attempts later, I added a few lines about how fabulous the place was and asked him to please make my colleagues as jealous as possible.

"Evening Ms. Douglas, do you have a moment?"

I looked up from the keyboard. "Hi, Kris. Something wrong?"

"Sorry to trouble you but would you mind stepping into my office?"

With the door closed, he turned to face me, his cheeks tinged with pink. "It's just that Mr. Hamilton complained the girl who cleans your room had been going through your personal possessions. He said she must have been looking for something to steal. I wanted to apologize. Of course I've let her go."

"You fired her?"

"I'm disappointed, of course, as I've had no complaints about her before."

"I see." *A girl who'd always done well had lost her job—no doubt a really important one to her—because Edward had accused her of theft.* "I'd like you to give her the job back."

"I don't understand."

"Maybe not our room. Could you find her others to clean?"

"But Mr. Hamilton—"

"If you say she's trustworthy, then perhaps Edward made a mistake."

"Thank you…she'll be thrilled. We all make mistakes, Ms. Douglas."

"Yes, I suppose we do…" I said more to the butterfly that floated past the window than to Kris.

I was approaching the end of the beach to get my sunset pictures. Why had Edward accused the cleaner of stealing? It was obvious she had no reason to disturb my letters. But why was *he* interested in them? They meant nothing to him—but everything to me. At least the cleaner had her job back.

I drew level with Falcon, then wandered towards the rocks a little further on. An islander's canoe was pulled up on the beach. A thin wooden pontoon-style stabilizer, held by bamboo arms was lashed to its side. I was surprised by the narrow hull, the crude workmanship.

The last of the sun brushed the horizon. A swarm of fireflies with their tiny lights flashed over the rocks. I watched them before raising my camera. Then a man—an elderly islander—got to his feet, the fireflies circling above him. He sprang off the rocks and walked over.

"I'm sorry, I didn't see you there. I got a couple of photos of the fireflies. Do you mind? You may be in them."

"You took my picture, lady?" he said quietly.

"If you're offended, I can delete them. Or if you'll let me keep them, I'd be happy to pay you something."

I took out my wallet and he stepped closer, staring at it. That's strange. Should I walk quickly away? But it was *his* island and I was the outsider. Opening the wallet, I pulled out a note but instead of taking it, he continued staring. Was I insulting him? Was that too much or should I have offered more?

"May I see that, lady?"

I'd brought Grandpa's strange wallet here because it had been in the padded envelope with Lizzie's letters when I'd packed for the trip. I was surprised at how well it repelled sand and water. But why was the old man interested in it? Still, it was *mine*. "Maybe it's better if I delete the—"

"Where did you get that?" he asked, his voice trembling.

"Excuse me?"

"Where did you buy it?"

"It was my grandfather's."

"You use a man's wallet?"

"It's about all I have of his."

"Let me see it, please."

The wallet had little cash in it. Surely there was no reason for him to steal it. No warning bells in my head, no butterflies in my stomach; there were still a few guests just down the beach from us. I didn't feel threatened, so I handed it to him.

He studied it in the failing light and then rubbed his fingers over the leather. His mouth dropped at the edges. He spoke softly. "Bad energy. Lady, it is better if it goes back."

"I don't understand..."

He was staring at me as he shook his head. He opened the wallet and handed me the money. Then he spun around and climbed back on the rocks, walking to the water's edge.

"Wait!" What was I to do? I wasn't going to get into a fight with anyone, let alone an islander who looked about eighty. I watched him lean down and heard some mumbled words. After a few minutes he returned and said, "It is done. I hope he forgives them."

"Them?" I asked.

Without answering my question, he walked past me, dragged the canoe into the water and climbed in. I lost sight of him as he paddled quickly around the headland.

Out of curiosity, I climbed onto the rocks and walked to where he'd knelt down. The wallet rested by the water under a scattering of purple flower petals. They reminded me of the morning glory the little girl had given me when we arrived.

Well, it *is* the only thing I have of Grandpa's, I thought, picking it up.

I'd taken a few steps when I felt it—a cold edge to the breeze. I shivered and headed back wondering if rain was expected.

I met Kris coming out of the canvas equipment tent with a baby sleeping in a sling across his chest. He introduced me to Luna who gurgled in her sleep. He asked if everything was okay and I described my encounter with the elderly man.

"Don't worry about it," he said quietly, as we walked back in the gloaming. "I know who he is. He can behave a little strangely but I've never heard of him doing anything untoward."

"I'm sure I've seen him before," I said. "Yes, at the airstrip when we arrived."

"We call him 'Firefly Bob'. He's stuck in the past and the world's moved on without him. But one thing's worth remembering: Forget everything you know when trying to understand the locals. They have a completely different view of how the world works."

"Interesting...and there may be a story in there too. Do you think there's anyone who could tell me—"

"Well, that's what Emma keeps reminding me. And you know what? The more time I spend here, the more I find myself questioning everything I've been taught. That's why we want her..." He stroked the baby's blond curls. "...to be exposed to some of their beliefs. It isn't, after all, the South Pacific islanders who are destroying our planet."

"Are you saying you believe their legends?"

"Well, here's something to think about: The ocean floor around the islands was first surveyed in the Seventies and they found a deep trench—"

"Yes, we fished over it."

"So how do you explain—oh!" Luna was writhing in her sling. Kris stroked her forehead and made a C-shape with his hand, touching his chin and moving it quickly away.

"Hot?" he asked her.

He saw my puzzled expression. "We're starting the baby sign language early. Worked like a charm for Emma's sister. It lets babies communicate without crying."

"The trench?"

"Oh yes, Firefly Bob claims he's known about it since childhood. It's quite possible because Emma read about it in a book on local legends that was published in the 1930s. Apparently that's why he says we're on sacred ground but he won't say anything more. He just gets upset. Paddles away shaking his head at our ignorance."

"He made me feel about two inches tall."

"Emma too. She had all but given up on her doctorate and was about to fly back to Auckland when she met yours truly. The rest, as they say, is history."

"Does Emma believe there's a legend? Or know anything about Fonu?"

"You'll have to ask her."

CHAPTER THIRTEEN

I pulled my deckchair under the parasol, angling it at the ocean as the morning sun crept across the cloudless sky. To my right the sun glinted on Falcon's deck fittings; beyond lay the rocks. Closing my eyes, I saw the old man again. What had been so special about the wallet? Why had he scattered flower petals around it and said something about someone forgiving *them*. Who was he referring to?

How arrogant of me to have thought it was the money. I'd arrived here knowing nothing of the islanders' beliefs and customs, and through my ignorance, I'd managed to offend someone, a very nice someone who had said I was special and given me a purple flower on the day he welcomed me to his country. And I had no idea what I'd done wrong. While that would probably delight Bear, it concerned me.

I reminded myself I was here to report on Thurston Morfil. I was waiting for an interview over which I had no control, which might happen in days or weeks, but at every turn, a local legend, this boy Fonu and a strange rock kept cropping up. To keep me busy and satisfy my curiosity, why not see what I could uncover about the legend? It seemed interesting and who knows, it might even provide some background to the Morfil report.

"Good morning Ms. Douglas."

"Hi Kris, I wish you'd call me Teal."

"With pleasure."

"I've been thinking. If I wanted to do some research on the islands, get a feel for their history and politics—would the library on the main island be a good place to start? Is there anything closer?"

"We have a little lending library on the shelf over there for guests, but yes, the only real library is on the main island. Emma's been there and she mentioned it's got a couple of useful books, although current politics is all about one man."

"Thurston Morfil?"

"Someone's done their homework. I can ring and get them to reserve them for you."

"I'd appreciate that. Are they open Saturdays?"

"I'll check. I'll drop you on Tofua'a and you can get the island hopper to the main island. Oh, just remembered: I've got an old scrapbook somewhere. A previous resort owner put it together years ago. I'll dig it out—it may be helpful too." With a smile he was on his way.

My windsurfer glided through the ripples as I approached the gap in the reef. A few dozen yards later, the playful aquamarine surrendered to a somber navy blue. I dropped the sail, and drifted thirty feet above the dark coral of the drop off, my shadow passing over hovering fish, clumps of weed. I sat cross-legged on the windsurfer board enjoying the silence, the tranquility—not really thinking, just being there. A dark shape moved from the coral and approached the surface. I shielded my eyes from the glare.

A small head poked through the surface, gulped air.

"Hello, turtle," I said, as its splayed flippers slid back and forth, carrying it ever closer. I sat very still, willing it towards me.

A mechanical roar behind me made me turn. A jet ski, a plume of water spurting behind it, was charging towards me. I braced myself as Edward flew past. He waved, shouted something and when the windsurfer had stopped rocking, the turtle was gone—an empty dorito bag in its place. As I lifted the sail to return to the beach, Edward was heading straight out to sea.

The sun warmed my tired muscles; soon it would dry my swimsuit. Sun block applied, I pulled the rim of my hat down and relaxed onto my beach chair.

"Excuse me, lady. But Mr. Hamilton…"

I opened my eyes. One of the beach attendants was now standing over me. "Yes?"

"I told him to stay close, stay inside the reef. But…"

I sat up and looked in the direction the young man indicated. "I can't see him."

"He is stuck on the rock." He handed me binoculars and I stared through their fogged lenses. Adjusting the focus on Whaling Rock, I saw a stationary jet ski beside it and a lump on the rock that could only be Bear.

"What on earth is he doing there?"

"I told him that jet ski wasn't running right but he didn't listen. Now he's stuck in a bad place."

"Can't you get him? Tow him back with another jet ski?"

"Not me, lady."

"Are the tides too strong?"

The youth shook his head and stared at his feet.

"Okay. There must be a beach manager. Could you take me to him or her?"

"Beach manager?" he asked.

"Great! Now what are we going to do? I suppose I'll have to—"

From the corner of my eye, I saw Perry emerge from the cabin of Falcon. He stretched his arms, and balanced on the stern like a brown 'T'. Then he dived in. I admired the precision, reflected in the tidy splash and waited for him to reappear, but the surface remained unbroken. Had something happened? Was he okay?

The boy stood in the surf. Why was he smiling? How could someone hold their breath *that* long?

"Where is he?" I asked, wading in knee deep.

"Mr. Perry always does this. He's copying an island tradition," the beach attendant explained.

My stomach started to clench. *Since when did drowning become an island tradition?* Finally, a dark shape joined the foaming white of the surf. A head appeared and then Perry stood in front of us, the surf pulling at his thighs, his pale trunks breaking the bronze of his sculpted body. He flicked his head and a spray of water caught the sunlight before his hands swept back the wavy curls. I found myself mesmerized as his diaphragm rose and fell with each breath.

The beach attendant walked over to Perry who glanced out to sea, then at me. After a flashing smile, the boy helped him slide a jet ski parked on the beach into the water. Raising the binoculars, I watched the spouting wake as he charged towards the rock. He stopped beside it and it was some time before Bear stood up and clambered down. They returned to the beach in tandem, linked by a straining rope, with Perry towing Bear who sat astride his broken jet ski.

When Perry finally reached the water's edge in front of me and switched off the engine, I asked, "Why on earth did you go there, Bear?"

"Last I heard it's still a free world."

Perry shook his head in frustration. I thanked him as he pulled his jet ski back up the beach near me. Bear rolled off the broken jet ski and wallowed on his back, spurting water from his mouth.

Perry nodded his head in Bear's direction. "Look, I think he's had enough sun but he won't take my advice. Maybe he'll listen to you." He strode past me towards the bar, as Bear lumbered up the beach to where I sat on the beach chair.

"One thing I *don't* need is to be lectured by a tuna-obsessed gym bunny."

"You need to get out of the sun."

"I can't stand this damn island. Going to check emails. Some of us have work to do."

When he was out of sight, I wrapped my sarong around me and walked up to the bar, my beach bag over my shoulder. Perry was writing in a note book.

"Sorry to disturb you," I said.

"You're not disturbing me at all. I was just recording a double pilot whale sighting."

"I wanted to apologize. And to say 'thanks'. "

"Don't worry about it. Can I get you something?"

"It's *me* who should be getting *you* something."

He motioned to the bartender. "Toka, please make the lady a Horseshoe Whisperer." He turned to me. "A little something I concocted. It's on The Blue Beluga's menu."

"I'd love to try it."

"Think I'll join you. Toka, please make two."

"Coming right up, Mr. Perry."

Toka sliced and blended fruit, tilted bottles and crushed ice. He presented the cocktail with a slice of pineapple and a mini fanfare.

There was a hint of sweetness: I tasted rum, orange, coconut. "It's delicious. Really, it is."

"So pleased you like it. It cost me three liver transplants to perfect. Oh, I heard you had a strange encounter with Firefly Bob."

"I took a couple of photos of him by mistake. I offered to pay for them but he walked off with my wallet instead!"

"I've seen him pose for pictures before, so don't worry—you didn't commit some terrible crime."

I took a sip. "While we weren't talking about it, the beach attendant said something about an island tradition...which is why you insist on swimming ashore underwater."

He laughed. "Oh, *that*. Apparently the young men here did that in an ancient rite of passage. Anyway, we'll have to make sure you stay in old Bob's good books. Next time I see him, I'll launch a PR offensive."

"Thanks. May I ask you something?"

He turned to face me. "Sounds serious."

I laughed. "I'm curious as to why you're here. Apart from counting starfish, that is."

"It's rewarding work, you know."

"I bet."

"I used to suffer from wandering albatross syndrome. Not much to keep me in England so I ended up stateside. Then I found this place, it and...it called to me," he said softly.

"You feel more settled here than in Manhattan?" I looked around. "I think I can buy that."

"I split my time between the two. They couldn't be more different. Yet strangely, I sort of sense I belong here. I don't know whether I should tell you this…"

Touching a finger to my lips, I said, "I can keep a secret."

"Just a moment." He picked up his drink and took three gulps.

"Uh-oh." I raised mine too.

Now he was patting the water drops on the bar with a napkin.

"Look, if this is too personal I…"

He turned to face me. "I really hope I get the chance to tell you the whole story before you leave. All I can say now is something strange is going on. But same question at you. Of all the gin joints in all the towns in all the world you walk into mine. Why?"

I laughed, though I registered a serious edge to the question. I wanted to answer but hesitated in case I said something wrong and spoiled the moment. I started carefully. "Because a charming man who does a terrible Bogart impersonation recommended it?"

"Violet wasn't impressed either."

That's the second time he'd mentioned her—had I detected a fondness in his voice when he said her name? Who was she? His wife? Girlfriend? And why was he trying to impress her? He was speaking again.

"Something tells me there's more to you being here than me recommending it," Perry said.

Okay, I can ask about Violet later. All we're doing is talking, having a drink. Right?

"You won't laugh?"

He placed a hand on his heart. "Perry's honor."

"I'm not sure where to start."

"The end would be my third choice."

If I tell him everything, will he think I'm crazy?

"Please tell me, I won't think you're mad."

"Now you're reading my mind!"

He stared at me and I'd seen that expression before—when we were drifting with the whales. His intensity felt a little disarming but I desperately wanted to tell *someone*. So I told Perry, a man I'd only just met, about my job, how work for me had to be about making a difference…and that I seemed to be thwarted at every turn. I described how close I had been to Grandma Lizzie and mentioned her story telling.

Then I took a deep breath and told him about the music—the music at the awards ceremony *and* the music I'd heard waking from dreams. I studied him as I spoke, searching for clues that he was uncomfortable or bored, ready to change course at the first frown and pretend the whole thing was a joke. But his expression never changed and when I hesitated, he nodded encouragement. I told him it was as if I'd been summoned to this remote corner of the planet.

Finally, he let a long breath escape in a controlled sigh. Then he sat quite still, without speaking.

"I'm sorry, I've said too much. I'd better go." I slipped off the chair and started walking. Now, I thought, I've ruined everything.

"Teal, wait!"

"I have to…check on Edward."

He gently took my wrist and he turned me to face him. Why was my heart thumping?

"You don't understand." He looked around without letting go. He moved closer. Satisfied no one could hear, he whispered, "That's why I'm here. I feel like I was summoned too."

CHAPTER FOURTEEN

As I walked across the bedroom in our A-frame the next morning, I noticed my hand had settled on my wrist where Perry had touched it.

I leafed through Kris's scrapbook on the desk which contained photos, dinner menus, some tide tables and newspaper cuttings. One cutting entitled *Court Rejects Islander's Property Claim—Again!* was so faded I couldn't read past the first line. Another addressed the fledgling tourist industry, a third featured local wildlife. Not one of the yellowed articles was dated this millennium but I kept turning pages and studying photos in the hope that something might prove to be useful background material.

I smiled at the hairstyles in a set of black and white wedding photos and laughed at the Bermuda shorts of the men playing golf at low tide on a vast sand-flat (location unknown). I learned they'd extended Horseshoe's jetty in 1972 and renovated the bar two years later. Smiling faces, deep suntans, an occasional islander staring cautiously at the camera. But nothing much on local history. There was a flap at the back and I felt inside it. Paper? I pulled out several sheets: the staple that once bound them had left a rusty stain. I counted five pages, but the last was torn in half. Were pages missing?

The font looked old—perhaps it was *Carbon Type*. In places the ink was faint. Words had been crossed out and ragged lines lead to illegible margin jottings. I made a mental note to read this document after I'd read the newspaper articles.

A flatulent emission from the other side of the room broke my concentration.

"Teal?"

"I'm going for a jog, see you at breakfast," I answered. I replaced the document in the scrapbook, checked my waistpack was secure and slipped out of the room. Outside I inhaled the scented damp of the post-dawn tropics. A few tendon-lengthening stretches later, I was running along the sand.

I nodded to the beach cleaners who'd raked the garbage into mounds along the high tide line. A sandy path took me through knee-high scrub, palms providing shade as I side-stepped fallen coconuts. Soon I reached the beach at the back of the island and slowed to admire the azure of the open ocean. Three sets of push ups, sit ups, lunges and crunches later, I followed the path back to re-emerge on the main beach.

Birds dipped and wheeled above Whaling Rock, but a sudden movement made them veer away. Despite the haze, I could see a lone figure standing there, facing the shore, arms limp at his sides. A tingle ran down my spine. The man raised a dark arm and then pointed. At me.

Looking around, I confirmed I was the only person on the beach. I rubbed my eyes. Now he waved, with long, deliberate strokes of the air. It struck me that most people wave with the upper arm but this was different. He kept his arm straight and it described generous semi-circles above his shoulder. The way you'd wave if you wanted someone to see you from far away.

I was glued to the spot. Why was he waving? Who was he? I noticed that no jet ski or boat was tied up to the rock. How had he gotten there? Was he stranded? From this distance, surely he couldn't see who I was. *Could he?*

A cracking twig made me turn. A beach cleaner emerged from the scrub dragging a bulging garbage bag.

"Excuse me," I said. "That person on the rock. Do—"

He shaded his eyes with his hand. "No one there, lady," he said before walking away.

I rubbed my eyes and checked again. Gulls hovered once more over the unbroken strip of stone—with no man in sight.

I glanced at my watch. If I kept Bear waiting at breakfast...well, we both knew he'd start without me. Turning, I began a second loop of the scrubby track that led to the back of the island.

This back beach had a more aggressive slope; clumps of seaweed and driftwood lay scattered on the unruly sand. Gulls pecked along the tide line as I settled with my back against a boulder. Smooth and warm, it offered a welcome additional barrier between me and our A-frame on the other side of the island. *And* it reminded me of a secret place I had discovered with Grandma, where we had devoured our picnics. I pulled a tissue from my pocket and wiped my hands. Then I lifted the envelopes from my waist-pack. The ribbon fell away and I opened Letter Two.

"I'm sorry Grandma, this is the first chance I've had to be alone..."

What on earth was he up to? How could anyone work on reigniting the spark if one of the parties wasn't even around to be sparked?

"Have you been chasing Mucus Media? They don't sound very on top of it. Send you all this way and—"

"I wish Morfil's PA would return my calls."

"Anyway, you'll have James Bond to look after you."

"Well, at least I'll—*what?*"

"I've seen how you look at him."

I felt the heat in my face. All I'd done was talk to Perry who was polite, charming. Unlike Edward, who corrected or dismissed everything I said, Perry seemed to enjoy our discussions.

"Don't be ridiculous!" I said.

"Methinks the lady doth protest too much."

"I don't see—"

"William Shakespeare."

This time he wasn't getting away with it: "Get your facts first, and then you can distort them as much as you please."

"Facts? I saw—"

"Mark Twain."

*   *   *

"Join us for breakfast, Angel?"

I looked up at Nancy, who was yawning. "Sorry, I was miles away," I said.

"We saw you sitting all alone."

"You look tired, Nancy."

"Bad night's sleep. Woken in the middle of the night by weird noises. Anyway, Frank said you looked like a gal with a problem. Come and tell us all about it?"

"What sort of weird noises?"

"Don't worry about it, Angel."

Why doesn't she want to talk about it? "I'd love to have breakfast with you. Promise you won't laugh if I tell you what just happened to me?"

"Depends if it's funny," Nancy said as we strolled to her table. She stared at Frank. "Whatever's wrong, dear? You look...green."

Frank drained his orange juice in one giant swig as I smiled hello.

"Excuse me," he said with a grimace. He pushed his fork into the crinkly mass on his plate. "Whatever *this* is, it's disgusting."

"Teal's going to tell us what just happened to her." Nancy pointed to her forehead. "Remember, worrying causes frowning and frowning causes wrinkles. If you're not careful, you'll end up like me."

"Love you just the way you are," Frank said gently.

Nancy winked at me. "See how well trained he is?"

Frank lowered his coffee cup. "Will I burn in hell for thinking instant coffee's fine—so long as you don't start off believing it's coffee? Okay, shoot, Teal—I'm all ears."

"Can I get a treble espresso here?" Nancy asked.

"There isn't an easy way of saying this but...I think I saw a ghost."

"Don't we just love ghost stories, Frank?"

"Sure do!"

I described the man on the rock as they stared. Then Frank patted the back of my hand.

"What did Edward say?"

"Didn't tell him."

"Well dear, *we* believe you," said Frank.

"I was wondering if what I saw had anything to do with the legend no one wants to talk about."

"Oh, don't you just love this island? Wildlife and whales, strange noises in the night and now a ghost too!" Nancy said.

Their excitement was infectious. Soon the conversation changed direction and Frank said he'd taken photos of eleven bird species, dolphins (one was jumping), two species of bat and a *giant* coconut crab with claws as big as his hands. Nancy had been writing postcards, working on her vitamin D replenishment (AKA her killer tan) and tomorrow they planned a trip to the local market.

"No luck with the skink yet?" Nancy asked him.

"To see one would make my day."

"You absolutely *must* check out the market with us. Kris says there are all sorts of fun things to see," Nancy said to me.

"And *buy*, if I know my wife."

I told them I'd love to. Frank looked at me and said, "So tell us about Teal. What brings you to Horseshoe?"

I explained I was here to interview a local VIP, as part of a big public relations exercise for my company. A glowing piece would ensure me a promotion and a welcome pay rise. I told them I didn't know why Bear had agreed to come—that he'd seemed surprisingly keen. But the choice of resort was mine.

I wondered whether I should mention that I'd met Perry in New York and that he'd actually recommended The Sun and Moon. No, I decided. A ghost story was enough for now.

"And what if you *don't* write a glowing piece?" asked Frank.

"Journalistic integrity is everything. We're required to be forthright, objective, professional. We—"

"Sounds to me like the girl's gonna get fired," said Nancy, yawning again.

"Why not have a nap this afternoon, Pumpkin?"

"Never heard anything like it in my entire life. The same noise repeated, over and over. If they were words, I sure couldn't understand them."

Thinking of the mysterious music, I asked, "Did it drift in from the ocean? Was it slow, sad...like a tune?"

"No. Fast and only one note. I can't describe its mood. But after an hour of it, I sure could describe mine! Why, Angel?"

It didn't sound like the same thing. But what on earth could it have been? "Just an idea...don't worry about it."

"It's a shame I sold *The Bugle*," Frank said.

"The Bugle?"

"Our east coast newspaper, I could have offered you a job."

"You aren't kidding—if I screw up, it'll be the end of my career in the big city. And they're cranking up the pressure: They want the report yesterday."

"Hmm," said Frank. "And what's this VIP's name?"

"Thurston Morfil."

A look passed between them but as quickly as I spotted it, it was gone.

"When are you interviewing him, Angel?" asked Nancy, gulping her jet black coffee that had just arrived.

"No idea. I'm still waiting for a call."

"Now if you're any good with words, maybe you can help me with this." Nancy pulled a piece of paper from her pocket. "Frank left it under my pillow. M—Y—I—T—D—R—I—T—M—P."

"Is it code?"

"Sort of." She looked at her watch, then at her husband. "You haven't won that dollar yet. I've still got five minutes."

Frank laughed. "Anyway Teal, why not find out more about the ghost and write about that?"

"Where there's a ghost, there's a story," added Nancy. "Just imagine, it could be about love, intrigue, betrayal, revenge. What fun!"

"Not sure who'd read it."

"*We* would, wouldn't we, Pumpkin?"

"Sure! You must give it a catchy title. How about 'The Specter of Horseshoe Island'? I'm shivering already!"

I smiled. "Okay, same question to you guys. What brings you here?"

Frank leant forward, making a tent with his fingers. "After a lifetime in business, we decided to catch up on the things we'd missed out on, like travel. You know, see the world, try to give something back."

"What line of work were you in, Frank?"

"If there was a pie, he had a finger in it."

He leaned back. "I guess I kept pretty busy."

"What Mr. Modesty isn't telling you is that he kept a lot of people in work."

"And *you're* being modest, Pumpkin. Tell Teal about *Green Wingers*."

"I started a little business with my bestie, Anne, selling garden ornaments which we sold through my garden center. Life-size concrete angels, in fact."

"*Little* as in sales in all fifty states, plus Canada and Turkmenistan."

"Turkmenistan?"

"Your guess is as good as ours," Frank said.

"Frank, you'll have me blushing."

"Have you ever seen an angel, Nancy?"

"No, but Anne has. Her home's full of books and paintings of angels. We thought making our statues might attract more of the celestial host. Have you ever seen one, Teal?"

"I'd like to—but I'm not sure I believe in them." Looking at them in turn, I asked, "How did you get interested in wildlife?"

"Frank owned a pet shop. One day we realized the right place to see animals was in the wild."

"Now that I'm retired, I'm photographing and recording everything. Last year it was West Africa, the year before, Australia. I forward my findings to a contact at the Smithsonian. No idea how useful it is but she's always so grateful, so encouraging. I hope to get some whale shots here."

I nodded.

"That nice Perry who lives on the sailboat..." Nancy gestured towards Falcon. "He was telling us about the whales here. In the old days, hundreds of them spent the summer frolicking between the islands."

"We saw sperm whales two days ago with Perry. It...made me...cry."

"There should be humpbacks too, this time of year," Frank said. "He was telling us that he recognizes individuals by their flukes—their tails—because each one is different. The whales return year after year to mate and give birth. But they feed only in the Antarctic."

Emma walked into the dining room. I watched as she greeted her guests, one table at a time.

"Whales don't interest Edward and anyway he's going away. But *we* could go whale watching."

"Try and stop me," said Nancy. "And our own Ansel Adams might get the photo of a lifetime that he's always dreamed of—Edward's going away? Whatever for, dear?"

Seeing the tears in my eyes, she quickly changed subject.

Frank fiddled with his camera. "I'm entering a little competition back home. First prize is five hundred bucks!"

"I bet you're quite the expert."

Emma glided over. "Another perfect morning in paradise. How's everyone today? Chilled?"

"A little tired, dear," said Nancy. "Love what you've done to your hands! What is that, a tattoo?"

"Indian henna. Beautiful, eh? It fades in a couple of weeks so planning something *way* more intricate next time. This came for Edward, Teal-babe." She handed me a manila envelope. "I just missed the boys. Edward's on Coconut with Kris—airstrip bound."

"I'm sure it can wait till he gets back."

"Where's he going, dear?" asked Frank.

I shrugged, looking down at my hands. "He didn't say goodbye."

Nancy leaned forward and squeezed my arm. "That's what my ex used to do, Angel. Disappeared for days at a time 'on business'. Can you guess what he was doing?"

"Oh, Bear would never do *that!* Anyway, I'm here trying to salvage our relationship. Isn't that the right thing to do?"

"Dear Teal…why are you trying so hard to save it?" Frank asked.

"It's just that—well, my other two relationships were disasters. If this one fails too, I might as well join a nunnery. Or surround myself with cats."

"There's nothing wrong with cats, they're delightful, but Angel, it's high time you started having some fun. Meet you at the beach bar at noon?"

"I really should do some online research."

"Dudes, please excuse me but I'm off to chant," Emma beamed.

"I'm a 'dude'?" Frank asked, with a laugh.

"Chant?" Nancy added.

"The Lotus Sutra from Nichiren Daishonin Buddhism: 'Nam myoho renge kyo'. Later peeps." Emma and her sandalwood cloud wafted off to the next table.

Nancy laughed. "That's one mystery solved. It was her chanting on the beach," Nancy said. Then she looked at me. "Meant to tell you—that divine Perry has a tattoo in an unexpected place!"

Frank rolled his eyes in mock horror.

"God's my witness, he just happened to climb out of the surf in front of me and—"

"She was standing there pretending to admire his boat," Frank added, his finger tapping the table.

"Oh, Franklin darling—" Her hand slipped around his shoulders and she squeezed him. "He doesn't compare to you."

"Sure!"

She laughed. In a conspiratorial whisper, she said, "His trunks had slipped a little. Couldn't see the tattoo properly before he pulled them up."

I felt a surge of optimism. It might only be for a few days but I'd come all this way and yes, I *was* going to start enjoying myself. Had I really expected Edward to sit still for three weeks? If he *was* chasing another deal, perhaps I should be…grateful. It would give me time to think. And maybe he was working so hard because he was thinking of our future.

"Noon at the bar, it is," I said.

Nancy threw her hands up in delight. "M—Y—I—T—D—R—I—T—M—P: Meet you in the dining room in ten minutes, Pumpkin!"

Frank laughed. "Darn. That puts you three bucks ahead."

*　　*　　*

I dropped the manila envelope on the table next to the bed and changed into a black one-piece swimsuit, catching my reflection in the full length mirror. Yes, the new gym routine had paid off—I now felt I had more energy to meet all my deadlines and pursue any story that Malcolm or Sir Basil could throw at me. Or follow up story ideas of my own—like the Specter of Horseshoe Island, for starters.

Who had waved at me from the rock? And there was Lizzie's mysterious letter that told me to get an ally and investigate the past. Bear was leaving for a few days (for reasons unknown). And had I imagined the look that passed between Frank and Nancy when I mentioned Thurston Morfil? What was *that* about? Clearly, there was more than one mystery swirling around this paradise…

"If you're watching Grandma, please send a sign…because I feel I'm in way over my head."

I looked around for a new hiding place for my precious letters. I checked behind another picture (too obvious), under the mattress (severe danger of being crushed) and behind the shower-room cabinet (spiders?). I settled on the dresser, slipping them in the space between the back of the drawer and the wall.

I checked the time. Two hours to get some work done. Soon the sun would be too hot out front, so I settled in the shade on one of the log benches behind the A-frame. With Kris's scrapbook open beside me, I took notes on my MacBook as I worked through the newspaper articles.

When I had completed my notes, I slid the typed document out of the flap at the back of the scrapbook Kris had given me and began reading.

1941: The islanders watched in silence as a boy strode past the line of unsmiling warriors. Eyes cast down, he approached The Great Chief of the Islands who sat on the throne they had carried down to the beach. Despite his age, the Chief was a big man, with sinewed arms and a straight back. If anyone thought the bowler hat he wore over his silvered hair looked strange, they dared not say so.

It was a gift, along with the case of whisky, from the foreigners whose ship 'Aroha' was now anchored beyond the reef. As the wind carried a mixture of shouting and strange music onshore, the Chief remembered what the ship's captain had told him and his chest puffed with pride: In New Zealand, only the most powerful and respected chiefs were entitled to wear this style of hat.

The boy bowed to the Chief who tapped the sand with a brass-topped cane. The old man's eyes scrutinized the muscular teenager before him. His voice trembled with fury.

"Fonu—"

So—this story was about that kid who died. Interesting! But 1941 was a long time ago. How could this have any relevance to the modern resort or provide useful background for the Morfil report? Only one way to find out.

"Fonu…you cannot swim or paddle a canoe. Last night you were seen with the basket weaver Losa again. You carve animal images from driftwood that serve no purpose and spend your days in the village listening to the old, the broken, and to women. You have, in fact, defied me at every turn for sixteen years. Even in birth you nearly killed your mother with your refusal to arrive. Sixteen years is too long for a father to wait for a son's obedience. For devotion. For any sign that you will prove a worthy heir.

"Losa will share your fate. You, my son who is not a son, will be paddled to the rock today in front of our people—by Losa, a girl. There you both will wait as the Blood Moon and tide rise—"

"Father, you know that to send us to that rock at high tide can mean only one thing—"

"Silence! The time has come when you must prove yourselves worthy to remain among us. You will wait until the whales come. Captain Jackson has placed rocket-flares in the canoe. You will fire them over the whales so Jackson's ship can give chase."

Fonu stared across the beach to the canoe held steady by a young woman standing in the water, her paddle checked across the gunnels. Crinkly hair tumbled over glistening shoulders—he knew its softness, its scent…and he remembered the fire in her questioning eyes last night.

He also knew that her slimness belied her strength. A surge of excitement crept into his stomach, to be extinguished by a wave of sorrow. A single night of fumbling, of locked limbs and hammered breathing. One brief journey into a forbidden world, with promises of more that would now probably never be fulfilled.

I checked my watch again. Poor Fonu and Losa, I thought. The briefest taste of love. And I worried about my relationship! But their tragedy would have to wait because I should have met Frank and Nancy at the bar ten minutes ago.

I put the document away, grabbed my beach bag and hurried out the door.

CHAPTER FIFTEEN

A dozen guests lounged at the bar with more scattered on the beach, but to my relief Frank and Nancy had yet to arrive—so I wasn't the only one adopting the more relaxed island time! Perry, however, was there, poring over the blues and yellows of a marine chart.

"Hi!" I said.

He looked up and smiled. "Did the sun just break through the clouds?"

"Frank and Nancy said to meet them here."

"I was waiting for them too. Never mind, I suppose I'll have to make do with you."

"The charming Englishman!" I laughed. "What's the chart for?" It offered the perfect excuse to stand next to him. I saw different colored Xs with numbers beside them crawling across the curling paper.

"My whale sightings this year. Look—here's Horseshoe at about five degrees south and one hundred and seventy-two degrees east. So each X has a code number, GPS coordinates and the date of the sighting. If I spot a whale in another location, I join the Xs with a dotted line. So far I've recorded eleven humpbacks, two pods of sperm whales, one group of false killer whales, some short-finned pilot whales and a few beaked whales. Plenty of dolphins too, as you can see. Later I'll transfer all this to my computer."

I nodded.

"But I'm boring you."

"How does it compare with last year?"

"Down, I'm afraid. And down on 2011 too. May I get you a drink?"

"Thanks. Whatever you're having. Do you get beluga whales here?"

"No, they live in cold water. Arctic and subarctic species."

"So why the pub name?"

"I did post-graduate research on them—they have a special place in my heart."

Perry's gaze moved from me to the chart, and then I guess, to a world of melting iceflows and cracking glaciers.

"I love their faces. The skull bones aren't fused as in other whales so they can make a wide range of expressions…in captivity they've been known to mimic people's voices."

"Wow! They sound so cute."

"It's more than that. I worked with a whale called Molly. After a while I realized something was going on…a kind of special bond. If I arrived unhappy, she would follow me round the pool and splash me when I wasn't looking. Then she'd mimic my laughing. It always worked."

"Did it work both ways? Could you tell what mood she was in?"

"You know what? Towards the end, I used to feel that I could."

"Someone once sent me a Youtube video of an orca mimicking the noise of an outboard engine," I said.

"I've seen that one!" His voice thickened. "But sadly, the whole thing…well, it's not good news. We study belugas as a 'sentinel' species because they reflect an ecosystem's health. Did you know they suffer terribly from cancer? Many whales are riddled with toxins, heavy metals such as lead, cadmium, chromium, mercury. It's an absolute disgrace."

"Is that why you named the restaurant the *Blue* Beluga? Blue as in sad."

"Sometimes I used to feel Molly was carrying the sadness of her entire species around with her. I've been working on an action plan to address it."

"Is that even possible?"

"All I can do is try. But here are my thoughts: To start with we need to build awareness. That creates a motivated following that puts pressure on governments and industry. Don't buy from this company or vote for that politician. What polluting corporates and their crony governments forget is that everything is interconnected. The land, the oceans, orangutans, krill, bats, ants, plankton, bacteria…and homo not very sapiens. Almost no one knows about the poisoned belugas—"

"Out of sight, out of mind. I guess belugas don't vote."

"The point is, it's like that game, Jenga. You have a tower of bricks and you keep pulling them away one at a time. There comes a point when the tower collapses. The loser's the person who pulls out the last brick."

"For a whole planet, I guess the loser's gonna be everyone."

"The pub…its mission is to raise awareness. It's no good ramming the ocean's problems down people's throats, everyone has enough on their plate already. So I try to be subtle about it: The menu is eco-friendly, on quiz night I insist on a couple of environmental questions. Wildlife and conservation charities get a discount if they dine there and a portion of profits goes back to them. And I plow most of my remaining profits back into my marine conservation work. I must confess I can be a bit of a gadget freak though," he said, twisting the bezel of his dive watch. "I'm always open to new ideas, if you have any suggestions."

"Are you making progress?"

"Hard to say. What I dream of…" His hand swept above the chart. "…is to create marine sanctuaries around the world in critical places—like right here—to give the ocean a chance to recover. With the lack of political will and the fast-buck attitude to the oceans, we're up against some pretty steep obstacles."

"Do you target politicians?"

"Yes…but it's frustratingly slow going. The few guys who aren't in the pockets of corporates won't stick their heads above the parapet unless it will win them votes. Forget the idea of living in a democracy—it doesn't seem to work that way. I'll give you an example. Next year, the US navy, sanctioned by the president, is set to start testing new laser sonar and weapons systems that Greenpeace estimate will kill and injure 138,500 whales and dolphins. This acoustic holocaust is dressed up by the US government, as usual, in terms of national security."

"Maybe I can help? I am a journalist, after all."

"Thank you. I…" He ran a hand through his still damp hair. "I imagine a two pronged attack. The first involves educating people and getting millions to sign petitions that address specific issues which can be thrust in front of the lawmakers. Look, ocean charities have proved again and again that pressure can work.

"Then after building awareness, what we need is a commitment from the UN and governments to start implementing an international marine sanctuaries program. Places to give our marine environment a chance to heal." He stared at the ocean. In a far-away voice, he said, "Once…there were so many whales they were a hazard to shipping."

"Now there are so many ships they're a hazard to whales?"

He nodded.

"Seems to me," I began, "I want to *write about* wrongs. You want to *right* wrongs."

"We all need to play a part."

Pointing at the chart, I asked, "Most of the whales are in groups. But this one?"

"He's an old Humpback they call *Solomon*. Very inquisitive, gentle. Comes up to boats and loves eyeballing people. He's never come close enough to touch though. Been coming here for years but the poor fellow has a harpoon stuck in his back. Some cruel idiot with a speargun…"

"That's dreadful. Can anything be done?"

"The blubber there's about six inches thick so some of the spear's in muscle tissue. I emailed some experts and they agreed it was best to leave it alone."

I felt at ease with Perry. He was so natural, so unassuming. Quite a contrast to…and now I had a few days without Edward…then I pushed some quite vivid and unbidden thoughts aside. Perry probably had a wife and kids back home—and he'd mentioned someone called Violet. Apart from my work, I was here to focus on Edward and me. It was fine to talk to Perry—and that's all I was doing.

Perry rolled up the chart. "I have to get back to the good ship Falcon. Violet's due her foot rub."

"Violet?" I asked. Despite what I'd just told myself, I felt my world crashing around me.

"Coming?"

"Where?"

"To meet her."

I looked at Falcon and sighed. "No, I don't think so. But thanks anyway. I'll just…" …*throw myself into the nearest volcano.*

"Nonsense. You'll get on like a house on fire. Come on!" He took my hand and ignoring my protests, pulled me towards the surf.

"It's a bit of a swim but I promise I'll rescue you if you get kidnapped by a herd of malevolent seahorses."

"Herd?"

"Trust me, I'm a marine biologist."

"I really don't want to be any trouble. I'll wait for Frank and Nancy. They'll wonder where I—"

"We can always swim back if they turn up."

We were up to our knees in bubbles.

"You haven't taken your sandals off," I said.

"You should buy a pair and wear them when swimming. Just in case."

"Of what?"

"*Synanceia verrucosa.* The stonefish. So-named because they're the splitting image of a—"

"Banana?" *I wish he wouldn't smile like that.*

"Where the sand's clear it's fairly safe but they can bury themselves. If you see what you think's a rock, don't touch it. Venomous spines. Unimaginably painful. If you're lucky a shark will hear your screams and eat you." He was staring at me. "Come on, you'll enjoy the swim."

Why weren't Frank and Nancy at the bar yet? I should make an excuse and wait for them.

We were swimming slowly, and I couldn't help but admire the grace in his strokes, how the water curled over his broad shoulders. Had he had lessons, or even competed? He looked as stable as an aircraft carrier. "You swim pretty well," I said.

"I was thinking the same about you."

He flipped onto his back, wavelets parting around his head. "You'll adore Violet."

The beach was far behind and Falcon loomed closer. I should say I had work to do, questions to prepare for my VIP interview. That might—

"She beats me at chess three times out of four. Unless I cheat. Maybe you'd like to challenge her?"

It was too late—we were nearly there. And I didn't know a rook from a prawn.

"I adore boobies. Ever seen one?"

"Excuse me?" I spluttered, choking on a mouthful of seawater.

We were treading water at Falcon's stern. Perry called, "Violet!" and climbed aboard. I hesitated, still treading water, still wondering whether to follow, aching to turn back and bolt for shore. It was his smile that made me take his offered hand. I felt the reserves of power in his body, I noticed the way his triceps flexed as he hauled me up.

"Violet? Where are you, dearest?"

I waited for her to climb from the cabin, bracing myself to meet the inevitable Miss World, with brains. Instead, a bird swooped low. A large seabird with blue feet.

"Where have you been, you naughty girl?"

She landed on the deck beside him and folded her elegant wings.

"Now best behavior because we have an important guest," he said.

"*That's* Violet?" (And I'm *important?*)

He nodded. "Violet, this is Teal. Best manners now or no foot rub." He looked at me and smiled. "Everything alright, Teal?" he asked innocently.

I managed a strangled "yes".

"She's my blue-footed booby stow-away."

"We've met before. But...how did you two meet?"

"Storm off the Galapagos. Force thirty-two on the Beaufort Scale that normally stops at twelve. Million foot waves. I was bailing below deck and when I came up, there she was, crouching in the cockpit. Poor thing had hurt her wing. So I nursed her back to health and now she won't leave. Problem was I was wearing bright blue trainers that day."

"I don't understand."

"Boobies choose their mates by the color of their feet and mine were nearly neon. I think she may have proposed marriage in seagull."

The bird's body was white, her wings dark. The feathers were flecked gray around drunk rolling eyes. She stood, her head tilted. Then she lifted a foot and thrust her head way back.

"She's sky pointing—means she's jealous," said Perry.

"Looks more like twerking to me!"

He laughed. "Okay, bird. Lunch time!"

He went below, returning with a container of raw fish. He tossed a piece towards her which she caught and gulped down. "Next time I'm near the Galapagos, I'll slow down on feeding her over time. Hopefully she'll fly home. And I won't wear the blue shoes."

We settled either side of a table in the cockpit, on which lay a strange looking pair of binoculars, complete with head straps.

"What are those?"

He lifted them, his voice dancing with excitement. "The Exelis PVS-7. With third generation image intensifier tube and autogated gain control. Super cool." He saw my puzzled look. "Sorry—my last birthday and Christmas present from me to me. Night vision goggles. I keep a couple of pairs onboard for night work."

An hour later, we were still talking, Violet strutting along the deck as if auditioning for the Ministry of Silly Walks. Perry rigged a sun canopy and despite the heat, there was nowhere I would rather have been.

"So tell me about your beautiful boat."

"Been sailing since I was tiny. Being close to the ocean always appealed to me. In a sailboat you are working with the elements but in a motorboat, against them. I found Falcon by chance in a New English boatyard. It was built between the wars and had been neglected for decades. The hull was holed, varnish long gone, sails rotted. Not water-logged though, the boards were still true. I thought it would be a tragedy to lose this boat and I was looking for a project..."

"What type of project were you looking for?"

"Something that included traveling, around the world perhaps. I had a Master's in Marine Science and I loved the fact it was such an elegant old thing. When I scraped the grime off the stern, and saw the name, well...that was the clincher."

I remembered the Amazing Anastasia and the falcon she'd seen outside her window. I wanted to tell Perry—but I needed to hear his story first. "Go on."

"My name's *Peregrine*. As in Peregrine Falcon, the fastest creature on earth. And then there's my ring name. I used to box as an amateur. My nickname was The Falcon because they said I was fast. Why are you staring at me?"

"Your nose looks pretty straight to me."

"You think anyone ever landed a punch on me when I was doing 270 mph in reverse?"

"I'm sure you're much braver than that."

"Well, you'll never know as I don't fight anymore. Pledge of peace and all that."

"May I tell you something, Perry?"

The corners of his eyes flexed. "Depends…"

"Have you ever had a tarot reading?"

"When I was a boy, a fortune teller at a country fair lured me into her tent and told me to choose a card. I remember it was the Tower. She told me I was too young to understand what it meant but one day, when the time was right, I'd find out."

"And?"

He laughed. "I forgot all about it!"

"Talking of towers, you mentioned the bricks in Jenga. Do you think the card means something's about to collapse?"

"Could be. If it is, I need to find out *what's* about to collapse. Planet Earth maybe, but that seems too specific to a card I was given decades ago." His tone changed. "Note to self: Research meaning of Tower tarot card online."

"The night at The Blue Beluga…" I was watching him closely and felt sure I could tell him more.

"…I'd found an old raffle prize. A tarot reading. Normally I'd ignore tarot too, but…"

"Desperate times call for desperate measures?"

"Something like that." I drew a deep breath. "The tarot reader said to look out for a falcon. And then you recommended this place, and I find out it's your name and the name of your boat."

"I know where you're coming from. I set off intending to circumnavigate, doing research as I went. But this was as far as I got. It's my seventh season. I keep coming back hoping to work out what's going on."

I explained Grandma's letters, how she taught me to recognize signs.

"I've had strange coincidences too. One or two at first. The more you notice them, the more you see."

"That's what she used to say! And she suggested I get myself an ally. I don't suppose you could possibly think of anyone who might be prepared to perform this onerous role?"

"Teal, we all need allies." He held out his hand and though I expected an electric shock, instead I felt the firm grip of reassurance. "I'd suggest a blood pact, but I don't think you'd be impressed if I fainted," he said.

"My hero!"

We sat there in silence, but it wasn't one of those embarrassing times when you search for something to say. We floated in the heat of the day and the gentle breeze that fanned us in a beautiful boat on a turquoise ocean. When he asked if I was okay, I answered with a smile.

Later, the turning tide swung the boat around. Whaling Rock lay exposed, waves lapping its base. I noticed Perry studying it too.

He propped himself on an elbow. "That's a very mysterious lump of rock."

I sat up. "Tell me about it. Someone was waving at me from it this morning but when I looked back, he was gone."

"Talk to Firefly Bob—if there's a legend about disappearing men on the island, he'll know it. I tell you what, next time I run into him, I'll ask." As he moved, his trunks shifted and I found my eyes drawn to the suntan line at his waist. He caught me looking.

"You looking at my tattoo?" he asked with mock suspicion.

"I didn't mean to stare. But I can only see the top of it. What is it?"

He laughed, pulling his trunks higher. "A symbol—I find myself living my life by its values."

"Which are?"

"It means *mind, body, spirit.*"

"Why do you hide it away, *there?*"

"It's a…private thing. Not something I want to get into endless discussions with strangers over. Oh, I'm not including *you* in that!"

"I know you aren't."

"Back to the mystery man on the rock. Might be worth asking Emma too, as she's interrogated half the population." He glanced at his watch.

"Without success, apparently. Anyway, thanks so much, Perry. I've had an incredible time but I better head back."

"And I need to bait my fish traps and email some data."

"Bye, ally," I said.

He was beside me, very close. Leaning in, he kissed my forehead. It was gentle, over in a second. "Bye, ally," he whispered, stepping back. He smiled and the little lines around his eyes creased.

I drew in one long breath as I held his gaze. Diving in, I plunged deep, trailing an avalanche of bubbles.

When they had scattered, I swam hard underwater, the sand ahead of me lit by the beams of light that pierced the shifting waves above. Maintaining my depth, I worked my arms in long smooth strokes and aimed for the distant beach.

I held my course. I was about to kick for the surface when I had a thought: *Anything you can do, Peregrine…*

Now that I'd set myself a challenge, I couldn't quit. He'd be on deck, watching, wondering if I could do it. But it was further than I'd expected. My chest was heaving but I could tell that the distance between the surface and the sandy bottom was finally decreasing. Which meant I was getting close to shore. But close enough?

The sunbeams glinted through the waves, inviting me to burst up and breathe but I ignored them. Thumping in my chest; pounding in my ears. Weakening muscles. My strokes were short and jerky, the pressure tightened around my diaphragm but now I swam beneath a ceiling of broken foam. I had entered the surf. *Ten more strokes, you've got ten left in you!*

Standing, I gulped in air as the ocean pulled at my shaky legs. I forced myself to walk casually, as if it had been easy.

The "bravo" carried from way behind. "We'll make an islander of you yet!"

Without turning, I waved casually and walked up the beach. My legs nearly betrayed me as I dragged air into my lungs. But he wouldn't be able to see that from there. And it was *so* worth it!

Then I remembered the kiss. I had half expected one on my cheek. Maybe two, the way they do in France. But on my forehead? What did that mean? Well, whatever it meant, it was very—

Why was Toka, the bartender, approaching at speed?

"Excuse me, lady. Mrs. Davies has an important message for you."

I thanked him and hurried towards reception.

I found Emma in her office, eyes closed, swaying in a fug of transcendental smoke. A paisley bandana knotted above her forehead held battered headphones in place.

"You have a message for me, Emma?" I tapped her shoulder and she jumped.

She removed the headphones and the guitar riff from *Stairway to Heaven* flooded the room. I repeated the question while she lit a fresh incense stick.

"That's right, babe, Thurston Morfil's PA rang. Morfil had to jump on a plane, something about a conference in Fiji, or did she say Finland? She'll contact you as soon as he's back."

I thanked her for the message. Subjects who refused to be interviewed or even located were considered "challenges not problems" at Musculus Media. Sir Basil wasn't the sort of man who tolerated excuses so I'd have to email Malcolm and explain—a stop-gap for now—but it was all I could do.

Then I asked if she could spare five minutes for a weird story. "You know a bit about local legends, right?"

"Weird trumps Led Zep eight days of the week," she said, flopping in her chair. "Shoot."

I described the man on the rock, who may have looked like an old islander. How he'd waved, I was sure, at me. But I didn't know how he'd got there and suddenly he had vanished.

"That is indeed *mucho weirdo* because we had a guest last year, dudette was—Japanese, I think. Or Jamaican. Went round claiming she'd been summoned here. She saw someone, thought it was an old islander too, on that rock. Freaked out and legged it home the next day."

"Summoned here? Any theories?"

"Hallucinogenic fish poisoning or prototype Horseshoe Whisperers? But *you* don't strike me as a boozer…and now you're telling me the same thing happened to you."

"He was as real as you are."

"Hmmm. Looks like I need to disambiguate myself by re-reading that paper on modal Meinongianism and Actuality. Listen babe, the tribes wouldn't have fought tooth and nail over this sandbar if they didn't believe it was special. Problem is the last chief died decades ago and anyone who was alive then will be long dead. Except—"

"Go on."

"There's a rumor that I can't get to the bottom of, to do with something magical in the ocean. Whether it's fact or fiction, your guess is as good as mine."

"Is that what your thesis is about?"

"Sort of. It *was* on comparative death beliefs and experiences. What I call the 'Visiting Angel Phenomenon'. A lot of people in the West report seeing angels when they're about to snuff off their mortal coils."

"When Mom died two years ago, she lay there moaning and waving her arms in terror as if she was under attack from demons. It was really upsetting."

"I've heard of this too but I limit myself to the love and light side of the equation."

"Do the islanders report similar experiences?"

"Not that they'll talk about. But babe, it's crucial we stay open-minded about what any of us accept as real. There's a theory that people's near death experiences are conditioned by their beliefs and expectations. A Christian might describe seeing Christian-like angels, a Hindu would expect to see Yama, the Lord of Death, or Chitragupta, who keeps a record of everything the person's done in their—you're frowning, babe?"

"So, did I see a ghost, or not?" *Because I sure wasn't expecting to.*

"Listen, honey—if the locals claim that rock's got a resident ghost, and more than one person's seen it, then you've got my attention."

"Which means?"

"If I knew what the hell that meant, or *I* meant, I'd have finished my doctorate and be enjoying a congratulatory smoke."

She leaned forward, elbows on desk, chin in palms. "What *would* get my scholarly juices flowing would be if someone like you, with your Christian beliefs came here and experienced one of *their* near death experiences. Then we'd be talking collective unconscious, archetypes, morphic resonance, memes, visiting professorships and the Nobel Prize.

Hell, I bet they'd throw the Templeton Prize at me too."

"What's a Templeton?"

"A million dollars for a major contribution that affirms life's spiritual side. Imagine what we could do to this place with that much cash."

"So that's the Holy Grail," I said.

"Sure is. You better go, honey. I can see Frank and Nancy at the dock and Coconut chugs in five."

I was half way to the door when she said, "Not sure if I should say this but—that Thurston Morfil. Be careful—he shrinks my aura."

"Emma?"

But Led Zeppelin had reclaimed her attention.

CHAPTER SIXTEEN

With a spin of the wheel and a belch from the exhaust, Coconut settled against the jetty and Kris welcomed us to Thursday's highlight, the Tofua'a market. It was located on the same island the island hopper had deposited us on when we'd arrived. Canoes, powered by paddles or battered outboards, arrived as we disembarked. More canoes lined the beach; others, laden with produce, were leaving. Ahead, people thronged around the terminal building like ants at a sugar cube.

A battalion of excited islanders hurried with us towards the airstrip building, some pushed wheelbarrows, others supermarket trolleys laden with fruit, vegetables, clothing. A boy wobbled past with a not too fresh-looking fish bent across his slim shoulders. A woman sheltering beneath a golf umbrella balanced an enormous watermelon on her head; she walked with the poise of a catwalk model, buzzing children circling around her as if she were a kind of mobile hive.

In the terminal, the colorful crowd ebbed and flowed around makeshift stalls. A pulsing counter-flow of beach-bound islanders passed us. Nancy laughed when a patchwork dog bolted with its stolen prize, a stick-waving girl in pursuit. Two men with knotted faces argued about a sack of seed. Drawn in by the unfamiliar but exciting energy, I took a deep breath and continued strolling towards the market.

"Isn't this fun?" Nancy exclaimed.

"You bet!" said Frank.

We had entered a world of exotic smells—I recognized cinnamon and vanilla, which competed with the more robust aniseed and garlic, and fish. Rows of coconuts and pyramids of supermarket-reject tomatoes caught my eye. Nancy pointed out muddy yams and a pile of cassava roots which lay between wart-skinned lemons and plump papayas; I saw a mound of something that resembled giant spinach too. Violently colored beach bags, T-shirts and gaudy sunglasses competed with somber wood carvings and beautifully woven baskets. A corner stall offered beans, peppers and nutmeg along with a crate of shells, large and small.

Frank pointed at a stall built from balanced boxes. "I need photos of those fish."

They were stacked in a rainbow of overlapping roof tiles, with the larger (and meaner-looking) ones at the back. The middle ground comprised striped, silvery-blue *bonito* (according to Frank) and tiny fish that I would have expected to see in an aquarium, stared glassy-eyed from the front rows. With lazy strokes, a boy fanned a palm leaf at the flies, which synchronized their massed landings with his glances at a pretty girl opposite.

Frank pointed at a gleaming brown tiddler. "In forty years that fellow could have been another Black Jack." He pulled out a note book to record what he saw, occasionally confirming a local name with the stall owner.

A woman hurried past with a bucket of tuna heads. "Those make a delicious fish soup," Nancy said. She tapped Frank on the shoulder. "I'm dragging Teal off to find girly stuff. Catch you later, dearest."

She steered me toward a clothing stall. A tiny woman in a New England-winter-thick dress jumped up to boast about her wares. She smiled through blood red teeth.

"Chewing betel nuts," Nancy whispered.

The sarong I chose featured a school of hand-drawn tropical fish on a soft blue-green background. "That will look divine on you," Nancy said. "And Frank's gonna *love* this shirt." She lifted a jungle-themed extravaganza in a migraine of clashing colors.

Casually, she asked, "So—how'd it go with Perry?"

"We waited for you guys, you never showed."

"Change of plans." Nancy winked. "We thought you two should get better acquainted."

"You *set us up?*" I gasped. "Nancy, I'm practically married."

"Last I heard you weren't even engaged. Anyway, blame Frank—it was his idea. He's both a good judge of character and an old romantic." She nudged me with her elbow. "So— what's he like?"

I felt the warmth in my face. What was I meant to say? That he was fabulous and I couldn't get him out of my mind? That I fell asleep last night, wishing I'd met him when I'd first arrived in New York?

"For all I know, he's married."

"He isn't."

"Are you sure? I mean—" I asked, trying to appear nonchalant, knowing I'd broken eye contact.

"I asked Kris."

"Nancy!"

"Apparently he was pretty serious about a woman he dated at

university. Frank said he seemed reluctant to discuss it but something terrible happened. Frank *did* ascertain he's been single for quite a while."

A man like that, single? For quite a while?

"Come on, Angel—woman to woman? Is he as nice as he seems?"

"Keep a secret?"

"Sure can."

I said it very quietly. "Nicer."

She squeezed my arm as we strolled through the market. "I thought so, Frank had a long talk with him. Said he was a delight and a perfect gentleman. Knows every single thing about the ocean."

"Strange thing is we met at his eco-friendly pub-restaurant in New York a few weeks ago."

"He didn't mention it! Tell me all, Angel," she said in her most conspiratorial tone.

I kept the description of our pub encounter simple, ending with, "…so it was at his suggestion we came here."

"Bet you're glad you did!"

"Lots going on in my head just now."

"I can tell. Well, things have a way of sorting themselves out. You'll see."

"You and Frank seem so happy. What's your secret?"

"Second time round for both of us. Sure, we've had our problems, like anyone. Frank's work was getting to him. He was a workaholic, headed for an early grave. Then he had a minor stroke and thank heavens, he saw the light. We both sold up and retired."

"Is he okay now?"

"Should be. He takes his meds. A lot to do with letting go of the stress. My, what divine carvings."

A young man and woman sat whittling pieces of wood. Small boxes, some circular, others square or rectangular, lay at their feet, amongst a carpet of shavings. I lifted one. The pieces fitted loosely together, leaving a space inside.

"Called a swell box, lady. You put something inside, make a wish. You write something secret on the box then hold it underwater and the wood swells shut. When it opens your wish comes true," the boy said.

"How much for the round one?" Nancy asked.

"You must never tell anyone your wish or the magic won't work," the girl added.

"These remind me…I found a box in the street a few weeks ago. Thought it was glued shut, but maybe it's one of these?"

"In *New York*?"

Nancy lifted a curly-tailed reptile from a selection of carvings of stylized warriors and gods, canoes, birds, fish. We admired the mother-of-pearl inlays, the shell detailing.

The young woman beckoned us as she lifted an octopus and butterfly that fitted perfectly together, a tentacle slotting into a groove in the butterfly's abdomen.

"That's clever," I said.

"My brother and I are learning to do it," she explained.

Nancy struggled to attach a mouse to a hammerhead shark. "No, these don't join. But why fit a butterfly and octopus together?" she asked.

"No idea, lady."

"How many carvings can you interlock?" I asked the boy.

"Three or four. Then it gets too difficult."

"But there's that story—" the girl started. "And if *he* says it's true…"

"Everyone knows that's not true," the boy said, shaking his head. "You shouldn't believe all he says," he whispered.

A man's voice carried from behind the stall. "Just because you can't do it doesn't mean it can't be done!"

We looked around, but the voice's owner remained hidden.

"He's trying to teach us," the girl explained. "Says he used to be able to do it. But it may just be one of his stories."

I lifted a delicately carved, pearly-eyed turtle. "Oh, I like this one. So skillful."

"You're very talented," Nancy said, smiling at the young islander. He giggled in thanks and mumbled a price.

Nancy's attention shifted to a wooden flying fish bursting from a wave, while I reached for my wallet. As I offered the money, I noticed a movement at the corner of the stall. An islander stepped out and stared at me. Removing his sunglasses, I saw tears welling in his old eyes.

"Hello, you again?" I asked. "Are you alright?"

Bob pointed at the wallet. "Didn't I explain? Why do you still have that thing?"

"Because it's *mine*, and—" But something stopped me.

"You know this man, Angel? Is everything alright?"

"Is there a problem, Teal, Bob?"

I turned to see Kris behind us. "I don't know why he—"

"She still has that terrible thing!" the islander said, pointing at the wallet. "You offend him and you offend me. I tried to make it right with the Forgiving Ceremony, but I see you took it back."

Kris stepped between us. "Okay, Bob. This woman's a guest at my hotel and I'm sure she doesn't mean to offend anyone. But you'll have to explain what this is about. However passionate you are about this, I just can't have you upsetting my guests."

"You shouldn't even have guests. The island's not yours."

"How many times…. I'm sorry Bob, but that discussion's for

another time—"

"It always is," Bob said softly, staring at his feet.

"Bob, I didn't mean to upset you. Please explain the problem with the wallet to me?" I asked.

He mumbled the word "sacred" and that we didn't understand. Then he pointed again, staring at me hard. I stepped back, bracing myself for some terrible accusation. But surely all I'd done was retrieve my grandfather's wallet from a rock?

"That wallet is made from..."

"Yes?" I prompted.

"...whale..." He pointed at his groin.

I caught Nancy's baffled look.

"From whale penis," he said, his voice catching.

The softness of the leather triggered a tightening in my stomach and a wave of revulsion as the words sunk in.

"Are you sure? I...I had no idea."

"Oh, my!" Nancy said, staring wide-eyed at the wallet.

He was nodding slowly.

"That's why I tried to return it to the ocean. I told him you didn't know and you were sorry. Now he'll think I lied."

"*He?*" Nancy asked.

"That's terrible," I said. "I had no idea."

"It must go back. I feel great sadness," Bob said.

Kris came to my rescue. "Would you be happy returning it to the ocean, Teal?"

"Yes...yes, I suppose so."

"Bob, would you perform the ceremony again? Maybe I'll come too."

"Must be at sunset." Bob wiped his eyes with the back of his hand. "I will meet you at the same place tomorrow night. Maybe you aren't all so closed as old Bob thought." He walked away.

"Why did he say the hotel shouldn't be there?" I asked Kris.

"Claims only islanders should live on Horseshoe. Apparently the Japanese and Americans used it as a lookout during the war. Drove the islanders out and when peace was declared, it was sold to a Kiwi. Islanders weren't allowed back."

"Is that true?" asked Nancy.

"No idea. My lawyers tried to find out, but records were scarce...as you can imagine, not a lot written down. Now he sits alone at sunset staring out to sea. He can get a bit passionate. He's kind actually; he teaches the local children about the old days, the myths. No one else bothers now. Anyway, I'll be there tomorrow for moral support."

I looked again at the carved turtle in my hand, turning it over for the first time. Writing was cut into the underside of the shell. "Oh, that's a coincidence."

"What, Angel?"

"It says *Fonu.*"

"Well, it would. That means 'turtle'," said Kris.

CHAPTER SEVENTEEN

Perry had said thousands of whales once visited these islands—I tried to picture the ocean darkened by a navy of black backs, the air steamed with as many blows. What had happened to the sperm whales we'd seen? Had they moved on? Standing beside Coconut at the jetty, I realized it would be enough to see even one whale today. I knew I should probably be in my room doing research, emailing Malcolm, or chasing Thurston Morfil, but at least I had my laptop in my beach bag. Maybe I'd get some work done if things got slow?

"Wait for us!"

Kris smiled, "Last but not least. Get ready to cast off!"

"Sorry we're late. Frank forgot his cetacean ID chart."

Kris helped them aboard and said, "Nancy, Frank…let me introduce your fellow whale watchers. This is Lorraine and her daughter, Cecile, from Bordeaux."

I recognized the couple from the bar on the day we'd arrived. Lorraine, a mahogany-tanned forty-something, sheltered beneath a Hermes scarf and a haze of perfume. *"Bonjour,"* she said in a husky drawl, eyes locked on our captain, Kris. She drew heavily on a cigarette that poked from a black and gold cigarette holder.

Nancy smiled at Cecile, who went "pfff" and returned to the audible grunge music that journeyed from her MP3 to her multi-pierced ears.

Lorraine asked Kris, "Do you carry diving equipment, as I qualified last summer in Saint Tropez?"

Kris pointed to a chest inside the cabin. "Masks, fins, snorkels. If the whaling is slow, we might stop for a cooling dip over the reef." He continued his introductions. "And our honeymooners, Ming-Yue and Xu."

After saying hello, Ming-Yue pulled a camera from Xu's backpack.

"Holy smokes," Frank said stepping forward. "That a Seitz 6×17

Panoramic, young lady?"

"Yes."

"You must be pleased with it!"

"First time I use it. Xu gave it to me."

Frank turned to Nancy. "If we ever win the lottery, Pumpkin, that's the one for me."

He was soon exchanging opinions with the young couple about the pros and cons of various camera brands and traditional versus digital photography.

Kris scanned left and right with binoculars. Coconut plowed seaward beneath a bonito sky.

"Skipper," Frank shouted over the chug-cough of the engines. "What chance of a humpback?"

"Not bad—they're out here. It's calm so they'll be easier to spot. Wind's due to pick up this afternoon. Hard to see them when there's a lot of spray."

We cruised back and forth before heading south. Frank joined Kris on the flybridge and snippets of conversation, including *marine conservation*, *endangered species* and *protected habitat* drifted my way.

"What did you find out, dear?" Nancy asked, as Frank rejoined us in the cockpit.

"Well, Ming-Yue wants to be a photo-journalist. And some sobering facts from Kris. Did you know the humpback population fell by ninety percent before the ban in '66? What's disgusts me is that scientists estimate the Antarctic blue whale population fell ninety-nine per cent because of illegal Soviet whaling. Some whale populations are so depleted they have no chance of rebuilding."

"Isn't there any good news?" I asked.

"I was on the International Whaling Commission website last night. Let me check my notes." He pulled a notepad from his pocket and began reading. "The Gulf of California blue whale population is growing three per cent annually…some humpback populations are recovering strongly at ten per cent…eastern North Pacific fin whales are increasing at four to five per cent…the Argentina, Brazil, South Africa and Australian populations of southern right whales are growing at seven to eight per cent…"

Cecile had removed her headphones and appeared to be listening. When I asked her if she'd seen a whale before, she replied, "I hate boats."

"This old tub makes such a racket, the whales can hear us an ocean away. I'm cutting the engines and we'll try a drift. I'm afraid it may feel pretty hot without the breeze," Kris called from the flybridge.

Coconut settled, the last of its wake ambling towards the horizon. The piercing sun glinted on a surface of flexing mirrors. A jellyfish, its back split by a purple vein, floated past; tiny fish darted around its trailing tentacles. The silence was broken only by the massaging gurgle of water on hull. Soon I was yawning.

A shadow flashed on the deck and a familiar squawk interrupted my thoughts. The bird hovered astern. Ming-Yue raised her camera.

"Hi, Violet!" I said. If she's here, maybe Falcon was close by, I thought.

"There's Perry," said Kris, pointing at a sailboat a couple of miles away. "I'll get him on the boat radio."

Lorraine's powder compact was out, inches from her face as she patted and pouted.

"He is coming here?" she asked, clicking the compact shut.

A broken radio conversation from the flybridge reached us. Then Kris said, "Eyes peeled, people. That was Perry. He said he spotted a whale that may be injured. It's heading this way."

I wiped my sunglasses, climbed up beside Kris and scanned the water from there.

"Here it comes," said Kris. "A humpback."

"*Mon Dieu!*" Lorraine pointed at the giant gliding twenty feet below us.

We threw ourselves against one gunnel, then the other as it passed in silent majesty beneath us. With a tilt of its body, the whale released a stream of bubbles.

"That whale's in trouble. Something wrapped around his fin," Kris said.

A knotted mass of netting trailed along the animal's flank. "There must be something we can do!" I said. "Is that a spear in his back? It's Solomon!"

"I can't risk starting the engines, they'll scare it. I'll ask Perry if he has any ideas."

"Got a knife, son?" Frank asked, pulling off his shirt.

"Over my dead body, Franklin Washington Butler. Don't even *think* of swimming with that whale." Nancy said.

"But, Pumpkin—"

"Don't argue with a woman who's just given up sugar!"

"Wait for Perry. He's worked with whales," Kris said.

"You going in there with it?" Frank asked Kris.

"No way—can't abandon ship."

"He'll need help," I said. "I'll go…"

"Way too dangerous, Angel."

"Dear Lord, it must be suffering" said Frank, as the whale stilled on the surface and blew a massive blowhole sigh.

"It's like he's asking for help," I whispered.

"Look!" shouted Lorraine. "*C'est magnifique,*" she said, before glancing back at Falcon.

"We can't just sit here, he could swim off," I said. *Now's our chance. Hurry Perry, please hurry!*

The whale hung motionless; a clumped ligature of nylon bound the base of his knobbly fin. Pale, gaping wounds cut deep into its flanks.

"The poor creature. That netting's strangling him!" I said.

We stared at the whale, then at each other. *Someone has to do something and Perry's a long way away.* First I checked that all eyes were on the whale, then slipped unseen into the cabin. I found the equipment chest, pulled out a mask, fins and knife and crept out the cabin door. At the far side of the boat from the others, I lowered myself as quietly as I could into the water.

"Teal, come back—are you crazy?" yelled Kris.

Nancy shouted "Angel!" But Frank waved a thumbs up.

The shouting receded as I dived overboard and swam underwater towards the colossal slab of gray. The sperm whales hadn't prepared me for the vastness of the humpback whale that extended before me. As his fifty foot bulk swamped my vision, I felt infinitely small, insignificant. And at the same time, profoundly privileged to be in his presence.

I marveled at the whale that hung tail down, suspended like a leaning tower, his head brushing the surface. A pale underside blended into a dark back, before sweeping into a vast tail. The head and fins were covered in lumps; a small fin broke the broad dorsal expanse. I recoiled at the damage I could see caused by the garroting tangle of nylon. Little fish, some jacketed in vivid stripes, darted around open wounds. Closer now, I swam with long, smooth strokes, hoping not to scare Solomon.

I positioned myself by his eye, to let him study me as I tried to project my thoughts to him. "I won't hurt you." I reached out and rubbed my hand gently along his head. The texture was firm and smooth. "Solomon, I want to help you."

I grasped the net but the serrated knife made no impression on the nylon which was set like stone. I surfaced to grab a breath of air, and dived again to saw and pull, but only a few strands came away. Solomon hovered motionless beside me. Did he understand I was trying to help?

I surfaced again to see Kris waving from the flybridge. The other guests were shouting at me to return.

I pushed my palm at them. "Stay back...please!"

"Teal, it's too dangerous," shouted Kris.

A blinding flash of light from Coconut's cockpit made me shield my eyes. It came a second time—this time it lingered.

"Lorraine!" I shouted, "No!"

But Solomon was already moving.

"Look out for its tail. Get back! Get back!" Kris shouted.

I spun in a vortex of blue. Rolling, I tried to steady myself, the knife tumbling into the depths. I paddled upwards, surfacing in time to see Solomon's tail, like a jet's back wings, waving a leisurely goodbye.

"You could have been killed, Angel!" said Nancy, as I clambered onto the swim platform. She helped me over the transom and wrapped a towel tightly around me.

"Bravest thing I ever saw," Frank said.

"*Mon Dieu*. You are crazy!" Cecile said, cuffing her forehead. "You risk your life for a *fish?*"

Kris picked up the mask. "The glass is cracked. If the tail had hit your head—"

"Lorraine frightened him—"

"There are sharks out here. Man eaters. You don't know how lucky you are."

"*Coconut, Coconut. This is Falcon, Falcon. Suggest channel seven two. Over.*"

Kris scrambled up to the flybridge.

Nancy came closer, her voice level. "Kris's right, you know. Oceanic whitetip sharks, super aggressive. He was explaining—"

"I don't care, I—"

"Fortunately, it's only midday. He said late afternoon's when they feed—when their primitive brains flick a switch and they become killing machines. But Teal, really—that's not something I'd risk my life on. You might meet a shark out here on Massachusetts time whose dinner bell goes off early. I was terrified for you, Angel."

But I hardly listened. Since when had my life been important? Instead, I imagined the submerged humpback, the net tearing into his body…the yawning wounds and parasitic fish. Would the magnificent whale slow as infection overwhelmed him? Then I pictured the sharks, all daggered teeth and raked bodies, circling, probing, charging…ripping. Returning again and again. I was about to turn away to hide my tears when Nancy placed her hands on my shoulders.

"Teal, you've got to take care of yourself first and *then* you can take care of others. Otherwise there'll be no Teal left to take care of anyone."

"I couldn't leave him. I had to help him—doesn't anyone understand?" I asked, leaning to sob into her shoulder.

Nancy enveloped me in a Lizzie-like hug. She whispered, "Trust me. Frank and I understand, dear."

CHAPTER EIGHTEEN

"I looked through the photos and was able to identify it by its flukes. It's definitely Solomon," Perry said, while we sat at the bar later that afternoon. The joviality of the other guests around us jarred after the somber scenes of earlier in the day.

"I was on my way—what spooked him?" Perry asked, lifting his drink.

"Lorraine had her powder compact out. The sun flashed on the mirror. Or it may have been the way her red lipstick clashed with her tangerine eye shadow. Oh, I shouldn't have said that, but I'm just so upset that she scared him away. I wanted to help."

"That netting's bad news for any whale, but for an old whale like him..." added Kris.

"The question is—how can we help that poor animal?" asked Frank.

"I've informed the IWC, the IWPO and a couple of whale charities of the sighting, as well as WHOI."

He saw my expression.

"The International Whaling Commission, the International Whale Protection Organization and Woods Hole."

"Woods Hole...isn't that the oceanographic place in Massachusetts?" Nancy asked.

"Yup. I did my second degree there—it's where I learned the difference between a left hook and a fish hook."

"I had you as an Oxford-type," said Frank.

Perry looked around the table, a little shyly, I thought. "Well, yes...Oxford was great fun and I did lots of sport there but Woods Hole was where I knuckled down and worked."

"Tell me the truth. What are Solomon's chances of survival?" I asked.

"In my opinion, he didn't look too distressed, but long-term, his prospects aren't good. Especially if he encounters Orcas. And I'm afraid that as he weakens, he'll become more vulnerable to ship strike."

"How often does this sort of thing happen?" Nancy asked.

"Too often," Perry said. "The whaling ban has helped population growth. But so many whales are still lost to nets, ship strike, and noise pollution from ships and sonar. It stops them communicating with each other, probably confuses them, causes mass strandings."

"I'm sorry to leave, but if you'll excuse me, it's time for Luna's bedtime story," Kris said.

"Oh yes, we better go too," said Nancy brightly.

"But I'm ready for another—" Frank started.

"Franklin, T—W—T—B—A."

Nancy took his arm and led him away, Frank shaking his head. Then he stopped. "Got it!" he said, before he waved goodbye over his shoulder.

Perry was torturing a chunk of pineapple with a toothpick.

"So…" I said, hoping he'd run with the ball.

"So… nice sarong."

"Thank you. Bought it at the local market. Wait till you see the shirt Nancy bought Frank."

"I had an interesting chat with him. He's knowledgeable about wildlife. I couldn't have identified Solomon without his photos." His tone changed. "Kris said you tried to free him."

"Are you mad at me too?"

He tapped the bar with his finger. Finally he said, "You're brave…but yes."

"Someone had to do something."

"I'm relieved you weren't hurt. Imagine the headline: *Tourist drowned by whale.* Kris and Emma would have been *thrilled* that the authorities had a perfect excuse not to renew their lease."

"You're all heart!"

"Seriously, I'm impressed—and it takes a lot to impress me, these days. But please promise me you'll never just jump in like that again. Not alone, not without at least—"

"So, what were you doing out there today?"

"Promise, and I'll tell you."

"Okay. Deal."

"There's an incredibly rare cetacean called Omura's whale that was only formally recognized as a separate species in 2003." His eyes shone like Dooby Scoo's, the time he shredded the brand new couch. "They've been identified a couple of times in these waters. A yachtsman reported an odd looking whale a couple of days ago, so I went to investigate."

"It must be like looking for a needle in a haystack."

"That's a big problem. When you consider that over half the planet's covered by water more than two miles deep, it surprises me new species aren't discovered more often. Take the colossal squid. Science first knew about it from chunks of tentacle recovered from the belly of a sperm whale in the 1920s. It wasn't until 1981 that the next one was positively identified. You know what it uses to hunt prey and admire undiscovered species of benthic holothurians? Stereoscopic ocular photophores powered by the oxidization of luciferin!"

"Come on! Everybody knows *that!*"

"Sorry. Light-emitting organs in its eyes. Is that cool or what?"

"Do you wonder what other creatures are waiting to be discovered?"

"Keeps me awake at night. Take the giant octopus—tentacles forty, fifty feet long...pulls down small boats. Rips propellers off nuclear submarines. In Norwegian folklore it's called the *kraken.*"

"You're just—"

"Seriously, I was involved in what became known as the *Joan Ormond-Kelso Encounter.* You probably heard about it."

"No, I don't think so."

"One of those chain link ferries got stuck half way across a fjord in Norway, summer of 2008. Something wrapped around the ferry, brought it to a complete stop. Suddenly these huge blistered tentacles came up and pulled a couple of cars over the side. Joan was a tourist, she got dragged in."

"*Was* a tourist? That's terrible!"

Perry took a sip of his drink and when he looked up, I saw deep furrows across his forehead, a distant, pained look in his eyes. When finally he spoke, his voice trembled. "I was on the ferry...powerless to help."

"I'm sorry."

"But she was very lucky. She was saved."

"How?"

"A school of red herrings swam by. They did the only thing possible. They—"

"*Red* herrings?"

"...Tickled it to death."

"Now wait a minute..." There was something in his expression. And *red herrings?* I laughed uncertainly. The way his mouth trembled—why was he trying not to laugh?

"The clue was in the name."

"Joan?"

"Joan Ormond-Kelso Encounter. It's an acronym."

I spelled it out, "J—O—K—E". My attempt at an incinerating glare only made him laugh harder.

He reached out, his hand settled on my wrist. "Forgive me, Teal? I couldn't resist...your expression!"

I lowered my voice. "Be careful—revenge is a dish best served cold."

"In which case you must be my guest for dinner aboard Falcon. Tomorrow, maybe?"

"What time do you serve?" I asked.

"What time do you eat?"

"Oh, wait. I have to go into town. Library research. And then write up my findings—"

"Hmmm." He stroked his chin, in exaggerated concentration. "I may be able to play around with my hectic research schedule. If I delayed my submission on exogenous depression in orphaned mantis shrimps.... Would Sunday work for you?"

"That would be great, I've got so many questions I'd love to ask about the island."

"Perfect."

"You've got a date! But I have to run. Performing a wallet ceremony with Firefly Bob in ten minutes."

"A *what?*"

I told him I'd explain later and slipped away.

*   *   *

I had wrapped the wallet in a plastic bag—out of respect, I didn't want to touch it. The idea that someone could do *that* to a whale. What an appalling insult.

But my thoughts returned to Perry. What I knew about him was that he owned a pub in New York and had gone to Oxford University. He had a qualification in marine biology and spent much of his time on a small island in a remote part of the South Pacific. *You missed a small detail, Teal: He's single.*

Bob and Kris were waiting for me in the lengthening shadows.

"Good evening," I said, keeping my voice formal.

"You are just in time, lady." Bob nodded at the setting sun.

I handed him the wallet. He sprung onto the rocks and climbed down to where the swell bubbled and shushed. *Men half his age aren't that agile!* He waited until the sun touched the horizon, then delicately placed the wallet on a flat rock. He reached into his pocket and scattered purple petals over it again.

"You must pray." He closed his eyes, lifted his arms and began to chant in a language I didn't recognize. Self-consciously, I looked down, and asked in silence for the spirit of the whale to forgive the men who had killed and dishonored it. I finished by explaining I had not known what the wallet was made of, and offered my sincerest apologies.

I watched the wallet tremble beneath a push of water. Then a wave, shaped like foaming fingers, reached up and grasped it. The wallet spun in a wandering eddy and settled deeper in the water.

Bob turned to face me. "The ocean has reclaimed it."

"May I ask you something? Who were you praying to?"

"You prayed fine, lady. But they killed that whale long ago. I don't think our prayers reached him."

"How do you know that?"

"Because nothing came back. Tomorrow I will pray again, and the next day, and I will keep praying. One day that whale's spirit will hear because he will be listening."

I studied the leaden calm of the ocean as the scent of bougainvillea surrendered to the evening's saline humidity. My thoughts were in turmoil—this old man had reminded me how little I knew about so many things.

A gentle cough and Kris stepped forward. "Thank you for including me, Bob. A beautiful ceremony. But if you'll excuse me, I have to get back and do some admin."

I waited until Kris was out of sight, then faced Bob. "I've heard there's a legend about Whaling Rock. Will you tell me about it? I'd be very grateful."

Bob gave me one of his strange looks before facing the ocean, eyes closed. I shifted from foot to foot, aware of the deep draw of his breathing. Finally, he turned to me.

"No."

He walked past and jumped from the rocks onto the beach.

"But…why not?"

Bob pushed his canoe into the surf, then climbed aboard. Soon he was paddling into the last of the light, but his voice carried as if he was still standing beside me. "Because he says you aren't ready yet."

"Who is *he*?" I called.

But Bob had already disappeared around the headland.

CHAPTER NINETEEN

I rushed breakfast—fresh pineapple and black coffee—because I had a boat to catch, then a flight to the main island. I met Frank and Nancy as I hurried from the dining room.

"Looks like you survived last night, Angel," Nancy said.

"Bob's okay. He's a gentle soul, a little upset by the modern world."

"Anything interesting happen?"

I told them quickly, finishing with, "But he refused to tell me the legend."

"D'you think he's a beer short of a six-pack?" asked Frank.

"I'm afraid I *did* laugh inside at what I didn't understand, at first. It's easy to do. I feel bad about it now. Especially when I saw the conviction with which he holds his beliefs—whatever they may be." My thoughts returned to the ceremony, and the wallet sinking into the depths. Bob had claimed he knew what I'd prayed for. Maybe it was obvious? Or was he pretending? But who, if anyone, had Bob been listening to? A god? An ancestor?

"A penny for them?" Frank asked softly.

I told him how embarrassed I was to have carried that wallet.

"That's nothing, Teal. I heard some Russian clowns covered the inside of their SUVs with whale penis leather. Onassis specified sperm whale foreskin for the barstools on his yacht. And they did it on purpose. You didn't know."

*   *   *

If the ride in Coconut from Horseshoe to Tofua'a had been bumpy, the island hopper flight to the main island was worse. I checked my laptop and camera before disembarking from the plane. A sweating mechanic wiped oil from its wing while another man, spanner in hand, raised the engine cowling and scratched his head. They had six hours to fix the leak before I flew back. Neither seemed too concerned. Just another regular day and another regular check-up, it seemed.

So this was the main island, which I'd glimpsed through patchy cloud as our Airbus had begun its final approach a week ago. I crossed the tarmac and walked through the modern terminal building, which looked smaller, shabbier than when we'd arrived. I smiled at the thought of soon being surrounded by books. Solving puzzles and drawing pictures with words— telling the world about it—was what I loved most. Investigative journalism was my dream job, and if I could just write a command-performance report, I'd be a step closer to achieving it.

With care I settled onto the meltingly hot seat of a contraption that combined motorbike and buggy in a three-wheeled configuration. The writing on its side boasted: *Island Taxi*. I felt grateful for the sun shade, less so for the broken seatbelt. The driver said the library was five minutes away as he gunned the engine. Palms skyward, he mouthed *Muffler broken* and we roared off into the morning traffic.

Twenty minutes later we pulled up outside a modest green building perched between an architecturally abrupt church and a burnt out school bus. A sign jutting from a strip of withered lawn read *Maintained by the Peace Corps*. Relishing the silence, I paid the driver and asked, "Have you heard of Thurston Morfil?"

"Why you want to know, lady?"

"I'm a journalist and I'm doing a story. Interested in what the locals think of him."

"You police?"

I laughed, though I wasn't sure if he was joking. "No."

Looking around, he said, "That Mr. Morfil is a powerful man."

"I know. Is he...liked? Respected?"

"I think he's a great man." He gunned the engine and accelerated away.

Inside the library, my eyes adjusted slowly to the dim interior, a welcome relief from the glare of the street.

The empty chairs reminded me of school cast-offs. Piles of curly-cornered magazines topped the wooded tables. Warped shelves housed a few hardbacks and yellowed paperbacks. Other occupants included a skinny young man who stared out of the window and a buzzing fly.

A stern islander fanned herself beneath a bulb-free light socket. She pushed her Elton John glasses into her white hair and greeted me with an index finger to her lips.

"Good morning," I said softly. "Kris Davies at the Sun and Moon said you'd put some reference books aside for me on local history and politics. My name's Teal Douglas."

Without turning, she bellowed, "Jerome, bring what I put out for the lady." She leaned back on her throne and continued to scrutinize me, breaking into a betel nut smile.

Jerome returned with a pile of books, flip-flops slapping the concrete. She didn't look at him. "Not those. The one on the reserved table...not that table. The one by the window." She completed her instructions with a series of headshakes and tuts.

"They should have named that one Fonu," she muttered. Arms crossed, she added, "We close at twelve o'clock today."

"But the sign said—"

"Eleven, if no one else comes in."

"That reminds me...do you have anything on this Fonu? His name keeps coming up and I'm looking for background info for—"

"I put the best book out for you on politics. That was what Mr. Davies asked for. Read the last chapter."

I took my laptop from my bag and settled at a table beneath the only fan.

"Fan broken," she said, before I asked.

The book, a fairly recent publication, featured events post-independence. The last chapter was titled, *Thurston Morfil—A Friend to All*.

I began reading:

After taking a First Class Honors Degree from Cambridge University, Mr. Morfil enjoyed a prestigious career in the City of London, settling in the islands in the Eighties, having fallen in love with them when vacationing here in his youth. With financial backing from a small group of elite London investors, he established The Islands Development and Consulting Corporation (IDCC), which gained its well-deserved pre-eminence in a range of industries including mining, tourism, fisheries and transport.

The book informed me IDCC was "the first point of contact for overseas investors". Who wrote this stuff? Morfil was described as a VIP, friend and confidante of former and current ministers and prime ministers, the Governor Generals of Australia and New Zealand, and was known to represent numerous prestigious foreign corporations here. *Quite impressive, Thurston. But I'm still waiting for that interview.*

My watch said ten fifty so I perused the library's shelves until I found a section marked *Local Cookery and Religion*. I lifted a promising-looking but tattered hardback. The prolog described the author (a former merchant seaman who'd settled here in the 1930s) and his fascination with the islands. His research included naval and city records, as well as some detailed documentation of islander narratives. *So the islanders were more forthcoming back then....* I carried Captain George Goodfellow's *Myth and Legends of an Arcane Paradise* to the yawning librarian.

"May I keep this for a few days?"

Outside, the midday heat engulfed me as I stepped around a dusty Mercedes that blocked my path. The driver's thick arms poked from his short-sleeved shirt. A policeman's cap lay on the dashboard behind an insect-speckled windshield. On the far side, the passenger door swung open to reveal a copper man in a quicksilver suit. His eyes were hidden behind reflective sunglasses as he approached.

"Good morning, ma'am," he said, standing too close to me.

"Hello."

"ID."

"Is there a problem?" I asked, reaching for my wallet.

He motioned to the driver who also stepped from the car. His shirt buttons strained over a bulging chest, a tattooed bicep twitched as his hand engulfed my wallet. *What's going on? Is something wrong?*

"P-passport's back at the hotel," I explained, my voice curiously quiet. My driver's license and credit cards were laid on the car bonnet and photographed. I was photographed too. The book I carried was inspected.

"Why you reading this nonsense?" the silver-suited copper asked.

"I'm interested in myths and legends," I answered carefully.

He flipped through my notebook and rifled through the contents of my bag. "Which hotel?"

"Can we do this in the shade?"

He repeated the question.

I could feel the sweat on my forehead, as a rivulet worked its way down my back. "The Sun and Moon. Horseshoe Island."

The driver returned to the car and spoke softly into the radio. After a minute he nodded at his boss who walked back to the car. "Enjoy your holiday, Ms. Douglas," he said. With a scrunch of gravel, they were gone.

Fanning my face, I went back into the library.

"What was all that about?" I asked the librarian who had just scurried away from the window.

"Didn't see nothing, lady."

Of course you didn't. "Can you order me a taxi?"

My flight wasn't till four. Nearly five hours to check out the capital. The taxi took me past ex-colonial and government buildings (no photographs allowed), the docks (no photographs allowed), and the central market (no photographs allowed). My driver steered the bumping three-wheeler out of town to skirt a copra factory, all the while shouting a monotone commentary over his shoulder. Wild flowers flashed from the scrub grass, hump-shouldered cattle, bell-necked goats and broken fencing whizzed past. But I couldn't get the encounter with the police out of my mind.

Who had told them I was there—or did they simply enjoy throwing their weight around? Hardly good for the tourist industry.

There was more: Though I couldn't be sure because he'd worn sunglasses, I felt certain the detective had never taken his eyes off me as the contents of my wallet were checked. So how had he known my name?

*   *   *

Turning onto the airport road with twenty minutes to spare before my flight, we watched the glinting body of a commercial airliner slip through the clouds and dip towards the runway.

"International flight arriving," my driver explained.

Fifteen minutes later I had seated myself in the dripping sauna that was the island hopper, praying for the thrum of the air con. The just-arrived Airbus was parked beside us and I watched as the passenger door swung open to repeat a familiar ritual: pallid tourists stepping excitedly into the sunlight, hesitating at the heat blast, then descending the disembarkation stairs. I was about to turn away when I spotted a familiar face.

Casually at first, then with increasing intensity I stared at her strawberry blonde hair, full figure and gravity-defying chest, before other passengers obscured my view. The wide-brimmed hat made recognition difficult, but the tight skirt and high heels were a dead giveaway. *What on earth are you doing* here *Triple-F Fiona Taylor?*

CHAPTER TWENTY

My dreams fused leering, distorted faces with police uniforms and warnings. It wasn't yet dawn as I stretched myself awake, glad to find myself curled up on the bed and not in the baking hot sun outside the library.

Why had the police behaved like that? Since when was being interested in Thurston Morfil some sort of crime? Who had tipped them off? The librarian had known. So had the taxi driver. Come to think of it, so had Frank and Nancy. Even Kris.

Now you're being ridiculous, Teal!

However I tried to explain it to myself, something did feel very wrong.

Too wound up to go back to sleep, I lifted my MacBook off the night table and rearranged the pillows to prop up my back. I flicked between the two blank documents that gleamed at me from my laptop, one entitled *Thurston Morfil, Island Savior*, the other, *A South Pacific Ghost Story*. I glanced through my notes and began to add what background I could to story number one. I'd checked my emails last night and a new one from Malcolm had informed me Sir Basil required a draft report on Morfil ASAP. "Come on guys, be reasonable!" I remember saying as I wondered what to write back.

I'd decided I'd reply this afternoon, taking advantage of the sixteen hours I was ahead of New York (when Malcolm should be asleep) to tell him that much of the background material was in place but Morfil's PA still hadn't made contact. I'd suggest Malcolm could help me out by doing some Morfil chasing himself. With luck that should buy a little time. Then I wondered, if this was so important to Sir Basil, why didn't *he* push Thurston Morfil to set up a meeting?

My chairman had described his friend in a positive way, but a few doubts had crept into my mind. Nothing definitive—not yet. Just an uneasy feeling because the initial feedback I was getting on Thurston Morfil didn't seem to fit Sir Basil's opinion of the man. Did they *really* want me to dig around, or did they assume that once I was seduced by the beaches, the ocean, and saturated with a continuous flow of rum punches, I'd lazily confirm Thane's opinion of Morfil? Now, in true Musculus tradition, the pressure was being ratcheted up. It was almost as if they wanted me to submit the first draft before I'd interviewed him. Something told me I could trust Perry absolutely, so I decided to bounce my concerns off him.

The sky blushed in post-dawn pink, but my glance out of the window also revealed a bank of dark clouds that were swelling offshore. Rain? Was it coming this way? Did it matter if I got soaked? It was as good a time as any for a jog. I slipped into my jogging clothes, anticipating the quiet of the early morning, which cleared my thoughts, reenergised my mind, and fed my resolve.

On the track that snaked to the back of the island, the breeze whipped at the surf and pulled strands of hair from my ponytail across my face. Sea birds worked the wave tops, sand-colored crabs scattered before my footfalls. I stopped and leaned against a palm trunk and took in the curl of the beach, my gaze following it to where it met scrub. Did something just move there? Too distant to be sure, I jogged on. But whoever, or whatever I'd seen had melted into the undergrowth. Closer now, there it was again—a man—in the broken light. Was it the figure who had waved at me from the rock? What was he doing here, alone on this remote corner of the island, at this hour?

And what was that...thumping noise?

While I wondered, a cloud slipped across the sun. The light dimmed as the first drops of rain, large and warm, tapped my shoulders.

Of course, I could jog back and ask Kris, but I was intrigued. And the scrub would provide cover. I cut back into the undergrowth and crouching, tiptoed forward. When a twig snapped, I froze but the sound was masked by the breeze and the surf. Unfortunately, though the grasses may have concealed me, they also hid the object of my curiosity. I parted some brush and gazed into a small clearing.

There he was.

My first reaction was to call out in surprise. But I was transfixed by the athleticism, and by the way his tanned muscles bulged and troughed under a gloss of moisture. Gloved hands pummeled depressions in a punch bag, which juddered and swung with each impact. Feather-light feet danced one way, then another. Though his head bobbed, his eyes were steely-locked on his mark. It went on and on, the pace rising and falling.

The rain became more persistent; the drops were large, warm and left mini craters in the sand. But my attention was on the precision of the man's balance, the variation in attack, the compelling relationship he shared with his inanimate opponent, the punch bag. As my world narrowed to a strip of rain-pelted scrub, I found myself captivated by an animalistic poetry I'd never imagined a man could possess.

"Oh," I said weakly.

Perry spun around. Our eyes met.

"Mr. Balboa, I presume?" I joked, my breathing quicker than it should have been.

"Welcome to the gym at the end of the world."

"That was incredible. Really!"

"The product, I'm afraid, of a wasted youth. But it's my favorite form of exercise, I try to do it every day—"

"And you're not even breathing hard."

He smiled as he wiped a hand across his wet brow. "I love rain," he said, glancing at the sky.

My eyes wandered down to his flat stomach.

"I...I wish I could hit like that!"

"Want a lesson?"

"Seriously? Well, I won't be any good—and the rain's getting heavier..."

Perry removed the gloves and offered them to me with a smile.

"I'm game if you are," he said, the water drops shimmering on his skin.

He started with my stance and addressed my feet, the position of my hips, chest, arms and head, until everything was where he wanted it. Or as close as he could get it. With him standing so close, I found myself struggling to concentrate. I thought the rain, which now forced him to raise his voice, would cool the air. So why was steam rising off the boulders that bordered his makeshift gym?

He placed his hands on my wet shoulders to demonstrate the rotation with a hooked punch. Then he held my fist as he uncurled my arm in slow motion, using phrases such as *body alignment* and *focused acceleration*. Prisms of color swum in the raindrops that clung to his eyelashes. I studied a water drop that meandered down his nose—for seconds it balanced on the very tip before dropping.

"Are you paying attention?"

"Sorry!"

I watched with fascination as he now slid the gloves on me. Velcro fastened, he announced that the next world champ was ready.

"Ding, ding!"

His soaked hair was flattened against his head. Streams ran off his hanging curls. As the rain built, a sheen of water slipped down his torso, soaking his trunks.

"Ding, ding?"

I couldn't remember a thing. But I pushed out my arm, the glove patting the bag, which remained motionless.

"Knockout!" he shouted.

I laughed. "What went wrong?"

We revisited the basics, which Perry made look so easy. He'd stand one side of me to study my feet, then move in front to make sure I was keeping my elbows in and my chin tucked behind my lead shoulder. I think he said something about punching from the ground, involving the whole body. Angles and levers. Slowly, I was improving and enjoying myself too. As the bag chirped and twitched, my feet squelched in my sneakers.

"That's enough for your first time. Or your muscles will be sore tomorrow."

I ran through all he'd taught me and hit the bag again, this time, with all my force. It jumped a few inches, casting a spray of droplets.

"Bravo! I would have felt that one!"

He walked over to a rock and retrieved a towel. "Soaking wet," he said, ringing it out. He returned and offered it to me.

"Not much point," I said, with a laugh. I took it anyway and patted my face as the rain died away.

Then I said, "A bag can't defend itself. It must be much more difficult to hit a person."

"Ah—that problem is solved with Perry's first rule of boxing, which states that when throwing the first punch, you must 'take your opponent's mind'."

"Which means?"

He flashed his hand in front of my face. "You blinked. An automatic response. So, if I pull back my right hand, for a fraction of a second your brain will think I'm loading a punch. Then I jab you with my left. Works every time."

"How many Perry boxing rules are there?"

"Thousands! But seriously, I'm impressed—I wanted to see how long you could keep going. Your stamina's good!"

"Thanks," I said. "This sure is tiring!"

"Yes. I need to go and lie down for a few hours, before I don my chef's apron," he said.

"Why?"

"I'm exhausted."

"But you're the fittest man I know."

"I was ready to collapse. If you hadn't spoken when you did…"

"You knew I was watching? But I approached on your blind side."

"I saw you on the beach. So I…er…tried a lot harder!"

*　　　*　　　*

Three dresses were draped over the bed, their hems aligned with different shoes. A gold and coral necklace and hooped earrings moved from one combination to the next as I tried to decide. Were my choices too formal for a sailboat dinner? Was I sending the wrong message? Should I go in shorts and a T-shirt? And what makeup should I wear? Or none at all?

The white cotton shift dress with emerald bamboo pattern edged out the others, because I loved the gold detailing at the hem and bust, and how well the jewelry worked with it. Informal but fun; classy but understated. I slipped my cork-soled wedge sandals into my beach bag and donned flip-flops for the walk there and the tender trip. I'd kept my makeup simple: a brush of eye shadow and a hint of natural-colored lipstick. I tucked two reference books and my laptop in beside my sandals—a professional touch and reminder of the evening's purpose. But why was there a flutter in my stomach—that nervous rush that sharpened the senses?

The mirror confirmed my belief I'd made the right choice. Sitting on the edge of the bed, I stared at the ceiling and said, "Grandma Lizzie, please bring me luck tonight."

I still had half an hour to kill. I opened *Myth and Legends of an Arcane Paradise* and checked the appendix for references to Fonu. Disappointed, I picked up Kris's scrapbook and pulled out the document. Yes, I remembered—Fonu was about to be rowed by Losa to the Whaling Rock to act as lookouts for a bunch of New Zealand whalers. And they were expected to die.

I wondered if the mood of the story was what I needed right now. But, with a deep breath, I began reading anyway.

> *"Father," he said carefully, "I have spent my life working tirelessly to make you proud of me. I have listened to you, the greatest Chief of all. Many times you reminded me that there is one truth that rides above all others. I have not forgotten it: That every creature is sacred, that everything depends on everything else. To kill the whales will destroy the trust that exists between them and us. It will destroy the trust you told me goes back to when the first men walked the earth. This is what my wise father taught me and this is why I oppose the killing of our whale brothers that these foreigners have planned."*
>
> *He glanced again across the beach to the beautiful Losa and straightened his back. "Father, I will go to the rock proudly with her!"*
>
> *The old man allowed himself a smile. This son—who could not paddle, who could not even swim, who spoke nonsense with the same determination with which he carved pointless items—spoke passionately...and well.*

But the elders had not bestowed the title of Great Chief upon the old man lightly. He remembered the "X" he'd marked at the bottom of something the foreigners called a "contract". They had given him the bowler hat then, in recognition of his wisdom. They told him he had been clever agreeing to the terms so quickly; by doing so, Captain Jackson had promised not to talk to other chiefs. Yes! Now he would be remembered long after his death for the most important deal in his people's history: guns for whales. Guns to keep the other tribes at bay after he died, when he could no longer direct his warriors in battle. Guns that would protect his people until they chose a new chief. Guns that would prove a substitute for his charming but disappointing son.

His hand slipped to the side of his grass skirt, to a secret pocket, and came back grasping a carved whale.

"Fonu, you carved this when you were seven. Your skill was great—but what I wanted, what I had prayed for, was a son who made me proud. A son who could lead my people in battle. With your older brother dead and my advancing years..." His voice thickened. "Three was too young for you to watch what happened to Taufa. Nonetheless, a Chief's son must still swim. He must still paddle. And fight. From the earliest age he must assume the responsibility of assuring his people's safety, before his own selfish wants. If you marry the daughter of the neighboring chief as I have decreed, on my death, they will leave you in peace." His hand landed heavily on Fonu's shoulder. "By now you should have got over Taufa's death. And be ready to take his place."

Memories of his only brother rose up to ambush Fonu's thoughts: Taufa had been pretending he was a manta ray as they'd laughed and splashed in the shallows, shortly after a passing storm had churned up the water. Was it because they were having so much fun that they had forgotten the warnings?

His big brother had stepped back, unaware of the stonefish buried in the sand. Fonu caught his breath as Taufa's screams tore through him again. He remembered them carrying the writhing boy away. It was the last time Fonu had seen him.

Fonu breathed deeply. "Great Chief, we all know that in your lifetime, you have conquered many islands—"

A round-bellied elder interrupted. "Including this one, the most sacred of them all."

"They say that your wisdom has brought many triumphs. That no man has ever fooled you or—"

The elder raised his hand. "We all know what Father Xavier said. That our Great Chief is as wise as the wisest king in his Bible book."

Fonu shook his head at the elder. "I am not here to ask my father to choose which woman is the mother of a baby. I am here to ask that if I prove myself worthy, he will call off the whale hunt. That he will send the whaling ship back to New Zealand. That at least in our waters, the gun on its front stays silent." Under his breath, he added, "I do not know why you trust the foreigners, Father. Especially that man Jackson who makes promises while his eyes admit his lies."

The Chief dropped the carved whale on the sand. "I have other carvers. This must stop. And still you won't tell me why the first carving you gave me was a whale."

Fonu shrugged. "I have tried to explain, but you won't listen. A voice came to me in a dream. It carried a warning and told me about a great circle that I saw with my own eyes. All the animals, all the plants—"

The Chief drew himself to his full height and stepped nearer the boy. He was shaking with rage as their eyes drew level.

"I have told you this before—it is very simple. The gods leave us driftwood on the falling tide to fuel our fires, not for carving animals. They also fill the ocean with fish for us to eat. The cattle I traded for fish with the foreigners provide milk and meat. The gods also give us bees. From them we get—"

"Honey?"

An adrenal wave of panic engulfed me. I tried to picture Lizzie's smiling face to counter it. I breathed in deeply as the door burst open.

"I'm back! Haw, haw."

I exhaled slowly. *Stay calm, Teal. Even here, murder's a crime.*

I tried to smile.

"It's shower time," he said, his hand buried wrist-deep in a family-sized bag of tortilla chips.

His clothing, item by item, hit the floor as he stomped past. A sweat-ringed shirt landed on my pillow. From the shower-room he bellowed, "Aren't you curious how it went?"

"How did it—whatever you were doing—go?" I asked, trying to echo his excitement.

"Excellently! Anything interesting happen while I was away?"

Gurgling pipes, escaping steam, Bear "singing". The shower room door slammed shut.

"I swam with a whale…saw Fiona at the airport…returned my grandfather's wallet to the ocean…was nearly arrested…and…the hottest man on earth invited me on a date." *Which you've just ruined.*

The singing and gurgling pipes continued. Then the shower switched off and Bear reappeared, dripping water on the floor.

"Well, that all sounds nice. Have to shoot off again soon."

"I don't know where you went, I—"

"Any mail for me?"

"Oh, yes—I forgot." I pointed at the manila envelope on the table.

"Anything else going on?"

"I've been doing background research. I have an interview booked tonight and—"

"Cancel it. Glad you got my email but no need to dress up on my account. Kris found a bottle of adequate champagne." While admiring himself in the mirror, he missed my blank look.

"You said you're leaving Tuesday. Where—"

"Must you sound so excited?"

"Curious what you're up to. That's all."

"That dreary couple still here?"

"Frank and Nancy? They aren't dreary, they—"

There was a knock at the door.

"That'll be room service. I ordered dinner—hoping this place can't ruin New Zealand lamb."

He walked over and opened the door. "Take it 'round the back of the hut. Set up the table there, we'll eat outside," he said to the room service waiter. "Call me when it's ready."

"In which case we'll need these." I lifted two cushions and followed the waiter outside. Stopping at the side of the hut, I glanced down the beach. From this distance, it looked like pin pricks of light (candles?) decorated Falcon's cockpit. A man sat motionless on the sand—was that a bird beside him? He was staring out to sea.

CHAPTER TWENTY-ONE

The next morning, I was waiting in our room for Bear who had wanted to watch the fish feeding again. I had chosen instead to battle with the nearly empty page of the Morfil document on my laptop.

When Bear returned, he complained about an over-dressed French mother and her whining daughter. He'd forgotten we'd met Lorraine and Cecile at the start of our vacation, preferring to haw, haw himself into a frenzy after comparing the teenager's complexion with an unsolved Rubik's cube. Other onlookers had apparently included an Australian family. He mimicked their exclamations of surprise (adding "mate" after every other word) when Black Jack had wolfed down an unfortunate fish.

"That surly French girl makes a better door than a window. But I got some great photos after I pushed her off the jetty."

"You're not serious!"

"Made it look like an accident, haw, haw!"

Scrolling through the images, he beamed at his artistry before inviting me to look.

"Slower. I can't see them," I said.

"I'm looking for the best one. There—isn't it great? I think I'll send it."

"What's so interesting about that fish?"

"What?"

"Who are you sending photos of Black Jack to?"

"Don't you worry your pretty face about it."

He marched past and out the door.

"Meet me in the dining room in ten."

After Bear had rushed through breakfast and disappeared off to the business center, I settled alone under a parasol with a three-day-old newspaper. I skimmed a piece on massaged unemployment figures and seethed at a story that exposed huge bonuses for chieftains of a loss-making, taxpayer recapitalised bank. The crossword caught my eye, but I was soon struggling with a clue: *Mexican brew lights up your day?*

My gaze drifted to Falcon's now empty mooring. "I'm so sorry, Perry," I whispered.

Was he out there checking his specimen traps? Searching for Solomon? More likely he was disappointed, probably annoyed with me, as he had every right to be. Had he sailed off to another island never to return? Maybe he planned to wait there until we'd gone home. With that selfish, unreliable American woman brushed from his thoughts, he'd return to continue his important research work. The first time I'd stood someone up in my entire life…and it had to be *him!* My laptop languished in my beach bag as I scanned the horizon in search of a set of sails. I wondered how I could get a message to him, to explain what had happened. To say sorry.

"Hi, Angel. My, you're looking glum. What's wrong?"

I told Nancy about last night's research meeting that wasn't.

"Don't we girls just love research meetings on yachts covered from one end to the other with tea lights!"

"Oh, Nancy."

"Frank was up early, said that Falcon crept out of here at first light. That crazy bird was flying behind it."

"What should I do? I don't have his email."

"You said Perry had a pub? Doesn't it have a website?"

"Yes?"

"Contact him via the website. I'm sure he'll understand."

"Nancy, you're a genius!" On an impulse, I leaned over and hugged her.

She picked up the newspaper. "Hmmm. Haven't done a crossword all vacation."

I was scanning the horizon again when she said, "Five letters. *Double header introduces periodic digital change.* Hmm. I think that's 'digital' as in 'digits' or numbers. Periodic is a regular passage of time like a month or year. Calendar years have four digits which change at the start of the New Year, which is January. And the god 'Janus' is usually depicted with two heads, so it must be *Janus!*" She wrote on the paper before announcing, "Obviously eight down is *torpedo.*" Moments later, "*Elephant.* Think you'll fool an old bird like me with an anagram, do you?"

Over the next few minutes I heard *obfuscation, dialect* and watched with fascination as she alternated between writing and staring over my shoulder. She dropped the paper beside me with a chuckle.

"Wow! I'm impressed!"

She was rubbing her hands. "It was nothing, Angel."

I explained I'd given up at one across.

"*Mexican brew lights up your day?* A brew is a beer. The day is lit by the sun and there's a Mexican beer called 'Sol', which is an alternative word for sun...from the Latin, Angel. Archaic—as in 'solar system'. So the answer has to be 'Sol'."

"Seems obvious now!" I laughed, marveling at the skill of crossword junkies.

"It's one way we fossils keep our minds active. The fun ones are the anagrams, you should give it a try. Who knows? Even an elite journalist like you might improve your vocabulary."

"When it comes to word puzzles, I think my mind has a mind of its own," I said.

"All the more reason to get started then! Okay, try this: Take the name of this hotel, drop the 'and', see how many seven letter words you can come up with. Then try it with 'sol' instead of 'sun'."

I laughed. "If you insist! By the way, I worked out your code the other day, T—W—T—B—A: They want to be alone."

"Even that blue-footed bird can see what's going on between you two."

I sighed. "But I'm so worried. I stood Perry up. He was sitting on the beach..."

"I'm so glad you like him, Angel. I was scared you were falling into the same trap it took me eighteen years to escape from."

"...staring out over the water."

"I married the wrong guy first time round because I thought there was no one else for me. Suitors weren't exactly beating a path to my door and I was scared I'd end up alone. When he finally ran off, I had plenty of time on my own. For the first time in my life, I learned to get to know myself. And you know what?"

"You decided you liked yourself?"

Nancy smiled. "Angel, the right man will allow you to *value* yourself. Then you'll look back on all this and be amazed you put up with Edward for so long. It'll work out, dear. Trust me."

"I hope so...is he really so awf—"

"Yes! Come on, a little smile, just a little one for me?"

"But my job's on the line too. I'm under pressure to interview Thurston Morfil, even though they *know* he's abroad. And nobody returns my calls or says when he'll be back. And...and what's Edward's up to? He comes and goes without warning." I lowered my voice. "I'm not sure I trust him anymore."

"You trusted him before?"

I described the comings and goings, the secrecy...the photos he took

135

of Black Jack before adding, "And I'm sure I saw his assistant Fiona at the airport on Saturday."

"Oh my! I'll talk to Frank—two heads are better than one. In the meantime, try to think about other things—you're supposed to be on vacation, after all. I do need to find Frank. Help him with his crab survey, no it's Monday. Beetle count."

There's more to you than meets the eye, Nancy. "Thanks for being a friend," I said as she got up to leave.

I arranged the letters of *moon* and *sun* on the page and started playing around with them, trying to find even one seven letter word. After five minutes I gave up. But when I substituted *sol,* a name jumped off the page at me.

"Good heavens!" I said. "I wasn't expecting that!"

CHAPTER TWENTY-TWO

The afternoon sun crawled over my face, reddening the back of my closed eyes. It felt good to stretch out on the bed. Bear had left this morning in a self-important flurry, ignoring my questions about where he was going. Or when he'd return. I was about to get up when my eyelids darkened: I assumed a cloud had passed in front of the sun. How strange, I thought, that the background sound of little waves breaking on the beach had fallen silent too.

Then I heard it: sad distant notes at the edge of my mind. They dipped and slurred in an illogical harmony that repeated over and over. Absorbed, I let it carry me along. What instrument possessed so unique a sound, so wide a range? Suddenly a dreadful crescendo—part moan part scream—ripped through my head. Then nothing.

I sat up and looked around, half expecting to be confronted by something magical or other-worldly, but my simple room was unchanged. I swung my legs over the edge of the bed, feeling an actual shiver run up my spine.

"Grandma, did you ever hear it end like *that?*" I asked out loud.

Could the music have something to do with Horseshoe Island? But Grandma had heard it thousands of miles away in Nantucket. Perry felt he'd been summoned here too. How—why, would it be here? And the first time I'd heard it had been—New York. The music, it seemed, could be anywhere. My fingers twisted Grandma's lucky ring.

It was not until much later that I noticed the piece of paper that had been slipped under the door. Sand grains peppered my feet as I unfolded it. The writing was scratchy and child-like; there were smudges too. In places the paper was damp and a tiny shell was sello-taped to a corner.

Dear Ms. Teal,
Pery asked me to fly this over. I am sorrie if it is a little wet but I
droppped it wen playing tide and seak with a jelliefish. Peree says he
understands why you coodn't make dinner becauze that nice Nancee
explained and all is forgivin. He went away for a wile, so not to be in
the way but wen his highly-traned spy Herman the Hermit Crab
informed him the coaste was clear, he upped ankor and returned. If
your busy shedyule permitts, he would be onoured to pik you up in the
tender at seven twonite from the beech for diner aboard the good ship
Falkon.
Your blue-footed frend,
Violet
PS.. Do you like the shel? I foundd it at low tide in Zanzibar (oops, I
meant Zansibarr).

I read it again, laughing as I went. Then I checked my watch. *Dear
Lord—the time!* I showered and dressed quickly.

Twenty minutes later I was dressed and walking on the sand with my
MacBook in my beach bag and my heart in my mouth.

*   *   *

A feathery breeze mixed the island's scents and exhaled them, along with an
occasional moth, across Falcon's elegant cockpit. We sat at a teak table
sipping a chilled rosé.

Perry asked if I liked the wine as if he meant it, and I smiled a *Very
much.* It felt good to have someone value my opinion. He took a sip, which
he sloshed around his mouth, making a variety of strange faces. Then he
announced it offered an obtusely aromatic nose, marked by hints of wild
strawberry and burnt jet fuel that blended cautiously into a damp meadow
of subtly unexpected rewards.

I laughed, "I didn't expect to be dining with a wine connoisseur."

"I haven't used that line in years—I memorized it to confuse
pompous wine waiters. I was hoping it would impress you," he said quietly.

Mission accomplished! "I can't get over how amazing it is that we *did*
finally meet. I am trying to resist saying 'it's a small world'."

"Sometimes you have to give destiny a helping hand," he said gently.

"Meaning?"

"You don't think I suggested this place out of a desire to support the
local tourist industry, do you?"

"Perry!" I said with mock firmness. Softly, I added, "I'm glad you
did. But you know what? Despite your jokes, sometimes you strike me as a
serious guy."

He put the wine down and our eyes met.

"The truth?"

"Please," I said carefully.

"What do you notice about this shirt?"

Strange question. Was that a flash of vulnerability in his eyes? "I see a frayed collar...and initials." I leaned in. "PANTS?"

"Peregrine Anstruther Norcliffe Tremayne Stanley. Would you believe?"

"That's enough names for a whole family!"

"I was called *Knickers* at school."

"Is that your subtle way of telling me you come from an ancient family?"

"It's not about what one's family did. It's about who *you* are."

Perry refilled our glasses. He sipped his, raising his eyebrows as if constructing another erudite description, but he hesitated. That's when I noticed the palest crescent of a scar by his eye.

"Looks like someone landed a punch on you."

"Sort of..."

I reached out and squeezed his wrist. "If you don't want to tell me..."

"My father used to beat me up. I lived in constant fear when I was young. The thing I remember most clearly about him?"

"What?"

"The look in his eye. The enjoyment he got from it. I learned to box to defend myself."

I moved my hand over the back of his. "That's ghastly. Did you ever have to defend yourself against him?"

"Once, when I was fifteen, he swung a punch at me, I ducked and popped him one. Broke his nose, blood everywhere. I thought he'd *kill* me. Instead he collapsed and cried like a baby."

"Did the beatings stop?"

"He withdrew further into the bottle. We buried him six months later."

"They do say close family is a relative term."

"Very good, Teal!"

"Please go on."

"I kept up the serious boxing, right through Oxford. Then I ran off to Woods Hole. Decided to be a marine biologist, rather than a bishop or an ambassador or a politician, as my family had expected of me." He sipped from his glass, and smiling, asked me to tell him my story.

"One last question. The boxing—how far did you take it?"

"I had plenty of amateur wins. I was in the final of a championship, shadow boxing in front of a mirror, when a terrible realization came to me. My expression—I looked just like my father. Same eyes, enjoyment, brutality. Okay, I was fighting in a ring and there were rules, but I realized I enjoyed the sport for the wrong reason. Suddenly I knew I couldn't box anymore."

"So you walked out of the championship?"

"Don't be silly. I won in the first round, but I never boxed again. My opponent was out cold for five minutes and his mother was ringside."

"Was he alright?"

"I went to hospital with his family and they did a brain scan. He was fine but I felt sick…terrified. Now I'm a complete pacifist. Nothing will make me fight again."

"But isn't it a useful skill to have, just in case?"

"In theory, but nothing's so important you can't talk it through. A drunk threw a punch at me in the pub. I didn't fight back. I went home with a thick lip, but at least I hadn't retaliated." Fingers entwined, he stretched his arms in front of him.

"Your turn. Fascinate me," he said.

"I don't know. I'm not that interesting."

"Three interesting facts—or the bird gets your grub!"

He stood to light the candles. When he sat, he slid closer, the light flickering in his eyes. "And what about you—any scars?"

I showed him a mark on the back of my hand. "Car accident."

"Ouch. Anyone hurt?"

"I'm afraid so—my sister. She died."

"My goodness. I'm sorry Teal," he said, turning to face me, wide-eyed.

"One of those tragedies that…happen."

I had to concentrate to hear what he said next.

"Yes. I can relate to that."

"Perry?"

"Her name was Kimberly. Car crash on the way to the airport."

"They say time heals but in my experience…"

"She was really into magic."

I took a deep breath and tried to sound jollier.

"Sometimes, I lie awake in bed and wonder what happens to us when we die."

"I spend enough time wondering what's going to happen to me while I'm living."

"Seriously, is Grandma up there? Sometimes I feel she's watching, trying to help. Probably frustrated by the mistakes I make…and my mother, will I see her again?"

"You lost her too? Your father?"

"Abandoned Mom when I was two. Ran off with her cousin. Never heard from them again."

I saw his expression. "I don't remember him. What I do remember are the bad things Mom used to say about him. But I don't know who was to blame—did she drive him away or did she become bitter because he'd abandoned us?"

"Sounds like we've both been through the mill. Left with lots of unanswerable questions. It's appealing to think our loved ones will be waiting for us. But thousands of charlatans have grown rich on the desperation of the bereaved."

"Heaven or hell? Or just blackness. Nothing. Emma's thesis is about this…but something tells me she'll never finish it," I said.

"I think she's been sidetracked by her aquaculture garden."

"Is she actually growing anything…*legal?*"

"She says you can feed the world's starving with seaweed. She's always testing local varieties on guests."

"So that's the revolting crinkly stuff that keeps appearing on my plate!"

He laughed. "Why do you think I never dine there?"

"I thought you were avoiding Madame Ooh-la-la."

He laughed. "That too!"

Something in Perry's manner unlocked the story inside me, and the words flowed. "Carly was Mom's favorite. Mom didn't…like me—I reminded her of Dad. Carly was the only one allowed to sit up front in the car, but that day I'd managed to swap places with her. I just wanted to sit next to Mom. I wanted so much for her to love me, so I was talking to her when—"

"How old were you?"

"Six. Carly was eight. A car smashed into us at a junction. She died instantly. After that, Mom used to say that if I hadn't changed places…"

He held my eyes. "If you don't mind me saying, sounds like you were a little crushed too."

Perry had listened to everything and I'd watched him thinking, responding, sharing my pain. "I'm sorry. If I made you uncomfortable."

"Thank you for trusting me with your story, Teal. Any other family?"

"My grandmother was like a mother to me."

"And your grandfather?"

"Grandpa was an artist. He died when I was young. Grandma used to say his work was always laden with meaning. But he was never discovered, so life was tough for them. Grandma used to laugh about it— she'd say they were 'banana sandwich poor'."

Perry and I sat there until the last of the sun's rays filtered over the horizon.

"I think it's time for grub," he said, jumping up. With a squeeze of my shoulder, he climbed into the cabin.

I heard the tinkle of cutlery, lids being placed on saucepans, cupboard doors slamming and something hitting the floor, followed by an "oops!".

Then he called out, "Ladies and gentlemen of the press, assorted non-believers, boys and girls...prepare to be amazed!" He reappeared in the hatch holding a small tray, which he passed up to me. "Keep you from being bored, see how many you can identify."

Mini walls sectioned the tray into compartments. "Perry's weird and wonderful collection of aquatic curios," he said as he disappeared below again.

"Okay. I see a pretty shell—"

"Ah, the Glory of the Sea cone shell," said a slightly muffled voice from the galley. "Truly beautiful, but it packs a hidden, highly venomous harpoon inside it, which it uses to immobilize prey. Never pick up a live one."

"Yikes. And what's this?" I described what resembled a notched arrowhead, about four inches long.

"Barb from an Amazon stingray. You don't want to—"

"I think I can guess! Oh, is this a shark tooth?"

"White? Large downward hook, two small hooks on the side?"

"Yup."

"No. That's the hook from the sucker of a colossal squid. Once a poor fish is caught in those tentacles, there's no escape."

"And here's a gold doubloon."

"Found it on a beach in the Caribbean. It's dated 1595, the reign of Philip the Second of Spain. Spent a month searching for the rest of the hoard but no luck."

I laughed. "And one compartment's empty."

"Oh, yes."

"What was in it?"

He appeared at the hatch, and said in a mock-serious voice, "An incredible and unique pearl from the Gulf of Mannar, which is between India and Sri Lanka—won it with the last roll of the dice in a backgammon tournament in Mumbai."

"What did it look like?"

"Let's just say..."

He ducked back into the cabin but turned at the last moment. "...it captured a prayer and a dream."

"Very cryptic!" *And romantic!*

"Some people claim pearls are unlucky, because they're made by the oyster to protect itself when something sharp gets into its shell. It coats them with mother of pearl, or *nacre*, as it's called. For me, they're about overcoming pain, adversity, about a brighter future. Turning situations, even bad ones, around. So I think they're lucky."

"I prefer your view. What happened to it?"

He returned with a napkin draped over his arm and his face fell. "I put it in a box, which I lost somewhere in New York a few weeks ago. Anyway, tonight's special: seafood platter, for...*two*. If the yellowfin sashimi was any fresher, it would jump overboard."

I laughed. "You remembered! Thank you, Perry!" Then a thought came to me. "In a box? A little wooden box? You lost it in New York a few weeks ago? Do you remember where?"

"Had it with me at a conservation meeting on Park Avenue. When I got back to the pub, I couldn't find it. An idiot in a Ferrari plowed into the back of me at Lexington and 45th. I think it must have flown out of my pocket."

"This is incredible. Were you in a cab?"

"How could you know that?"

"Because I *saw* you!"

"You *saw* me? I remember coming out of the Waldorf, how disappointed I was with the meeting. Oh yes, and a crazy woman in a red dress running down the street waving. I told the cab driver to get out of there as fast as possible and the Ferrari driver decided to race. Where were *you*?"

"I..."

"Walking past? Wait a minute...you're not...?"

"The crazy woman in red? No. I was not. I was the glammed-up, impulsive do-gooder in the scarlet ball gown trying to return your box. I was at the Waldorf. You dropped it next to me!"

"Oh, it was *you!*" His eyes opened wider and we laughed.

"That's amazing," he finally said. "To think we nearly met before the pub. So, what became of the box?"

"Wait a second. The box had my name on it! How on earth could you have known—"

"I didn't."

"Oh! *That's* why you looked astonished when I introduced myself on the fishing boat—you were as shocked as me that you'd carved my name on a box. So why *did* you—?"

"Not allowed to tell you or the magic won't happen."

"Wait—that's...what they told us in the market: You put something symbolic inside and scratch a coded message on the base. That's why it wouldn't open. It's a swell box, isn't it?"

He nodded. "I tell you what. The man I bought it from didn't say I couldn't give you a clue as to why I wrote TEAL on it. So I'll see if I can think something up."

"I wonder what became of it. I remember showing it to my

143

BEN STARLING

colleagues at my award ceremony. Can't remember if I got it back. Unless..."
"Unless?"
"I brought Grandma's handbag with me. It might be in there—I'll check when I get back to the room."
"Fingers crossed—you have to find it. In case it opens."
He grabbed my wrist, pulling me towards him. "Shhhhh, listen," he whispered, facing the reef.
"What is it?"
"I heard a blow."
"You mean—"
"That's a whale."
A whale? Now? Please go away Mr. or Ms. Whale before Perry ups anchor and tries to follow you. I want him all to myself tonight.
Silver confetti sparkled on the waves that radiated gently towards us. As the boat rocked, I found myself leaning against Perry. His arm slipped around my shoulder—it felt like the most natural thing in the world.
A great shape broke the surface inside the reef, a cone head that balanced, tilting and rotating before it slipped underwater.
"That's Solomon and he's checking us out," Perry said. "Never seen him inside the reef before. Keep still."
We waited until another blow, softer and closer this time, broke the silence. Now Solomon was beside Falcon. He raised his vast head from the water towards us.
"I've never seen one do that at night. It's called *spy-hopping*."
"There's only one word to describe it." I whispered.
"Magical?"
I squeezed him.

144

CHAPTER TWENTY-THREE

The tea lights on Falcon's deck blinked as brightly as the stars above that looked almost low enough to touch.

"That was so delicious." I clinked glasses with Perry.

"Delighted you enjoyed it. I thought I might fail on the tuna, but I caught a little one at four o'clock. The ocean gods obviously wanted our evening to be a success."

"Please be sure to thank them from me. You know what? I've noticed that we refer to Solomon as 'he' but the others use 'it'."

"Interesting you say that. I've worked around whales and dolphins for years and from day one it was obvious that they were intelligent, sentient beings, so I always think of them as individuals. I know Solomon is male because I once got close to him when he was singing—only male humpbacks sing. I was overjoyed when India recently declared that dolphins were 'non-human persons'. I'm praying other nations will follow suit—at the very least, stop imprisoning them in tiny tanks for people's fun and profit." He lifted a pad of paper. "I now feel a compelling need to commemorate this epic evening with an equally epic poem."

"You're a poet?"

"Nope. An artist...well, I sketch a bit."

"May I see your work?"

"Afraid I lent it to a friend. As soon as he's finished with it..."

"And the poetry?"

He wrote, looked up at the sky then shook his head, crossed it out and started again.

"How long have you been writing poetry?"

He checked his watch. "Two and a half minutes."

I laughed. "How's it going, Mr. Longfellow?"

"There was a young lady called Teal, who swam like a demented eel…"

"Uh-oh. This could degenerate into something rude!"

He tapped his head. "Back to the drawing board. I need to brush up on my iambic pentameters. But I'll make you a promise. Before you leave, I'll have completed a masterpiece Percy Bysshe Shelley would be proud of." His voice grew quiet. "If I'm lucky, you too."

"I can't wait! As it's getting late, may I ask you something?"

He put down his pencil and entwined his fingers behind his head. "Shoot."

"You said the other day that you thought you'd been summoned here."

"That's right."

"The journalist in me thinks there's a story at Horseshoe, but I can't put my finger on it. Something to do with the Whaling Rock and that boy Fonu. Other than the humpback, does the name *Solomon* hold any significance for you?"

He didn't answer immediately. "For some reason, it *is* ringing a faint bell."

I told him about the tarot cards and the name of the hotel. "When Nancy gave me an anagram to solve, the only word that came to me was 'Solomon'."

"You think there's a connection between the cards, the hotel and the whale? I mean, other than the name?"

"I'm probably ascribing meaning to what's just coincidence. But Grandma *did* teach me to look for signs. And it's like the name Solomon is a clue to something important. Problem is, Bob's the only one who may have answers but he won't talk. And there's something else. Seems like he's not the only one around here who doesn't want me asking questions. When I went to the library, the police were waiting for me. It was as if they wanted to scare me off."

"What were you researching?"

"I was looking for information on a local businessman called Thurston Morfil."

"Well, at least I can shed light on one mystery." He lowered his voice and looked around the boat, as if someone might be listening. "Just checking that whale wasn't eavesdropping on us."

I laughed.

"Seriously, the guy's a crook. Controls this place through a network of informers. Nothing happens here without his approval. And he has important friends abroad too. If you were asking questions about him, he would have heard."

"But I'm meant to be writing a glowing report on him. He's an old friend of my chairman and sits on our International Advisory Board. Now they're putting pressure on me to deliver, but I can't even get an interview with him."

"Any idea why your boss wants the report?"

"They're getting Musculus ready for an IPO. Basil's about to make a squillion from it. For the next few months, there mustn't be any hint of a scandal, but now you're telling me his old pal Morfil is bad news. One other thought crossed my mind—Basil mentioned Morfil deserves to have been knighted by now. Maybe Basil's checking him out for that too, before he recommends him to the people who award honors."

"Either your boss is honest and wants an accurate appraisal, or he's a crook too, expecting you to rubber stamp Morfil. But why would he go to the trouble and expense of sending you here if he didn't want the truth? My guess is, he knows you're good. Maybe it's a first step in the due diligence process?"

"At the award ceremony, a journalist asked Thane about a rumor that all wasn't well at Musculus. Maybe there's a connection. Is Morfil really *that* bad?"

"Remember that Korean longliner when we were fishing? I said the Minister of Fisheries turned a blind eye. It's because he answers to Morfil, they all do. You can bet the Koreans are stuffing one of his secret bank accounts with money. The trouble is getting evidence."

"You're trying?"

"It's difficult when you're constantly being watched."

"Who by?"

"Maybe the same person who tipped off the police that you were asking about Morfil. Could be a maid, a beach cleaner, a bartender. They're probably all in his pocket. I spend half the year here trying to escape big city commercialism. But with every passing day, I have more concerns about this place."

"Tomorrow I'll—"

"Wait a minute! I *knew* it came up recently," he said. "You remember the quiz that night in the Blue Beluga? My team came second because we got the last answer wrong."

"Yes?"

"It cost us the regional final—'Who wrote the book of Ecclesiastes?'"

"Edward didn't know that one either."

He spoke slowly. "It was King *Solomon*."

We looked at each other. I was unsure what to say. Finally, I said, "If Edward had known that answer, he would have gotten to choose the hotel, and I wouldn't be here now. In fact, *we* wouldn't have met again."

"That proves I was right about something."

"What?"

"I never pictured Edward in Bible study group." He grinned. "Seriously though, please be careful. Morfil is at the peak of his career. He has a lot to lose if you expose him."

"I could understand that if he was in the States or Europe. But this place isn't exactly one of the world's thriving economies. By GDP, one hundred and seventy-eighth out of a hundred and ninety-three, if I remember correctly. So why—"

"Teal, a few years ago a journalist started asking questions. He was roughed up, his visa canceled and he left on the next flight. I don't want the same thing to happen to you."

*   *   *

"Thank you for walking me back," I said. "You're a gentleman."

It was that awkward moment—how would the evening end? With a kiss, a hug? Perry was unusually quiet and suddenly I had no idea what to say either. My fingers fumbled with the key, before I pushed open the door.

"Do you want to check that handbag?"

"Oh, of course, the swell box. Won't take long."

I walked in and left the door open, but he didn't follow. The handbag was in the cupboard. I carried it back to Perry before I opened it.

"If we're lucky—yes! It's here!" I said, handing the box to him in the half light.

He inspected it and shook it gently. "Still swollen shut." He looked at me. "It's amazing to be reunited with it. Teal, you're a marvel. However can I thank you?"

I'm sure you can think of something...

"I'll put it in the sun. Then it should dry out and hopefully open one auspicious day."

Then he stepped forward. The night air warmed as the stars outlined his silhouette. He stood very close and kissed me lightly on both cheeks. "That's how we kiss goodnight in Europe," he said quietly. My eyes were closed when he kissed me again. This time on the forehead. Softly. Lingering.

When I opened them, he was stepping back.

"That was a Perry kiss. I save it for special people. Goodnight, Teal. Thank you for an *epic* evening."

"Th-thank *you* Perry, it was amazing and—" I said to the retreating figure who was soon swallowed by the darkness. A dozen thoughts swirled in my head.

And one in my heart.

CHAPTER TWENTY-FOUR

I'd told myself the veranda would make a pleasant place to work before the day heated up, but in an hour I'd typed only one paragraph. And it needed editing. Sleep had come with difficulty—why hadn't I noticed how uncomfortable the bed was before? I found myself glancing down the beach at Falcon as I relived every detail of last night. Tiny waves curled onto the sand, the rhythm gentle, soothing, bell like.

Bell like?

I rushed in and grabbed the phone.

"Putting a call through. Please hold."

I cradled the receiver and waited. After a series of clicks, I heard, "...don't be late."

"Hello? You were cut off—who is this?" I asked, as I tried to recognize the owner of the crisp English accent.

"...At eleven-thirty sharp today."

"There's a lot of static on the line. Do you have the right person?"

"Teal Douglas?"

"Yes. Who is this?"

"Ruth Entwhistle. I'm Thurston Morfil's senior diary secretary."

"Oh, hello. Could you repeat what you just said, please?"

"Mr. Morfil can see you for forty-five minutes at eleven-thirty today. Please write down the address. And don't be late or try to extend the interview as he's flying out immediately afterwards."

I glanced around. Oh, no—my laptop was on the veranda.

"Suite One, the Coral Business Complex, Commercial Street—"

"Got it! That's the IDCC headquarters? Hello? Hello?" But the line was dead.

I checked my watch, grabbed the phone and dialed reception.

"Hi Kris. Could you run me over to Tofua'a in Coconut at nine-thirty? I need to catch the island hopper to the main island. And can you book me a seat, returning this afternoon?"

"No problem."

I hurried to the shower room to get ready.

Twenty minutes later I dropped my iPhone and laptop in my handbag. Finally, the real purpose of my trip loomed and I couldn't afford to screw it up. I had added a slim gold chain to a lightweight navy business suit, an open neck cream shirt and black pumps. I was just leaving the room when the phone rang again.

"Hello?"

"Teal? It's Malcolm. I'm hoping you've got good news for me."

"Malcolm? Yes—I'm on my way out to interview Thurston Morfil!"

"Listen, Citizen Thane summoned me again yesterday after he'd met with his investment bankers and lawyers. Never seen him so stony-faced. Wanted to know what the devil you were up to. He's getting very impatient. So am I."

"But Morfil's been traveling. Now he's back. Got a plane to catch—bye!"

"Wait! Teal, Sir Basil expects five thousand of your best words on his desk by Friday. He wants background, history, the man's bio, all his business deals. Who he knows, mixes with socially, at work, in government. Guestimate his wealth and tell Sir Basil how he fills his spare time. He wants to know what people think of Morfil. Provide corroborating interviews, links to newspaper articles, photos and relevant websites. Hell, you might as well find out which side he butters his toast, before Sir Basil asks."

"Are you serious? It's already Wednesday morning, here."

"So crack some all-nighters. I don't know—cut a few corners if you have to. Just don't let me down."

I hung up and was opening the door when the phone rang again. I rushed back.

"Malcolm, if I cut corners, I'll end up going round in circles. Then you'll—"

"Teal?"

"Bear? Can't talk now. Rushing. I have my interview with Morfil."

"That dreary couple. What did you say their names were?"

A warning bell rang in my head. "Why on earth are you ringing me to ask me this?"

"I need their names."

"I have a boat—and a flight to catch. Jim and Mary, okay?"

"What's their surname?"

"I'm sorry, you're breaking up. Their what?"

"I can hear you fine. I said—"

Click.

What was that about? I wasn't proud I'd lied, but his tone had sounded serious. Almost threatening. Luckily there was the usual static on the line. I could always say he misheard me and he knew calls get dropped here all the time.

Coconut was waiting at the jetty. Kris wasn't. I groaned in frustration, checked my watch again and hurried back towards reception. All this rushing around in a business suit was the last thing I needed before the interview. And time was tight enough as it was.

"Kris?"

"No sign of Emma. No idea where she is," he said in a faraway voice as he stroked Luna's head that poked out above from the top of her denim sling. "Does she feel a little hot to you? Do you think she's catching something?"

I touched her forehead. "Hard to say," I said, as the baby's eyes held mine.

"Word on the street is that Bob's the local shaman. Emma doesn't like western medicine so maybe we'll ask him. Does Daddy's baby seahorse feel a little icky-poo?" he asked, blowing gently on her face.

"Kris, I'm sorry to change the subject but I'll miss the flight! It's my interview with Thurston Morfil. Is there someone else who can take me? I have to—"

"You're *interviewing* Thurstonella?"

"Why do you call him that?"

He ran his fingers through his hair and pouted. In a clipped English accent and operatic voice, he said, "Dear lady, it behooves me to apologize energetically for my recondite grasp of the matters to which you kindly allude, though their verisimilitude is without question beyond all reasonable doubt."

"Kris?"

"It'll make sense when you meet him. But I'm afraid I can't leave the hotel unattended. He checked the wall clock. Emma's breasts are eleven and a half minutes late."

"Oh. I see." I didn't but sometimes even the most rigidly schedule-bound of us have to learn to go with the flow. Kris too, I thought impatiently.

"LSD's feeding time."

Ten minutes later we were still in reception waiting for Emma's breasts. Kris put in a call and was told the island hopper would be on time (apparently, for the first time this century) and couldn't be delayed because it had some VIPs from the World Bank on board. I asked him to turn up the fan as I paced back and forth. All this way, one shot at the interview and now I was going to miss it. Borrowing from Cecile, I let out a melodramatic pfffff and stared out the window at Coconut.

My tapping foot did the trick.

"Wait! I've got it!" Kris walked over to a mini-fridge and opened the door. "Had this installed for emergencies." Out came a gallon jug. "That's baby formula but it's only half full. Do you think it's enough?"

"Were you planning to give her a drink or bathe her in it?"

Emma skipped in. "Hi peeps! Why the long faces? Is my little princess hungry?" Baby transfer complete, she placed a gulping Luna on her breast. "Later. Termite nest in room nine needs to be lovingly relocated, or this time, I think our Andorran guests really will fly home."

"Andorran? How exotic."

"Trust me, I have a great eye for accents," she said, leaving.

Kris grabbed the boat keys off a hook. Then he stopped, pulled open a drawer and handed me a hammer. "We'll need this."

"Why?"

But Kris was already twelve steps out the door, striding towards Coconut bobbing gently by the jetty. I hurried after him, praying Morfil's office had air con.

CHAPTER TWENTY-FIVE

It didn't.

CHAPTER TWENTY-SIX

Despite the importance of the assignment and the limited time available, I relaxed into the leather seat of the car in which Thurston Morfil and I were now being driven.

Morfil's body was fashioned from a series of interlocking rectangles, each slimmer than the last. The square-jawed face that protruded from the worsted pinstripe suit radiated cool. Clumps of gold secured the shirt's lilac cuffs, which he adjusted until they protruded *just so* beyond the jacket sleeves. Diamond studs performed the same function down the front of his pleated shirt. A thick cigar and purple bowtie added pomp. He waved his arms to emphasize his old-world diction and my first impression was of an enthusiastic, elongated Lego-man. I found myself intrigued as much by his charm as by his theater.

"Forgive me if it was a trifle warm in my office, Ms. Douglas. Though I am exceptionally fortunate in never feeling the heat, I do hate to see a lady looking uncomfortable."

I swept my damp hair from my face. As I crossed my legs to hide an oil stain on my skirt, I caught him studying the smudge of grease on my wrist. Hardly the impressive entry I'd planned. I hoped he wouldn't report back to Sir Basil. "Boat problems, I'm afraid. Kris made me thump the engine with a hammer every twenty seconds to stop it seizing."

"The endless mechanical tribulations of island living. Fortunately, my estimable Lexus—incidentally the only one in the islands, and the only *gold* one between here and New Zealand—has the most excellent air conditioning system, don't you think? If the air feels a trifle frigid, do let me know. We'll take a leisurely drive, and you must question me on any subject. Don't be shy, now, dear lady." Manicured fingers patted my knee. I was glad my skirt was long enough to cover it. Then he drew on his cigar and flooded the car with smoke.

"Very thoughtful of you, Mr. Morfil—" I stifled a cough.

"Permit me to apologize profoundly for the last minute nature of our meeting."

"I only just made it!" I laughed.

"No need to stand on ceremony, my friends call me Thurston," he said, adjusting the tortoiseshell sunglasses perched on his silvery crown.

"Thank you, Thurston." I lifted my laptop from my bag and opened the document with the questions I'd prepared. With my iPhone on the seat between us, I hit record. "And it's Teal. Before we start, I'm curious...how do you get the car serviced?"

"Lexus dispatch mechanics from Australia and fly in the parts. Why they should treat this simple, unworthy old codger so well remains a complete mystery to me. Who knows? Perhaps it has something to do with the dedication I have shown to my professional career all these years and, if I may say so, to my exemplary reputation for loyalty, hard work and fairness. Naturally, I remain humbled and most grateful for life's kindnesses, large and small." He laughed with a falsetto screech.

"Sir Basil speaks highly of you. I understand you've known each other since your university days."

"We rowed together on the varsity team."

"Cambridge, wasn't it?" *The year Oxford won by ten lengths, Wikipedia informed me.*

I jumped when the driver blasted the horn. An islander on a battered motorbike swerved off the road, coming to a halt in a cloud of dust. I was watching him in the rear window when Morfil spoke.

"I see you're admiring my rose gold Daytona Cosmograph. It's a Rolex, you know. An undeserved birthday gift from your generous chairman. We were sporting team mates then, business colleagues and inseparable friends ever since."

"Please explain your decision to move here as I understand you had a successful career in London."

"I'm glad you've taken the trouble to do your research. I worked in a merchant bank—similar to what you Americans call an investment bank—advising companies, putting deals together. One of my clients was a major mining conglomerate. You'll appreciate my circumspection but names aren't necessary in this instance. They sent me to a number of their...shall we call them...*problematic* facilities?" He turned to face me. "For some time rumors circulated that I had a penchant for locking the warring factions in disused mine shafts until they agreed to work together." He grinned. "Of course, etiquette prevents me commenting on the veracity—or otherwise—of what any half-decent defamation barrister wouldn't hesitate to describe as a 'gross calumny'."

I laughed politely, as it seemed to be expected.

"One positive consequence was that I learned a thing or two about mining. No formal mining qualifications, you understand."

I nodded to indicate how impressed I was. I had found over the years that the best way to get a subject talking was to remain steadfastly mute and let them fill in the silences.

"I discovered I had a knack for sorting things out. Enamored of the South Pacific and bored of enriching others, I assembled a team of financial backers and migrated here. What excites me is growing fledgling economies, bringing employment and a better quality of life to communities the rest of the world has overlooked. The first step is to develop revenue-relevant infrastructure—"

"Could you give me examples?"

"Airports, roads, dockyard facilities...which opens the export and import markets, followed by tourism. And of course the icing on the gateau has been the numerous commercial successes with which I have been rewarded. Last year, I was privileged to be able to donate a state-of-the-art operating theater for the hospital and to appoint two full-time Western surgeons."

"You mentioned 'infrastructure'...."

"Indeed I did." He pushed a button at his elbow and the glass partition that separated us from the driver, slid down. "Tangaroa—"

"Yes, sir, Mr. Morfil?"

"Take the coast road and turn onto Windward."

With the tinted partition lowered, I could see the man's bull neck, a mangled ear.

"He used to play rugby for New Zealand," Morfil explained. "A disagreement with a referee ended his career."

The Lexus slowed to take a turn, and the driver blasted the horn at a group of islanders crossing the road. Two oncoming cars and an island taxi pulled over at our approach.

"You seem to be well known."

"Over there, beyond that Japanese freighter. You see those cranes with IDCC on them? I'm proud to say I arranged financing for the redevelopment of the docks. We cut a deeper, wider channel, built a small container facility, refrigerated warehousing and a canning factory. You'll know about our fish, but have you heard of 'copra'?"

"Dried coconut, isn't it?"

"Indeed it is." He turned to admire his docks. "Many people congratulate me for single-handedly developing the islands' copra export market. At the risk of sounding immodest..." he puffed again on his cigar, "...I used my international connections to increase the size of the industry ten-fold in as many years. With logging on the decline, it's an important export now. But, within eighteen months, I predict seafood will overtake it."

"Is the fishing sustainable?"

"Allow me to enlighten you about my new cannery, which has been operational for three months now. I'm also involved with the financing of a modern fishing fleet. Together these will create hundreds of jobs and exploit the boundless riches of the ocean. I must admit I *do* enjoy a modest flush of pride at my not insignificant achievement."

"That's very impressive, but I wanted to ask about the longliners. I understand they're seriously damaging the habitat."

Morfil threw a hand up to his brow in mock anguish. "Tut, tut, dear lady. What can I say? There are naysayers out there who are predisposed to finding fault—so-called environmentalists. But believe me when I say they have hidden agendas. I assure you, there isn't a single piece of substantiated evidence that proves longlining is doing harm here."

"I thought the turtles, the albatrosses, the sharks—"

"Hush! These alarmist claims have been made many times. Which is why, at my own not inconsiderable expense, I commissioned a detailed scientific study into the matter. It concluded that any decreases in animal populations were entirely natural. All populations peak and trough…but, of course, there are people who don't want you to hear this. They'd prefer to stand in the way of economic progress."

I may not be qualified to review your detailed scientific study, Thurston—but I know someone who is. "Could you email me a copy of the report?"

"Come now, dear Teal, why ever would you want to trouble yourself with something so tedious? After all, it's quite scientific…graphs and numbers. That sort of thing." He patted my knee again.

I smiled sweetly. "In case Sir Basil asks if I've read it. I need to have covered all the bases. But between you and me, I'll only have time to skim it." *Which is true, but something tells me Perry will read every word.*

He pulled a bottle green notepad from his breast pocket. "Made from a local lizard. I send the skins to a little man in Bristol who does a wonderful job dying them," he explained.

"It's very attractive. Skink?" I asked.

"Indeed so. Are you a herpetologist?"

"A lucky guess."

Flowery writing gushed from the fountain pen. *Purple* ink?

"Some accuse me of being old fashioned, but I find this 'aide memoire' entirely reliable. You'll have it tomorrow via electronic mail."

"Please tell me about the whales."

"There was a fledgling whaling industry here before the war. Now, of course, they're super-protected, as they should be. Every year some blaggard approaches me trying to kill whales for what they claim are scientific purposes. Promises of wealth, anonymity. I always send them packing."

"I meant whale-watching."

"Ah, whale-*watching*, dear lady! Eco-tourism, very important, you know. It's growing nicely, helping get us on the tourist map. I believe Horseshoe runs trips. Have you been?"

"Yes, it was incredible."

"You see, there are plenty out there." He flashed a smile.

"What about the dolphins? I've heard the islanders harvest them for food, some are still exported to seaquariums and—"

"Utter balderdash, and you may quote me on that. I wonder who told you this. The islanders have a long tradition of respecting the ocean, especially the dolphins that they see as their spirit brothers. I, for one, wouldn't hesitate to bring this to my close friend, the Prime Minister's attention, if I was aware of, or even suspected such appalling activity. Regarding people who delight in rumor-mongering: If you'll excuse the conjoined metaphor, 'before adopting the moral high ground, remember pride comes before a fall.'"

"You're saying—"

"The very notion that our flippered cousins could possibly come to harm here! Forgive me if I don't dignify that statement with a detailed answer. In any event, the matter is eloquently addressed in my report. But enough about me, tell me about *you*. Are you enjoying yourself in our modest paradise?"

I laughed. "If you don't mind, I still have a few more questions."

"And how is that old rogue, Thane?"

I watched him intently but he gave nothing away. "As charming as ever," I said carefully.

"Do you like souvenirs?" Before I'd answered, he glanced at his watch and the partition slid down again. "To the cannery, and hurry, man!" He turned to me. "I have a second office there."

The Lexus lurched forward, horn blaring. "Use the lights too, the lights!" he shouted.

From somewhere, a pair of police motor cycles, sirens wailing, slipped in front of us. I thought we were being pulled over; instead their riders gestured violently at the scattering traffic.

Ten minutes later a saluting security guard raised a barrier and we pulled up outside a single story building appended to a warehouse. The words *Gold Fin Marine Resources Ltd.* appeared in gilded letters across a green awning, which incorporated a logo of entwined tunas. Morfil punched a code into the wall-mounted security pad and mechanical deadlocks whirred. The door clicked open.

"Impressive, Thurston. I didn't realize you'd need this much security for a fish factory."

"Dear lady, by the end of next week I'll have a first class security camera and alarm system fitted, linked to police headquarters," he said over his shoulder.

Framed certificates and photos of Morfil shaking hands with dignitaries lined the walls. A pile of tuna cans covered half the desk, an open nautical chart, the other. On the chart lay a roll of labels, and a few more cans.

"May I?" I asked raising my camera.

"A moment, please." Morfil adjusted his bowtie in a wall mirror and stroked a comb through his hair. When I'd confirmed his bald patch didn't show, he arranged his face in an *Invest in me* smile.

He checked the digital image. "No, no! Take more, and be sure to get the Prime Minister's photo in the background."

Twenty photos later, he nodded his satisfaction and handed me a can of tuna. "Let me know what you think."

We were leaving when I asked, "Could you spare another? For friends…"

"Quick, then."

I rushed over and grabbed a second. When I turned, he was blocking my exit.

"Not that one," he said firmly.

He took it from me and walked around the desk, dropping it in a drawer.

"I'm sorry, I didn't—"

"Typographical error on the label, dear lady," he explained, before reconstructing the smile and handing me another can. I dropped them in my bag and we walked back to the car.

Tangaroa opened my door.

"Airport!"

Inside the car, I watched Morfil closely. "May I ask you about an incident on Saturday? The police stopped and questioned me. I had mentioned your name, the next thing I knew—"

"Word of this innocent misunderstanding did reach me. A case of mistaken identity. A woman tourist was suspected of selling drugs here; unfortunately, you matched her description. And drugs are something we do not tolerate." He took my hand and turned to me. "On behalf of each and every one of our two hundred thousand-strong population, I most humbly apologize."

I laughed, retrieving my hand. "Accepted."

We passed a small industrial facility that Morfil said he owned, then he pointed out a distant island. "That's our latest development: *The Coral Palm Resort*, which will be one of the very finest in the Pacific. It will be environmentally neutral and wellbeing-themed."

"Coral Palm rings a bell. Isn't there a turtle nesting site on the beach?"

"A deranged islander just sent me a petition with about twenty signatures claiming that." He squealed his falsetto laugh. "There was a page of illiterate scrawl demanding something about islanders and visitors needing to work together to save the local wildlife."

One of those signatures was mine!

"If we'd had more time today, I would have had the car driven inland and shown you the new irrigation system, and some most promising mine workings." He tapped his cufflinks. "Fashioned from our own gold, you know."

I nodded at the diamond studs. "And those?"

He lowered the partition. "Phone the airport and tell them to hold the Auckland flight."

He laughed. "No, a gift from a dear Angolan friend."

"You've been most helpful, one last question. Your international connections and relationship with Musculus. Could you describe—"

"Dear lady," he said. "When do you leave our modest paradise?"

"On the fourteenth."

Tangaroa slowed the car, easing to a halt in front of the main doors of the airport terminal.

"Perhaps I will be blessed with good fortune and our paths will cross again."

After running a comb through his bouffant hair again, he patted it affectionately. He checked his bowtie in the window reflection and intoned, "Farewell, dear lady," as Tangaroa opened the door. Morfil beamed as he got out of the car and strode into the airport, smiling at everyone. "Bring my bags," he boomed at a line of rigid porters.

I lifted a tuna can, trying to compare it in my mind's eye with the one he'd taken from me. I'd only glanced at that one, but my investigative radar had detected *something* about the label was different. I sat back in the leather seat, trying to reconstruct the image of the other tuna can, just like Lizzie used to make me practice when we'd played memory games.

Another thought struck me: As Thurston Morfil, millionaire, VIP, island economic savior, hospital benefactor, Musculus advisor, and potential British Knight of the Realm, had walked smiling and waving into the airport—not one islander had smiled back.

CHAPTER TWENTY-SEVEN

Perry stood at Falcon's helm as soft light flooded the morning. The sails stretched taut in isometric counterbalance to the playful breeze. Four miles offshore, it felt as though the ocean approved of Falcon, caressing and encouraging the yacht's gentle progress. Where Coconut bulldozed and Tango sprinted, Falcon's was a soft motion, the timbers that formed the hull working with, not against the waves. Perry, shirtless, motionless, seemed to be a part of the boat. A part of the sky and ocean too.

And I shouldn't have been here. I should have been in my room transcribing, typing, researching—or even risking looking for other people to interview who knew Morfil. The interview hadn't gone as I'd expected. It had left me with more questions than I had started with. Now I was faced with every journalist's worst nightmare: trying to write a story when pieces were still missing, as the deadline galloped ever closer.

"Dolphins!" I exclaimed, nodding at the shapes greyhounding in. The ocean came to life as they materialized around us, cavorting at Falcon's bow as they took turns surfacing, diving under the boat and accelerating away. Astern, one jumped like a missile before crashing back onto a wave. Another rolled on its side, its tail beating as it charged away.

A minute later they were gone.

Perry had promised to tell me everything he knew about the islands. That counted as research, didn't it? He was about the closest thing to a local I could find who would actually answer my questions. And of course, I'd brought my laptop.

I was still thinking about what Malcolm had said Sir Basil required. Was he bluffing? Surely Sir Basil knew most of this already. Malcolm had mentioned Sir Basil had met with his advisors. My guess was they were double checking anyone associated with the company, so that no skeletons tumbled from the Musculus closet in the build up to the IPO. Bad news could delay things, affect the share price. And be embarrassing.

I needed some time, some space to let my intuition guide my next move. Perhaps, sailing with Perry wasn't the worst idea in the world. And when he'd placed his hands on my shoulders and explained that Violet wanted to discuss the mysterious activity she'd spotted from a hundred feet above Morfil's office, well, how could I refuse?

I opened my laptop and placed my iPhone by Perry. As the Morfil interview played, I typed it into a new document. When it finished, Perry said, "I never did understand the case for building a cannery there."

"I could easily submit an incomplete report and make the deadline—but to get to the bottom of this, even if it's only to prove nothing sinister *is* going on, I need more time."

Then Perry smiled—one of those smiles that repositions you at the center of the universe. Behind him a flying fish launching itself on a pillow of air and skittered across the surface. When its improbable glide ended in an inelegant splash, I refocused on Perry, feeling a lump in my throat. I turned so he wouldn't see—big girls don't cry—but that was when I knew he was at the center of *my* universe.

Little by little, I could feel myself letting go, as minutes became hours, as the morning wandered into afternoon, and as the courage to dream replaced years of emptiness. As I dreamed, the wind shushed to stillness and Falcon settled on the water becalmed, like a leaf on a pond.

Perry pointed at a dark, kink-winged bird; I learned that because its head was pointing down, it was tracking fish. Later, he whispered 'Turtle', but all I saw were brown fractals shattering beneath the boiling water.

When the breeze returned, he spun the wheel and leaned forward to release some rope from a winch. Falcon veered away, the sails luffing as the boom swished across the cockpit. Perry showed me how to loop ropes around the winch on the new leeward side, then pull them taut till the sails regained their crisp shape. Falcon once again picked up speed as we cut through the waves.

Perry's attention shifted to a long, flat rock, a half mile away. His brow furrowed as he spun the wheel, and Falcon headed towards it. He muttered something before checking the GPS. "There aren't rocks there…"

Soon we were alongside. A fin broke the slate gray back. Above, screeching gulls hovered and dived.

"The netting's killing him."

Then I understood. "Solomon!"

Perry ducked into the cabin and emerged clutching masks, fins, knives. "Teal, I shouldn't ask you, you should say *no*, but I can't do this on my own. And as you two are already acquainted…"

"Just try to stop me," I said.

"It could be dangerous."

He checked the sky, then his watch. He ran to the bow and leaned over, searching left and right.

"What are you doing?"

"You don't want to know."

"Perry?"

He turned to me.

"You were checking for sharks, weren't you?"

"Didn't see any."

"Then we're wasting time."

When we'd lowered the sails, he pulled a long rope from a locker and fastened one end around a thick belt at his waist. He joined us together with a second length. I watched him complete the knot.

"As long as the wind doesn't pick up, we'll be fine. If it does, Falcon will drag and we'll be pulled away from Solomon. But there's no way I can risk us being separated from the yacht this far out."

I followed Perry down the transom ladder and slipped into the water beside him. The ocean opened around us in piercing cathedrals of blue. The light stabbed in, dappling the whale's flanks. Brown netting undulated in the water like a living thing, as Solomon hung motionless. The darting fish had grown in size and number; the wounds cut deeper.

I swam up to Solomon's eye. I could see the tiredness there, I could sense his plea for help. I rubbed his head, his firm skin yielding to my fingers as the huge eyelid twitched. His great body though, remained still. I projected a thought, promising we'd do whatever we could, hoping he'd understand.

Perry was cutting and sawing; I repositioned myself beside him as we struggled to untangle the matted netting that had set like concrete. Puffs of algae bloomed as the rope yielded inches at a time. A buoyancy float broke free, then a gnarl unraveled. I heaved at a length of rope that ran like an artery into the nylon parasite's knotted heart.

"That's a good idea," Perry shouted between gulps of air. He found the rope's twin, cutting and pulling as we drifted with the leviathan. My fingers felt raw, my arms ached, but each time a tangled clump broke free, my spirits soared.

"We can't be too long—the light's going," Perry shouted.

I glanced around, surprised it was late afternoon. Level again with the whale's head, I passed his black eye and found myself speaking. "Don't be scared. Please stay still." Then Solomon blew, a soft thunder that vibrated the full length of his body.

"I know," I said. "Not too long now."

"There's one crucial knot—seems to be holding everything together," Perry said. "If you hold it away from his side, I'll cut. But it's locked under his fin."

We dived together, curling into a wall of shadow. Perry pointed, I lifted, he sawed. We surfaced, breathed, dived again; a signal here, a look there…complete understanding of a shared purpose.

Many dives later, the netting finally belched in surrender. By flexing, Solomon helped jettison the nylon. Though the wounds glowed deep, he was moving now. The snarled mass spiraled into the depths. We trod water to one side, anticipating the sweep of the vast tail. A long blow, deep and full of strength, echoed through us as he accelerated towards his uncertain future. I turned to Perry, teary, speechless, elated. We high-fived, then laughing, I swam into his arms.

He laughed with me. "We did it! You were incredible, Teal! Look!"

I turned, gasping at the titanic splash in front of us. Then Solomon breached again—his entire body teetered on the surface before he crashed back in an explosion of liquid thunder.

"Try and convince me he isn't jumping for joy," Perry said.

"I know!"

I tried to kiss his cheek but our masks collided. I laughed and went in at a more extreme angle.

"Teal, we have a problem," he whispered in my ear.

I'll take my mask off. I reached for the rubber strap behind my head.

"No, keep it on. But—no jerky movements." He was looking underwater and I followed his eye line to a smear of white-tipped gray twenty feet below. Blunt muscularity, bold energy. Nausea flooded my stomach, setting off a ringing in my head.

"Don't scream. Try to relax, we can get to Falcon. Swim smoothly." We were two boat lengths away as the shark swept past in a thick broadside of attitude. I tried to mimic Perry's smooth strokes, though I wanted to throw myself into a manic crawl. Why was he swimming so slowly? Any second I expected the beast to double back, charge. It would be too fast, too strong.

"Climb on board. I'll watch for Jaws, but I think he missed his chance."

With jelly-weak limbs, I clambered aboard. Perry was right behind me. We collapsed on deck, breathing hard, laughing, crying.

A movement in the corner of my eye made me look around. Solomon had returned so quietly that we had almost missed him. But now we were standing, holding each other as the whale held his head above the waves, balanced on outstretched fins.

"Hello, old friend," Perry said. Then he added, "I think he wanted to check we were okay."

"Or to say thank you?"

I squeezed Perry's hand as the whale studied us.

"My name's Teal." I reached out, wanting to touch him again, to complete the encounter, but he was out of reach. Then he slipped down to settled lengthways, far longer than our boat, before his mighty tail powered him away.

"We need to get back," Perry finally said, kissing my forehead softly. "I hadn't forgotten I owed you a kiss."

Pushed by an unseen force, I moved close to him, and he stayed there. I brought my body in until we touched. My hands slipped around his waist, my head rested on his shoulder. In the electric silence, he stayed quite still. I trembled. Had I gone too far?

My fingers crept around his back and I pulled him closer. We stayed that way, swaying gently. *He hasn't pushed me away yet.* Were his fingers moving, just a little? *He hasn't pushed me away, yet.* He sighed, long and deep into my hair. *He hasn't pushed me away...*

He brushed my cheek, the same fingertip tracing the line of my jaw. His breath fanned my face as, all gentleness and strength, his thumb brushed across my lips. He kissed the corners of my mouth, one at a time. We pressed closer, deeper. His hand settled on the small of my back and then, slowly, ever so slowly, his mouth found mine. He stole my air, my fear. And my heart.

"I love you, Teal," he whispered, in my ear.

When his words had swum through every cell in my body, I tightened my grip and answered, "I love you, Perry."

CHAPTER TWENTY-EIGHT

I was sipping my steaming Americano in the business center. Like me forty minutes ago, the computer blinked on and off as it struggled to wake. Unlike me, it hadn't been up until four in the morning writing the first draft of the Morfil report. I opened the first of three emails. A one-liner from Malcolm read: "I know you won't let me down, Teal."

It would be so easy to download my report and hit send. Then I could relax, enjoy the sun, the sea and...Perry. But my stomach was churning because I knew things didn't add up. The thoughts that had kept me awake (when I wasn't thinking about Perry) returned: How badly did I want to be an investigative journalist? A good one? If they could pressure me into submitting sloppy work this early in my career, what did that augur for the future?

The second email was from Ruth Entwhistle. *I'm impressed with your office's efficiency, Thurston.* The attached PDF was headed: "A Regional Environmental Impact Report on a South Pacific Fishery."

A photo of Thurston Morfil—hands clasped in front of him, smiling from behind a huge desk—occupied the first page. Beneath it, we were reminded that he was Chairman and Chief Executive of *The Islands Development and Consulting Corporation (IDCC)*. I skimmed the list of contents and flipped though blocks of text, split with impressive looking tables, pie charts, bar charts, graphs, photos. I scanned the bullet-pointed summary and read the conclusion aloud:

> *"Due to their remoteness and the influence of both the South Equatorial Current and South Pacific Gyre, the islands enjoy a varied and highly robust ecosystem. This report recognizes and applauds the IDCC's ongoing commitment to protecting its fisheries from industrial-scale exploitation by foreign interests. Compared with*

neighboring island nations, commercial exploitation of pelagic species has been expertly managed and is modest. It is the reporting committee's conclusion that a twelve-fold increase in the harvesting of marine species, primarily the tunas listed in Table 7(iii), will be sustainable for the foreseeable future."

I began typing:

Dear Perry,
For some strange reason the email I sent Violet bounced back. I used violet.b.f.booby@kosmic-kalamari.com. Could you please forward the attached Environmental Impact Report from Thurston Morfil to her, as she promised to review it?
Your favorite duck xox.

The final email was from Sammie. She'd attached a photo of Koji, a cat she'd just brought home from the rescue center. I knew it was her way of asking how my vacation was going, so I emailed back a few superlatives, and noted that the fluffy orange feline was adorable.

Then I replied to Malcolm. "Thanks for your vote of confidence! I am nearly there with the report but, as I know you expect nothing short of complete professionalism from me, I am awaiting a second opinion on a research paper Mr. Morfil commissioned, before I submit. It won't be long now. You know you can trust me. Teal."

*　　　*　　　*

The sand beneath my feet felt softer today. Was the sky a shade bluer too? I covered the ground from the business center to the restaurant as if on air, to find Nancy finishing her mango-pineapple-granola-yogurt fruit bowl. She explained that Frank was in their room sorting photos. He was excited by one of waking fruit bats that he thought might be a prize winner.

When I mentioned, as casually as I could, that we'd nearly been attacked by a shark, her mouth fell open.

"Dear Lord have mercy!"

"Perry was explaining how lucky we were it was only one."

"That's one too many, Angel."

"It's a serious problem. The longliners are killing sharks in their millions for shark fin soup. They cut off the fins and even if the animal isn't dead, they throw it back to die. Twenty years ago we'd have been attacked by dozens of sharks."

"Well, I'm just a teeny-weeny bit grateful to those fishermen right now. If I had to choose between you and some old shark—"

"That's the dilemma. I may owe my life to the shark finners, but Perry explained if you stay calm, the shark will probably ignore you. He said that if you kill them all, then there won't be any predators to eat the next rung down the food chain: the fish that feed on plankton. Then this population explodes and all the plankton gets eaten."

"What's wrong with that? Then *we* can eat the plankton feeders."

"I asked the same question. Apparently, seventy percent of the oxygen we breathe is converted from carbon dioxide by plankton, not by trees. We may think we can just eat the extra fish, but history reminds us that whenever humans have played God, it comes back to bite us. Perry gave me lots of examples like cane toads in Australia, the Kudzu vine in the US, the Asian tiger mosquito."

"Don't tell Perry, but I'm still glad that shark left hungry. By the way, Angel, have you heard? Starts at seven. *The* social event of the South Pacific. *Everyone* will be there...I heard a plane load of Hollywood A-Listers are flying in, and Harper's Bazaar are sending their best photographers."

I laughed. "In which case, I think I'll have an early night."

"Traditional music, a fire dance, roast pig on a spit. You name it." She stopped scooping mangoes. "Was there something you wanted to share with me, Angel? You know Frank was moth collecting on the rocks last night and he saw Falcon return..." she coughed quietly, "...quite late."

"That was *Frank* jumping around that light, waving something like a madman? We thought Firefly Bob was performing a ceremony."

"That was a butterfly net. Frank is the most discreet man I know...however, he may just possibly, though he of course isn't completely sure, but he thought he might've seen—"

I felt the heat rising in my face. "He *watched* us?"

Nancy squeezed my wrist. "Oh Angel, I'm so excited for you both! I invited Perry to join us at our table."

"It was only—a goodnight kiss."

"*Only*? Twelve minutes and forty-four seconds by Frank's watch, young lady!"

*   *   *

I puffed up the pillows behind me and opened the laptop. I re-read the first draft of the Morfil piece, tweaking a sentence here, a phrase there. But my heart wasn't in it because I still needed to hear back from Perry about the environmental impact report. What if he agreed the report was nonsense? Would I include that information, without knowing what Morfil was actually up to? How had Malcolm reacted to my last email? Had it bought me more time...or was a letter of dismissal already sitting on my desk?

For all practical purposes, all I could do was more background research. The scrapbook lay beside me. Who knows, maybe it contained something useful? I closed my laptop and took out Fonu's story, which had slipped to the back of my mind. I began reading where I'd left off:

I have told you this before—it is very simple. The gods give us fish to eat. The cattle I traded with the foreigners provide milk and meat. From bees we get honey."

The Chief pointed his cane at a clump of trees set well back from the beach. Partly hidden by foliage, bathed in shadow, the twin prows of a great war canoe arched skyward.

He spoke in a guttural whisper that the whole beach heard.

"I ordered the canoe built the day your brother was born. With double hulls that hold fifty warriors, and twin thrones, with the most detailed carvings and finest paintwork, it is the most magnificent canoe ever seen in the islands. It is a canoe fitting for the handover of power from a great chief to his son. But my only surviving son refuses to learn to swim or paddle, in fact he fears the ocean. So it sits under those trees collecting rats and bird droppings. With nothing to celebrate, I should have ordered it burned when your brother died."

Fonu spoke softly. "Father, you have not answered my question. If I prove myself worthy, will you call off the whalers?"

"Worthy? When I was your age, I swam the length of thirty canoes underwater." He laughed. "Who can stop the unstoppable? Even if these whalers were to leave, more of them would come—as many as the waves of the ocean. I have made allies with these men to protect my people. I trade whales for guns because guns will bring peace. Fonu, you ask the impossible."

Fonu bowed. "Impossible is a good reason to try. And yes, I ask for it. But if I achieve the impossible—if I swim the length of forty canoes underwater—will you call off the whalers?"

The Chief placed his hand on his son's shoulder. "No one can swim forty canoe lengths under water. No one. Especially not you. You are a strange boy, and you disappoint me." Then he whispered, "But I will miss you."

"So be it," Fonu said, and walked down to the canoe. His heart fluttered when Losa smiled at him. He longed to hold her as he had last night, to feel her warm body, to hear her moans. He whispered that it would be alright, as he pushed the canoe into deeper water, hopped in ahead of her and lifted his paddle.

"By what magic?" an elder asked.

"But he knows how to paddle!" another added.

The Chief watched them. He was as surprised as anyone that his son did not fear the ocean and that he could handle the canoe. When he saw that Fonu showed no shame in being piloted by a woman, he shook his head.

The Chief's expression tightened as Fonu and Losa approached the distant rock, because the rising tide meant one thing: In a few hours his son and the girl would be swept off it.

The Great Chief of the Islands stood alone on the beach long after the crowd had dispersed. He recalled what Father Xavier had told him: Jesus Christ was more powerful than all island gods. When he saw the foreigners' clothes, their ships and tools, their guns, he knew the priest was right. "What do the lives of a few whales matter compared with my people's future?"

He was grinding his teeth as he removed the bowler hat. He ran his fingers over the felt, then he stroked the soft silk that lined it. He replaced the hat. "Why does my son doubt me—me! The Great Chief of the Islands?"

He swung the cane with all his strength and it splintered on the sand. Then he sat, with his head in his hands to hide his tears—

The phone was ringing.

"Teal, do you have *any* idea what time it is here? I've been trying to get you all day!"

"Malcolm! I'm sorry, I—"

"I'm seriously regretting recommending you for an assignment you seem to think is some sort of jaunt. Sir Basil's summoned me again, I've never been spoken to like that! Have you for one moment considered what this could do to *my* prospects here?"

"Malcolm, I've written…some of the report but I'm sorry. I just can't, I won't send it as it is. It's incomplete. I should know more tonight."

"What's happening tonight? Don't tell me, a party, no doubt."

"In fact I'm meeting someone—whose opinion I value highly—about Morfil. And there's an opportunity to do some more background research."

"Background research? I need foreground, and I need it now!"

"I'm afraid I have very little control over the timeline. I'm doing my best." I waited for a reply. "Malcolm?"

"I'm sorry I raised my voice." A long sigh. "Listen darling, you know I trust you. But send me something. Whatever you've got. I'll show it to Sir Basil."

"I'll do what I can. Promise. Malcolm, I must go." I hung up.

I'd never heard Malcolm so upset. I closed the curling pages of the scrapbook and took some deep breaths. Send what I had? That just wasn't possible. With important people involved, late or otherwise, I had to be certain of the report's accuracy. For all our sakes.

"Fonu, I'll try to get back to you if…and when I can," I said, as I headed for the shower.

CHAPTER TWENTY-NINE

The tables described a large semicircle on the beach. To one side, a split pig rotated above a flaming pit, sparks spiraling skyward. Waiters came and went, hotel guests clustered around the buffet. Kris, microphone in hand, welcomed us to a celebration of island culture.

"And it's my pleasure to introduce *Frigate Bird*—the most authentic island dance troupe. So authentic that if one of their cannibal warriors starts giving you strange looks.... And ladies and gentlemen, boys and girls, you'll notice there's a wooden spear on your tables. Please don't do anything with them yet—apparently a surprise has been added to tonight's entertainment."

Bare-chested islanders blew on pan pipes. A man's enormous tummy wobbled as he tonked out a bouncy rhythm from an instrument comprising lashed-together bamboos; his twin beat a vast drum. The grass-skirted women, shelled and adorned in brown and white feathers, swayed like snake-hipped swans.

"Great shirt, Frank!" Perry said.

"Nancy bought it in the market." He slouched in his chair. "I promised I'd wear it at least once," he whispered.

"Aw, it looks great," Nancy laughed. "Takes years off you!"

"I'm scared it will," he said, beheading a giant prawn. "So, Teal. Why don't you tell us about Thurston Morfil?"

A waiter took my soup bowl and presented us each with a Horseshoe Whisperer.

"Compliments of Mr. Kris," he explained.

"I *love* that shirt," I said, winking at Nancy. Frank slouched deeper in his chair.

I described the encounter as Perry listened, leaning forward on his elbows. I finished with, "The guy doesn't add up."

"Did he give you his dolphin-friendly speech?" asked Perry.

"You could attach 'friendly' to everything he said. It wasn't so much an interview as a PR offensive."

"When I google-earthed the docks, I saw a rectangular structure," Perry said.

"What size?" asked Frank.

"Maybe a hundred by forty feet."

"It can be only one thing," said Nancy. "It's as we feared. Disgusting!"

Perry's tone dropped and he looked at me. "There've been rumors for years that they export dolphins to the Middle East. I think it must be a new holding pen too."

"Can't think what else it could be," added Frank, his fist striking the table. "Unless they're investing in their Olympic water polo team."

"What about the cannery, Teal? Did you see it?" Perry asked.

"I saw his office—that's all. But I got a couple of cans of tuna. I thought they might prove useful."

"Did the operation look legitimate?" Frank asked.

"Something *has* been bothering me." I described how Morfil had reacted when I took the second tuna can, his explanation of a printing error. "But if you had a few misprinted labels, wouldn't you be giving *those* away, because you can't sell them? Why snatch it back?"

"Did you see what the typo was?" Perry asked.

"Afraid not."

Kris's voice came over the microphone. "Ladies and gentlemen, now it's the men's turn. Please welcome the *Red Snapper Warriors* who will perform their famous *Flame Dance*. And kids," he added, "Please don't try this at home."

The lighting dimmed, leaving us illuminated by crackling perimeter torches. The performers crouched, hunched, scowled. Protruding tongues waggled. Wooden weapons glinted and body paint shone. Perry explained that the menacing spike lashed to their foreheads came from the local hornbill. "Traditionally, they fill them with the hair of their elders. Some sort of magic."

The dance began with each warrior twirling a flaming torch. As they stomped back and forth, I thought how well rehearsed the performers were, sliding from one routine to the next. The performance built to a series of crescendos in front of the applauding audience.

Emma came over, and smiled at Frank. "*Groovy* shirt, bro!"

"Nancy bought it in the…" Frank mumbled.

"Great soup, Emma," I said. "What kind was it?"

"No idea. I think it started life as banana bread."

"Any idea what the spears are for?" Nancy asked her.

173

"Afraid not. Apparently it's a surprise."

"Is this dance authentic?" I asked Emma.

"More of a hodgepodge of gyrations and smiles put together for tourists. The authentic stuff's gone the way of the local skink. A few old islanders try to keep the traditions alive, but the young are more turned on by their phones and running shoes. Oh, if any of you lovelies finds Kris's mic, please yell."

"I was reading about island legends from a 1930s book," I began. "Apparently, Horseshoe sits on a magical axis between life and death. This place has huge significance for their culture."

"I've read that book too. Problem is finding someone who'll tell us more," Emma said.

"Someone trustworthy." I added.

"Too right, Teal-babe. Beware the helpful islander who then demands payment. Lots of them around, making it up as they go along. To them, tourists are rich and gullible, and deserve what they get because they're responsible for global warming, pollution, rising sea levels, less fish. It's their revenge. How do we know the well-meaning author of *Myths and Legends of an Arcane Paradise* wasn't conned too? My tutor's mantra was: 'Those who know won't talk and those who talk won't know'. Sadly, he's been quite ill since he licked that Amazonian toad. But they say his new book out-insights the great Evans-Pritchard. It's a bummer that kind of toad doesn't live around here..."

"You can't be serious?" I asked.

"You're right. I should wait until I've finished breast feeding. Problem is, like it or not, tourism may be the most cost-effective way of developing this economy. To get money to build schools, roads, hospitals, the islanders are forced to work with the visitors. But in the past, foreigners have done so much harm that there's little trust."

A line of flame-waving cannibals stomped towards our table.

Nancy pointed at her tummy. "All fat and gristle, boys. But these love birds..."

"Nancy!" I protested as I squeezed Perry's arm.

Perry leaned in. "Don't worry. They don't eat scrawny tourists but they may cube you for their fish traps."

"Look—a new member of the troupe. Yikes! Check out *Mr. Angry!*" I said.

"They're pretending they don't know him, I love it!" Nancy added.

One by one the dancers stilled. They drifted away, as the new arrival lunged forward in a series of head-thrusting growls. The pipes and drum fell silent too. The dried grasses of the newcomer's skirt trailed in the sand and *shhhhhhed* to his jerking movements. A curved oval of yellowed wood hid his face. Stylized eyes, black, white and manic glared above a downturned mouth. The light glinted on the inlayed shells that adorned the rectangle of timber that covered his chest. He shook his arms, his feet thumping the sand after each high-kneed step. Spinning, he faced one table, then another, waving his arms, as he threw imaginary spears at the holidaymakers. A child started crying, a father waved the performer away.

When he had "attacked" the last table, which was occupied by a group of boisterous Australians, he shouted, "Now you must kill me!" The tremble in his voice was magnified by the speakers.

He pointed at a wooden spear. The tourist beside it put down his beer can and took aim. The spear arced over the man's shoulder.

"That's one mystery solved," Perry whispered, pointing at the raised microphone in the performer's hand. "I hope Kris's insurance covers being impaled on a spear."

One by one the spears sailed towards the performer, a few came close. Finally, one struck him in the chest. "Bull's-eye!" someone shouted and people cheered. He caught it and wobbled backwards. Head gyrating, he stumbled and moaned. Back and forth he staggered as he re-enacted his death torment, one table at a time. Then he collapsed and lay still.

In the silence, Nancy whispered, "Are we meant to clap?"

"Look, he's getting up," Perry said.

The masked man raised the microphone. "You come. Every year. But you never stop to think."

"This is getting a little strange," Frank said.

A woman shouted, "But it's my first time!" Her table joined in with her laughing.

"Tonight I performed a dance called 'The Silent Dawn' because something evil is coming this way."

"What does he mean by that?" I asked.

"It will arrive soon. We must all try to stop it. If we don't—"

Kris hurried over to the masked man, ushering him towards the musicians. "Thank you, thank you—very entertaining—"

The man slipped away from Kris and ran back. He shouted, "You must never forget that time always—"

Kris grabbed the microphone and lifted the mask off the mysterious dancer's head.

The audience gasped. How could someone so old be so agile, so energetic? The old man's head drooped.

"Thank you Bob, that was…wonderful! Ladies and gentlemen, give it up for our own Firefly Bob and our first ever audience participation event! A real treat. Now please, it's Frigate Bird's turn. Bob, they charge by the hour, so please let them play!" Kris said into the mic.

Bob produced a roll of paper from under his skirt. "If your guests sign this, it will help. If I give it to the Prime Minister…to show how many of us care."

"It looks like a petition. What's it say, Bob?" Kris read slowly. "We have signed this because it is best for all of us to keep them out." He looked at Bob. "Who's *them* Bob?"

"I don't know yet."

The answer brought a murmur from the audience. A few people laughed nervously.

Kris's hand settled on Bob's shoulder. "I tell you what Bob, I'll put it in reception. Anyone who wants to sign it, can. You can collect it in a few days."

Perry leaned over to me. "Poor fellow. He means well. But a *paper* petition?"

"What was that about 'time'?" Nancy asked.

"No idea," Perry said.

The old islander turned, and head bowed, shuffled away. Kris followed a pace behind as the guests glanced awkwardly at each other. Some spoke of their surprise, others were more sympathetic. The father of the crying child shouted, "Mate, make sure that old fool don't come back!"

"That loudmouth should show some respect," Perry growled.

Frank then said exactly what I was thinking: "He feels very strongly about something—and no one understands what."

"That seems to include him," Nancy added with a sigh.

Emma was now with the band, imploring the musicians to resume playing as the guests shifted and murmured. First one pan pipe, then another fluted gently. The dancing started again, but the evening needed rebuilding. Frank and Nancy looked happy enough though, holding hands, nodding in time to the music.

"Is Bob okay?" Perry asked Kris, who was now standing at my shoulder.

"I don't think so. He gets more upset each year. Hey, Frank. That's quite a shirt!"

Frank mumbled something and slouched lower still.

"Where's Bob?" I asked.

"Paddled off, muttering and crying. I feel awful but I have zero influence over island governance. Anyway, I hope it didn't spoil your evening," Kris said. "His petition's in reception, but I'm damned if I know what he's trying to achieve with it. Or who he thinks is coming this way."

Slowly, the party picked up again. The roast pork was lean, rich and smoky; the tropical salads glistened under mangoes and cashews, and Frank's choice of Koonunga Hill cabernet merlot complemented all.

The performers regrouped and completed their act to cheers and claps. Frank and Nancy giggled like kids. When the speakers switched to Western music, they were the first guests twisting on the sand.

"Fortunately, I've been taking dancing lessons," Perry said deadpan. "So I'd be honored if you'd accept my invitation to waft you around the dance floor. Make that around the beach."

"Of course."

"They were break dance lessons. For every two minutes I dance, I need a twenty minute break."

I should have known he'd dance beautifully.

"Doing my best," he said, ten minutes later.

"Your best is...perfect," I said, smiling at Ming-Yue and Xu who were making little effort to dance—instead they rocked gently back and forth, wrapped tightly around each other, gazing into each others' eyes.

The music ended, and Nancy spoke to the bandleader. Now she hurried back. She winked at me as the next dance began—a slow one.

I feigned shock, swooned in delight.

Perry held me in his strong arms. I fitted so well there. He led me gently around as the last of the day's heat seeped up my legs from the soft sand.

Back at the table, Frank and Nancy hugged us goodnight, with an excuse about taking a walk along the beach in search of a marine organism that glowed in the dark.

I sat next to Perry, leaning against him as the other guests drifted away.

We watched as Kris strode towards us, negotiating the empty chairs.

"I'm sorry to disturb you, Teal...I told him you were busy, but he said you had to hear this now. I hope I've done the right—"

"Who, Kris?" Perry asked.

"Bob, he came back all flustered and excited. Can he have a quick word with you?"

"Couldn't it wait?" Perry asked.

"I better see what he wants. Send search parties if I'm not back in five." I kissed his cheek and whispered, "Whatever it is, it's important to him. I hope I find something to believe in as passionately, one day."

I walked with Kris towards reception, and around the back of the building where we found Bob.

"Hello, lady," he said softly, freezing me with one of his stares. "I wanted to thank you."

"What for, Bob?"

His old eyes held mine. He lowered his voice so Kris wouldn't hear. Just then a firefly flashed above his head. Soon others joined it.

"For saving the old whale."

Back at the table, Perry said how pleased he was that I'd returned so soon. Then he asked what was so important it couldn't wait until tomorrow.

"Perry, I didn't realize you'd told anyone about the humpback."

"I didn't. I thought it was our secret. Why?"

*   *   *

We stood outside my room. The evening was about to end, I guessed, with a long hug and a Perry kiss on my forehead. Such a gentle gesture—that sent me reeling.

But I needed more. I pulled him close, my mouth brushing his. He held me against him, my hands roving over the muscles in his back. Then I broke away.

"That's called a Teal kiss," I said. "Good night, Perry."

"But?"

"Soon," I whispered.

He kissed me gently on the forehead. "I understand. It's killing me, but—"

"Shhhhh."

Back in my room, I wondered if word would get back to Edward about how Perry and I had danced. Had anyone seen us holding hands? Probably not, I thought. And Edward hadn't exactly made friends since we arrived. Even if he did find out, would he care? He'd hardly spent a moment with me and showed no interest in changing.

I stood there, remembering John and Maxwell, my boyfriends before Edward. I'd felt the same flat, nervous way around them too. With Perry, it was so different. There was no pressure, no belittling. And something else: the deep sense of *belonging* that entwined us. Is that what people meant when they talked about finding their soul mate?

Like a film in fast forward, I re-played the last three years of my life, my three years with Edward. I paused occasionally when I remembered a good time. But the pauses became less frequent. How long had it been since Edward and I had really enjoyed each other's company? And if I was painfully honest with myself, *had I ever?*

I was getting into bed when I remembered what I'd forgotten: I didn't ask Perry if he'd read Morfil's report.

CHAPTER THIRTY

The bedside clock said seven-fifteen, Saturday morning—that meant three-fifteen, Friday afternoon, New York time. I opened the drawer of the table it sat on and pulled out the scrapbook.

"Okay, Fonu," I said, "Tell me what happens to someone who doesn't toe the party line, asks questions he's not supposed to, and doesn't trust the most powerful man on this island chain. I need a few tips."

They were near the rock when the girl pointed at the matting that lay in the bottom of the canoe. "The rope is under there. I traded it with a foreigner for my shell collection."

"When this is over, I will give you the best shell collection anyone has seen, Losa."

"You don't have to do that, Fonu. All I want is you."

The waves bucked the canoe as she steered it to a halt beside the rock. Losa shivered under the dark clouds that pressed the horizon. They climbed onto the algae-covered surface that slanted upward to a knuckle of stone.

"We could try to lash the canoe onto the rock—but it might break free and knock us off. Better to secure it with a tether and push into the lee of the rock—it should be a little calmer there," Losa said.

They roped the box of rocket flares and paddles to the knuckle, knotting the remaining cord around their waists. Then they curled around each other, tensed against the rasping breeze and rising tide. Across the waves, at the far end of the island, the Aroha, rolled in the swell.

"That ship frightens me, with that huge cannon on the front," Losa said.

"It would frighten anyone, but Jackson said it was only a

converted freighter. The other whaling ships are worse—they have a tall tower and can spot whales from a great distance. They are faster than that one too."

Beside the rock, the waves splashed into the bucking canoe and it settled deep in the water until its gunnels were barely visible.

"My father is a great man but he is...stubborn," Fonu said.

He leaned forward, the rope chafing his side, and kissed her. "If we die, at least we are together. Which means—"

"Don't talk about such things now." Losa said, pressing her cheek against his shoulder.

"I want us to be together. Always," he said softly, squeezing her hands. Gently, he brushed a tear from her eyelashes, before adding, "I pray that both of us live or die here. To have to make a choice—"

They huddled together, sharing their warmth. Their fear. Their hope. Birds wheeled overhead, screeching as the spray built. The first wave crashed over them at noon but the ropes held true and they stayed bound to the rock.

Over the next hour, they were swept off their feet many times— soon the rising waves hurled them against the jagged knuckle too. Sometimes Fonu gripped Losa in the torrent or she braced herself against the rock and he, despite his tortured muscles, clung to her. The final wave of a furious set pounded the rock, wrestling the scrabbling pair towards the churning ocean. But the ropes held, and with bloodied fingers, they hunched together again, blinded by the brine, deafened by the howling roar.

For an uplifting, magical moment it seemed the ocean gods had paused. Was that sunlight overhead? Had the wind dropped too? Fonu laughed, thanking the gods for calling off the maelstrom. He stood and pulled Losa up beside him.

"I think—" he started.

"Fonu—look!" Losa cried.

A giant wave, black as night, taller even than the Chief's hut galloped in, harnessing a sustained, redoubled fury. Fonu wrapped Losa's rope tight around his wrist, as their arms gripped each other.

"Don't let me go!" she cried.

Transfixed, they watched the water pull back from the rock, the ocean dropping to expose streaming weed, dripping coral. There was an eerie silence in the seconds before the foaming monster reared to an impossible height.

Then the wave cascaded its wrath on them, rolling them over and over. Fonu cracked his head on stone, his consciousness seeping back as he lay stretched across the rock. Lights flashed in his head and he choked out a mouthful of iron-tasting sea water. Then he gasped.

Losa wasn't there.

He pulled her rope until its frayed end rested in his torn hands.

As the water poured from the rock, Fonu cried out her name, dragging himself onto all fours. He ignored the pain in his knees and the blood that coursed from his nose. He forced himself upright.

"Fonu!" he heard above the bellow of the surf. "Help me!"

Losa's hands clung to the very edge of the rock face, her body obscured by the boiling water. He crawled over and dived forward to grab them. As his cold, raw fingers grasped her wrists, he willed strength into his failing arms. She released the rock to grip him, shouting again, "Don't let me go!"

Then another surge of water, as angry as the last, seized her from behind.

There was a knock on my front door.

"Good morning, beautiful!" Perry said, wrapping me in a tight hug and swinging me round. As the door swung closed, he started to kiss me. Groggily, I dragged my mind away from Fonu and Losa, then with rising interest, began to explore the burst of mint toothpaste on his lips. Though my research was meant to be my top priority, my arms seemed to have forgotten. Completely.

"Great timing!" I mumbled into his shoulder, "Saved from a double drowning."

"What?"

"Down, boy! Not just now…I…oh my!"

But Perry was kissing my neck, working his way gently to my earlobes. Nibbling. His hands kneaded my shoulders…my shoulders needed his hands.

Somehow, against all the odds, a tiny bit of sanity bubbled to the surface somewhere in a remote corner of my brain.

Wriggling free, I fanned my face. "Perry, behave!" I said, failing to sound stern, with my outstretched hand against his chest. I jabbed him playfully on the sternum when he came too close.

"To business! I have a small mystery I want to run past you. Did you get a chance to read Morfil's environmental assessment?"

"Spoil sport. Yes, I did. Complete nonsense. Amazing what you can dress up as science if you're prepared to pay for it. Waiting to hear what Woods Hole think of it too."

"As I feared. That means…I probably won't have a job to go back to. Had it been okay, I could have appended it to my Morfil report and given the guy a guarded thumbs up. Now I have to find out what's going on and re-plan my report. Problem is I'm out of time."

"Was that the small mystery you were referring to?"

I took his hand, led him to the table by the front door and showed him my souvenirs from the Morfil interview. He picked up the tuna cans, turning and inspecting them.

"Remember I said Morfil took one back—said it was mislabeled?"

He nodded. "This looks like any other tinned tuna," he said.

"If nothing comes from this, at least a holiday present's sorted out."

"Who are they for?"

"Sammie. She can feed it to her cats who have developed quite discerning palates—their bodies are about ninety-five percent take-out sashimi and five percent organic catnip."

"I have to admit, *Gold Fin Tuna* is a great brand name," he said.

"Why?"

"Bluefin tuna is the best, yellowfin second best. No such thing as a gold fin...but it implies quality." He tapped the label. "That's a sick joke, though. Dolphin *friendly!*"

"I saw that."

"These tins are identical. It's a shame you didn't get a better look at the other one."

"Wait a minute." I lifted my camera and began scrolling back through the images I'd taken in Morfil's office in the LCD panel. "If we're lucky—because he made me take about forty thousand extra photos of him...yes, here it is!"

Morfil beamed from his desk, the cans piled shoulder-high behind him.

I pointed. "Those are the normal ones, these are the misprinted labels. If I enlarge this photo..."

We studied the image. Then he lifted one of the cans and checked it.

"Interesting," he said, pointing at the camera screen.

"I can see—it's super-pixilated but, I think there's an extra letter. An *E*. Does that mean anything to you, Perry?"

"Afraid not."

"So why didn't Morfil want me taking a can with a typo on it?" I asked.

"Did anything else strike you as different or strange? Wait a minute," he said as I scrolled through more photos. "Why does he have *that* chart open on his desk?"

"What do you mean?"

"It's of the trench we fished over. He's even highlighted it." He played around with the zoom. "Hmmm, as Winston Churchill said..."

"A riddle wrapped in a mystery inside an enigma?"

"Hey, you're good! Okay, back to my question about anything striking you as odd."

I played the Morfil interview back carefully: his endless self-promotion, his vanity, his eagerness for more photos, how he grabbed back the "wrong" can from me and his unconvincing explanation. Finally, I recalled how he'd walked into the airport, big smiling, big waving, only to be completely ignored.

Then it hit me: There *had* been something different.

"This may sound silly but…I think, the other can was heavier."

CHAPTER THIRTY-ONE

"Where've you been? Nice of you to be here to greet me." Bear said, as I entered the room. A towel quivered around his waist, a cigar poked from his mouth. A second towel—mine—was wrapped around his neck.

"W—welcome back, Bear, I went for a walk. Took some photos of the sunset and the back of the island."

"With that Percy guy, no doubt."

"Can't you smoke that outside?"

"I have news. The *Apex Predator* arrives tomorrow and we're invited to dinner on Monday. I want you glammed-up. Do something about your hair. Wear some makeup. You don't need to say much—try to look pretty. And I'd appreciate it if you kept you opinions to yourself."

I'd heard this all before—most recently before I'd attended his last office party. I bit my lip, steadied my breathing.

Bear patted his belly. "Not too bad. Local stuff?"

The empty tuna cans lay on the table beside a flattened bag of tortilla chips.

As I stared at them, my hands tightened. But then I wondered if it mattered. Whatever was going on in the factory, the answer wasn't in *those* cans—or in Bear's stomach—because Morfil wouldn't have given them to me.

"I'm glad you enjoyed them. I take it the Apex Predator is someone's boat?"

"It's not a boat. It's a *mega yacht.*" He rolled his eyes. "The second biggest of The Dragon's four yachts."

The name sounded vaguely familiar. "Who's he?"

"Dan. Dan Dragan. We were talking about him in that crappy fish pub. Can't you remember a single—"

"Oh, *him*—the billionaire arms manufacturer."

184

"I meant what I said about best behavior." Under his breath he added, "God knows why, but his wife wants to meet you. And leave the journalistic Teal behind. This is strictly social."

"What if your glammed-up partner chooses not to behave?"

He stepped closer, his eyes narrowing as a vein bulged in his forehead. His voice dropped. "Don't play games with me, Teal. What's gotten into you? Just be your normal self—the adoring partner who knows how lucky she is to have me. There's nothing wrong with you when you behave properly."

The old Teal—the Teal of even a few days ago—would probably have apologized immediately. But something was swelling inside me. It felt like a cool pillar was extending up my spine, and my whole being was strengthened by it. Clear. Stiff. For the first time ever, Bear's criticisms didn't make something inside me collapse. Instead, his words bounced off. Maybe I didn't care anymore? But how could that be? He'd been my rock, and the sole person in New York I had turned to for support these past three years. I inhaled slowly and changed tack.

"But why on earth has he come all this way if—"

"Oh, and get my suitcase packed. I've had more than enough of the S and M resort." He stopped and grinned. Then he bellowed with laughter.

"Haw, haw. The S and M—geddit? How appropriate!" He stomped past and out the door. Once outside, he stretched his arms and cracked his knuckles over his head. "Yesssss," he said with a chuckle. "Just let them try and stop me now."

He was back, dressing. "Look what Danny Boy gave me: a silk cravat." He secured it around his neck, dropping my towel on the floor.

"You told me you hated cravats. You said any man who wore one was a—"

"Never let it be said that Edward Hamilton III is inflexible in his choice of fashion." He positioned himself in front of the mirror. "Not bad, even if I say so myself." Then he turned to me.

"Get a move on, Teal. I'm hungry."

CHAPTER THIRTY-TWO

I jogged back from the surf, invigorated by my swim. The softer light, the absence of shouting tourists, wayward Frisbees and screaming jet skis made the early morning so special. I did a quick calculation before I entered our A-frame. Today was day fifteen. That meant I had only six days left before I'd be boarding that international flight, on my way home to face Malcolm and Sir Basil.

My report was overdue and I was still miles away from finishing it. At least I now had allies and we were doing what we could, as fast as we could. Would that enable us to unravel what on earth was going on here— soon enough to save my job?

I passed Edward, who was still in bed, on my way to shower. A dribble trickled from his vibrating mouth as he copulated with someone in his dream. We hadn't had anything to drink last night, he hadn't been especially tired. Why had he forgotten to remove the cravat? It had slipped a little...what was that where his chin bulged against his neck? A...*bruise?*

I leaned over, reached out and touched the silk. It clung tightly, and my first pull produced a grunt as he shifted in his sleep. I picked at it in the dim light, and it moved a little. Yes, that looked like a fading bruise. I needed to be sure so I worked on the knot and revealed more: a few days old but it could only be...a love bite.

The shock charged through me like a bolt of electricity. I wanted to punch him, kick him out of bed, throw him out of the room. Anywhere away from me. I'd put up with his demands and no-shows for year after repulsive year, and now he'd cheated on me!

Then I remembered I'd kissed Perry.

An arm came over and flapped across my shoulders, pinning me. I tried to move but was held fast. And maybe the hickey was all that had happened? Maybe I was wrong. Maybe—*wake up, since when is a love bite ever all that happened?*

I grasped his wrist and lifted, squirmed. Then he burbled in dream-speak.

"Fixi...please..."

Fixi?

I dragged myself from under his arm, tore a sheet of paper from a note pad and grabbed a pen. *Fixi—is that Fiona? Fiona Taylor—Triple-F Fiona? If it was, then I did see her at the airport!*

I marched into the shower-room and rummaged in my cosmetic bag. My hand shook as I wrote on the sheet in big capital letters. After leaving a tube of foundation on the note, I stormed back past the sprawled Edward and out of the A-frame. Stomping Bear-like along the beach, I kicked the sand. *Yes, of course he's been having an affair—that's why he's shown no interest in me for weeks. Make that months. Make that years.*

Falcon drew me like a magnet because, right now, I needed someone to talk to.

*   *   *

"You wrote *what?*" asked Perry, as we walked along the beach.

"'If you must return resembling a loved-up, blotchy-skinned elephant seal, you may find this makeup hides your hickey better than your hero's gauche cravat.'"

"Your doctorate in diplomacy was money well spent."

"Should I go back and tear it up, pretend I haven't seen the love bite? Maybe I made a mistake—I mean, if I've just accused him of having an affair, then I'm not going to want to have dinner with him on that yacht. I'd be raging with fury or sulking in my room, or getting drunk."

Perry picked up a shell and threw it into the surf. "I'd love to accompany you aboard—it would be fascinating to meet Dragan—a man I've been hearing things about for years. Sadly, I'm not invited. I really want to know why he's here. His type don't come to a place like this because they happen to be passing through. If you don't go to dinner tomorrow, we may never know."

"Or we'll find out too late. Okay, I can just about manage to play it cool a little longer."

Back at the A-frame, I opened the door and tiptoed in. Bear was still in bed. I crept past into the shower-room. I scrunched my declaration of war in my hand and returned the makeup to my cosmetic bag.

When I came out, he was sitting up, rubbing his eyes.

"Morning," I said casually. "Sleep well?"

"No."

He cleared his throat, then staggered out of bed towards the shower-room. At the door he stopped. "Everything okay? You been out already? You seem nervous."

"A lungful of morning air."

He pointed. "What's that?"

"What?"

"In your hand."

"Oh, this." I unfolded the paper and looked innocently at it. "I made a mistake with my research. So annoying, now I'll have to ask Kris—"

He walked into the shower-room and slammed the door. "You looked like you had a guilty secret," he shouted over the rush of water from the shower head.

*   *   *

The guests and staff had gathered on the sand outside the Sun and Moon's bar with their cameras, phones and iPads. When a young beach attendant started shouting, more guests and staff soon arrived. Some pointed, others stared slack-jawed. I heard something about lottery jackpots being way too small to afford it. One man suggested it was a cruise ship; his wife insisted it was the plaything of a Russian oligarch. Nancy, fanning her face, looked in an entirely different direction.

She whispered she'd never seen anything like it either. I turned—to see Perry, up to his knees in foam, pulling up his swimsuit.

"Are you alright, Nancy?"

"Oh my…I saw his…"

"Nancy!"

"…tattoo."

Beyond the reef, Apex Predator, black of hull, cream of superstructure, glinted beneath a forest of aerials, spinning radars and glistening domes. Its glass was dark-smoked, its hull raked to an aggressive conclusion. It boasted gratuitous muscularity in its bulging excesses—a tactless, other-worldly icon that broadcast its owner's Ozymandian contempt in dozens of ways. Including matching bow and stern helicopters.

The mega yacht dropped anchor, the clank of chain carrying to the crowd. Aboard, white-uniformed crew darted about. A door lifted in the hull and a sleek tender slipped out.

Bear stood a hundred yards away from me, at the end of the jetty. He turned to view the crowd—I pictured his chest, bloated with pride, before the tender arrived to skim him over to the yacht. Nancy clinked glasses with Frank and smiled at me.

"May I ask your advice?"

"Anything, Angel."

I told them about the love bite, and how I'd nearly confronted Bear, but had changed my mind because I wanted to meet Dragan. That I didn't know whether Edward knew I'd seen the hickey. That I'd had my doubts for some time, and didn't understand why he'd left for places unknown in the middle of *our* vacation, in *our* time. Or that maybe I'd known it was wrong for years, but had ignored the signs.

I finished with, "If you try hard enough, you can make it work with anyone, right?"

"Of course not," said Nancy. "You can't turn glass into diamond. Find yourself a diamond, Angel. You deserve it. "

"Can you describe his personal assistant?" Frank asked, as I considered Nancy's advice. Why were they smiling nervously? Why had she slipped her hand into Frank's?

"Fiona's...strawberry blonde. Average height but wears heels. Very curvy. Why?"

"Does she chew gum?"

"How did you know that?"

"We went back to the market the other day. I'm afraid we saw her," Frank said.

"So she *is* here. But why?"

Frank cleared his throat. "I'm afraid it gets worse. She was arm in arm with Edward. I'm sorry, dear," Frank added, squeezing my hand in support.

I repeated Frank's words to myself. Was this why he'd agreed to come with me to the South Pacific, on a vacation he clearly hated every minute of? He'd stashed Fiona away in another resort and was sneaking back and forth. And yet, why go to all that trouble? Maybe he was doing it because of the thrill of cheating behind my back. Or was there another reason? Slowly, finally, my stomach unclenched as I realized I no longer cared.

But relief came too. At least now it would be easy to leave. No more guilt and no more trying. Bile wicked the back of my throat. It wasn't like I had lost—because there had never ever been a chance of winning. One more evening, one final dinner. I could get through that. And with luck, I'd never have to see him again.

Frank spoke softly. "Perry told us what you're planning. It could be dangerous. You'll be alone on that yacht with those people, and none of us know what they're capable of."

"Angel, nobody's pressuring you into going to that dinner. We're both worried."

"I know what you're thinking and in a worst case scenario, you might be right. But I've trained for this and I'm ready. I've always wanted to be investigative and here's my chance. It's all about risk assessment, taking precautions, contingency planning. I'm a good swimmer, it's not *too* far back to land. I've seen police boats here. And Perry will be waiting on the beach with a jet ski, if I need rescuing. You're right, it's a risk—but life's a risk. In the end, investigative isn't just about getting the story, it's about doing some good in the world. And I haven't done that before. Tomorrow I might fail…but I'm going to try."

"It's true that the answer to what's going on may be on the yacht," Frank said. "If you do go—"

"I'm going."

"We're not talking ghosts on rocks, this time, Angel," Nancy added. "These people could be a law unto themselves, especially if they're close to influential islanders…like Thurston Morfil."

"Good point. I can't believe Morfil doesn't know Dragan's here and hasn't made contact. By going, I might be able to find out more about Morfil. He might even be at the dinner!"

"Well, you can get to the bottom of it, if anyone can," Frank said. "I believe in you."

"I believe in you too, Teal. But I'll be praying." Nancy looked down at an orange ladybird that landed on her knee. "And I don't even believe in God," she said softly.

The tender returned. Docked. Bear climbed out.

"What's he carrying?" asked Nancy.

"One of those aluminum suitcases," Frank answered. "You know, the type photographers use."

"And what looks like…a shovel," Nancy added.

They turned to me inquiringly.

I shrugged. "He isn't into photography. Or gardening."

*   *   *

Long after Frank and Nancy had excused themselves and wandered hand in hand back to their A-frame, I lingered on the beach. Finally, I settled on the sand opposite Falcon's empty mooring. I pictured the yacht far offshore, Perry shirtless at the helm, the spray, Violet hovering behind. Was he tracking whales? Counting dolphins? I thought back over the last few weeks and remembered how Grandma said life could change in a moment.

I needed to re-establish my link with her, to hold her letters again, to read them slowly, smell the remnants of her perfume before it faded away. The tender was heading back to Apex Predator with Bear aboard once again. Why so much to-ing and fro-ing? The good news was he'd be away for a few hours. And after tonight, I hoped, for ever…

The first thing I saw on entering our room was the dress draped over the bed. The note read:

Wear the Tiffany earrings with this dress. You'll get your precious letters back when you start behaving. You cause a scene, try to screw things up at dinner or play anything other than the doting partner and you'll regret it. I trust I've made myself clear.

I gasped. A little dizzy, my bare feet crunched on the tortilla crumbs that linked the bed to the dresser. I pulled out the drawer but the letters were gone. Instead, there was a folded piece of notepaper. I smoothed it out and read aloud. "I mean it."

With my heart pounding in my chest, I paced the room then stormed outside to gulp the salty air before returning. Flopping in a chair, I fought back tears.

It was my fault—I should have listened to Grandma. She had given me any number of subtle and not so subtle warnings. But I'd been so blinded by my desire to win my mother's approval that I hadn't saved any space to find out what would please me. Now I was paying for it. I may never see Lizzie's letters again—never get to read the last one. Lizzie's last letter. For all I knew, Bear had already thrown them in the ocean.

When I had calmed down, I rubbed Grandma's ring. The metal was reassuringly firm, warm. Thanks Lizzie, I thought. Yes, I know—I *must* play it cool tonight.

I walked back to the bed and picked up the dress. Black. Lace shoulders. I held it in front of the full length mirror. Way too short, it plunged in front and was practically see-through. *Perfect*, I thought, throwing it onto the floor.

And hour later the tender vomited Edward into my evening. He threw open the door and stomped sand into the room, before dropping into a chair.

"The senator's leaving tomorrow, my stateroom won't be ready till then, so I'll be sleeping here tonight. Like the dress?"

"Well, it's not exactly what—"

"Good."

"And what shoes are you planning to wear?"

"I've got just the right ones."

"Okay."

"Look Bear, if it's that important to you, I won't let you down, but those letters are incredibly important to me."

"Excellent. Then you'll behave."

CHAPTER THIRTY-THREE

The sand scrunch-squeaked under my sneakers as I jogged on the track beneath the palms, emerging once again from the scrub at the far end of the beach. My thoughts weren't on the pace, or on dodging the fallen coconuts, but on whether Malcolm had been contacted by Sir Basil over the weekend. If he had, what had been said?

Sure, Morfil wasn't what he appeared to be, but then what successful businessman was? Looking for new people to interview would only alert the police, who would report back to Morfil. He'd then complain to Sir Basil that after he'd kindly slotted me into his super-busy schedule, I'd thanked him by snooping around behind his back. Forget my promotion and raise, my dream of switching to investigative. If my old job *was* even still there, it was hanging by a thread.

I jumped over a depression in the sand and turned for home. How long would Malcolm fight in my corner? The point must be fast approaching when he felt my actions were threatening *his* future at Musculus. Maybe that point had already been reached.

On the jetty, a small crowd was dispersing after the daily fish feeding. Someone was waving at me from the beach end of the jetty. Was it Frank? I altered course towards him, wondering what Black Jack had seized today.

"Morning, Frank," I said, high-stepping on the spot to keep my cardio up.

"I think he over-slept."

"Who?"

"Black Jack. First morning he's been a no-show."

"How disappointing," I said. "I guess everyone needs a day off."

"And another ship's arriving."

Apex Predator had swung with the tide, and lay stern to. Beyond it, a plume of filthy smoke heralded the arrival of another large vessel. With a goodbye wave, I turned back to the beach to start my second island circuit.

Bear had been shaving when I left, but a vague memory or part of a dream played on my mind. It involved him rolling off the bed and creeping out of the room, just as the first dawn rays filtered in. But when I'd woken, the usual gurgling thunder confirmed he still lay beside me.

At a fork in the track, I stared along the beach at Falcon. Was Perry aboard? I headed towards the back of the island—was he at his gym? But all I found there was a lizard that scurried up the punch bag. I pictured Perry boxing: the springy balance, taut muscles, blurring hand speed. Was he still asleep? This beautiful man at his most vulnerable—was he a cuddler? Did he smile when he dreamed? Did he sleep naked? Mmm…did he sleep naked?

I jogged in the mottled light beneath a row of palms at the end of the beach. There were the rocks the wallet had been placed on and beyond them, Falcon. But my eye was drawn to something I hadn't noticed before: a boulder in the surf. Above it hovered a pair of cackling gulls; one dropped. It pecked at the rock and flew off. That's strange, I thought. And why had more gulls arrived? Closer now, I saw how each wave rocked the dark shape, so it couldn't be a boulder. With growing curiosity, I jogged over.

It took time for my brain to accept what lay in front of me. Scales covered the giant body, the fins were coarse-spined. But there was no head. Instead, a shattered mass trailed globular entrails that flowed back and forth with the surf.

"Black Jack? What…what happened?" My jaw tightened.

Another gull landed. With a squawk it began to peck and pull.

"You poor thing. I'm so sorry. This is terrib—"

"I saw the gulls."

"Perry!"

He squeezed my shoulder before hurrying past. Kneeling, he reached into the wound.

"Teal, could you…?"

I joined him and found grip at the base of a fin. We waited for the right wave and surfed the fish higher up the sand.

"Here comes Kris," I said.

"Oh god, how did *that* happen?" he said, running the last few yards. "Propeller?" He dropped beside Perry who was elbow deep, working his hands inside the flesh.

"I felt something before…here it is." He pulled until his arm slipped free. He held a metal rod which he washed in the surf.

"That's a harpoon," Kris said.

"Never seen one like it," Perry said, sniffing the flared end before running his finger inside it. It came back black. "What the hell? Cordite?"

"An *exploding* harpoon?" Kris suggested.

"Yes," Perry said, "but why would—Teal, are you alright?"

It had been a possibility, but I'd dismissed it. Even he—even *they* wouldn't do such a thing. To the Sun and Moon's oldest and most famous resident. To Kris and Emma's livelihood. I glanced at our hut, then at Apex Predator and swore under my breath. Shaking my head, I whispered, "Edward Hamilton, you were no angel before, but what has this Dan Dragan turned you into?"

"Teal?" asked Kris.

I told them about the conversation I'd had with Bear in The Blue Beluga—of Dragan's arms company and the exploding speargun developed for the Israelis. How I thought Bear had slipped out of bed before dawn this morning.

"It can't all be coincidence, can it?" I asked.

Perry pointed. "Here comes the tender to collect Edward. And, no doubt, the evidence."

In the distance, I could see Bear striding towards the end of the jetty. Two men dressed in white uniforms followed him, carrying his suitcases.

"Edward's got that photographer's box with him again," Perry said. "The harpoon gun must be in it."

"And one of the crew's carrying the shovel," I said. "I guess he meant to bury Black Jack, so no one would know."

Kris muttered he'd join us later and hurried towards the hotel's office. Perry and I walked back to my A-frame. It took only seconds to confirm Bear's possessions were gone. By the time I looked out of the window, the tender was tethered alongside Apex Predator. A large commercial vessel sat nearby.

"Looks like a survey ship," Perry said. "Must belong to Dragan. Otherwise why would it anchor so close to his yacht?"

"Why would he be surveying this backwater?" I asked.

He kissed my forehead, his fingertips sliding featherlike down my cheek, leaving a tingling energy line behind.

"You smell of fish, mister!"

"Sorry! You definitely going to dinner on that thing?"

"After he stole my letters, and now *this*—try and stop me!"

I held the dress up and explained I had to attend dinner in this cha-cha belly dancer outfit, and behave impeccably if I wanted to get the letters back.

"You know what? You'll look great! Stunning! I can't wait to—oh. No, no. You're right. I mean…not your style at all. It would look awful on you…um, totally wrong color," Perry said, grinning from ear to ear.

"Perry?"

His face darkened. "He stole your letters to keep you in line?

Surprise, surprise, he's a blackmailer too." Then a light flashed in his eyes. "You know I almost find myself *liking* this guy."

"What do you mean?"

"He makes me look *really* good!" He saw my expression. "I'm sorry."

"It's just that I don't know why I ever—" Warm tears trickled down my cheeks. "I'm such an idiot. How could I have fallen for him?"

He wrapped his arms around me and whispered, "Please don't beat yourself up. You were vulnerable, we all are sometimes. He took advantage of you. You're a kind person, Teal. Kind people don't do well with giant rats."

"He was a *super* rat."

I pressed closer, burying myself in the warmth, awash in his honeysuckle-mango and grouper scent. Yes, definitely a cuddler.

"I wish I'd been invited to Dragan's, maybe I could have helped."

"You *are* helping."

"Doing my best." Minutes passed, and I realized I hadn't enjoyed such contentment since…the last time Grandma hugged me. He tickled my ribs, then darted out of reach when I tried to tickle back. "Perry, that's cheating!"

"I love your giggle."

"It's still cheating."

He took my hands in his. I found myself studying his face, his eyes, his mouth. Especially his mouth. I had to concentrate to hear his words. "…and be sure to charm Dragan. Then corner Edward in front of him, think of something that will force him to return the letters. You can do it."

I squeezed his hands.

There was a knock at the door. Kris entered, his face tight.

"Emma told me one of the beach cleaners saw Edward on the end of the jetty very early. He wasn't close enough to see what he was doing, but he heard a muffled explosion."

"Dear God," I said.

"I'm told I'm pretty easy going, but these selfish, cruel, arrogant people…" Kris took a deep breath. "…have gone too far. Somehow, someway…"

"I know," I said. "We're working on it."

CHAPTER THIRTY-FOUR

The thrum-thrum of the helicopter that had beaten us to Apex Predator faded as the crew tied the tender alongside. With the outboards cut and chopper silent, it brought a moment of peace until I picked up the pervasive hum of electronics aboard the mega yacht. I inhaled deeply, steadied myself and looked up.

Apex Predator bulged above me, its extremities shielded by sweeping curves and generous overhangs. So smooth was the steel, so lustrous the black paintwork, that the ocean was mirrored in the hull, just as the vessel itself was reflected in the dark water. Wish I'd brought my camera. Wish I wasn't so nervous. Wish Perry was with me.

Inside the yacht, the bite of the air con surprised me. With nothing to cover my shoulders, I felt an immediate chill.

Two young women (blonde, tight uniforms, legs) stepped forward. One cradled a linen-wrapped green bottle; the other balanced a cut crystal glass on a Louis Quatorze tray.

"Champagne, ma'am?"

A serious-looking man, (walkie talkie, razor burn) welcomed me aboard and ushered me towards a glass elevator. Its panels were engraved with scenes from a tiger hunt: elephants, maharajas in wicker baskets, rifles, with the great cat crouching in the foreground. We purred upwards through several decks.

The elevator door hissed open, and the steward led me along a hallway inlaid with marble. In the perfumed chill of fresh jasmine, we passed a dozen sculptured bronzes, a display of carved Japanese ivory and line of oil paintings. Was that a *Monet?*

An albino peacock held pride of place in a full length cabinet that included every shape and size of stuffed bird. I recognized pelicans, owls, swans, an ibis, necking doves (the label proclaimed *Two birds with one stone.*

Or shot.), and a delicate hummingbird (broken beak). What struck me as creepy was that every single bird was...white.

My breathing quickened as my escort led me towards yet another door, flanked by matching polar bears. It opened, and I stepped into...Heaven.

Not in the literal sense. It was more the way that nearly everything—the carpet and marble surround, the walls, sofas, curtains, ceiling—was Violet's tummy-white. White lacquers, silks, leathers. The only relief came from the animal skins (heads intact) that lay spread-eagled on the floor and the furs (spots, roundels, stripes) that draped over the furniture. A clutch of people sat at the end of the room: three men, an elderly woman. And a gum-chewing strawberry blonde. A flash of fury stopped me dead in my tracks. *Her!*

"Evening, my darling," a beaming Edward said, arms outstretched. "You look lovely, as always. But what on earth, haw, haw?" They all stared at my shoes.

I found my most innocent voice. "I read somewhere you can't wear stilettos on a boat. They damage the wooden decks. So tonight I wore my best sneakers."

"Come and give the luckiest man alive a kiss."

After he'd air-pecked both cheeks, he bellowed, "It's a *yacht,* darling! Now, let me introduce our hostess, Mrs. Dragan."

"How do you do?" I shook the diamond and ruby encrusted fingers as Dracula nails stabbed my palm. Swathed in mists of magenta chiffon, she adjusted the mink stole draped over her shoulders.

"What divine perfume. May I ask what it is?" I asked.

"Imperial Majesty by Clive Christian. I *never* wear anything else even though Daniel's always complaining about the price. And you must call me 'Zelda'," she said in a perfect Kissinger.

"Thank you. Zelda."

"And how thoughtful of you to think of our decking. What size are you? Perhaps I could lend you something a little more elegant."

"That's kind of you but...I've caught Edward's athlete's foot. I'd hate to pass it on," I said quietly.

Edward cleared his throat. "You've met Thurston Morfil before."

"Delighted our paths should cross again, dear lady. And so soon."

"What an unexpected surprise. Was it you arriving in the helicopter, Thurston?"

"Indeed so, straight from the airport. And permit me to introduce our host, Mr. Dan Dragan."

"It's a pleasure, sir," I said, smiling demurely at the conservatively dressed man in front of me. Charcoal suit, crisp white shirt, black silk tie. Something lupine in the streaky gray hair and pointy nose.

Cold fingers grasped mine. Don't pull free—let him release you, I told myself as his eyes drifted down, calculated, then flicked to another part of me. Despite the revealing dress, I felt I was being evaluated, not ogled.

I stepped back, hoping to re-establish a little distance between us, but he slithered forward to bathe me in the aroma of his tomato juice breath. Finally, in a soft voice, he said, "Charming. You may call me Dan. Edward has spoken highly of you." He released my hand and said, "Where are my manners? You know Ms. Taylor, of course?"

I couldn't meet Fiona's eyes, but smiled at the lynx pelt over her shoulders.

"I wasn't expecting to see you here, Fiona. I thought—"

"A man can't be expected to function without his personal assistant," Edward said.

"I arrived yesterday," she said.

The conversation turned to the quaintness of the Sun and Moon (Edward interrupting to haw, haw after repeating his sadomasochism joke), the remoteness of the island and our fishing trip. When I said I'd seen whales, Dragan's head tilted, as if to hear better.

"Was the whale watching with that jolly English fellow?" Edward gushed.

"You can tell me about the whales over dinner," Dragan said. "Sixteen guests left yesterday. More arrive tomorrow but when there are few of us aboard, Zelda prefers the intimacy of our Sky Dining Room."

Dragan offered his arm. With a swallow, I took it.

"Zelda insists on meeting my business associates and their partners—even the more trivial ones. At first I resisted inviting you, Teal, as I have an aversion to people in your profession."

"I'm sorry to hear that," I said.

"But we're all friends tonight. Isn't that so?" he said, smiling.

"Of course," I answered, catching Edward's shifty gaze.

"Thurston?" he added, without looking.

"We certainly are, Dan."

"Indeed...we...are," Dragan repeated.

"Teal," Zelda said, "You let me know the minute he starts bullying you."

"I'm sure I'll be fine. Won't I, Dan?"

"Shame you can't sleep aboard, dear," she added.

"Excuse me?"

Dragan now studied Edward, though his words were for me. "Your motion sickness, Teal. But don't worry, I'll return him in a few days." He was facing me. "I hope you like lobster."

"Very much." Motion sickness? It wasn't *me* double-fisting Stugeron and Dramamine on that round-the-island corporate sailing event last

August.

I looked at Zelda. "I just *love* what you've done with the interior. Was it you, or did you use a famous designer?"

"The theme was all my idea, but I engaged the divine Leonardo Leonardi of Fifth Avenue to sort out the detail."

Never heard of him. "I might have guessed!"

"I see we're going to get along just fine," Zelda said, adjusting her mink. "Be sure to tell me if you feel chilled, dear. There's plenty more where this one came from."

I thanked her as we stepped into another sparkling elevator that wafted us three levels higher to emerge above the twinkling ocean.

We walked along a corridor, and Daniel stopped in front of a glass-fronted alcove. The stuffed deer within had huge ears and dark eyes.

"Mule deer," he stated, "See that scar on its neck? That animal caused me a lot of problems. Had to kill it twice."

"With that thing?" I pointed at the weapon fixed to the wall, above the deer.

"The crossbow's an effective and silent killer, in the right hands. You can take an animal in someone's garden at night and they'll never know. I started my hunting career with that, so I get a buzz every time I walk past it."

Zelda seated me on Dragan's right. Fiona took her place on his left with Edward and Morfil either side of our hostess. Gold cutlery. Gold-rimmed plates and glasses. *AP* (in gold) embroidered, stamped, carved, chiseled, embossed, glued and welded onto every available surface. Memories of Malcolm pouring champagne at the award ceremony returned as the crew poured from the right, served from the left—and left.

When the appetizer of smoked arctic char arrived (marinated in Barrique de Ponciano Porfidio tequila, the menu card declared), Dragan ordered us to report any fish bones. "Chef's fined $500 per bone," he explained. "Four and he's history. On my third chef this year. Picked this one up a few weeks back at the Carlisle, after he did something interesting with foie gras and veal. You know what the beauty of veal is, Edward?"

"Not sure I do, sir."

Zelda spoke. "He claims it doesn't count as red meat."

"Of course it doesn't! I limit myself to a couple of steaks a year, at most," Edward said patting his stomach, before repeating his weight versus height joke.

Then he *ooohed* and *aaahed* at the wines as I micro-sipped my champagne and returned the glass to the depression its base had made in the monogrammed table cloth. I was encouraged by how much the others, except for our host, drank. My sobriety might offer me some advantage. And right now, I needed every advantage I could get.

Morfil complimented our hostess on the outstanding lobster. "You prefer these to the local ones?" he asked Dragan.

"They've got claws. The local ones don't," Zelda explained, anticipating my question.

"Maine lobster. Best in the world," Dragan said. "Holding tank below deck. By my calculations we'll have only...eighty-two left. If the crew haven't been stealing them. The local seafood sucks."

"But the tuna's delicious," I offered, prodding the ginger-sprinkled, orchid-sculpted carrot that bobbed in my tasting bowl of lemongrass-infused Bouillabaisse bouillon.

"You're right, Dan. I ate a local mackerel the other night. I'd choose cold water fish every time," Edward said.

"Speaking of which," said Dragan, pointedly turning away from Edward and addressing Morfil. "The prototype's on its way. Arriving for my big day with the cargoed-up *Wunpa Cent*. Those damned expensive design modifications better work."

"I had the designs double-checked by a highly recommended naval architect. He confirmed stability wouldn't be compromised and that those Taiwanese fellows did a first class job, right down to the davits and reinforced decking. Naturally, I side-stepped his questions as to the precise nature of our venture. We're still starting with ten?"

"*I'm* still starting with *one*. If it works okay, then ten. I'll add more trawlers as soon as the business model's proved itself."

"What's a davit, Dan?" asked Edward, between mouthfuls.

Dragan put down his knife and fork and stared at Edward. The temperature plunged.

"Sorry sir, none of my business." Had Edward's cheeks actually flushed? "B-by the way, my suspicions were correct about that irritating husband and wife—I had another copy flown in, it's in my stateroom," he said.

"Please get it," Dragan said quietly, without looking at Edward. "Now."

"I'll go," offered Fiona. "That's my job," she said, fluttering her eyelashes at Edward.

"Thanks, Fixi."

Fixi! The name he'd mentioned in his sleep! And what did he mean by having another copy flown in? Could it be the manila envelope that had arrived for him while he was away? And why did "Fixi" know where things were in Edward's *stateroom?*

"You look chilly, dear," Zelda said, pulling her stole close around her neck.

"I'm fine," I said, rubbing the goose bumps on my arms. "Perhaps if the air con—"

Dragan's palm settled on my shoulder as he turned slightly and arched an eyebrow. A steward hurried over. She leaned down and he whispered in her ear.

"Right away, Mr. Dragan."

"Tell me more about my other investment, Thurston. I see you're wearing a damn fine pair of cufflinks. What news from the mines?" Dragan asked.

Morfil twiddled the chunk of gold that bound a ruffled cuff. "None of them are economic, I'm afraid, Dan. Gold's spread too thin. But it was worth checking."

"And those?"

"Harrods. Bought them on my last visit to Old London Town."

Dragan turned to face me, his eyes still on Morfil. "Don't you love it when someone tells you it was 'worth checking'? Three million bucks of *my* money for a bunch of exploratory mines...and he writes it off with a smile."

"Relax, Dan. *Poseidon* will pay you back in spades," Morfil said calmly, holding Dragan's stare.

"At least two hundred million a year, like dear old Teodoro, eh?"

"Precisely."

"The cogs well oiled?"

"Every last one."

"How many times have I told you not to leave the ladies out of a conversation, Daniel?" Zelda asked.

Dragan sipped from his tomato juice. "One sticky gear can throw everything out. Isn't that so, Thurston?"

Morfil stopped chewing and nodded.

"Everyone has their price. Isn't that so, Edward?" Dragan added.

"If you say so, sir, haw, haw!"

In the silence that followed, Dragan's eyes flicked between Edward and Morfil, as he chewed. He swallowed, patted his lips with his napkin.

Poseidon? Teodoro? I don't remember ever attending a meeting, let alone a social function, quite like this. Ever.

The steward returned, handing me a tissue-wrapped package. I unfolded it, feeling its luxuriant softness. The letters *AP* were embroidered repeatedly around the border of the white shawl. "Cashmere?" I asked.

"Certainly not! Tell her, Thurston."

"What? Oh yes, Dan. Well, it's um, *vicuña*, an Andean animal—"

"Camelid."

"Thank you, Dan. Camelid. The softest and most expensive textile in the world."

"Put it on," Dragan insisted.

"That's very kind of you, thank you. Yes, much better now."

"Consider it a small memento of your evening."

"I couldn't keep it, Mr. Dragan."

"Nonsense!"

Fiona was back. She handed Dragan a copy of Time magazine. The cover looked strangely familiar.

"Page sixty-two," Edward said after clearing his throat.

I remembered that when we'd arrived, Frank dropped his copy of Time overboard and Edward claimed it wasn't an accident. That's where I'd seen it before.

We sat in silence as Dragan read, his face immobile, his eyes darting back and forth. If he was self-conscious as everyone watched him, he didn't show it. He closed the magazine, placed it on the table and looked at Edward.

"Time ranks our friends thirty-first of fifty. Someone tell me one single way they've made a difference."

He looked first at Morfil, then Edward. "As usual, they'll achieve nothing."

Edward haw, hawed, Morfil ran his fingers through his hair, Zelda rolled her eyes and Fiona leaned back, drawing Edward's eyes to her cleavage. *More secrets?* I glanced at the magazine cover and read the headline: *We List the World's Top Fifty Environmentalists.*

What was I supposed to report to Basil Thane now? That I didn't trust Morfil one inch, not to mention this Dragan? Despite the alarm bells that were ringing in my head, I still had no idea what was going on.

"So how did you meet my husband?" Zelda asked Edward.

"I contacted Dan with an idea. He was gracious enough to meet me to discuss it."

Dragan turned to me. "When your sixty-fifth birthday is imminent, it's important to celebrate in style. I already had one…*amusement*…planned. Edward had what started as a mildly interesting idea, but it became exponentially more attractive the more I considered it."

"I'm not sure I understand. *Two* birthday celebrations?" I asked brightly.

Dragan paused, a lobster-laden fork hovering over his plate. He looked at me appraisingly for a stretched moment. Then: "The Dan and Zelda Dragan Foundation amused me for a while, and it keeps Zelda as busy as she wants to be. But now I—"

"What does it support?" I asked.

"When I shot my world's record third Javan rhino—"

"That's incredible, haw, haw!"

"I already had the world's largest collection of albino specimens. I was looking for something special. The crowning glory."

"Which is?" I asked more casually this time.

Dragan intertwined his fingers. "This thing runs smoothly and we'll take it from there, Edward. Got it?"

"Trust me, it will. Everything's set up."

Casual hadn't worked. "This is *so* exciting. What *is* it you are going to do?" I asked, all smiles.

"Young lady, the planet's full of environmentalists, pacifists, vegans, religious nuts, conspiracy theorists, astral projectors. Collectively they inhabit a fantasy world I refer to as 'La-la Land'. I, on the other hand, have no delusions about the natural order of things. Hence the name of this yacht. Does a lion cry when it eviscerates a young zebra?"

Morfil laughed. "Dan, remember she's a journalist."

"I hadn't forgotten. I will say this: If my successes can be attributed to anything—"

"No, let me, Dan, haw, haw! I would say it's Dan's unique ability to identify and harness commercial opportunities missed by the lobotomized masses."

"Why not give the young lady an example, Edward."

"Let me see…Dan was a pioneer in the krill mining industry. Such is the tsunami of jealousy that attaches to anything Dan does, that it attracted nothing but trouble."

"Krill mining?" I asked.

Dragan held his hand up to silence Edward. "Shrimps. Trillions of them that swim around pointlessly until they die. An unexploited resource. So we catch a few and put them to various uses."

"I think I understand," I said, making a mental note to mention this to Perry.

Zelda interrupted my thoughts. "Edward, how long have you two been together?"

"Must be…almost two years," he said.

"Three."

"A lovely girl like this? So why haven't you put a ring on her finger, young man?"

"Oh, I *intend* to. Just as soon as she—"

"'Grants my little request, haw, haw.'—Is that what you were going to say, Bear?" I said, winking at him.

"And what might that be?" Morfil asked, perking up and pulling his chair closer to the table.

"Why don't you tell them about Dr. Mortimer's two for one offer, dearest?"

"Oh, Teal—I'm sure they're not interested in our private business, haw, haw!"

I looked at Zelda. "He wants me to have a boob job."

"Makes sense," Dragan said. "I just bought a company that makes implants."

"Teal, dear, what would you say is the most important thing in a relationship?" Zelda asked.

I didn't need to think of my answer. "You're always reminding me, aren't you, *darling*?" Edward's eyes narrowed. "Go on, *you* tell everyone."

"Well," he started slowly. "It could be several things."

I laughed. "You don't have to be shy. Tell them!"

He glanced around the table. "I…"

"Great strapping businessman but he gets tongue-tied when talking about love. Integrity, isn't it darling? Being able to trust a person completely. That's what you always say matters most. That and…" I said coyly, "…sex appeal." I was only able to look Edward in the eye because I was imagining Perry climbing from the surf instead.

"You'll have me blushing."

"Integrity is so important," Zelda agreed. Morfil nodded with enthusiasm.

"Oh darling, before I forget…" I said.

"Yes?"

"Thank you for looking after my letters. But I need them back now."

"What letters are these?" Zelda asked.

"From my late grandmother. Edward promised to keep them safe."

"I imagine they're quite precious," Zelda said.

"But…" Edward started.

His face tightened as everyone turned to stare at him.

"Edward! Why are you still sitting there?" Zelda asked.

He rose, an eye twitching. "Be right back."

"With divorce rates at nearly fifty percent, it's sensible to get to know each other first," Dragan said. "I was lucky. It was love at first sight for us, wasn't it, Princess?"

"Maybe for you," she answered, winking at me.

Zelda launched into a lecture on the sanctity of marriage, the commitment one person makes to another that must be honored for life. She touched on the mission of the Dan and Zelda Dragan Foundation, how, via a twelve-step program, it counseled couples and promoted strong bonds in relationships.

"I explained it over and over to Grant. I told him straight. I tried using analogy," she said. "He just didn't get it."

"Who's Grant?" I asked.

"My fourth husband. But you know what? The quarter million it cost to set up DZDF was money well spent…which matches Daniel's other charitable support."

I turned to Dragan. "What other foundations do you support, Daniel?"

Zelda spoke first. "He doesn't really talk about it. But Daniel supports a post-traumatic stress disorder charity. Did you know about one in three people who experience a terrible event go on to develop PTSD?"

Had Dragan's face tightened? "I'm sure they aren't interested in—" he began.

"It's only recently that we're beginning to learn the terrible harm it does. Take for example our returning soldiers. The damage can show up in many different ways…"

"I'm sure they don't want to hear about this," Daniel said, leaning back with his arms crossed.

"You know Daniel received the Silver Star for bravery in Vietnam. But when he came home, there was almost no support. PTSE wasn't understood then."

"I'm impressed, Daniel," I said.

Zelda continued. "Many of them suffered terribly. Did you know some of our boys used to sleep with hairdryers under the bed?"

"I don't understand," I said, looking at Dragan.

"Bedwetting is associated with PTSD. Can you imagine the shame, the humiliation for a full-grown man when he suddenly starts wetting the bed?"

"The hairdryer?" I asked.

"So they could tidy up after themselves if they had an accident," she explained.

Edward returned with Grandma's letters and dropped them in front of me.

"Thanks, Bear," I said, blowing him a kiss. I checked they were all there, before placing them in a zipped compartment in my bag.

Dragan motioned to a steward to freshen my glass.

"I'll have her champagne. She's watching her weight," Edward said.

"Whatever made you think that, dearest?" I asked. "But you're right, no thank you. I need a clear head for tomorrow. Pressing deadline."

After dinner, we retired to the adjoining Sky Lounge for coffee and liqueurs. I was glad I *didn't* suffer from motion sickness because the combination of bleached crocodile skin walls and modern art sent a flutter through my stomach. Dragan pointed out a Kandinsky and a pair of Picassos, before enumerating the impressionists he owned. He poured Fiona a Henri IV Cognac Grande Champagne in a bucket-sized balloon glass.

"So Edward," began Zelda. "I hope you spoil your lovely lady."

He cleared his throat. "In my modest way. Those earrings, for example. I always say a beautiful woman can't have too much jewelry. Isn't that right, honey?"

"I remember you mentioning that," I said, wondering where the over-sized earrings Fiona was wearing came from. "Zelda and Dan, it's been absolutely lovely but I'm afraid I should get back to the island. Duty calls."

"It was a pleasure seeing you again, Teal. How's your piece on me coming along?" Morfil asked, as he kissed my cheek.

"Very well, but Sir Basil has brought the deadline forward. He's very keen to read it. So an early start tomorrow."

"Well, we can't have you upsetting our favorite Knight of the Realm, can we? If, dear lady, I can be of further service…"

I smiled and thanked Zelda again for such a wonderful evening aboard her fantastic ocean liner. Edward rolled his eyes, and the others laughed. I nodded at Fiona before turning to Dragan.

"What can I say? You have been so kind, and thank you for keeping an eye on Edward."

"He may have potential. We'll know soon enough."

He may have potential? We'll know soon enough? Whatever they were up to, it was imminent. The problem was, I still hadn't worked out what it was.

"Darling, would you mind escorting me to the tender?"

"Of course," Edward said, offering his arm.

We made our way in silence but I couldn't stop smiling. He saw, and I knew it annoyed him. Finally he asked what the hell was so funny.

I ignored him.

"So you got the letters back. Big deal."

"I really like the way my sneakers complement this lap-dancer ensemble. Your taste is impeccable."

"Next time Zelda Dragan offers you shoes, you don't pretend to have athlete's foot. Got it?"

"What makes you think there'll be a next time?"

Before I stepped aboard the tender, I kissed him on both cheeks. Then I blasted him with my Anne Hathaway smile.

"I naively thought you came here to save our relationship. I'd love to be able to say it's been a pleasure knowing you."

"But—"

I took off the earrings and thrust them into his hand. "I don't want these. Goodbye, Edward Hamilton."

"You didn't think they were real, did you? Haw, haw!" he shouted as the tender reversed away from the yacht.

I opened my handbag and checked again that Grandma's letters really were there. Then I tapped the record "stop" button on my iPhone. I let the throb of the engines carry my words away: "Did I do okay, Lizzie?"

CHAPTER THIRTY-FIVE

Even before the moon broke free to wash a hesitant pewter along the beach, I knew where I'd find Perry: sitting on the sand opposite Falcon.

"Counting sheep?" I asked, dropping my hand on his shoulder.

"I was worried," he said softly.

"Walk?"

We set off along the track that led to the back of the island and soon reached the beach there. Far away, the resort's lights twinkled through the palm fronds.

"Would you like to tell me about it?" Perry asked.

"I recorded everything. Half the time Dragan spoke in code, and he sure enjoyed making Morfil and Edward squirm. Edward's come up with some sort of career-defining idea for Dragan, that's why Edward's here. Problem is, I have no idea what it is. Oh, and after boasting to me that there's gold here, Morfil told Dragan there wasn't enough to justify mining it."

"Can I listen to the recording tomorrow? I imagine you're exhausted," he said.

"I don't have the strength to walk another step."

"Nor do I." We sat on the sand, and I spread the shawl across our shoulders. "Dragan gave it to me—I wanted to throw it in the ocean but Violet might like it for her nest," I said, nuzzling closer and resting my head on his shoulder.

"I missed you," he whispered.

"I missed *you*," I answered, my fingers flexing against his ribs. I shivered.

"Cold?"

"No."

He turned towards me and slipped an arm around my waist. There was no distance between us, the curves of my body found their mirror in his. The warm air wrapped around us, deflecting the breeze that rode in on the surf. We held each other under the flickering stars as the waves settled to a respectful plush and the noises of the resort died.

But he was still too far away.

Perry whispered, "Teal…I…love…you," and the distance vanished. His warm hands settled on my cheeks, tilting my face. He kissed me gently on the forehead and my pulse quickened.

My hands kneaded his back, fingers circling his muscles, tracing the vertebra of his spine through the soft cotton of his shirt. His firm chest settled against me, and I slid a hand behind his neck and massaged him closer, as I replayed his words in my mind.

Then a butterfly fluttered doubt in my stomach. But it was a false friend, a relic of the unworthy Teal my mother had created in my mind. It had returned to whisper that this couldn't be happening, not to *me*—that I didn't deserve to have something, someone so special. That I was a mistake. I deserved the Edwards of this world. But I breathed in Perry, and exhaled my doubts into the night.

Then I heard it. Closer than before—the music—but this time it danced its song. There were still no words—but a quicker, more joyous beat. A river welled inside me, surging through my body. Courage, certainty. And a glimpse of something immortal banished any remnants of doubt. I waded into the unknown as the world and its problems, pulled back.

"I love you, Peregrine."

I dropped the shawl and lay on it, pulling him down on top of me. The cool sand tickled my legs one grain at a time. Sighing, we blended as I swept the curls of his hair at the base of his neck. Thighs, tummies, hands, shadows locked, unlocked. Locked again. Propped on elbows above me, his kisses came at random, in unguided, clumsy desperation. Mine too. His fingers dragged, caressed my skin, teased as he nibbled my neck, my ears, my soul.

Someone moaned. His lips brushed my eyelashes and we stilled, our pounding hearts pressed close. His tongue drifted along my lips, probed and met mine. Then deeper, swirling kisses and clashing noses. I angled my face and we breathed shared air. We slipped and teased in the eye of the storm. Powerless to resist, unwilling to try, I welcomed the craving that burned inside. He tasted of fire and water. Of eternity.

The storm returned and he moved over me, framed by stars. A hand flattened beneath my back, lifting my hips as he pulled at the last of my dress, my panties. Had the surf risen, was hot wind boiling around us? Fumbling. I tried to help, but I was frantic too. I closed my eyes and felt the universe slide in as we melted into another world. A brief stillness, gasps. My hands gripped his buttocks—then shared rhythms, kisses. Some were long, insistent; others, as light as settling dust. The moaning was back. Louder. But somehow...further away. Then he stopped and whispered in my ear.

"T—too excited."

I giggled, stroked his neck. "It's alright."

Perry rolled onto his back and gently lifted me onto him. His hand slid between us. He teased and stroked, my rhythms countering his slicking fingers. He arched upwards and kissed my breasts, his hot tongue circling. Then he shifted and I glided onto him, his hands now gripped my hips, my knees gouging troughs in the sand. Nothing else mattered as our frenzy built. Locked together, I cried out. His breathing deepened as he tensed, driving upward. I prolonged the moment, holding him as he groaned. The night, the beach, the island faded away as we balanced there, my body, my mind wracked by shuddering.

He cupped my head and we lay still as our breathing settled. I snuggled against his chest, my fingers tracing the line of his cheek, his jaw, rasping lightly against the stubble. I stroked his damp hair, his shoulders as breath by breath, we relaxed. When he sighed, I nuzzled closer. Yes. He was real.

He folded his arms around my shoulders, his legs held mine.

"You're my prisoner," he whispered.

"I hope it's a long sentence."

"Is *life* long enough?"

"No."

I lay there, safe beneath his weight, his heat, vaguely aware of the churning surf and the first notes of bird dawnsong.

*   *   *

I woke in Perry's arms on Falcon, naked but safe in the darkness. Perry stirred behind me and nuzzled the back of my neck. I dropped my hand onto his knee, my fingers circling slowly higher. "Good morning, mister."

"I slept like a baby. Did you?" he asked, pulling me closer.

"Never better," I whispered.

"Shame to waste the *whole* morning," he added playfully.

"You make an excellent point—"

"I make an excellent omelet too!"

"What's the rush?"

We made love again slowly, last night's urgency replaced with teasing, savoring.

It was noon before we showered and dressed. Perry handed me a bowl and six eggs.

"Can you crack these—wait, where's Violet?"

"In the water. She wouldn't make eye contact with me when I wished her good morning," I answered.

Perry laughed, and I began whisking.

"Oh, there might be some cheese in the fridge. I was given some by a passing yacht a couple of…"

I handed him the bowl and opened the fridge. "Got it. I love blue cheese."

"…months ago."

"It's not meant to be this color, is it?"

"Possibly not. Would you believe me if I told you the yacht was called the Alexander Fleming?"

I laughed.

We sat in the cockpit; the omelet was light and fluffy. I complimented him between two large glugs of coffee before saying, "I suppose we ought to get down to business—"

"More? You've exhausted me!"

"What I meant…anything more on Morfil's report?"

Perry's foot rubbed mine beneath the table. "Give me two minutes. I'm busy watching you eat."

"In the unlikely event I have a job to go back to. After seeing Morfil with Dragan, I'm certain I'm on to something."

"Okay, I heard back from Woods Hole. They agree the report skates around the truth, flounders in its logic and exists *solely* as—"

"Perry!"

"It's gibberish. This fishery is already under enormous pressure. Professor Mizugawa pointed out they usually can the lower quality tunas, like albacore and skipjack. But the local fish population doesn't justify building a cannery."

I pulled my iPhone from my bag and hit play. "It's a bit faint at times because it was on my lap but there's something about trawlers on the recording. It's quite long. I'll skip through the boring bits," I said.

We listened together. He frowned and shook his head when Dragan mentioned the krill mining, muttering that they were destroying the base of the food-chain.

When the recording ended, he said, "Quite a collection of low-lifes."

"Tell me about it."

"You did so well—I could never have got through the evening without blowing a gasket. The recording raises a lot of questions."

"Such as?"

He lifted his note pad. "For example, 'compromise stability…reinforced decking and davits'. What's that about?"

"Exactly! So…what *is* a davit?"

"A small crane carried on a ship. So this is the prototype of a trawler and it's on its way for testing. But what are they planning to lift onto a ship that needs a reinforced deck? There's mention of adding more trawlers when the business model has proved itself, but we don't know what the intended cargo is. And there's nothing about these waters that justifies a fleet of trawlers, let alone modified ones. A trawler's a trawler, a tuna's a tuna. And that bit about someone called Teodoro and two hundred mill a year. Any idea who he is?"

"Afraid not," I said.

"What we know is Dragan and his survey ship are here because of all this, and Poseidon is the code word. But what on earth are they up to?"

He tapped the pad with the pencil. After a minute, he said, "Drawing a complete blank. No reports of ocean floor minerals here and I can't think what else it could be."

"What about a pipeline—maybe gas or oil from somewhere to somewhere else. A terminal here?"

"Interesting idea but why use trawlers? I'll check the map and geology just in case. Anything else of interest?"

I told him about the Time magazine Frank dropped overboard.

Perry read from his notes. "'There's no such thing as coincidence. As usual, they'll achieve nothing.' So some people who featured in Time are trying to stop Dragan. Sounds as if Frank may know who they are."

"We'll need to ask him. My journalistic intuition's on red alert. Clearly, Morfil's involved. Which means one thing. I need to check out his office."

"Correction: Make that *we* need to check it out as we make a pretty good team."

I smiled. "Thanks—the support will be most welcome."

"Getting there undetected will be difficult. Morfil would know if we took the island hopper because of his spy network. We'd be arrested in five minutes. Make that *impossible*. I hate to admit it but I'm stumped."

"It doesn't look good, does it?"

"And even if we got there, how would we get into his office?" Then he asked, "Teal, why are you smiling?"

CHAPTER THIRTY-SIX

The blue of the ocean sparkled in Perry's eyes while his fingers smoothed sunblock on my midriff, explaining sunburned tummies were the worst.

I had pushed the report to the deepest recesses of my mind because my world was upside down. And I liked that. Right now, as the afternoon sun warmed Falcon's cockpit, Thurston Morfil and Sir Basil Thane hardly existed.

"I was wondering if you'd like to move aboard Falcon, with me. I know it's cramped here and gets pretty hot in the day. I may not be the tidiest person but—"

I kissed him on the cheek. "Thank you. I'd love to, but something tells me it's better if they don't know about us, and you can be sure they'll be watching. As soon as Edward and Dragan have gone…"

"In which case, I'd like you to change rooms."

"The sooner the better. I don't trust Edward. Any of them, in fact. It could even be bugged."

"Look—smoke from the survey vessel. Is it moving?" Perry asked. "In the mood for a sail, Teal?"

"Rhetorical question?"

Sails fluttering in an uncertain breeze, we passed through the gap in the reef and followed the surveyor. "I can't keep up, but I want to know where they're going." He handed me binoculars.

I struggled to keep them level in the rolling ocean. "A few crew moving around."

"We can't get too close or we'll spook them."

"I can see its name. It's called…*The Bottom Line*."

"How predictable. Anything else?"

"Men on the stern. They may be watching us. They're removing a tarpaulin from something. Bright yellow. Round windows."

"Mini-sub?"

"Guess so."

"We'll just shadow them and try to look innocent. Prepare to tack." He turned the wheel and I released rope from a winch. The boom swung over our heads and I pulled in a rope on the other side till Perry said, "Perfect". When the sails filled again, we picked up speed.

"Feels like we're doing about ten miles per hour," I said.

"Actually, it only feels fast because you're close to the water. I'm guessing about three knots."

Fifteen minutes later, he tacked again and this time I was able to organize the ropes and set the sails on the new course with no help at all. The boat creaked and the water sloshed on Falcon's hull, and I wanted to stay here forever. But we were heading back towards The Bottom Line. Time to focus.

"I think it's slowing...yes, it's stopped. They're launching the sub. Okay, I've seen what I came for," Perry said.

Falcon's VHF radio crackled. *"Falcon, Falcon. This is survey vessel The Bottom Line, on channel sixteen. Falcon, you are in a restricted zone. You are required to exit the area immediately. Repeat. You are required to exit the area immediately. Over."*

I raised the binoculars. "Guys running around on deck. One's waving something. No, it can't be!"

"Leave immediately? What's that about?" Perry turned the wheel and Falcon's nose swung slowly away. "Just when you need wind, it dies!"

"Perry, some of them have...guns!"

"You sure? Why—there are no restricted zones around here!"

"Falcon. Falcon. This is survey vessel The Bottom Line. We are on official government business. You are required to exit the area immediately. If you fail to do so, your actions will be deemed hostile. Repeat. Your actions will be deemed hostile. Over."

"Hostile?" He turned to me. "Are they *on something*? Take the wheel!" He ducked below deck and returned with lifejackets.

"Put this on, just in case." He picked up the radio handset. "The Bottom Line. This is Falcon. Switch channel seven-two. Over."

Perry looked at me. "Don't they understand VHF protocol? Channel sixteen is the emergency channel. They should change immediately."

"The Bottom Line. This is Falcon on channel sixteen. Unaware area is restricted. Exiting area as fast as possible under sail but wind is unpredictable. Repeat, wind is unpredictable. Over."

I raised the binoculars. "They've launched some kind of motorboat. And I think...it's coming this way."

"They're probably just going to read us the riot act. Confirm our identity. Maybe issue some sort of fine—but what for? Teal, I don't know what they're—" He lifted the handset. "Sun and Moon. Sun and Moon.

213

This is Falcon on channel sixteen. Over."

The motorboat closed fast, bouncing from wave to wave, hurling spray with each impact. Engines hammering, the boat had soon halved the distance between.

"Quick, port side lazarette. Orange box."

I opened the locker under the cockpit seats Perry had indicated and passed him an orange box.

The flare gun was orange too. With horror I watched him load a stubby cartridge. "I hope we don't need this," he said.

"Yacht Falcon. Yacht Falcon. This is Sun and Moon. Switch channel seven-two."

"Yacht Falcon switching channel seven-two. Over."

"Falcon, Falcon, all okay out there, mate? Over."

"Survey vessel The Bottom Line claims we are in a restricted area and have launched a tender. Is this area restricted, Kris? Over."

"Not that I am aware of. Will await developments. Over."

"Thanks, chum. Yacht Falcon. Out." Perry replaced the handset.

I pointed at the charging tender. "Are they going to *ram* us?" I shouted, moving to the stern and copying Perry by snap-hooking the tether of my life jacket to one of the metal fittings by the wheel.

The motorboat bounded closer, aiming directly for the middle of Falcon's side. I could see the faces of the men who drove it, braced behind a raked windshield.

"They *can't* be serious." Perry said.

The motorboat reared above us like a stallion. I threw myself down as its engines screamed. At the last second it twisted sideways to flash past the stern. A sheet of spray flew over Falcon and we bucked in its wake. Then the tender turned and, pointing like a bull, charged again. It came flat and fast, shying away to cut across our bow. Falcon pitched and rolled in protest, water sloshing around the cockpit at our feet.

Perry said, "Hang on tight. They're just trying to scare us."

"It's working!" I said.

The tender stopped and swung its bow towards us again.

Perry stood, pointing at the sagging sails. "There's no wind, you *idiots*," he shouted. "If it's so important to you, we'll leave under power."

Two men dressed in white uniforms faced us. One of them was on the radio. Then the tender reared up and swung back towards the survey ship.

"Despite their efforts to terrify us, a piece of the jigsaw may just have fallen into place," Perry said slowly.

"Why do you say that?"

We were soaked and water was still draining off the deck. Perry bundled me in his arms. I hugged back.

"That was too close." He pulled back and framed my face with his hands, tracing my lips with his thumbs. "I. Can't. Lose. You."

I kissed his lips, my hand on his collar bone. "I'm fine. Really. But what do you now know?"

"Firstly, one of those men will be easy to identify—did you see his face?"

"Looked like he was seriously injured. His hair was sort of…lopsided." I said.

"Whatever they're up to, they're deadly serious about it. Not 'patch things up over a drink' sort of fellows, are they?"

"And secondly?"

Perry didn't smile. "I don't know what it means. But you remember that deep trench in the sea floor we fished over? The survey vessel just lowered the submarine into it."

CHAPTER THIRTY-SEVEN

"Thank you, Kris. This room's great."

"My pleasure," he said, adjusting Luna's sling. He rubbed her back until she burped, a smile meandering across her face. "Housekeeping, AKA yours truly, needs to bring fresh towels so I'll be back when I've fixed the shower in room seven. Meanwhile I'm still trying to make sense of what Perry told me about—"

There was a knock on the door.

I took Perry's hand and led him in. "Hello, mister." I whispered. "Nice to see you."

"I was saying to Teal, I can't believe they'd try to scare you guys like that. Thank God, no one was hurt," Kris said. "It used to be all peace and harmony around here. How could everything have changed so quickly?"

"Not *everything* that's going on around here's bad news," I said, slipping my arm around Perry's waist.

Kris's face lit up. "Wow! So it's official! I *was* wondering about you guys, but didn't want to pry."

I kissed Perry on the cheek.

"This calls for a celebration! I'll send over a bottle of my finest Chateau Horseshoe Cabernet Crab Claw."

"After my experience with the 2012, my doctor specifically—"

Kris laughed. "No offense, mate! But the way things are going, I may not have much to celebrate soon."

"Your lease?" Perry asked.

"I had to tell a party of divers Black Jack's dead. They canceled their booking."

"I'm sorry, chum," Perry said. His tone changed. "Maybe it was a test to see if the gun worked. Or do these people get a kick out of killing anything they can—the more endangered or precious, the better?"

"Or he just wanted to show off to Dragan," I suggested. "You should have seen the inside of the yacht. A taxidermist's wet dream."

Kris was pacing the room. "I found where the bastard hid the gun case—he dug a hole in a remote spot in the scrub and covered it with palms leaves and stones. Guess he didn't want to leave it in your room overnight, Teal."

"No way Dragan comes all this way to test a speargun. And why are they surveying the trench, talking modified trawlers and people being too late to stop them? I have a bad, bad feeling about this," I said. "And I'm meant to write up Morfil as a local hero, but he's up to his threaded eyebrows in it. I've *got* to take a look 'round his office—it's all I've got. But it has bars on the windows and a reinforced door. That's assuming I could get there undetected."

"He seems really worried about being burgled," Kris said.

"And he's about to add security cameras and an alarm system—he's got something to hide, I can feel it," I said.

"What's stupid is that by throwing their weight around, they've made you even more determined to get to the bottom of this," Perry said.

"Mate, they're probably watching us now. Who knows what surveillance equipment they've got on those vessels."

"Okay, so Morfil's office is on the main island. We know that flying there's way too risky, so it's by boat or not at all. We'll have to go at night and be back before dawn. But Coconut and Falcon are too slow. Wait a minute!" I stared at Kris.

"Don't even ask, Teal. You know the answer—"

"Come on, it's the only way," I said.

"I can't."

"She's right Kris. Spada's our only hope." Perry said.

"Sorry, guys." He looked at us in turn. "I really am."

"It can run seventy plus, long range fuel tanks, cuddy cabin. We'd be back before dawn—no problem!" Perry said.

"Correction. *Big* problem. Stefano may be in Rome but he'll go bananas if he finds out. I wouldn't let anyone else block my freezer with a swordfish, but my number one client gets whatever he wants around here and he knows it. I'm strictly banned from using his boat except in an emergency. And what if Thurstonella found out? Remember my lease is—"

"This *is* an emergency," I said.

"Killing Black Jack was repulsive. But it's not enough. I could lose everything. I can't risk doing that to Emma and Luna."

"Dragan's about to hit this place with a fleet of modified trawlers and you can bet he isn't doing it to feed the poor. Morfil's commissioned a laughable marine resource report. And bringing a survey vessel here—well, it's got to be something to do with the habitat, and my gut's screaming at me it's bad news," I continued.

"Come on, chum. If what they're doing decimates the eco-tourism—you won't have a resort to lose. We'll take heavy tackle. Pretend we're after broadbill." Perry turned to me. "Broadbill swordfish. You fish for them at night."

"At least *that* part of this mad plan makes a little sense," Kris said.

Perry squeezed my shoulder. "Problem solved!"

"Not so fast. Once they have you on radar, they'll launch a chopper—you won't be able to outrun *that*. As you ignored their last warning, they'll be a lot less friendly this time. Teal, you said you saw guns on the survey vessel. If you're right, I bet they aren't scared to use them. If they're prepared to charge Falcon and kill Black Jack, it's because they think they can do whatever they like. Remember, they've got the biggest guy in the islands in their pocket. For them, it's not a big step from killing a fish to killing a—"

"Can we jam their radar?" I asked.

"I don't know how to jam it—but I can lose it. We'll run in shadow," said Perry.

"You mean like some sort of cloaking device?" I asked.

"Yes—in a low tech way. Radar's blocked by solid objects like islands, so there are places they'd be blind. Called 'radar shadow'. We can head in one direction, slip behind an island and change course. We could run most of the way unseen. It's just the first few miles we'd be in the open."

"Mate, you'll be sitting ducks," Kris said, shaking his head. "Still too risky. And there's not much moon. What if you hit a reef?"

"Come on—you *know* Perry knows these waters backwards. And he's got night vision goggles on Falcon."

"So, let's say you *do* make it without crashing onto a reef. When you're close to land, someone will hear the engines."

Perry's brow creased. "I'll check the tide times, but we could come in on a flood tide just before high water, so we can cut the engines and paddle the last bit. We'll leave when it's falling. In complete silence."

"That's all very clever, but how exactly do you intend getting into Thurstonella's office?" Kris asked.

"We'll have to break in, grab and run. No other choice. Make it look like a cheap burglary. Away before they can respond," Perry said.

"Way too dangerous. What if the place has security guards?" Kris asked. "Did you see any, Teal?"

"Only a guy who raised the entrance barrier of the compound. I remember Morfil asked after someone called 'Benchley'."

"Any idea who that was?"

"Nope. But it's not an islander name, is it? Anyway, none of that means there'll be anyone there at night."

"None of that means there *won't* be, either," Kris said. "I hate to say this, but I'm not sure you *could* break in. Remember Teal said the door was reinforced and there were bars on the windows."

"See? It's not a plan, it's a kamikaze run. I'm sorry, mate. I'd love to help but..."

Perry looked down. "There *must* be a way. *Has* to be." His voice tailed away.

"We can get there unseen by running in radar shadow and dodge the reefs using night goggles. So the only problem's getting past the security door, right?" I asked.

"That's still a show-stopper," Kris said.

"What if you could get the door keypad number?" I asked in my most innocent tone.

"Brilliant! I'll phone Thurstonella and ask for it," Kris said dryly.

"I know the code," I said.

"You know the code?" Perry asked.

"I know the code."

"She knows the code?" Kris echoed.

"Apparently...she knows the code!" said Perry, putting an arm around me. Then he turned and looked at me, eyes wide. "What are you talking about, Teal?"

"When he showed me around his office, you don't think I just stood there, do you? I watched him punch in the code and I have a great memory."

Perry laughed. "That, I believe, is checkmate, chum!"

Before Kris could speak, my new hotel room phone rang. I picked it up. "Hello?"

"Where's my report on Thurston Morfil?"

"Excuse me?"

"Teal Douglas?"

"Sir...Sir Basil?"

"What's going on down there? Have you forgotten you're on an important assignment? And you're late."

"Not at all, it's just that—"

"Malcolm keeps trying to fob me off. Listen carefully because I'm not going to repeat this. It's 9 p.m. here. If I don't have it first thing tomorrow morning—that's 6 a.m. my time—well, I don't think I need to spell out what action I would take, Ms. Douglas."

"I fully understand. But—" The line went dead.

They were staring at me. "Great," I said, breathing deeply as I collected my thoughts. "He's super-hot for it. That should have been Sigvard, or Malcolm. Since when does Sir Basil Thane call the lowly foot soldiers? Now I've got the afternoon and evening to finish the report. But how can I when I have no idea what to put in it, and the only possible lead I have is Morfil's office?"

"Can you buy a few days? Tell him you're still researching?" Kris asked.

"Already played that card. Now I'm out of time. Morfil said the security cameras and alarm system would be fitted by the end of the week. Today's Wednesday and even that's cutting it a bit fine. It has to be tonight. So either I get a meaningless report to Sir Basil on time, or I ignore his deadline and lose my job."

"I'm sorry, but I still haven't said you can take Spada," Kris said. He frowned as he kissed Luna's forehead. "Don't bother growing up, little mermaid. Adulthood isn't all it's cracked up to be."

Then he stared at the wall and shook his head.

"Kris?" I asked.

"I was remembering how I ended up here. I thought this place would be a perfect antidote to the stress of my last job. Then you two team up and I'm back to square one!"

"What did you do before?" I asked.

"Eight years ago, I was scaling the greasy corporate ladder of an advertising agency. My life was fueled by the three 'Cs': cigarettes, caffeine and coke. Don't ask which kind of coke. The race was dead level coming up to the finishing line."

"What race?"

"Whether I'd make their youngest ever director or drop dead of a heart attack first. Then I spent a long weekend on a boat in the Bay of Islands for a stag party. Sandy, the best man—or *Sandals* as we called him— was a super grounded guy and there was no booze, no drugs, no strippers. I remember him asking me why I was working myself to death. He said if life was about anything, it was about choices. His exact words? 'The day will come when we must all decide who we are and what we believe in.'" He kissed the baby's forehead and whispered into her ear, "You know what, Luna? Godfather Sandals probably saved Daddy's life."

"Amazing story, Kris," I said.

"I wouldn't go *that* far. Mildly interesting, would be more accurate," Perry said with a mischievous smile.

"You don't understand. Basil Thane said the same thing to me about choices and deciding what we stand for. And Kris—"

"Walked into that one, didn't I?" Kris said.

"Afraid so. So—are you going to help us?"

"This calls for a head-clearing stroll along the beach. As this could impact on our futures, I have to bounce it off Emma." He said his goodbyes. "She's got the deciding vote."

Perry took my hand and pulled me close. When I didn't respond, he tipped my chin up with a finger.

"What's wrong?"

"Would you give me a minute?"

"Take your time."

I walked across the room, opened the door and stepped outside. I could see wavelets shushing around the delicate legs of a snow-white egret that stalked the shallows. I'll stay here until she catches a fish, I thought.

The bird rubbed its head on its shoulders then high-stepped as if walking on hot coals. It stopped and its neck inched forward. In a flash of silver beak, it stabbed the water and lifted a twisting minnow.

"Like it or not, Basil, I've made my decision," I said.

The egret turned its head and looked me straight in the eye.

Perry was leaning on the door frame when I returned. I slid my arms around him. As we kissed my fingers smoothed across his chest.

What we were planning was dangerous—of course it was. But around him, I didn't just feel safe—I felt *immortal.* Teal Douglas, sent here to interview a VIP, instead falls in love and starts planning a midnight raid on the VIP's office. I squeezed Perry and looked up into his eyes.

"Did I ever tell you my phobia?" I whispered in his ear.

"Nope."

"Clinophobia."

"Clinos? They're the worst."

"It's a gut wrenching, nerve tingling fear of…going to bed."

"Poor, poor Teal, that sounds *terrible.* Is there a treatment?" he asked, studying the bed with interest.

"Incurable. And it's *much* worse when I'm alone. In a new hotel room. Foot massages help."

"Alone? In a new hotel room?"

He scooped me up and tipped me onto the crisp sheets, where I bounced, giggling. Perry crawled beside me, then ran his thumb along the underside of my leg, from my hip all the way down to my heel.

"Do you think Emma will say yes?" I asked.

"To what?"

"To lending us Spada."

He lifted my foot to his shoulder and slowly, ever so slowly, began kissing the instep…

"What's a Spada?"

"No idea."

CHAPTER THIRTY-EIGHT

Frank put his drink down and rested his elbows on the beach bar to steady the binoculars. "Survey vessel's back beside the yacht and that's the third trip between them by tender. Whatever they're up to is keeping them busy."

"Any ideas?" Nancy asked.

"No," said Perry. "And a chopper was launched an hour ago. I fired off an email to Woods Hole on sea floor trenches, but they came up blank too. Oh, and Teal, I bounced your pipeline idea off them but they said it didn't add up." He slapped the bar. "I feel guilty admitting I wish I'd been in their mini-sub. Just to see what it's like down there!"

"I hope this doesn't sound too romantic..." I said.

They turned to face me.

"But could it be treasure? Obviously, it couldn't be another *Atocha*, not out here."

"Best idea I've heard all day," Frank said.

"Atocha?" asked Perry.

"A Spanish galleon that sank off the Florida Keys. They salvaged gazillions of dollars of gold and silver. Of course the Spanish came nowhere near here. But what if a ship with a valuable cargo *did* sink here, maybe in the war?"

"It's possible," Perry began. "But I haven't heard any rumors of treasure in these waters, so if you're right, they've hushed it up. Anyway, the trench is very deep. It would have to be super valuable to justify trying to recover something from it."

"Correct me if I'm rusty on my maritime law, but the trench isn't in international waters, so any treasure would belong to the islands—not to Dragan," said Frank.

"But Morfil can do what he likes around here," I said. "So maybe they'd just split the profits."

"But treasure isn't Dragan's style," Frank added.

We sat in silence until Nancy wondered aloud if there were records anywhere detailing local shipwrecks. Perry's distant look suggested he was in a mini-sub chasing halibut (or whatever swims down there). When I looked at Frank, I wondered about something he'd just said.

"Frank, you mentioned Dragan's *style*."

"Just a hunch. But an industrialist fiddling around with sunken treasure? Struck me as out of character."

Then Nancy said, "Every day I love this place more. Now it's got a new mystery to add to Teal's ghost."

"Oh, I may have figured out the ghost," I said. "I'm reading an old document on the story of Fonu. I think the ghost is him."

Emma breezed over. "Good morning, what a heaven-sent day!" She addressed Frank. "No problem with your flights. All organized."

"You're not leaving us, are you?" I asked.

"No. Just added an extra week. Unfinished business."

"Oh?" Perry asked.

"Migratory bird count. And I need better photos of local invertebrates."

"Okay—gotta fly, peeps. Levitation practice. If you need me, I'll be back down in an hour, thermal updrafts permitting."

Frank's mouth fell open.

Emma smiled. "Just kidding. I'm midwifing Seraphina. Her contractions have started and her last pregnancy was a multiple birth."

"How exciting, was it twins? Triplets?" Nancy asked.

"Quattrodecaplets," Emma said over her shoulder. "Fourteen baby stingrays."

When we'd stopped laughing, I looked at Frank. "May I ask you a question?"

"Shoot."

I hesitated, choosing my words with care.

"When we arrived you dropped a copy of Time over the side of Coconut—forgive me Frank—Edward said it wasn't an accident. I told him he was being ridiculous but at dinner on the yacht, he gave Dragan a copy of the same issue—I recognized the cover. They mentioned some people Dragan knew who were too late to stop him. Does that make any sense?"

Nancy came to his rescue. "Can I just say that...we've met Dragan before?"

"When you say *met*, do you mean *crossed swords*?" Perry asked.

Frank laughed. "Shucks. We've been rumbled, Pumpkin."

"Are you comfortable talking about it?" I asked.

"I'll make an exception. We don't like the way he runs his businesses. No sir, not one bit. So we bought one share in Dragan Global and one in quite a few other mega-corporations too. Means we can go to their annual stockholder meetings—they can't stop us attending. Or asking difficult questions."

"*They?*" I asked.

"We own one share in twenty-eight environmentally unethical corporations," Nancy explained. "We spend a lot of our time finding out what they're up to."

"Has Dragan ever been exposed?" Perry asked. "Journalists love stories like this."

"Too clever, too well connected. From Wall Street to the Senate to the Federal Reserve to Bilderberg to the Illuminati and I expect in hell itself, this guy's got powerful friends. Not only friends—people he has something on, people who owe him a favor. His network is global," Frank said.

"And Thurston Morfil? How does he fit in?" I asked.

"He's a nobody. Petty crook. Sure, he thinks he's a big shot around here but to Dragan he's as significant as a flea on a dog's butt. If you'll excuse my language," Frank added.

"So you two made Time's list of environmentalists," I said. "Congratulations!"

"We don't like drawing attention to ourselves, do we dear? That's why Frank had to drop the magazine overboard."

"So you're both here by chance?" I asked.

"Depends what you mean by chance. We spend a lot of time in pristine and struggling habitats. Sooner or later the Dragans of this world always show up," Frank said.

"Look," Nancy said, pointing.

A tender from Apex Predator sped towards the dock.

"Nice of them to ignore the speed limit," Perry said.

"May I, Frank?" Perry lifted the binoculars and followed them in. "Crew. Wonder what they want."

The tender docked and two men in naval whites jumped out. Then they strode towards us. Even from afar, I sensed the military precision in their strides as they straight-lined for the bar. They sat opposite us and ordered cold beers—emphasizing the word "cold". The one on the left was shorter and thick chested, with a forward slump of the shoulders and a backward slump of the forehead. Sandy hair stubbled across a bulldog face.

The other, wiry, olive-skinned, with a tilted beret of muddy hair and an angry scar that split his hairline, glared at us from his good eye.

After a few minutes, Bulldog nodded in our direction. "Sailing good around here, boy?"

"Can be," Perry answered cheerily.

"That wooden thing yours, is it?" Poodle asked.

"Chinese have a word for boats like that," Bulldog said.

"Very funny," said Perry.

I caught the look on Nancy's face as she squeezed Frank's hand.

"You need to update your charts, boy. There's a new restricted zone out there."

Perry turned his bar stool away. "As I was saying, Ms. Douglas, if you'll excuse me, I have to check the fishing equipment. My favorite rod needs attention."

"You ignoring my friendly advice, boy?"

"We have to get back too," Nancy said, as she pulled on Frank's arm.

"I'll walk with you, if you don't mind. I need to send an email," I said.

When they were beyond earshot, Perry said, "Those were the guys who half-sunk Falcon. So now Dragan's spying on us. My guess is ex-mercenaries. By their accents, maybe an Israeli and a South African."

"And maybe they aren't genuine crew," I suggested.

"Why do you say that?"

"The speargun was developed for the Israeli military, so they might work for them," I said.

Perry studied Apex Predator. "They could have Hitler, Bin Laden and Pol Pot aboard, for all we'd know."

"Is it a problem we've been seen together?" I asked.

"I'm sure they already know. But I fed them the line about fishing in case they spot us tonight. In fact, I'd better change the sparkplugs and oil in Spada's outboards, check it's all fueled up too. Then get the equipment loaded aboard."

"What time should we meet on the dock? I'll wear dark clothes." When he didn't respond, I asked, "Everything okay?"

"I rarely take so instant a dislike to anyone, but those two!"

Squeezing his hand, I said, "When this is over, I'll be able to give your favorite rod all the attention it deserves."

He laughed. "As it happens we have a long night ahead of us. We really should try to have a nap this afternoon."

CHAPTER THIRTY-NINE

Perry puffed up the pillows behind him and I settled back against his naked torso. His arms closed around mine as a rain shower beat against the windows of my new A-frame's bedroom. Like a crab burying itself in the sand, I wriggled to get more comfortable, to increase the number of places our bodies touched.

"Will the rain be a problem?" I asked.

"I checked—passing showers that will clear soon."

I sighed.

"You're worried about the Morfil story, aren't you?"

"I know there's stuff I don't know, but I don't know how much, or what it is I don't know. It's an epistemological conundrum."

"Wow!" Perry said. "I think, in your case, making love must *increase* blood flow to the brain. Oxford taught me some long words, but I've forgotten most of them."

"Any you remember?"

"Bet you don't know the meaning of...'eschatology'."

I asked him to spell it. "Just checking I didn't mishear you. Give me a clue?"

"Something I think about a lot."

"Me?" I asked, trying to sound serious.

"I was referring to its alternative meaning: the end of the world, the end of humankind. As in sorry, time's up. We screwed up."

"As in the end of Teal the journalist when Basil Thane doesn't get his report?"

He leaned over and kissed my shoulder. His fingers entwined with mine. "That could even be for the best. New beginnings and all that. Just like a passing storm that washes away the old and allows in the new."

"I don't follow."

"I suppose I'm posing a question. The planet's on the ropes. What could stop it getting knocked down for the count?"

"Some sort of counter attack? Wait—a disguised attack. What you said about 'taking your opponent's mind'?"

He laughed. "Makes sense. And you know what? I *do* have a theory."

"About how we can save the planet? I'm all ears."

He ran his fingers through my hair. "I don't know—it's so obvious, and yet when I used to tell people, they'd always laugh at me."

"I won't. I promise."

"Maybe one day. As long as you keep that promise." He kissed the top of my head. "I better be going," Perry said, rolling out of bed. I watched him dress, spellbound by the light slipping across his shoulders, his stomach. He leant over and kissed me gently on the lips. "I'll see myself out." He blew me another kiss before closing the door behind him.

Eschatology? Something that Perry thinks could stop the destruction of the whole planet from happening? I held the image of this man in my mind. The blue of his eyes, the spontaneous smile, the joking little boy, blessed with a panther's physique. And then there was his serious side.

"Yes, Lizzie. Life can change so suddenly, can't it?"

I climbed out of bed and returned with Kris's scrapbook. I didn't need more background, but I pretended to myself that Fonu's story might shed some unexpected light on Morfil, on what he and his buddies were up to. In fact, I was curious as to what became of the unfortunate Fonu and Losa who I had left clinging to Whaling Rock in a raging storm. Then another thought came: If I was really lucky, maybe these old typed pages held a clue to whatever was valuable in the ocean floor trench...

"Losa!" Fonu shouted. "Don't let go!"

He tightened his grip and heaved until his muscles screamed in pain, easing Losa closer. Then a towering wave reared up behind Fonu and collapsed on him in fury. Fonu tumbled forward, gulping air, as he struggled not to be swept off. One of Losa's hands was wrenched from his.

"Grab hold!" he shouted, his words smothered by spray. "You can do it!"

But the swell twisted her body, dragging her free hand beyond his reach.

The black ocean bulged around her as another great wave crashed over the rock.

"Fonu!" she spluttered, "I can't—"

"You must!"

A wall of water thundered over the rock, knocking Fonu flat. But he still held Losa, though her grip felt feeble as the waves bounced her against the unyielding stone. Then the water troughed around the rock, doubling Losa's weight.

"Hold on," he shouted, but her fingers slipped from his.

Fonu lunged forward, arms flailing as she disappeared into the cauldron. She surfaced twenty feet away, the current carrying her away.

"I must be with you," he yelled, unknotting the rope from his waist. "We will drown together. That way we will always be together in the Ocean of Souls."

"Fonu, we cannot both die. There is important work to do! I beg you not to join me. Not yet. Promise me—"

"Losa!" he shouted.

"Promise! Or all your carving—all we have learned—will be for nothing."

Losa's head disappeared in the churning foam. When she surfaced, her eyes were locked on his. Fonu saw her forehead was creased in pain, the terror in her bulging eyes. Then a whirlpool, like a black funnel opened around her, and with a guttural belch, dragged her down.

Fonu stood open-mouthed as the whirlpool clamped shut. Too cold to shiver, he sank down as his legs betrayed him. Tears streamed from his bloodshot eyes. "No!" he moaned. "No!"

With his hands clamped over his face, he sobbed. Once he thought he heard a voice—and he jumped up, searching near and far as he called her name, but there was no one there. He sobbed until he lost control of his breathing and convulsed like a choking man. Stooped, broken, he looked again at the ravaged ocean that had already dropped a foot with the tide. He shivered, staring at the settling waves, at the racing current that had carried Losa's body into its depths.

An hour later he spoke again, his voice level. "I will do this for you, Losa."

The canoe had capsized on its tether. He dragged it up the side of the rock, turned it over to drain the water and then pushed it back into the ocean.

The whales were close when he heard them blow.

A mother and calf—easy targets for the whalers—passed a stone's throw from the rock. Fonu sprung into the canoe and paddled towards the horizon. Losa was gone—he would not let them kill whales too.

Fonu drove himself on until his arms ached and his lungs screamed. The salt burned his blistered hands. He did not rest until he had put a great distance between him and the whales. Then he pulled a rocket-flare from the box; striking a match, fumbled with the fuse. He cursed—it was soaking wet.

Fonu pulled out the second rocket-flare and squinted at the distant island. Had they seen him leave the rock? Was that smoke climbing from Aroha's funnel? This time sparks sizzled from the fuse but, when they reached the base of the rocket, they spluttered and died.

Fonu angled the last rocket-flare towards the horizon—at an imaginary target furthest from Horseshoe. He twisted around to see Aroha had lifted anchor and was rolling forward. He struck the match.

"Please, please light!" he said.

I answered the telephone on the seventh ring.

"Hello?"

The voice was deep, heavily accented. "Ms. Teal Douglas? This is Chief Inspector Temotu. I am acting on recently acquired intelligence. Before I continue—would you like to call your lawyer?"

"What?"

"You are advised under mandate 452/b clause 7 of the Alien Criminal Justice Code that this conversation is being recorded. Your answers will be evaluated via polygraph and may be used in a court of law. Do you understand?"

"Are you *serious?*"

"First question: Do you like Four Seasons pizza with three cheeses and cold beer followed by—"

"Perry!" I laughed.

"Help! I need rescuing. Just leaving the bar."

"Who from?"

"Storage tent in twenty? Need to feed Violet first."

"See you there."

"Did I mention, I love you?"

"No, no, I don't believe so," I said.

"I love you, Teal."

"I love you, Perry."

The line went dead and for a minute I didn't move as I smiled at the warmth that flooded through me. I looked at the papers on my lap and then my watch. I had enough time to finish the story.

The last fuse burned well, and the rocket-flare shot from the canoe in a great hiss of sparks. It weaved across the sky ahead of a trail of smoke, dropping into the ocean nearly a mile away. Aroha's bow turned to follow the flare, just as Fonu had hoped. Now the whales would survive! Or at least they had a chance of surviving. Fonu picked up the paddle and began the long journey home, his mind awash with Losa. He wiped his eyes with the back of his hand and paddled on.

Why had it ended like this? What could he have done differently? Had his refusal to bow to his father's will cost Losa her life? He could have joined her in the ocean, for all eternity—but she'd begged him not to. She'd said he had important work to do and like a fool, a coward, he'd believed her. He laughed. "Important work? My carvings. All we have learned—what does any of that matter now?"

As he closed on Horseshoe, he whispered, "Losa, I wish you hadn't made me promise."

The threatening blue of the deeps blended with welcoming turquoise as Fonu paddled through the gap in the reef. The crowd had reassembled on the beach. When he was close enough for them to see that Losa was missing, he shipped the paddle and stood. He climbed carefully until one foot was on each gunnel, to raise himself as high above the water as possible. Though a hundred yards away, he tried to look into the eyes of each and every islander—those who had dismissed him, scorned him. The few who had supported him too. Until he faced his father. Then, holding the Chief's eyes, with a mighty spring, he dived off the canoe and plunged in.

The crowd watched the breaking surf in silence. In time, people spoke, at first in whispers. A boy said no one could hold their breath this long, a woman sobbed that he must have drowned. Another was certain he'd been devoured by a shark. A man shouted Fonu's name and others joined in. When the Chief raised his cane, they ignored him. But still Fonu did not appear.

Minutes passed. Finally an elder asked if warriors could be sent to find the body and retrieve the drifting canoe. The Chief sat quite still on the sand, his eyes locked on the surf.

Two warriors waded into the water, but the Chief called them back: He said that it was better the ocean, which had already claimed Losa, should keep his son too.

When the Great Chief of the Islands finally stood late that afternoon, the beach was deserted. It had taken sixteen years, but the curse of the whale that had died during Fonu's birth had come true.

Shoulders slumped, the Chief walked back to his hut. With a final glance at the ocean, he said, "My people will never forget this terrible day. And nor will I. They will remember it as the day my only surviving son, Fonu, showed he was not fit to be called an islander, let alone Chief."

I placed the document gently on the table beside me. Mystery solved—now I understood why Fonu was an outcast and a laughing stock. It made sense: the non-conformist son, the chief pulled in different directions by his paternal love and his deep sense of responsibility. A tragedy you could probably drop into any era and it would ring true. As I'd feared, it hadn't provided new insights into Thurston Morfil or the trench. What it had done, however, was remind me of the poignancy of love. I thought of Perry. *Thank you, Universe.*

I left the room and walked up the beach towards the bar and storage tent. I passed Lorraine who wobbled past in high heels and a floaty silk ensemble that looked way more Palm Beach than *this* beach. Ignoring my greeting, she was looking up and down the beach for someone.

The adventure ahead made me light-headed: a radar-dodging, high speed boat ride at night to search a VIP's office, back by dawn, hopefully undetected, with *him*. I knew that if we were arrested, with both Morfil and the government in Dragan's pocket, no one would come to our aid anytime soon. But it sure beat office politics, award ceremonies and deadlines!

Nearing the storage tent, a soft noise stopped me.

"Psssssssssssst!"

"Perry?"

I ducked through the canvas opening. "Why are you hiding in here?"

"Loitering within tent," he said.

"You sure you aren't loitering with intent?"

He laughed. "*That* can be arranged. That French woman gone?"

"I passed her a minute ago. She was heading for reception. With intent."

He lifted an enormous fishing reel to his ear and turned the handle, to better hear the silken purr of the ratchet. It clunked.

"My latest triumph," he said.

"You fixed it? And look, you clever man, you've even got some spare parts," I said, nodding at a couple of orphaned gears and washers on the woven mat beside him.

"Must they over-engineer everything?"

"Why are you playing the mechanic?"

"I was in here when those goons walked in and started nosing around. I had to look busy so I started taking the reel apart, as part of our cover. Now I need to work out how to put it back together properly."

"No, you don't," I said, moving closer.

"No, I don't."

I dropped down beside him on the mat. My fingers traced his lips, and I brought my face up to his. I kissed him as if we had all the time in the world. I tucked my hand inside his shirt to run my hands over his abs. His fingers, light as flitting butterflies, crept around my waist.

I broke free. "Coming up for air!" I gasped, fanning my face. "Wow! You do terrible things to my blood pressure."

When the room came back into focus, I said, "I like it here." I studied the stainless winches and coiled ropes, the orange-striped fenders, the gleaming fishing gear and barnacled propellers.

"It's a shady place for sunny people."

I laughed. "You know what I've noticed about you, Peregrine?"

"My exceptional charm, *savoir-faire*, erudition, integrity. No, wait...my six-pack?"

I kissed his nose gently. "That you make jokes when you're nervous."

"What do you call a three-legged lion with a—"

I took his hands and squeezed them, looking into his eyes. "It will work out." I hugged him, my cheek tickled by the curls beside his ear. Then I whispered, "Promise me you'll always make your jokes."

"As long as you laugh at them, even if they aren't funny."

"What do you think I've been doing all this time?"

I smelt orange and honey as his hand traced each vertebra of my spine; mine undid his jeans one zip tug at a time. "You smell good enough to eat." I whispered.

"Promises, promises!"

CHAPTER FORTY

They were waiting at the jetty, leaning against the pilings with their arms crossed. Bulldog held a walkie talkie; Poodle practiced his sneer. The front of Spada was heaped with equipment: coolers, blankets, waterproof clothing, charts, tackle boxes, gaffs and a bucket of water in which bobbed a block of white gunk.

"Jump in, Ms. Douglas, I'll pass you the rods. If you could pop them in the rod holders, please."

Poodle slouched over. "Looks like someone's going fishing."

"Let me take a wild guess. Harvard?" Perry asked.

"What?"

"Precisely."

"So...you goin' fishing or not?"

Perry dazzled Poodle with a smile, and started the engines: The three outboards gurgled, buzzed, urinated. "I liked how you handled him, Mr. Pacific Pacifist," I whispered.

I was casting off when I spotted Kris running towards us. He stopped breathlessly on the dock.

"Someone called Malcolm on the phone, long distance. I tried to explain you were unavailable. He said it was *imperative* you come straight to my office and take his call."

I looked at Perry. "You'll have to tell him...you couldn't find me."

"He's very worked up. I have to give him more."

"Tell him..." (Poodle sidled closer to listen to our conversation.) "...I've gone fishing."

As our boat swung towards open water, Bulldog raised the walkie talkie.

"Will Malcolm ever forgive me?"

"Well, he'll just have to wait. With luck, we fooled Dragan's muscle.

Anyway, here's my cunning fishing plan. There's an underwater seamount a couple of miles beyond the reef. An obvious place to fish at night because of the upwelling current. The bait tends to—" He looked at me. "Too much information?"

"One day, I want you to teach me *every last thing* about fishing."

"We'll drift over it. They'll think we've started fishing. If my calculations are right, we'll be close to their radar shadow. After half an hour they should be blind and then we can make our run for the main island. Anyway, I hope they get bored and stop watching us."

"Sounds perfect," I said.

"Spada, Spada, this is Sun and Moon. Keep an eye on engine two—it was running a bit hot the other day. Over."

"Sun and Moon, this is Spada. Understood. Thanks for the squid, Kris. Defrosting nicely. We'll start fishing over the seamount. Over."

"Remember the island record's two twenty pounds. Catch you in the morning. Sun and Moon out."

"Insurance?" I asked.

He nodded. "They'll be monitoring channel sixteen, so better safe than sorry. Okay, let's do this thing!"

Perry swept the throttles forward, and the engine notes hardened. The bow leveled out as the wind beat against us, and the ocean galloped past in a dark blur.

"That's only thirty-five!" Perry shouted. "Wait till we run for the main island."

"Stop!" I shouted, pointing.

He pulled the throttles back, our speed dropping as if he'd deployed a parachute.

"What's wrong?" he asked.

"Thought I saw something, over there. Yes, there it is again."

"Oh yes, I saw it—a blow."

A whale was wallowing in the agitated water. As we drew closer, a great knobbly fin broke the surface. Then it crashed down in a detonating slap.

"Humpback?" I asked.

"Hello, old friend," Perry said. Turning to me, "Why's he above the trench?"

"Solomon?"

"Yes."

I watched his fin rise again to wave and fall. He twisted his vast form to align himself with our boat.

"Solomon, it's great to see you too. I'm so sorry but we have to press on." Perry said.

"Take care," I called as we picked up speed again. But I couldn't take my eyes off Solomon and kept watching until he was lost in the fading light. An uneasy feeling stayed with me: It started in my gut and expanded to my diaphragm, to my head. I scanned the distant ocean but the old whale was gone. *Solomon, were you trying to tell us something?*

Perry clicked a switch and navigation lights flicked on, one overhead and two more to the sides: white, green and red.

"But they'll see us," I said.

"We want them to. For now."

He fiddled with the electronic fishfinder, then pulled back on the throttles. We came to rest as Perry looked around, checked his watch, cut the engines.

A few miles behind us, lights blinked on Horseshoe. The last of the sun's rays glowed pink on the distant clouds that had dumped rain on us earlier. To the south, an electrical storm scratched its jagged discharges on the horizon. I breathed in slowly, deeply, filling my lungs with the salty air, my ears with the silence. I found myself drawn by this ocean—by its swells, colors, warmth, the exotic life that made it their home—that differed in so many ways from the fascinatingly moody Atlantic of Nantucket Island I had grown up with. And yet, there was something about its persona that felt the same. It was as if it both were part of an endless, living thing.

"Seventy-one percent of the planet's covered by ocean," Perry said.

He leant over the side and swung a mass of weed aboard. Tiny shrimps cartwheeled from it. "Most people don't realize the critical role it plays." He shook it and an algae-covered bag fell on the deck. Despite the coating of beige slime, I was able to read *The Discount Hut*. Perry rubbed some slime away and the words *Always here for you!* appeared.

"But we're thousands of miles away," I said.

"Plastic doesn't decompose," said Perry. "It breaks down into smaller and smaller pieces or gets eaten, poisoning whatever eats it. Fish, turtle, bird, whale. I've seen research that estimates a trillion of the damn bags are discarded every year."

Perry scooped up the shrimps, and dropped them and the weed overboard. He turned towards me.

"Now we wait for the current to carry us past the end of that island, then they'll be blind. Pass me that small sports bag?"

When I pulled away the boxes to access it, I saw something bulky stretched beneath a nylon cover. My hand slipped under—it felt cold.

"What on earth is this, Perry?"

He laughed. "Emma's idea. I'll show you later," he said.

The sports bag contained the night goggles from Falcon. Head straps held them in place. They illuminated everything in a spectral green.

I swung around to face him. "The look suits you," I said.

He moved closer.

"Perry?"

"Don't smash them together," he whispered. "Or we'll be blind when it's dark."

"Eek! I'm being seduced by a Martian. Do you think this is a good idea? They may be watching," I said, as his hands slipped under my T-shirt. He led me into the cuddy cabin.

"We've got time to kill, and I'll let you in on a little secret: I find fishing *so* boring."

"Me too."

*　　*　　*

Fifteen minutes later, Perry paused. I kissed his neck then lips, as I gripped his waist. He lifted his hands off my shoulders, my hair still clinging to his damp forearms.

"What's wrong?"

He fanned his glowing face with his hand. "Just a short intermission. I need to confirm our rate of drift. And do a horizon check."

"Are you *serious*? The horizon's looking pretty good from here."

He laughed as he opened the cabin door. "I must check a supertanker isn't bearing down on us."

"I think one just was. On me."

*　　*　　*

"Should be safe now," Perry said, as we stepped from the cabin. "Time for warm clothing—at sixty the wind chill will be brutal."

"Aye aye, cap'n."

"Time to kill the lights."

He leaned in for a final kiss.

"Good luck, to both of us," I said softly.

"Always."

Perry turned the keys in the ignition, and I moved to stand beside him. We surged forward, running flat and fast.

"You call this teamwork?" I said into his ear. Dipping under his arm, I came up in front of him, my back snug against his chest. I dropped my hands on the wheel.

"Now, I do," he said.

The wind beat on my face, my ponytail streamed behind me. This was the most exciting thing I'd done in my entire life. Perry adjusted the throttles, then dropped his hands on mine—together we steered though the waves. He let me take the lead, but he was right there, just in case. Islands loomed dark, their proportions morphing before floating away.

"You're a natural," he said in my ear. "Rougher patch coming up," he said, easing the throttles, his hands back on mine. I braced against his stomach as we sliced through a quartering chop. He shouted that a current was running between these islands. Ten minutes later, the chop was forgotten and we picked up speed. He angled the bow for a lumpy headland and swung parallel to the island's surging reef. Then he checked his watch, adjusted the throttles and took his hands off mine.

"Helm's all yours," he said.

The wheel felt light, the boat responding instantly to my steering adjustments. The snarl of the engines gave the beast life.

As we skimmed around another headland, we passed a few bright lights twinkling on the water, perhaps two miles away.

"Islanders. Squid fishermen. They use lights to bring them to the surface," Perry explained.

"Will they have radio? Report an unidentified boat?"

"Unlikely. They don't even have engines."

We ran hard. Islands came and went. Earlier, the ocean had been dotted with occasional low-lying islets; now it restyled itself into bulky landmasses separated by water. The salt scent that swept over the bow grew earthy. Lights blinked here and there, and I found myself wondering about these passing mini-worlds: the loves, dramas, sufferings. Would any of *these* people pick up the phone to report a boat running without lights? Did they have phones?

Several miles distant, the lights of the island merged in a continuous glow. Perry pulled the throttles back to idle.

"It's twelve-fifteen. We'll run in quiet and slow, on one engine," he said.

Forty minutes later, I could make out individual buildings, a few street lights. We were closing on the docks that sprawled along an indentation in the coastline.

Perry said, "Looks like Morfil's thrown money at this place. That's a deep water dock to the right. Shipping containers and cranes. Boat repair area. Some modern-looking warehousing."

"Gas dock, too. Oil drums," I added. "Look left. Between that tall building and that wall," I said. "Is that what you google-earthed?"

"Yes."

"Can we start there? Won't take long. But there's a light on in the hut."

"If we're lucky, someone forgot to turn it off when they went home," he said.

And if we're unlucky, there's a room full of Kalashnikov-toting security guards.

He switched off the engines and retrieved two paddles from a storage locker in the cockpit. "Grab a blade."

The light shone from the upper floor of a small building. External steps descended to ground level. The compound spread out around it, revealing a scattering of low buildings and a long, flat-roofed warehouse. Morfil's office squatted in the far corner.

We paddled from different sides of the boat and when we found our rhythm, our progress improved.

"You're good—you've done this before?" Perry asked.

"A few times. Use your upper back and torso more, and arms less. Your arms are a little too bent."

"Offshore breeze doesn't help," Perry said, adjusting his motion. "But the compound looks quiet enough."

We stopped paddling in front of a chain link fence. Topped with razor wire, it blocked entry to a rectangular section of concrete along the seaward edge of the port facility.

"Looks new," I said.

The soft *pshhhh* that drifted to us from inside the watery compound was unmistakable. A moment later a dolphin came up to inspect us through the chain link that descended into the water. Another appeared beside it.

"As I feared—dolphin holding pen. Teal, can you hold us steady?" he whispered.

I braced Spada against the fencing.

A large padlock secured the chain link doors in front of us. Perry raised a hatch, opened a tool box and lifted out a pair of bolt cutters. The high carbon steel pincers guillotined the shiny metal, and the padlock dropped into the water.

"Good news—these doors haven't been alarmed yet," Perry whispered as he strained to drag them open. A dolphin's head slipped through the surface; it inspected us, then slipped away to circle around the back of the pen. A *pshhhh* was followed by a splash, and another head came up. A dolphin rolled beside it and more heads popped up.

"Don't know how many there are in here, but they're getting excited," Perry said.

"Soon have you all free," I said softly.

I was beside Perry, and I wiped my forehead as metal screamed on metal. Seconds later, barking split the night. Perry glanced at me, then at the lit window.

"That dog sounds big!" I said.

"And hungry!"

One pen door was now open. The barking grew wild, desperate. "It sounds stationary. Hope it's chained up!" I said.

After a scraping lurch, the second door to the dolphin pen slid open. Then an outside light flicked on. We froze. A man emerged to stand silhouetted under it, with a Rottweiler-great white shark crossbreed braced beside him. The beam from a powerful flashlight prowled the compound as the beast heaved on its leash.

"Back," Perry whispered. We pulled Spada along the fence, past the wall, until the boat crouched beneath the dock overhang.

Shoes scrunched gravel as the flashlight's beam swept the water in lazy crescents.

Heart pounding, I ducked low, pulling Perry beside me.

"We may have to leg it. Oh, damn," he whispered, staring upwards.

There it was: Spada's radio aerial sticking up way above the wall, informing the world, and the approaching night watchman, of our presence.

Perry rushed over, pulled a lever at the base of the aerial and it swung down. But the light, and the threshing drag of claw on gravel, came closer. Perry jumped across to the console, his hand dropping on the ignition.

I glanced at the water—at the wavelets that rippled away from the dock wall.

"Offshore wind," I whispered. "The dog can't smell us."

The animal growled, then its bark clattered from building to building.

The footsteps stopped. I looked at Perry and wiped my sweaty palms on my jeans. Surely the watchman would see the open gates?

"You drag me out here for nothin'?" The gravel scrunched again.

Was he coming closer?

I held my breath as we crouched still lower under the dock wall. Perry's triceps, and the sinews in his arms and neck, shone in the moonlight—he looked ready to jump up and tackle the watchman. But what about the dog? He flashed an encouraging smile at me as the sounds began to fade. He wiped his brow theatrically, adding a *phew* as together, we peered over the wall.

The watchman, a great refrigerator of a man, dragged the dog away. He swigged from a bottle, then wedged it under his spare arm. The light's beam bounced off buildings as he meandered back to the guardhouse.

"That isn't Coke Zero," I whispered.

The guard paused on the steps to swig from the bottle again, then shouldered the door and yanked the dog in behind him. The door slammed, and the light went out.

"With luck he's drunk, soon he'll be asleep. The dolphins should escape—they'll use echolocation to work out that their cage is open. Which is Morfil's office?"

I pointed. "Getting there will be easy—plenty of things to hide behind."

"I don't like that light above his front door," he whispered. "Or those street lights."

"We've got that sign and hedge to shield us. If the watchman's office has no rear facing windows, then—"

"You done this sort of thing before?"

"No comment."

Hand over hand, we pulled the boat around a corner, and tied it up. I patted my camera to check it hung secure on the lanyard around my neck. Then I scrambled onto the gunnel and rolled onto the top of the dock, with Perry a beat behind me. We skirted mounds of smelly garbage, stacks of empty pallets and a row of rusty oil drums, the night vision goggles lighting our way. From concrete wall to pallets to oil drums, we hugged the shadows. We dodged behind a stack of traffic cones and some wooden crates. Soon we pressed against a wall, with just one slim strip of open ground remaining between us and Morfil's office, which was bordered on our side by a scraggly hedge.

"Nearly there," I said, sliding forward. Then I grabbed Perry's wrist. "Oh no—Look!"

CHAPTER FORTY-ONE

The cold eye of a surveillance camera, bolted to the top corner of Morfil's office, pointed directly at us.

"You said the security cameras wouldn't be installed yet," Perry said.

"Morfil said end of the week."

We edged closer.

"I don't see one of those red lights on top, so let's hope it isn't wired in," I said. "He also said something about the security system being linked to the police station."

"Now you tell me!"

"I didn't want to alarm you."

"Very funny."

We stared at each other. Then he pulled his shirt over his head, holding it in front of his face like a tube. "I can just about see. Do the same. But we better move fast."

"How long do we have?"

"Police station's the other side of town. As long as there's no patrol car nearby—five minutes. Ten max," Perry said.

I checked my watch, then we ran to the front door. I punched in the code: *LetThemEatCake*. A click, whirring, and we were inside.

As before, tuna cans were piled on the left side of the desk. Three more cans and a roll of labels lay to their right, one of which Perry lifted.

"Here's that extra 'E' again. These cans read Gold *Fine* Tuna," Perry said. "So do these labels. So why keep using the wrong labels?"

"Because it's no mistake." I picked up a can and dropped it in my pocket.

"Morfil might notice one's missing."

"In which case…" I lifted a can from the larger pile and peeled a label from the roll, covering the old label. I placed it between the other two

241

cans.

"Genius—that's interesting," he said, a can in each hand. "You were right. The one with the strange label does feel heavier. Let's hope he doesn't notice the switch."

"That's one minute gone. Let's see what else is in here," I said, opening the upper half of the filing cabinet.

Perry lifted a large envelope from a desk drawer. "Postmarked Taiwan," he said.

"Which is where the prototype trawler is coming from."

He unfolded two large documents, spreading them across the desk. "Boat plans. This one's a trawler—seventy footer. Cab forward design, extra long cockpit. There's your davit and under-deck bracing. Bingo! It must be the one they were discussing."

"I'll take photos, but—" I lowered the window blinds behind me. "Camera flash," I explained.

Perry hurried to the opposite window and did likewise. I checked my watch. "That's two minutes."

Perry studied the second document. "*Way* bigger ship. Three hundred feet long. Looks like a purse seiner. Maybe there's other stuff in here."

He checked the contents of more drawers, and after I'd confirmed my images were satisfactory, I opened the lower half of the filing cabinet.

"Empty except for something under 'P'." I lifted an old, tattered photograph. "A volcano. Water filled, so it's extinct. I'll get a pic, may be useful," I said.

"There's writing on it," he said. "Faded but I can see *Anno*. Then something else but it's too faint."

"*Anno* means year. Could be the year the photo was taken," I suggested. "Oh, here's another one. It's of a track leading up the volcano." I placed it on the table, and the camera flashed. "Three and a half minutes."

Perry laughed. "I wasn't suggesting you photograph a patch of jungle!"

"Teal's first rule of investigative journalism: Never assume anything won't prove useful because assumption is error's Trojan horse. So I record evidence, potential evidence and things that make no sense at all."

"Did you hear that? Sounded like a car horn," he said, peering through the window blinds.

I joined him. A car's headlights flooded the compound in high beam. The horn blared again and barking came from the guardhouse.

"Police!" Perry whispered.

"No, looks like Morfil's car," I said, my heart hammering. "This place must be alarmed after all."

"If it is, I'd expect police, not him. Quick, get this stuff back," Perry said.

The car's horn blasted again.

"We've got till the watchman wakes up!" Perry whispered.

"Done!" I said, as I closed the filing cabinet, and he bundled the papers into the desk. I glanced out of the window again to see the watchman jogging towards the barrier, with the leashed dog beside him.

"Let's get out of here," Perry said.

The watchman raised the barrier. Opening the office door, I whispered, "On all fours," and we slipped out. The lock hissed shut behind us. We scrambled around the side of the building, and crouched with our backs pressed against the wall beside a pile of garbage bins, part sheltered by the scraggly hedge.

"Car's coming," Perry said, glancing around the corner of the building. We should run for it!"

"Where's the watchman?"

"Waiting at the barrier. With the dog."

I pulled him close beside me. "Don't move a muscle."

The Lexus pulled up twenty feet away, in front of the building; it's left side was just visible. I heard a car door open. Morfil's driver, Tangaroa, walked around, opened the passenger door and The Great Man himself stepped out. Morfil ran his fingers through his hair. Slowly he turned, until he'd scanned the entire compound. He reached inside the car and pulled out a briefcase.

Turning to the driver, he said, "You remembered Benchley's bone?"

"In the boot, boss."

"Okay. Wait here and keep your eyes open."

I heard the office door open. Tangaroa was so close... Would he get bored? Would he walk a few feet around the side of the building and see us? What then? And what if the watchman came over with that dog?

Oh no—*footsteps!*

We pressed together against the wall. Tangaroa now stood facing us, a foot beyond the hedge. His features shone eerily green. I prayed that hunched together we'd be mistaken for another mound of garbage. He started whistling. His hand dropped and...he unzipped his fly.

His bladder must have been painfully full. And what on earth had he been eating? Or drinking? I crinkled my nose. When finally he finished, he walked back to the car. A minute later I heard the office door open.

"Let's go," Morfil said.

The Lexus drove off, and the watchman raised the barrier. Then he trudged back towards the guardhouse with the dog, its head stooped under the weight of the huge bone it dragged.

"Bone? Looks like half a pig," I whispered.

"My foot's soaked," Perry said.

I stifled a laugh.

"Now can we get out of here?" Perry asked.

"Not so fast. When he's back in the guardhouse, we wait here for thirty minutes by my watch," I said, as the taillights snaked into the night. "With luck he'll pass out and that dog will fall asleep, full of Miss Piggy."

Man and dog were near the guardhouse now. He climbed the steps and pushed open the door. The light went out.

"He didn't close the door," Perry said.

"Let's hope the dog's chained up."

I squirmed, pushing my back into Perry's chest. His chin settled on my shoulder. "Just avoid that wet patch," he said. "Can't we move somewhere else?"

"Not yet."

He kissed my ear, then squeezed me. With my arms over his, I squeezed back. Allowing myself a deep sigh, I molded into him.

"Who'd have thought that a chance encounter and a few weeks later, the lady of my dreams would be in my arms, on the other side of the world?"

"That's nice."

"That's *nice*? Protocol dictates you now say something equally mushy to me."

"This is the nicest urine-scented hug I've ever had."

"Perfect!"

The night folded calmly around us, its silence broken only by the whirring of an occasional mosquito. I wondered whether our adventure would prove worthwhile—so far, we only had a can of tuna and some photos. But Morfil's arrival with a briefcase late at night had confirmed my fears about him. Something *was* wrong! I prayed we were carrying enough evidence to piece this thing, whatever it was, together. I settled deeper in Perry's arms. He yawned.

"If you want to sleep, I'll keep watch," I said.

"Sure?"

"But no snoring."

"Last of the great romantics," he said, nuzzling my neck and despite where I was, despite the urine and the trash, the saber-toothed hound and the fact that people like Morfil and Dragan even existed, I felt safe.

As I lay back on Perry, his warmth seeping through me, his breathing deepened. I whispered, "Get all the rest you can."

*   *   *

He woke with a jump. "What time...?"

"Time to scoot. By the way, you were so cute. As you dreamed, you twitched like a puppy."

He hugged me close.

"Nothing from the guardhouse. With luck, that rum's inside him and he's dead to the world," I said.

We helped each other up. Perry rubbed his face awake and scrambled his hair. I stretched my arms, rolled my shoulders as he hopped from leg to leg to get his circulation going.

We were moving again, retracing our steps in and out of shadows, around piles of junk, hugging buildings. As we dashed across the open ground towards Spada, I glanced back at the guardhouse. My heart jumped. Movement at the door—the dog was out. It sniffed the air.

I pointed, then dragged Perry into shadow.

The animal's head swung towards us.

"The wind's changed direction," Perry whispered.

With a howl, the dog bounded down the steps. It leapt onto the concrete and pointing directly at us, charged, the distance between us shrinking with surreal speed.

"Run!" I said.

We sprinted, the brute's course curling after its target like a missile tracks a jet.

At the dock wall, we sprang down into Spada. I landed on all fours. Perry was already standing tall in the back of the boat, squared up to the approaching monster. "Get behind me," he said.

The dog hurtled towards us, a mass of snarling, gravel-spraying muscle. It hunched ten feet away then launched itself. Foaming jaws, flashing teeth, glinting eyes…at Perry's throat.

I don't know what he did—something with his arm—but the dog changed course midair, and tumbled into the water beside the outboards. The splash soaked me. The snorting dog surfaced, and was now scrabbling at the side of the boat in search of a way to climb aboard.

"Boathook, Teal!"

I prodded the beast, strong-arming it away as it snapped at the hook. It locked on, jerking and shaking its head. When it turned side on, I yanked the boathook back and thrust at its ribs to fend it off. It swam around the boat again, clawing the hull with increasing fury. Then its ears went back, and its swimming slowed.

"It can't get in the boat or climb onto the dock—the wall's too high. What do we do, Perry?"

"I think it's admitted defeat. Over there," he pointed. "A small beach. If it can swim that far."

I shoved the animal's shoulder until it turned and swam off.

"Mangled boathook." I said ruefully.

"Let's go."

"Light's come on again," I said, as we pushed off. "Perry, the watchman's come out."

The ebb tide helped as we leaned into each stroke of our paddles, the boat swinging lazily with the current.

A *pshhhhh* made us turn. "Look!" I whispered as a dolphin rolled; it was joined by others that soon surrounded us. One flipped over, smacking the water with his tail. Another jumped high, to knife back in a splashless re-entry.

"You're very welcome," Perry said. "I'm disgusted they imprisoned you in the first place."

As suddenly as they appeared, they were gone and we drifted forward in silence. I stared back at the compound a hundred yards behind us. The watchman was still at the top of the steps. Between slurred curses, he hollered the dog's name.

"We made it!" Perry said. "If I'd known it would be *that* hairy—"

We hugged.

"We make quite a good team!" he said. "Okay, let's get this boat in gear."

"Only *quite* good?"

His hand dropped into his pocket and felt around. "That's strange."

"Perry?"

"Did I give you the keys?"

"Not funny."

"Oh god, I must have dropped them. Maybe when the dog...?"

We searched the cockpit and crevices along its deck. I moved forward and checked the piled equipment too.

He turned to me, "They must have fallen out when we were running. Teal?"

"Screwdriver, please." I knelt under the console, and removed a panel to be confronted by a bundle of wiring. The green imagery generated by the goggles blurred the color of the wires, so I used my finger to trace one back to the ignition. Other wires led to the batteries in a cubby-hole below deck. I found what I wanted, and a spark was followed by the whirr of a starter motor. One engine throbbed to life.

"Teal, you're *amazing*! Correction. We make a *great* team! Where on earth did you learn to do that?" he asked as we high-fived.

"Mike—Grandma's handyman—showed me when she lost her car keys."

"Thanks, Mike! What's he doing these days?"

"Six years for grand theft auto. As long as we're congratulating each other...what on earth did you do to the dog?"

"Oh, that. I treated his attack like a punch. Ducked its jaws, deflected its flight by pushing its body to the side. You don't need a lot of strength if you go with the direction of its energy. In boxing it's called a *parry*."

"Cool parry, Perry. Promise you'll teach me that move?"

"Deal, Teal. Except…I didn't get it quite right."

"Looked perfect to me."

He opened his hand; a flash of blood streaked his palm. "Barely a scratch."

I braced myself against a wash of dizziness. "Who knows what bacteria you could have picked up."

"First aid box under the console. Should be alcohol swabs."

The wound wasn't deep—and it cleaned easily. But the risk of infection was a serious threat I couldn't dismiss.

"They say a dog's mouth's cleaner than a human's," he said.

"Speak for yourself. Anyway, we need to get you on antibiotics to be safe."

"No, I'll be fine. I mean it's only—"

I placed my hands on his shoulders. "Peregrine, you're going on antibiotics, okay? Do it for me? Please?"

"I can't. I'm allergic to them."

"Seriously?"

"Don't worry, I'm a Stanley. I come from a long line of Stanleys. We're tough. Takes more than a mangy Pacific puppy to lay me low."

"We still need to get you checked by a doctor. What if it had *rabies?*"

"Then it would be the first recorded case in this part of the world. Promise, I'll be fine."

We crept seaward on one engine for ten minutes, the shore and dock installations blending into the island's silhouette.

A dolphin came up beside the boat, blew and submerged. I waited, but it didn't reappear.

"Do you think we're far enough out to start the other engines?" I asked, dropping down in front of the console again.

"Yes, would you do the honors?"

"I can't believe people would capture them," I said. "Confine them to a tiny cage."

"Many of them go mad in captivity. A Seaworld orca called Tilikum's killed three people."

"Do people know about this?" I asked as Engine Two whirred to life.

"Films like *The Cove* and *Blackfish* are helping. Did you know the Japanese slaughter over twenty thousand dolphins a year for food, even though the dolphins are so full of mercury they aren't safe to eat? Then, there's the grotesque annual slaughter of pilot whales in the Faroe Islands."

"That's Engine Three."

A searchlight came on.

"Since when has there been a searchlight *here*?" Perry asked.

The beam raked across the surface behind us, then it swept across our stern. Perry buried the throttles. Thrust by nine-hundred horses, Spada leapt forward, charging for the horizon. The chill wind buffeted my face.

Gripped by an exhilaration I'd never known before, I yelled, "Come on Morfil! Catch us if you can!"

*   *   *

We tore across the ocean surface like a white zip on dark fabric. I was in front of Perry again, steering, his arms gently holding me. A tilt of the wheel, a throttle adjustment and the boat, like a skimming missile, flew on as we blasted away from one world to return to another.

"We need to make up the time we lost," Perry shouted as he checked the instruments.

An hour later, Perry asked me to ease back on the throttles. The boat settled in the water. He was shifting the boxes and lifting the equipment in the bow.

"Help me with these?"

We pulled off a blanket. Water trickled from under a great fish. It lay dark and graceful, with a long bony spear that protruded from its snout.

"Marlin?" I asked.

"Broadbill swordfish. Emma's brainwave. Help me pull it to the back, we'll lay it across the cockpit."

Perry lifted the VHF handset. "Sun and Moon. Sun and Moon. This is Spada. Over."

Perry repeated the call, but no answer came. Then he added, "That's a shame 'cos I was going to tell you to put champagne on ice and get the scales ready. Spada out."

The islands were more dispersed now. As we rounded a headland, I could make out Horseshoe and beside it, the incongruous bulks of The Bottom Line and Apex Predator. A dark shape lifted from the yacht to hover above it.

"Chopper," Perry said. "Take your goggles off."

The helicopter came low and fast, swinging behind us with a building *dum-dum-dum*. A searchlight beam raked the cockpit as we ducked down and turned our backs. Perry waved a fist at them, pointed to his eyes and the searchlight died. The chopper veered away.

"Good, they must have seen the fish. Let's hope they fell for it. Okay, we'll be back in ten minutes."

"Ten minutes away from reading the inevitable email informing me I'm fired."

"Nonsense!" said Perry. "The business center's locked till eight."

"So why was Morfil sneaking into the cannery office in the middle of the night?"

"Something fishy going on?"

"Perry!"

"Ha! That briefcase—he was either smuggling something in, or out. Or both."

"Why do you say 'or both'?"

"No idea. It just sounded clever. But…"

I tapped my pocket. "My bet is the answer's in this tuna can."

CHAPTER FORTY-TWO

Holding hands, we sauntered towards the jetty where Apex Predator's tender was tied up. With Black Jack dead, I had wondered whether people would still bother to attend the daily fish feeding, but a few hardcore devotees were milling around the dock on which the giant swordfish hung head down from a gantry. Bulldog and Poodle were there too.

"Good morning, Teal, Perry," Kris announced warmly. "Looks like you had a grand night. How long was the fight?"

"Must have been *hours!*" I said.

People were taking photos of the fish. A few touched its skin and ran their fingers down its long bill. A tall man with a grinding voice described its feeding habits, as a small boy tugged his arm.

"When I saw it in Spada's cockpit, I thought it might be an island record. We got it on the scales as fast as possible," Kris said.

"And?"

"Two hundred and twenty pounds."

The boy broke free from his father and ran up to the fish. He poked its side. From the corner of my eye, I saw Bulldog muttering into his walkie talkie. A cigarette hung from Poodle's mouth as he walked over to examine the fish. He stubbed the cigarette out in the great fish's glazed eye.

"What do you think you're doing?" Kris asked.

Poodle turned. "You don't talk to me like that, boy."

"I'm going to have to ask you two to leave the island. It's private property, for guests only," Kris said. "And I'd appreciate it if you left without causing a scene. Don't come back."

Poodle slouched forward. "Wait till Mr. Morfil hears about this." He glared at Perry. "Fishing was good, was it?"

"See for yourself."

Poodle walked around Perry, the sneer distorting his unshaven face.

"Why's it so cold, Daddy?" the little boy asked, his arm buried elbow deep in the fish's mouth.

"Oh Jimmy, now you'll smell of fish!" his father said.

"To think we equaled the island record," Perry said breezily.

Bulldog touched the fish. "The kid's right. Why's it so damn cold?"

Perry smiled. "Deep water fish, caught at night. Dark skin. Low hemoglobin count at this time of year. Obviously an endothermic tissue response to the ambient temperature differential. It'll warm up in the sun."

Kris handed me a rod, and I stood beside the fish for photos. The goons stalked past, Bulldog barging into Perry's shoulder. A look flashed in Perry's eyes—a look I'd seen once before: when Edward had insulted him in the pub.

Bulldog stopped in front of Perry. "I may not know about fancy tissue responses but I know when something don't add up." He moved so close their faces nearly touched.

"I'll be watching you, boy."

"I recommend Listerine," said Perry.

Bulldog prodded Perry's chest. "For some guys it's drink, or skirt, or gambling. You know what does it for me?"

"Remember that bar in Bimini? Tell him how many we beat down," Poodle growled to his buddy.

"Stopped counting at eleven." Bulldog grinned as he patted Perry's cheek. "You look scared, boy." He spat on the ground. "Never met a Limey who *could* fight."

Perry didn't speak. Bulldog backed away, smirking. They jumped in their tender and roared away.

"And keep your speed to five knots near the jetty," Kris shouted.

"Missing you already," Perry added under his breath. Turning to Kris, he said, "A tie with the Italian's catch? What are the odds of *that?*"

"You alright?" I asked him. "I can't believe how restrained you were."

"Yes, yes, I'll be fine. When I've calmed down."

"You know what? I don't think I'd have minded if you'd thumped that idiot."

"He wasn't worth it."

"Isn't there anything you'd fight for?"

He leaned forward and kissed my forehead. With a smile, he said, "I can think of some*one* I'd defend."

"Thank you," I said quietly.

"We better get it back in the freezer," Kris said.

"And when you've done that, come to my room, Kris? Say half an hour?"

"Sure, Teal. See you there."

"I'll invite Frank and Nancy too. Something important to show you all."

*　　*　　*

I described our adventure. The tuna can lay between us on the table; Frank and Nancy asked questions. Kris lifted it, checked the label and frowned.

"Okay, drum roll please. Who'd like to open it?" I asked.

"Go on, Teal, all this is because of you," Frank said.

"Yes, you do it, Angel," Nancy added.

"Alright…and the contents of one can of *Gold Fine Tuna* is…" I pulled the ring and peeled back the lid.

"Who'd have guessed—regular tuna chunks!" Nancy said.

Perry pulled a multi-tool from his pocket. He poked the blade into the fish, then lifted out a ziplock bag from the bottom of the can. Gold glinted through the oil. He flipped the bag onto the table, sliced it open and poured out the contents. I counted nine nuggets and smaller pieces of gold including flecks as small as sand grains.

"I'd heard tuna was full of heavy metals," he said. "But this is ridiculous."

Frank lifted a nugget. "After Fukushima, you can add strontium, cesium and probably extinctium too." He lifted more gold. "I'm guessing the weight, but at say $1,300 an ounce, I'm thinking five to seven thousand dollars in this one can."

"Gold Fin, Gold Fine, *Fine Gold*," I said. "This time there were three cans on the desk. When I interviewed Morfil, only two."

"Two or three cans a day, so…" Perry added.

Frank cleared his throat. "Lower scenario of two cans at five grand a pop. If, and this is a big *if,* that's the *daily* haul, that's…$3.65 million a year."

"Let me guess, Frank. You owned a jewelry store?" I suggested.

"No, Angel. A pawnbroker's," Nancy said.

"Dragan said he had invested in a bunch of exploratory mines," I said.

"Well, it's possible," Frank said, "That there could be a lot more."

"But Morfil claimed it wasn't economic," I added.

"Surprise, surprise. Morfil's stealing the gold. Got a buyer, smuggles it out in re-labeled cans," Perry said. "Talk about no honor among thieves."

"But this doesn't fully explain the cannery, the trawlers or the offshore survey. There's still more to this," I said. "Let's take a closer look at the pics I took of the boats from Taiwan."

I scrolled though the photos, stopping, enlarging. I gave Perry the camera, and he studied the LCD panel before passing it to Kris. "What do you make of that, chum?"

"A trawler," Kris said, before adding, "Why does it need a *full beam* transom door? What are they planning to catch? *Whales?* And look—despite the photo's pixilation that looks like hydraulics under the deck. What's that about?"

Perry leaned over his shoulder. "I missed that. The end of the deck looks hinged. They plan to lift something heavy?"

Kris scrolled on to the purse seiner. "God help us all if they bring that thing here."

"May I?" asked Frank, reaching for the camera. "That's strange." He handed it to Perry, pointing to a feature of the boat's design. "What d'you make of those?"

Perry said, "Since when does a trawler need such big stabilizers?"

Nancy looked around the table. "All this effort to build a cannery as part of a gold smuggling operation may just about make sense." She shrugged. "But the rest of it sure doesn't. Any other photos, Teal?"

That was when I remembered the volcano. "Just an extinct volcano and a date I can't read," I said. "There's a lot of mist in the photo, so it would be hard to identify."

"May I?" asked Frank.

I handed him the camera.

"*Anno?*" he asked, before he scrolled to the next photo.

"This one looks like it was taken at the foot of the volcano," he said.

He adjusted the zoom and looked up. "That plant in the foreground is a member of the Euphorbiaceae, or spurge family."

"You old show-off!" Nancy said with a laugh. "You know he used to import rare—"

"Pumpkin, this could be important! It's a West African species—not found here. I'll bet anyone a dollar, hell, make that two bucks, that volcano's thousands of miles away."

"Can you be more precise?" Perry asked.

"Afraid not, son."

I looked up from the LCD panel. "Stolen gold. Okay, I get that. But why on earth does mister super-fastidious Thurston Morfil bother with photos of a West African volcano in his South Pacific office?"

CHAPTER FORTY-THREE

When they'd left, I turned to Perry and stretched, exaggerating a yawn. "I'm *so* tired," I said.

"But it's lunchtime," he said. "Oh, I get it. Bedtime story?"

"Yes, please."

Two hours later, I lay on top of him, my hands had slipped under his shoulders, my head rested on his chest. I wriggled just a little, as the aftershocks subsided. A film of sweat slicked us together in a secret intimacy. By hugging him, I kept out the world and its problems.

I nuzzled his ear. "*Once upon a time* doesn't constitute a story, mister."

"But you distracted me."

"So it's *my* fault?"

"You looked at me with those big, beautiful blue-green eyes. What was I to do?"

"Hmmm. First it's a promised poem. Now you can only manage four words of a story." I propped myself on an elbow, brushing a damp curl from his forehead. "What *are we* to do with you, Mr. Peregrine?"

"Violet was helping me with the poem, but she had a temper tantrum when I said it was for you."

"Poor thing. And this?"

I ran by hand gently over his tattoo. "You finally going to tell me what it means?"

"What does it look like to you?"

Elegant wings curled from a stylized body. "A butterfly. I see an angel too."

"Good answer."

"Why?"

"What you see tells me about you. People see different things. I am happy to confirm that you're probably safe around small children and puppies."

He raised his chin until his lips were almost, but not quite touching mine, and waited. I wiggled closer. Then he squeezed me against his chest, his hands meandering across my shoulders before his fingertips teased down my back.

Lying there, I knew that I had finally broken free.

*   *   *

It was late afternoon when the telephone interrupted my doze.

"H—hello?"

"Sorry to disturb you babe, it's Emma. Bob's here in reception, he's pretty excited. Insisted I ring you."

"Oh?"

"It's fine Bob, I'm talking to her—Teal, he wants to know if you and Perry are free tonight. Excuse me a second, he's talking again—Teal, he says it's important and the tide's just right. Yes, okay, Bob. Relax, bro— Says it must be tonight. Teal, you still there?"

"Yes, yes, Emma," I said, rubbing my eyes. "What does—"

"Bob? He's gone, Teal. But I've never seen him so *agitato*. He said to meet him at the usual place at seven, bring warm clothes. Can you get a message to Perry?"

"I'll do my best. Bye, thanks Emma."

I whispered in Perry's ear, but he didn't move.

"Come on lazy bones, wake up," I repeated, shaking him gently.

"I'm dying."

I kissed his ear, and settled for a floppy hug. "Emma just rang. We're meeting Bob at seven."

"Did she say why?"

"No, but apparently the tide will be just right."

"What's just right about half tide and falling?"

*   *   *

Bob was leaning against the prow of his canoe, which he'd pulled a short distance up the beach. He straightened up as we greeted him and handed us paddles. We pushed the canoe into the surf.

"At night, Bob?" Perry asked, but Bob was already aboard, gesturing for us to join him.

Perry leaned close to my ear, "I suppose you don't get to his age without knowing when it's safe to paddle around here."

"I think I can guess where he wants to go," I said.

"Me too."

Bob's paddle carved and fell, swirling the water in unison with the lap and slip of the waves. I tried to imitate him, but his relentless pace was exhausting. I soon felt the sting of my first blister. Perry's heavy breathing behind me broadcast *his* efforts. We cut through the troubled waters beyond the reef, where a lively current sped us on.

With the tide ebbing, Whaling Rock lay off our pitching bow, a dark shadow ringed with foam and soaked with mystery.

Bob held the canoe alongside and motioned for us to climb out.

I stood with Perry, feeling the smooth stone underfoot as Bob backed away in the canoe.

"Listen to me, because this is important. You must look deeply into his eye and open your hearts. Then will he let you in."

"Who are we waiting for, Bob?" Perry asked.

"Let us in? In *where*?" I added. But Bob didn't look back.

"I will return in a few hours," he called.

"I sure wouldn't like to be here alone," I said. "Thanks for being with me, Perry."

"This place is a bit creepy. What do you know about it?"

We sat down and I told him Fonu's story. Perry asked a few questions, jumped up when he said he had a cramp, then settled close beside me again. When I reached the end, he said, "Great—*and* you saw a ghost here. Uh-oh!"

"But why tonight?" I asked.

"Maybe it's the anniversary of his death. For what it's worth, I can't think of anyone I'd rather be with, waiting for a ghost on a rock in the middle of the Pacific Ocean."

I slipped my arm around his waist and leaned my head against his shoulder. "Funny where life takes you."

"If you let it."

I tilted my head back to study the heavens. "I wish Lizzie were here."

"She'd be proud of you."

"Thank you. Wish we had the night goggles," I said.

"Me too."

I sat bolt upright. "Did you hear that?" I whispered. "Was it scratching?"

He was on his feet, checking behind us. He dropped down and laughed. "Only an inquisitive crab."

"Thank you for teaching me…to like…no…to value myself."

"I've waited my whole life for *you*, Teal. Thanks for taking my resort recommendation seriously."

A breeze stirred, and he wrapped his arms around me, pulling me close, his chin on my shoulder.

"I want all of me to touch all of you," I said, stroking his hair.

"I want more."

I was still smiling when a half mile away, a great fin rose through the surface. It slapped down, as if in play. Then the dark shape of a whale's head nudged a crescent of waves.

The whale moved slowly. As he blew, he triggered the ocean's phosphorescence, which blinked and fluttered around him like a pulsing halo.

"I think it's Solomon," Perry whispered as I willed the leviathan closer.

Solomon came like an emissary from another world, encircled by swirling mandalas of light. It was as if he wanted to impress us, maybe play a game or share a secret.

"Cetacea are custodians of a watery planet ironically called Earth," said Perry.

"That's beautiful," I said.

The half-moon climbed higher, revealing the dark and pale of the whale's complexion. Through the water I saw the nobbled, cone head, the long pectoral fins that split and rejoined in a watery arabesque. A baritone of mist spouted from him, the vapor dissolving with reluctance, like a favorite dream.

"Hello, my friend," I said, when the whale arrived.

With graceful fin sweeps he balanced, his length lost in the depths. His glistening head protruded from the ocean. He was so close that I leaned out towards him and whispered, "Perry, hold me." I could just reach far enough for my hand to brush the whale's firm cheek.

Solomon's eye leveled on mine, a great orb that was marvelous in size, deeply lidded. Alive. Intelligent. Questioning. I pulled Perry closer—I needed him with me, and he reached out and stroked the whale too.

What had Bob said about *opening your heart*?

Perry's mouth moved with silent words as Solomon's black eye pulled me closer but I resisted. Fear? Uncertainty?

I strained to understand. Finally, I surrendered and let the energy settle where it needed to: in my heart. Then Solomon's eye opened wide and brightened. In it, I saw the stars above us. But when I looked closer, a feeling came: I wasn't studying the reflection of the night sky—it was as if the entire universe existed in the depths of the old humpback's eye. He was calling me to enter this world. In that moment of great calm, love flooded through me and I dissolved into his eye.

Bathed in a milky glow, I now floated in a lazy, drunken consciousness. I checked my arms and legs—they shimmered. When I commanded my fingers to move, they ignored me. Focusing on the darkness beyond, I knew I was not alone. But where was Perry?

I had no point of reference, yet I knew I was moving. Pale, watery presences drifted with me, flickering like dust specs in a beam of moonlight.

A pale coyote watched me as it glided by. Behind came a bent child, then a stately old woman. I saw angelfish and praying mantises, bonobo monkeys and harlequin-patterned pythons. As the spirit numbers grew, my body faded, persisting only in an outline of pulsing flashes. Waves of love swirled around me, through me, within me. I bathed in it as I drifted forward, searching for Perry.

Here, now, I knew infinite, unconditional love. I stilled in rapture at its presence, without need, without any desire to return to the physical world and its problems.

When I raised my hand, I found it had become a formless web of twinkling energy. From my heart, a silver thread stretched unbroken into the distance and I sensed Perry at its other end. Other threads, thin and fragile, radiated from me, a few waved broken like spider gossamer.

As my energy flowed down these threads, other threads returned it. Then everything slowed into juddering freeze-frame and with a gasp, I found myself perched on the edge of the rock again. I clamped my hand over my heart, willing the love to stay but it bled away.

"No!" I cried.

"Welcome back," Perry said, tears streaming down his cheeks, his arms around me.

"I didn't want to leave," I whispered.

"Nor did I."

The phosphorescence that encircled the rock twinkled like a living thing. At its perimeter Solomon swam hard, pushing a wave that bulged the surface. He rolled, waved a fin and sank from view.

"Goodbye," I said, wiping my eyes.

"I'm beginning to understand." I pulled Perry's arm close about me. "There's something down there—it's to do with the trench. I'm sure of it now."

"I didn't see it. Did you?"

"A glimpse, but I was far away and as soon as I saw it, I was back here. But I got a powerful feeling about it."

"Can you describe it?" he asked.

"Sort of. It was about the beginning and the end. Even the meaning of life and death. The damage we humans have done. I wanted to say, I should have said…sorry. But I know one thing for certain: If I ever return to that place, no power on earth could make me leave."

He took my hand in his, his fingers massaging my palm. "Sometimes words aren't that useful, are they? But I think you went deeper than me."

"It's like trying to remember a dream."

We stood, holding hands, hoping Solomon would return. The sparkles faded, the ocean slept. Then Perry drew me in, and brushed his lips across mine.

Running his fingers down the side of my face, he said, "Smiling and crying at the same time—not many people can do that."

A scud of cloud drifted across the moon, shading the rock until a freshening breeze dispersed it. There was Bob again—waiting. He may have been there for minutes, perhaps hours. Perry saw him first—the old islander in a simple canoe beside an ocean-swept rock.

"Bob, that was—"

But Bob raised his finger to his lips, and indicated we should take our places in the canoe. Perry and I crawled down the slippery rock, stepping onto a small ledge that jutted over the waves. We scrambled in beside Bob, picked up our paddles and began the rhythmic strokes that would take us home.

Bob steered the canoe through the surf, guiding and balancing with his paddle until a wave stranded us on the beach. We jumped out and pulled the canoe up to the seaweed line etched along the waterfront. Bob settled on the sand facing the ocean, and we sat opposite him. He looked at us in turn. Finally, he spoke.

"He invited both of you because you want to help." He leaned forward and lowered his voice. "So far you have solved nothing—but wanting to help is the first step."

"What was that place?" I asked.

"Humankind has known of it forever. Religions have different names for it. So do some of your mind doctors as well as the traditional healers and those who enter the spirit world using sacred plants."

"Does it have a name?" Perry asked.

"I call it the *Ocean of Souls*."

"I have never experienced such…love," Perry said quietly.

"The sky and the land use words you understand. But the ocean uses its own language. It is the source of pure, good love."

"Is there such a thing as *bad* love?" I asked.

"Love is love. But there are people who love the wrong things. The ones on the black yacht…they are prisoners of the shadows. But you tasted truth. He has been calling you for weeks."

Perry took my hand. "Sounds like a famous whale who's been calling in the Northern Pacific for decades at fifty-two hertz—the loneliest whale on earth. As most whales call at around seventeen, the other whales don't hear him. It's like…well, maybe they're not his target…"

"So, it was Solomon who's been calling us with music?" I asked. "But why did only a few of us hear him? Is he like Fifty-Two? *Is* he Fifty-Two? Can he choose who…?"

"We think Fifty-Two's a fin whale," Perry said, "or a fin-blue hybrid."

"He was calling your grandmother for longer."

"My grandmother? How do you know about her, Bob?"

"What you're saying, Bob, could re-write science books," Perry said.

"I do not think so, because there are many things your science will never explain. When you understand that everything is connected, in ways that cannot normally be seen or heard, then this kind of thing is no surprise." Bob looked me over slowly, thoughtfully. "It is Solomon who has been telling me what's going on in his world."

"The overfishing, the pollution, you mean?" Perry asked.

"The good things too."

"Bob, are you saying—"

Before I could finish, he replied, "What you are thinking is correct."

"Did Solomon tell you we cut the netting from him?"

"Yes. He did."

I looked at Perry. "So we were...*summoned* here? By a *whale*?"

Perry ran his hand through his hair. "I think my brain needs rebooting."

"At death every living thing returns to the Ocean of Souls to replenish their love. When we sleep, we can have short visits there too, to help rebuild us, to face the problems of living."

"I saw silver tendrils, attaching me to people," I said.

"Me too," Perry added.

"Those are the threads that bind us to those we love. But they break when we stop loving—though the broken thread stays with us always."

"Why did Solomon show *us?*" I asked.

"He knows things that people don't. Some he's been calling for years—the ones he thinks might care. He has been sending many messages recently. He thinks there is still hope. Because sometimes... sometimes...people answer."

"Can this be true?" I looked first at Bob, then Perry.

"What is truth? We must all choose what we believe. And I believe this to be true. You, of course, must choose for yourselves. You may decide, even after visiting the Ocean of Souls, that it isn't true. A trick of the mind, some might call it."

"Thank you, Bob—that was a humbling, life-changing experience. Really. And please thank Solomon." I said.

"I ask you to keep looking, asking questions. Solomon thinks you are close to finding out what is about to happen." He was facing me. "Another thing. You asked me to tell you about Fonu's story."

"Yes. But I read it in Kris's scrapbook."

"I remember telling it to a vacationing professor long ago. He must have typed it and that's where it ended up. I was worried that when I died, the story would be lost forever. Tell me, how did it end?"

"Losa was swept off the rock to her death. Fonu tried to swim ashore, but he drowned too."

"Yes, my memory does not fail me. The professor left before I finished the story. Would you like to hear more?"

"There's *more?*"

CHAPTER FORTY-FOUR

Bob cleared his throat.

"The sun was low when the Chief entered his hut. He gasped in surprise—standing in front of him was Fonu. "Are you a spirit? My son is dead. He drowned before my eyes!"

Fonu reached out and grasped his father's hand. When the old Chief felt his firm grip, he trembled. With broken words, he reminded his father that no one had ever fooled the Great Chief of the Islands.

Fonu explained that about a year before, he had noticed a beautiful girl in the village. He began to find excuses to walk past her hut, to catch a glimpse of her sitting in the doorway weaving baskets, to speak to her.

After a time, he and Losa had slipped down to the water at night where she had taught him to paddle and swim—she was no ordinary girl. With every lesson, he became more fascinated with her, more confident of himself, of his new-found skills. His attention had wandered when he wasn't with her until he found himself thinking about her throughout the day, counting the moments until nightfall. Soon he knew for certain that I loved her—that he wanted to spend the rest of his life with her.

When Fonu dived off the canoe, though the whole village had thought he was swimming towards the beach, he had in fact doubled back underwater and surfaced on the far side of the canoe. The wind and his kicking had carried Fonu, hidden behind the canoe, along the beach until he was opposite the Chief's hut. There he had filled his lungs and swum ashore, staying deep and remaining unseen.

"The distance underwater is more than forty canoe lengths—I have proved myself worthy." Fonu said. "You must now honor our

agreement, Father. Send the whalers away."

After a long pause, the Chief spoke.

"It is the curse of every leader to be unable to be all things to all people. And even great leaders make mistakes. It was wrong to promise you what I cannot give you. Leaders must sometimes sacrifice a small thing for the greater good. I do not do it lightly. But I cannot grant your request. Our people must have guns."

"Then I should have chosen to die with Losa! We would both be at peace now. But she begged me not to." With eyes cast down, he said, "I made a terrible mistake. Now I must live the rest of my life without her."

The Chief stared at his son, and it was some time before he spoke. "That scar on your arm..."

"Father?"

"A whale calf died the morning you were born. A shooting star passed across the dawn sky from the whale to the birthing hut. The whale had a scar like that on its fin."

Fonu glanced at his arm. "And you asked me why I carved you a whale?"

"I don't understand you, Fonu. I never have."

Fonu's eyes were glistening. "If the Great Chief truly wants to understand," said Fonu, "the answer waits in my hut." The boy bowed to his father. "I cannot live here any longer."

He walked down to the beach unseen by the rest of the village, fighting back tears. He boarded the canoe and pointed it at a distant island. Without looking back, he paddled away.

The Chief summoned his elders and they marched to Fonu's hut. When they entered, they saw before them a wooden ball, as tall as the Chief, made of intertwined wood carvings. There were animals of the land, air and ocean, insects and plants too.

"What does it mean?" the Chief asked. "This must have taken him years!"

The Chief grasped a wooden sea snake, which moved in his hand. He twisted, and it came away from the giant rat and pelican it was attached to. A hunched elder said they'd never seen such skillful carving. Another that there must be a great treasure hidden inside the globe.

The Chief removed a tiger and a tortoise. He reached into the hole he had created, but felt nothing.

An elder with ceremonial tattoos on his forearms coughed gently, "Great Chief—"

When the Chief looked around, he saw the man was flicking through the pages of a picture book filled with drawings of animals of every kind. "I found it in the corner," he said, "I remember when you gave it to him, years ago."

With increasing speed and jerky movements, the Chief tore away a carved tarantula and a strange bird with a long neck. He threw a goat and stingray across the hut, then a giant of an animal with humps on its back. When a man and a spiky plant came free, the Chief pushed his head into the hole, but it was too dark to see. He grasped a wild boar and a giant, wingless bird. He twisted it, and the globe collapsed into a mound of pieces.

The Chief dropped to his knees. "The treasure must be under here. Help me!" he shouted, flinging carvings behind him. Soon they were staring at the hut's sandy floor.

"Where is it?" the Chief shouted.

The Chief knelt in the center of the hut, surrounded by the wreck of the globe, stroking his silvery beard. The silence was broken when he commanded the elders to collect the carvings and bring them to his hut.

All that night the Chief and his most trusted advisors tried to rebuild the globe, but by morning they still had only a mound of carvings. The Chief paced back and forth, ignoring their questions.

When dawn came, he ordered his finest craftsmen resume work on the great war canoe. The thrones were to be polished, the double hulls cleaned and repainted. Any missing shell inlays and damaged timber must be replaced. Then he dismissed his elders, to continue to work on Fonu's globe, alone.

The food the elders left outside the Chief's hut went untouched. It was four days before he allowed anyone to enter. When he did finally accept visitors, his voice had grown calmer, his old eyes softer.

Finally, the canoe was ready. It took forty warriors to drag it down the beach. After all these years, the greatest war canoe ever seen in the islands was finally launched. At the Chief's insistence, there was no ceremony, no celebration—in fact, it was launched in silence.

The Chief had slept little, which may have explained his bloodshot eyes, the stoop in his back, why his hair looked whiter that day. It did not explain why, at the water's edge, he complimented the craftsmen, one-by-one, on their fine work, before thanking his elders for their many years of excellent guidance. He settled on a mighty throne in the war canoe, and asked them to place the sack of Fonu's carvings on the throne beside him. Then fifty of his finest warriors paddled the canoe towards the rock.

At the rock, the Chief climbed out, refusing any help with the sack. Doubled over by its weight, he clambered onto the rock. He sent the warriors on their way, ignoring their warnings of the rising tide, thanking them for bringing him here. He told them that he had depended on them, and they had served him well. The last thing they heard the Chief say as they began paddling away was that everything and everyone depended on everything and everyone else.

"Remove too many pieces," he said, "and the whole world collapses, never to be put back together again."

That night a terrible wailing carried to the island. When dawn arrived, the wind died and the tumultuous sea calmed. The most senior elder sent a canoe to fetch the Chief—but there was no sign of him. Or of the carvings.

The elders agreed the great canoe should be dragged ashore. Warriors collected the Chief's possessions and those of his son from their huts. Everything was placed inside the canoe which they set alight. It burned for two days and nights. The ash was allowed to cool before being rowed far offshore and cast into the ocean.

The New Zealanders aboard Aroha failed to kill a whale. Captain Jackson shouted that he had been tricked. When the Chief did not appear and Jackson was told that he refused to see him, Jackson sailed away.

"Next year," Jackson thundered, "I will return with a dozen whaling ships, with spotting towers and powerful engines. We will not have to rely again on islanders firing rockets from rocks..."

Bob's eyes refocused on us and he said, "A few weeks later the Second World War started in the Pacific. It spread to these islands—the Japanese and Americans fought bitterly over them. Many islanders died. Since then, no islander has lived here.

"So you see," Bob said, "that rock was named after the wails of the old Chief. It has nothing to do with whaling."

I was unable to hide the quaver in my voice. "I'm so sorry for Fonu. To have not joined Losa. It must have been such a difficult and painful decision."

"A beautiful and thought-provoking story," Perry added. "What became of Fonu? Did he find happiness?"

"No, he did not."

Bob reached out and took my hands in his. He held them firmly before repeating the gesture with Perry.

"Remember this," he said, staring at us in turn. "Life is but death's dreamtime. You returned from the Ocean of Souls before you learned the Final Truth. This is not the terrible thing it may seem. If Solomon does not invite you to learn more, you will learn it when you die. Everyone does."

CHAPTER FORTY-FIVE

My sleep-drenched thoughts were tuned to the waves that glugged on Falcon's hull. A sharp tapping broke the rhythm. I sat up, rubbing my eyes.

I had talked with Perry into the small hours, and we had fallen asleep in each other's arms. I stroked his hand as it rested on my tummy. Falcon's V-shaped berth wasn't large, but despite the heat, the closeness and the way my foot hung over the side, I loved everything about it—especially that I was sharing it with Perry.

I entwined my fingers in his and sat up when the tapping returned. My watch said it was nine-forty. I wrapped a towel around me. *Who could it be? Was it safe to answer?*

"Who is it?" I asked, sitting up, but received no answer. Through the skylight I glimpsed bright blue feet. I walked to the saloon and slid open the panels to open the hatch.

"Hello, Violet," I said. "Don't you know it's rude to wake people?"

She hopped and strutted, then raised a foot and lowered her head. Beating her wings, she rose into the air to hover above me.

"Alright, I'll see if there's any fish."

She was leaving with a strip of bonito when Perry's hand settled on my shoulder.

"Good morning, beautiful," he said, twisting the swell box cupped in his hand. "It needs more sun. How did you sleep?"

"I kept thinking about the Ocean of Souls. I wanted to recapture that feeling...of course, I couldn't. But just knowing it exists..."

"I'm afraid that for now, you'll have to make do with my ordinary, boring, every day, earthly love," he replied.

"However will I manage?" I asked. We climbed up on deck and looked at the sunlight glinting on Apex Predator, anchored a thousand yards away. "Are there any unchartered reefs around here?"

"One or two small ones. Why?"

"Can't they do something constructive like identify one by crashing onto it? They're casting a bad spell over the place."

"Breakfast?" Perry went back into the cabin and returned with a laden tray.

We sat at the cockpit table. He drizzled lime juice over a halved papaya as I poured the coffee.

"What's papaya without lime?" I mused.

"Why the frown?"

"Been thinking: That million dollar prize Dragan's offered Edward— it's to do with that speargun."

"Why do you say that?" Perry asked.

"Put yourself in Dragan's shoes. He's getting old and he's hunted everything out there—albino, defenseless, orphaned, critically endangered, tame, pregnant…you name it. Must be getting bored, looking for a crowning achievement for his repulsive blood lust, something that will offend normal people even more than usual. And I fear Edward's come up with the winning suggestion."

"But why here? There's nothing particularly unique, is there?" he asked. "Unless it's living deep in that ocean trench."

"I don't think it's to do with the trench—maybe Dragan was coming here anyway, and Edward simply added to his itinerary," I suggested.

A movement on the beach caught my eye. "Look, it's Frank—he's waving. He looks pretty excited."

"Quick," Perry said.

We dived in together and surfaced side by side, launching into front crawls. I stayed tight with him, pulling smoothly while admiring his rhythm and strength. I expected him to slow, but he surged on towards the beach. He lifted his head and smiled. Then he powered on, his form intact.

He climbed out in front of me, gripping the waist band of his swimming trunks.

Frank was hurrying towards us. "I think we've worked it out. Nancy's sending emails."

He beckoned us to follow him before stopping under a palm tree.

"This will do," he said, glancing around. "That photo of the volcano's been bothering me."

"Go on?" I said.

"It wasn't *anno* as in year, it was *anno* as in *Annobon! Annobon Island!*" he said triumphantly.

Perry looked at me and shrugged. "You'll have to give us more, Frank."

"The old name for *Pagalu Island.*"

"I've heard of it. That remote island off West Africa," Perry said.

267

"Isn't it part of Equatorial Guinea?" I added, "There was a failed coup there about ten years ago. And they had that hopeless swimmer, Eric the Eel, in the 2000 Olympics."

Frank turned to me. "What was the name of the guy Dragan mentioned at dinner? You know, makes two hundred mill a year."

"Teodoro," I said.

"Yes, that's him," Frank said.

"Hang on," Perry said. "There've been rumors about that place for years—"

"Pumpkin!"

Nancy arrived waving a sheet of paper. "I found a few stories, printer kept cutting out, but I printed one from Wikipedia:

The German edition of Der Spiegel of 28 August 2006 reported that the government of Equatorial Guinea sold permits to UK and US companies to bury 10 million metric tons toxic and 7 million metric tons radioactive waste on the island of Annobón. Teodoro Obiang Nguema Mbasogo supposedly receives 200 million US Dollars per year for renewed permits, while the population of Annobón lives in extreme poverty. The report also showed evidence that the whole island's ecosystem is about to collapse due to the massive waste dumping."

"That's appalling," Perry said. "But—"

"Wait, I get it," I said. "Dear God!"

"Oh no! They're going to dump...*here?*" Perry asked.

"In the ocean trench. Drums of toxic and nuclear waste, which will rust on the sea floor," Frank said, shaking his head.

"It'll wipe this place out! Half the Pacific too," Perry said. "Another Annobon."

Nancy lifted a second sheet of paper. *"Dragan Environmental Services...licensed to operate in forty-two countries...a long history of litigation...nothing proven in court but a frequent target for environmentalists."*

"Enough is enough," Frank said, his voice gravelly. "This time we'll stop him. Let's go, Pumpkin."

"Can that Dragan be for real?" I asked.

"The chilling part is he's as real as you or me," Frank said.

"But even he can't go around dumping poison in front of islanders and tourists. Can he?"

"Good point," Perry said. "So there's still a glimmer of hope. I mean, why invest in a cannery and fishing fleet if you're planning to wipe out the ecosystem?"

"We're still missing pieces, but we're getting close," I said. "Hey, look who it is." I nodded towards the two naval uniformed men who had slipped onto barstools on the hotel's terrace ahead of us. They glared at Frank and Nancy. Then they turned to look at us.

"Why does Dragan keep sending his muscle?" Perry asked. "And I thought Kris had banned them."

"Poodle's seen something," I said, following the man's pointing arm. "What are they up to?"

Bulldog spoke into his walkie talkie. Then he turned to Poodle.

"Hey, the boss is gonna love this—looks like a 'two birds with one stone' kinda day." They laughed and hurried away, leaving their beers unfinished. Minutes later their tender was speeding towards the mega yacht.

Perry saw my expression. "Quick, there are binoculars at the bar," he said.

We ran over as the tender closed on Apex Predator. There was a commotion on its deck as figures hurried back and forth.

"It's Dragan and Edward. Here comes Morfil. And…no! Please don't be thinking of doing *that!*"

"What is it, Perry?"

He handed me the binoculars. "Tell me I didn't see what I know I just saw."

Sky, then ocean flooded the lenses before I focused on Apex Predator. They were climbing aboard the tender and Edward was carrying—the small suitcase. Offshore, not even a mile away, the spray of a whale bloomed above a dark back.

"They've got it with them, the speargun!" I said. "And Poodle's carrying some sort of suit over his shoulder—bright orange. Perry?"

"Beats me."

I grabbed Perry's hand as we sprinted towards reception. "We have to tell Kris and borrow a boat. We have to stop them."

"They can't be about to—"

"Yes. They're going to *kill that whale!*"

Kris was on the phone. He ended the call as soon as he saw our expressions.

"We need a boat. Dragan's setting off on a whale hunt. We have to stop him. Spada available?" Perry asked, chest heaving.

"Take Coconut. Catch!" He threw the keys. "Try not to lose them this time! Oh wait, it's loaded with—"

"Tell Frank and Nancy we're in pursuit," I called as we ran from the office. To Perry I said, "I'll need my camera."

"Keep the port engine's revs below 2,000—it may be about to seize. And keep me updated on the VHF. I'll do whatever I can from here," Kris shouted back.

Outside, Perry said, "Meet you at the jetty. We've got zero minutes to lose."

I ignored the bemused sunbathers as I pounded along the beach. Bursting into my room, I grabbed my camera and then dashed out again, heading for the jetty.

"Okay, let's do this!" Perry said as I jumped aboard. "Watch out for the—"

The cockpit was full of boxes of seaweed. My foot squelched in one.

"Emma's latest harvest," Perry said.

I stood beside him on the flybridge as he reversed away from the dock and swung Coconut seaward. "Come on, old thing!" He pushed the throttles down. The engines roared as the boat churned forward. A hammering vibration echoed through the hull.

"Ten knots, that's tops. Oil pressure and temperature okay. So far, so good."

A terrible thought flashed into my head. "Which whale are they following?"

"Not sure, but they're heading straight out. With luck it dived and they've lost it."

It was twenty minutes before the gap between us and the tender began to narrow.

"They've slowed. Don't know if that's a good or bad sign," Perry said. "Look—there's another ship on the horizon. A big one."

"I wish Coconut was quicker!"

We were a hundred yards away when they turned. "They've seen us." I lifted the camera. "Better get busy."

"And look," Perry said. "A trawler's approaching. That big ship's a purse seiner. Why's it just sitting way out there? And sending a trawler over here? Here, take the wheel." Perry jumped down the ladder, three rungs at a time. He landed in the cockpit and lifted a deck hatch. "Engine's in trouble. We may lose it."

"You can do it!" I shouted, patting Coconut's instrument console encouragingly. Smoke billowed from the hatch, and the little boat charged on.

Perry was beside me again. "Is that guy—"

"Yes, that's Dragan," I said.

"He's holding…the speargun."

"He isn't holding it—he's *pointing* it. At that whale! Oh no, I think it's Solomon and they're sneaking right up on him. Don't sit there Solomon, please *dive!*"

But the whale wallowed in the ocean. A great fin came out and waved, before it settled back in the water. Then he blew as the tender edged closer.

"With luck, our engine noise will frighten him." Then Perry shouted,

"Please Solomon, get out of here!"

"Can you get between them? I need to get photos."

"No time."

Perry held the throttles down and the belching smoke was joined by a clattering roar.

Dragan studied us before he turned back to face the whale. As he brought the speargun to his shoulder and leveled the sights on Solomon, we slewed alongside. Perry killed the engines.

"She's taking photos," he yelled. "You harm that whale and an hour from now they'll be all over the internet."

Dragan lowered the speargun. "Your boat's smoking. You'd be safer here. Do join us," he said.

I shouted. "Let the whale go first."

Dragan nodded at Poodle, whose hand slipped under his shirt. It returned gripping a black pistol which he pointed at me.

Dragan beckoned us. "No need to RSVP. And do bring the camera."

Poodle waved the pistol. "Hands where I can see them."

Edward and Bulldog held the boats together as we climbed in. I couldn't bring myself to look at Edward who stood beside Morfil.

"Push that tub away! Smoking boats make me uncomfortable," Dragan said.

Dragan stepped forward and brought his face up to mine. He spoke calmly. "You, young lady, have become an irritation."

"Whale's surfaced, Dan. Dumb animal's still in range," Edward said.

Dragan turned to look. "What's that in its back?"

"Looks like an old harpoon, Sir," Poodle answered.

"Of all the whales out here, why do I get this one?"

Dragan turned to Poodle. "Give me that gun and cover them with this." He handed Poodle the speargun.

Grasping the pistol, Dragan spoke softly. "So we find ourselves in the middle of nowhere, temporarily inconvenienced by you two. It makes no difference. Allow me to explain: This is a Beretta model 92FS nine millimeter semi-automatic. Effective lethal range, sixty yards. The hollow point bullet will blow an orange-sized hole in someone. But in many situations, it's quite ineffective. Observe."

He pointed the gun at the water and pulled the trigger. I jumped as the *boom* ripped through the air.

"See those bubbles? Density of the water stops the bullet dead in a couple of feet."

"Your point is?" Perry asked.

"My point is…" He aimed the pistol at the whale. "Watch closely."

"Don't!" Perry shouted. "Look, can't we discuss this like civilized people?"

"The camera, please," Dragan said.

"No way," I said, my hand tightening around it. "Please be reasonable, we—"

The crack of the pistol reverberated through my head. A jet of vapor shot from Solomon's blow-hole and his tail slapped the water, the crash carrying like a second gun shot.

Dragan laughed. "It didn't even feel it."

"It's against the law, they're protected. The world will find out!" I shouted.

Dragan shook his head. "The great journalist—but I'm afraid you're misinformed. Thurston, explain."

Morfil cleared his throat. "Dan's correct. This country was never a signatory to the 1946 International Convention for the Regulation of Whaling, or the 1956 protocol. Those agreements recognize the rights of indigenous people to hunt whales in limited numbers. Hunting is also permitted for scientific purposes."

"And my line of scientific enquiry involves establishing pain thresholds in humpback whales."

"But you've never announced an intention to hunt whales here. You can't just—" Perry began.

"Excuse me, but I think you'll find...we just did," Dragan said.

"What about the whale watching here? You'll destroy a fledgling industry that could bring thousands of extra tourists," I said.

"I *never* thought of that! We'll just have to sing songs around the camp fire, and think up another way for me to make money out of this sweaty backwater. Oh, wait a minute. I already have!"

"Haw, haw!"

Dragan's hand shot out and grabbed my camera.

"Wait! That's mine!"

He threw it into the ocean.

"That's company equipment," I said.

"Send me the bill."

"What are you planning to do? Kill us? Even you with your connections won't get away with it," I said, trying to inject confidence into my voice.

"Oh, it's a beautiful day for a killing. But kill *you? Now?*" He laughed. "You underestimate me."

"And I'm going to earn a nice few bucks, haw, haw!"

"Look, would you mind putting the guns away?" Perry said, "There must be a way we can sort—"

"We're wasting time." Dragan handed the pistol to Edward. "I find these toys so *unfulfilling.*" He took the speargun from Poodle.

I hadn't looked at it before, but I now noticed Perry studying it.

"You designed it?" he asked.

"Sure I did. And my overpaid engineers built it. You see the challenge with special operations is their requirement for a weapon that packs a punch above *and* below the water."

"Looks impressive. How does it work?" I glanced at Perry and added, "I have to admit it's cool."

"Edward, explain."

"Yes, Dan. The thing is, it's made from a very light and strong material, and the spears are filled with explosive and the gun part, that's um, made from, um—"

"Edward…"

"Yes, Dan?"

"Shut up."

A smiling Dragan turned the speargun over in his hand, his fingers stroked it.

"Six rotating barrels built around a central barrel. Machine pistol frame. Uses parts from the Uzi, thirty-shot magazine, forty-five caliber ACP round. Resembles the Russian ADS underwater assault rifle, I hear you say, but let me explain why it's superior…"

"They're just trying to buy time, Mr. Dragan," Poodle said.

Dragan fell silent.

"Sorry, sir."

The whale still wallowed beside the boat.

"The clever part's the speargun." He pulled a spear from the barrel. "Bottom two inches are hollow, filled with propellant, primer located on the end. SMG did it with twenty-two caliber blanks but slow reload. With this, the diver has six spears in a quiver, held together with ethafoam spacers. Reload time: five seconds."

"Can he reload underwater?" I asked.

"Excellent question. Short answer, yes. And here's the best part. See how the spear swells at the end? Full of explosive. Underwater cannon. Blow a man in two, sink a small boat—"

"Blow a dumb grouper's head off, haw, haw."

"Bet that made you feel like a real hero," Perry said.

"Ah, look," Dragan said, pointing the spear gun at the trawler that had stopped a quarter mile away. "Our colleagues have taken up position. Now, Edward. What's your side bet?"

"I say three."

"Three *what?*" I asked.

"My in-depth research leads me to wager three shots to kill this whale," Edward said. "If I'm right, Dan will double my million."

Perry's voice quivered with rage, "You murdered one of the largest recorded goliath groupers as part of a sadistic *bet?*" His eyes held Dragan's.

"Now you're going to kill a defenseless old whale? And not any whale. A whale that can—"

Dragan's arm flashed up with the speargun. His left hand braced the foregrip as he took aim.

"No!" I shouted and lunged forward.

I right-hooked Dragan on the shoulder with all my strength, rotating with the punch as Perry had taught me. He tipped forward. An arm flailed as he fought to regain his balance.

The speargun flew from his hand, splashing beside the whale. Poodle was on me in seconds, dragging me back in an arm lock as Bulldog helped Dragan up.

"Bravo, Teal!" Perry shouted.

"Not so fast," Edward said, his gun level with my chest.

CHAPTER FORTY-SIX

Dragan exhaled slowly. He stared at me as he tucked his shirt back in. Pointing at a locker, he clicked his fingers. Why was Dragan smiling as Poodle opened it?

"If my memory serves me, you'll find the Mark One in there, behind my suit. Pass them to me," he said as Poodle retrieved the orange suit I'd seen him carrying to the tender earlier.

"You're going swim—" The words died when I saw what else Poodle lifted.

Dragan laughed. "An earlier prototype of the *Columbine*—inferior safety catch and trigger mechanism but fully functional. And no, I have no intention of swimming."

I glanced at an open-mouthed Perry.

"Now where was I?" Dragan asked, with the speargun at his shoulder and the whale stationary in the water.

"How convenient of this whale to have swum over here."

"Over *here*?" Perry asked. "We're nearly above the trench."

"Correct, young man. And the trawler's waiting above it."

"Wait till your shareholders—Wall Street—hear about this," Perry said. "Great PR, Dragan, killing an old whale."

He adjusted his aim. Without turning, he said, "The whale's just the icing on my cake. Anyway, it'll blow over because, at the end of the day, all anyone cares about is the bottom line. Anyone who matters, that is."

"No, don't!" I shouted.

The speargun bucked and a silver streak flashed from the barrel. Solomon's body shook violently, and his tail slapped. A terrible noise, part moan, part scream, ripped through my head. He blew, the vapor misting pink. Then, as if in slow motion, he dived.

Perry lowered his hands from his eyes, "I—I can't believe you did that," he said, his voice breaking.

Dragan pointed at a brown stain in the water. "Fascinating. So blood *is* thicker than water. Now we must be patient. When he surfaces, I'll finish him." He motioned to Perry, jerking his thumb over his shoulder.

"Get the resort on the radio. Tell them we're all fine here. I recommend you give nothing away."

"If I refuse?"

Dragan sighed. "Ever seen what an exploding harpoon does to a woman's face?"

Perry moved to the console and lifted the VHF mouthpiece. Dragan said, "Good move, because I wasn't bluffing."

"Sun and Moon, Sun and Moon, this is Apex Predator tender, Apex Predator tender on channel sixteen. Over."

"Apex Predator tender, this is Sun and Moon. That you Perry? You making friends out there? Over."

"All's fine here, mate. With my friend, Mr. Dragan, now. Coconut broke down, so we're on his tender. We'll be here a while longer. Over."

"Roger. Keep me posted, chum. Out."

Dragan turned to Edward. "Till now, I couldn't decide which was the more rewarding: The silverback gorilla I bagged in Virunga or the mother and baby elephant I killed with consecutive shots in the Selous. For your information, those are game reserves in Congo and Tanzania, respectively." His pitch rose. "But whales are a whole new ball game! Quite a birthday I'm having!"

Perry clenched his fists and glared at Dragan.

If only Perry could have got a message to Kris. If only Dragan had missed. If only he didn't have a spare Columbine. If only.

Dragan addressed Morfil. "Any new intel on the break-in at the compound?"

"Local activists. Smashed a padlock, opened the pen gates. No real damage."

"Security cameras?"

"Weren't wired up."

"Gates? Activists? Security cameras? Anyone would think you had something to hide," Perry said.

"You sure the office was secure?" Dragan asked.

Morfil nodded. "Nothing missing."

I looked at Perry who was inspecting his finger nails.

"Forgive me for changing the subject, Thurston," Perry said casually. "Is it true that they *can* find *gold* in these parts?"

"Why would you ask—" Morfil's eyes narrowed. "One or two…isolated nuggets but in…unequivocally uncommercial quantities."

"By the way, I've emailed the first draft of my report on you,

276

Thurston," I lied. "Lots of unanswered questions. I imagine the updated version will *fascinate* Sir Basil. And you too, Dragan."

"Never seen you sweat," Dragan said, his eyebrow arched as Morfil patted his brow with a silk handkerchief.

"I'm struggling with a trifling malady, which will pass. But Daniel, I've been reflecting on this situation and perhaps...unlikely as it seems...they are correct. Killing a whale might indeed jeopardize our tourist industry. Why don't we drop them off on some isolated island for er...a picnic?"

"So you can come back and kill Solomon? Afraid that doesn't work for us," I said.

"Thurston, you need to toughen up. It'll be their word against mine, and like every other time, it will be easy to convince a court they're lying. Remember, I do not select my attorneys from the Boy Scouts."

"But *in front of them,* Dan?"

"You seem to hold all the cards, Mr. Dragan. I have one question. What *are* you surveying for?" I asked.

"As an exclusive contract was signed this very morning, I can divulge that we're here prospecting for rare earth elements. Why don't you report on *that,* my little journalist-ette? A brilliant scientist I know predicts the trench is littered with mineral nodules. An estimated—"

"This brilliant scientist—could he be called Teodoro Obiang Nguema Mbasogo?" I asked.

"And what does this genius estimate you'll earn from it? Let me take a wild guess: over two hundred million a year?" Perry added.

Dragan didn't flinch. His eyes flicked between us, as he flexed his fingers on the speargun.

"But you're in plain view of the island," I said. "You'll be seen."

"Will I?"

"Careful, Dan—" Morfil began.

"It *could* attract the attentions of irritating environmentalists. The authorities? I don't lose sleep worrying about them. Anyway, they'll never know."

"Don't bet on it!" Perry said.

"Those Davies people might as well pack up and leave. First thing I'm gonna do is bulldoze their zero-star resort."

"You don't own Horseshoe. Kris and Emma have a lease—you can't do that!" I said.

"Can't I? Tell him, Thurston."

"Dan's correct. He's the new leaseholder of Horseshoe Island. I signed the contract after breakfast. The seven day eviction notice will be served tomorrow. Force will be used if necessary."

"How *can* you let him destroy a great resort? It's a *gold*en opportunity to improve the place, modernize it," Perry said, glaring at Morfil.

Morfil dabbed at his brow with his handkerchief again.

"We get it, Dragan," I said. "We know what you plan to do here, even your code name Poseidon."

"Give the woman a coconut."

"But even *you* won't want the world finding out. Imagine the litigation, pressure groups, demonstrations, media attention. It'll go viral on the internet. Killing a whale's one thing, but dumping waste here—well, that's a whole new ball game. And there's no way you can disguise what you're doing," Perry added.

"You think it'll be the first time twenty hairy-legged women hold a demonstration outside my HQ, or start a Facebook page nobody joins? Can you see me trembling?"

He turned to Edward. "Any sign of that whale?"

"Not yet, Dan."

Dragan studied us in turn. "Nevertheless, I will congratulate you on working it out. But you missed the best part."

"Dan, they don't need to know the details," Morfil said.

Dragan silenced him with a stare. "I don't expect to attract attention because the cannery and fishing fleet will act as cover. I'll use purse seiners as long-range freighters. They'll carry the drums here in their fish holds. The first purse seiner's sitting out there and that trawler's carrying ten drums, five toxic, five radioactive. And who do you think's about to get the fun job of tipping them over the side? And no, this thing is not a diving suit."

"So, that's the second part of your birthday treat? You murder a whale, then you kill an entire ocean?" Perry shouted. "I appeal to you, Mr. Dragan. Surely you can understand that—"

"You're only sixty-five once, young man."

"But—" I started.

"I hold signed contracts with eight long-term customers from six developed nations who are desperate for us to dispose of their waste, and I'm negotiating with more. The demand's there—I haven't spent a cent on marketing, word just spread. And I make ten times the profit from nuclear as toxic. Dear me, it feels good to be in demand."

I shook my head as I spoke. "So, the drums are transferred to the trawlers from the purse seiners, out of sight of land. Then the trawlers will come in close and dump them in the trench, while pretending to fish. Is that it? But it can be rough out there…"

"That's why the trawlers need big stabilizers. Then they come in, fill the trench with all that beautiful waste and my pockets with gold." The pitch of his voice rose. "The trawlers can go fishing too, sell their catch here. Some of it will be canned. And when the purse seiners have unloaded their cargoes, they will be free to fish out of sight of land."

"Where I guess they'll use those fish aggregating devices that are destroying fish stocks," I said.

"I do like to embrace all technological advances. Then the trawlers will return to the countries they collected the waste from to sell the fish. That way their holds will be full on both legs of the journey. Simple, elegant, clever, if I do say so myself."

"But there aren't enough fish here," I said.

"My scientists beg to differ," Morfil said.

"They'd have found limitless tuna stocks on the moon, if you'd paid them enough," I said.

"In which case I'd better get started there too, before someone else clears the place out."

"What if the drums miss, land in shallow water? No matter where they land, they'll rust and leak within a few years," Perry said through gritted teeth. "It's complete lunacy, you'll cause an environmental catastrophe! The drums will contaminate the fish holds too. You even plan to sell this fish around the world?"

"Perfect business model, young man. How convenient that the countries that produce the most waste pay the highest price for sushi. Sort of divine justice." He laughed. "Your problem is you're sentimental. Population forecasters have been warning for years that we need to lose a few billion people for Planet Earth to survive. As politicians are so impotent, it falls to me to accept the challenge."

I glanced at Perry; cords bulged in his neck. "It may not be us...but someone will stop you, Dragan." A thought had been nagging me. "Now that we know, what are you going to do to us?" I added.

"That whale up again?"

"No sign, boss," Bulldog said. "Shouldn't be too long."

"Young lady, I am fortunate that I have always enjoyed complete clarity in my business visions. Where others worry, judge, moralize, procrastinate, Dan Dragan acts."

"You haven't answered her question," Perry said.

"I disagree. Must I spell it out? I'd be delighted if after today's sport, you both joined me aboard my yacht to celebrate." He turned to Morfil. "I can imagine your report to the Chief of Police, Thurston. How these love birds went skinny dipping at night, after a heavy meal. Was it the sharks? Cramp, perhaps? Sadly their bodies were never recovered."

Perry said, "You're a lunatic, Dragan. You'll never—"

"But a very rich one."

I looked at Perry and mouthed *Don't push him.*

"What do you plan to do with a dead whale?" Perry asked.

"Edward, tell them about my new trophy room," Dragan said,

scanning the ocean.

"Dan's renamed a wing of his ranch the *Leviathan Room*. Viewing by private invitation only."

I stared at Edward, then Dragan. "You're planning to stuff a *whale*?"

"Couldn't find a team of taxidermists who'd do it. Did you know expanding gasses cause rotting whales to explode? Inconvenient. Flat deck on The Bottom Line's stern's been prepared to accept the carcass. Cameras will record coloration, and then we'll make a giant mold, and build a fiberglass replica like museums do. You'll be amazed at the level of detail achievable these days—right down to scars, warts and harpoon holes." He turned to Morfil, who had retreated to the far end of the boat. "You've gone unusually quiet, Thurston. Everything okay, old buddy?"

"Yes, yes," Morfil said.

"Then you cast the carcass adrift?" Perry asked.

"Of course not. I have a Japanese customer lined up. He's just waiting for my call. In the name of scientific research, you understand—"

"Haw, haw!"

"I can almost taste the whale sashimi now. And I bet those school kids can too," Dragan added.

"Kids?" I asked.

"Sure. They love it."

"You know whale meat's full of mercury?" Perry asked.

"Someone fetch my Stradivarius."

"Haw, haw!"

Perry's hand slipped into mine.

Dragan was speaking again. "Some time ago, I attended one of those tedious charity functions at the Natural History Museum in London. I slipped away and you know what I found in an exhibition room? A life-sized model of a whale. Ever since, I've always wanted a whale of my own, and you know what?" His voice dropped an octave. "Soon I will."

"When I was a child, I used to spend weekends there—with a sketch book," Perry said, quietly.

I prayed for the roar of the local police boat's engines, blue flashing lights, sirens. No one knew we were in trouble. No one would come. I looked at Morfil. Was our knowing about the gold a hollow bargaining tool? If we told Dragan, it might torpedo that deal, but would it make any difference to how he treated *us*? There was one way to find out.

"Thurston, isn't there something you want to get off your chest?" I asked.

"Or off your cuffs?" Perry added.

"If this represents a preposterous insinuation concerning—"

"Some kind of idiot, am I?" Dragan began. "I've long suspected you, Thurston, *old buddy*. You think I don't have people on my payroll in the mines, the cannery?"

"But Daniel—" Morfil blanched.

"I've got people tracing the gold too—I'll know who your buyer is in a day or two." He looked at Perry. "You think I didn't notice your *can* and *gold* wordplay?"

He turned back to Morfil. "I'm not surprised by you, Thurston. I knew you were cheap when you accepted my eighty-twenty offer. Now it's ninety-nine to one, in my favor. Take it or leave it."

"But—"

"Plenty more Third World countries with ocean trenches, deep water canyons, volcanoes—nothing very special about this place. I'll have your answer when the whale's dead. Oh look, we have a visitor."

A large bird was gliding towards us. Her front was white, her feet were Grandma's favorite shade of blue. She hovered astern, head tilting from side to side. Edward slipped the safety off the nine millimeter, and grasping it with both hands, leveled the sights on Violet.

"For God's sake!" Perry shouted. "That's my bird!"

"It's a pet!" I screamed as the gun boomed.

"Damn boat's rocking." *Boom!*

Violet veered sideways. "Fly away, please fly away, Violet!" Perry shouted, waving his arms.

"Don't move," Bulldog said, covering us with another pistol.

Boom! "Haw, haw, I got her!"

A feather sprung from Violet's wing, and she jumped a foot in the air. Then she dropped before lifting and wheeling away. *Boom! Boom! Boom!*

"You missed!" Perry shouted, as she soared off. "That was just shock wave."

"If I'd had a shotgun…" Edward muttered, lowering the pistol.

"I thought you said you could handle a gun," Dragan said.

Poodle was pointing. "Splashing over there, boss. Near the trawler. The whale's come up beside it." He laughed. "And he don't look too happy."

"It probably thinks the trawler guys will protect it," Bulldog added with a snigger.

Dragan stroked the Columbine. "Did I mention the advanced polymer construction? It weighs only half a pound more than a standard Uzi but air chambers guarantee neutral density underwater. We're wasting time—let's have some fun."

The tender picked up speed. A wave of nausea swept through me. Was Solomon in pain? Bleeding to death? Solomon, the whale that had changed my understanding of life and death, of love. Then it came to me: He was trying to help. As I watched, his fin broke the surface and slapped down.

"He's trying to warn us," I said. "He knows what's about to happened." A tear ran down my cheek, which Perry wiped gently away.

"Aw, how touching, haw, haw!"

"Mr. Dragan, there must be another way. Leave the whale alone. Forget the dumping. This place is a fragile paradise and you're about to destroy it. The planet desperately needs habitats like this. For those who come after us. For your kids!" Perry said.

"I hate kids."

"Edward, please—make this man see sense!" I implored.

"But Teal, he strikes me as eminently sensible. Your recent choices, however…" He nodded at Perry. "…seem poorly thought out."

We slowed near the trawler. Its cockpit was filled with black drums and men in orange suits.

Poodle swung the bow upwind of the whale and cut the engines. We drifted in silence.

Dragan climbed into his orange suit. He pulled the zip half way up, and left the hood hanging at his neck. I recognized the radioactive warning symbol below the words *Dragan Environmental Services*.

"Get out of here, Solomon!" I shouted. I took Perry's hand again. He squeezed back.

Dragan turned to face the humpback. The words "Birthday Boy" were printed in bold across the back of his hazardous waste suit.

Now, Solomon lay broadside, a boat length away, his fin close enough to brush the trawler. A mighty sigh misted the air pink. The huge, gentle eye—the portal to another world—watched us.

"I think he wants to block Dragan from getting into the trawler," I whispered.

"Or he's trying to protect the trench," Perry said.

Dragan raised the Columbine.

CHAPTER FORTY-SEVEN

With the speargun trained on Solomon's head, Dragan shouted to the trawler. "First five drums of radioactive—line 'em up!"

Two men ran to the back of the boat. The transom door swung open, exposing the barrels.

"Geiger counter reading?" Dragan shouted.

Someone called back, "Within safe limits, boss."

"There's no such things as safe. The saltwater will—" Perry shouted.

"Trust me. Those drums are made from sixteenth inch Dragan steel. I would have specified eighth inch, but in these difficult economic times, I find it prudent to make savings wherever I can."

I jumped at the whip-crack: Another steel rod flashed from the barrel. Then came a muffled boom, and Solomon shook in a great spasm that propelled concentric waves from his thrashing body. Again, that appalling noise, part moan, part scream, pulsed through the air.

I gasped as I saw his eye flex. Then slowly it opened wide and his tail began to beat.

"Solomon," I shouted, "Please, swim away!"

Perry rushed forward. "Dive Solomon, for God's sake dive!" He lunged in front of Dragan. "That's enough...it's over! You'll have to go through me to get to him."

"Stand aside young man." He turned to Bulldog. "Kindly assist our guest."

Arms splayed, roaring, Bulldog charged. Perry sidestepped and whipped a punch under the man's jaw. Bulldog grunted, bounced off the side of the boat, and was raising his arms to protect his face when another punch buried itself in his ribs. A protracted squeak escaped as, blood dripping from his mouth, he sank to his knees, as if in prayer.

Poodle closed in. His hand dropped to his ankle. When it returned, he was grasping a knife. He snaked it in front of Perry, switching from hand to hand. "Never did learn the Queensberry Rules," he said as he edged closer, crouched, menacing, his back to me.

"My money's *isn't* on lover-boy, haw, haw!"

"Oh dear, Dan, can't you—" said Morfil, who was cringing in the back of the boat.

As Poodle advanced on Perry, I forced myself to think. *Do something!*

Poodle swiped the knife at Perry who jumped back—but Poodle stepped forward. Perry had nowhere to go.

"How many times you think you can make me miss?"

I was trying to remember. Back on the beach, the boxing lesson. What was it Perry had said when I asked him the secret to landing a punch?

Perry's eyes were locked on the blade. I jumped behind Poodle and Perry's eyes flicked right to meet mine. An involuntary movement. He mouthed *Keep back*—it was enough. Poodle half-turned, the knife still. In that second, he offered Perry his blind side.

The punches, some straight, others curled, rocked Poodle's head back and forth like a cork on waves. A sweeping hook spun him to face me. Eyes rolling, he collapsed like a thermited tower, and the knife clattered onto the deck.

Edward aimed the gun at Perry. "Knife over the side. Now!"

I heard the *plish* of steel on water.

"I seriously did *not* want to do that," Perry said, grinning from ear to ear.

"Nice uppercut. Perhaps I should offer you a job, young man."

"You couldn't afford me."

"Try me."

"My price? Leave the whale alone and don't dump here. Or anywhere else."

"You're right. I can't afford you."

The goons dragged themselves up. Bulldog spat blood from his mouth; Poodle wobbled like a Friday night wino.

"Call yourselves bodyguards?"

Solomon still lay there with an unnatural tilt to his body. He circled a pectoral fin but over-corrected, the blood that seeped from him staining the purity of the ocean.

"Edward, keep our melodramatic guests covered."

Dragan raised the speargun to his shoulder, but Perry stepped across and blocked his line of sight again.

"As I said, it's over, Dragan."

"No, Perry! It's too dangerous. Please—"

"What have we here? A game of chicken?" Dragan asked. "That's fine, because it's one of my favorites!"

"Perry, move!" I insisted.

Dragan shouted at the men on the trawler. "I'll be there in a minute. Raise the platform, but don't you dare tilt it!"

The rear of the trawler's deck rose slowly, raising the line of drums at its stern. Dragan turned to me. "Because today, that's *my* job."

His focus returned to Perry. "I'll count to three, young man," he said quietly.

"It's over, Dragan. Look behind you," Perry said calmly.

"Oldest trick in the book— One."

"Boss, boat coming. Blue flashing lights," said Poodle.

"How long before it gets here?" Dragan asked without looking, the speargun level with Perry's chest. "And that's *two.*"

"Mr. Dragan there's no point now. Please, see sense! It's not worth it. You'll lose everything!" I said.

"A few minutes, boss."

He pulled the suit's zip up to his chin and the hood over his head. "Still plenty of time to finish both jobs."

"Move, Perry, *please* move. For me, for us!"

"Boat getting closer, boss."

"Two and a half."

"Police waving, boss."

"Dear God, Perry, *move!*"

"I warned you. Three!"

I leapt forward, spinning around to face Dragan, with Perry behind me, shielded. "If you kill Perry, you'll have to kill me too." I saw the surprise on Dragan's face, the snout of the speargun that pointed at my chest. Perry's hands landed on my shoulders. I braced myself so he couldn't push me away.

"No Teal, it's—" he said.

"I'm not moving!"

My eyes held Dragan's. I could sense the calculating mind within their darkness. I braced myself for the explosion. For the end.

But Dragan was smiling. "Like I said. There are plenty more remote places run by crooks." He lowered the Columbine.

"What are you doing, Dan?" Edward shrieked.

"Calculated decision, Edward. That was my best poker face but— looks like you won't be earning that million, my friend."

The crack tore through my brain. Everything became a spinning turmoil. The scene before me slowed, froze. I felt no thump in the chest, no pain as the man with the speargun shouted silent words. Smoke corkscrewed innocently from the shiny thing in the chubby man's hand. His mouth fell open. "Haw, haw!"

Haw, haw? The faces in the white uniforms stared at each other.

A screaming in the sky as the hands slid off my shoulders, and someone slumped behind me. When I turned, my mind struggled with the broken shape that lay in hyper-focus. A shot of dizziness, my legs buckled, and I went down too.

The spit of scarlet on the shirt wasn't large. He'd survive, I told myself.

I cupped his chin, hugged his face. "You're going to be alright." I looked up at the sky. "Dear God, let him live. You can't do this—not to *him!*"

I shivered when his mouth lolled, cried out at the red bubbles that foamed there. Perry's eyes held mine with confused serenity.

"I'm…so sorry, Teal. I'm a fool, it's my fault and you're so brave. But I couldn't let—"

"No, don't try to speak. We'll get you to a hospital, save your strength. We'll—" I moved my hand to his back to support him, and my fingers settled in something warm, sticky. I leaned closer, dreading what I'd see. I gasped at the blood.

With heavily lidded eyes, he looked around the boat. A frown furrowed his forehead. To no one, he asked, "Why do they kill and kill? Please tell me why."

"Not now, save your strength."

"Has Violet been fed today?"

"Perry," I sobbed.

His gaze sheared in and out of focus. A question, then a half-smile lit his face.

"You're very beautiful."

"You don't have to say that now."

"Are those feathers real?"

"Violet's not here. Just try to—"

"How do you do that with the light?"

"I don't understand. Please rest—"

His voice rasped. "Can't you see her?" he asked. "Silly Teal, behind you. There's…an angel."

I grasped his hand, "Don't leave me Perry. You can't—"

He moved his head closer to mine, the effort rippling through his sagging torso. He gripped my hand, but his strength was ebbing. I looked into his eyes—at the sparkling blue, at the calm that had settled in them, as the light there dimmed.

"Shhhhhh," he said, smiling.

"Perry—"

"Teal, I'll wait for you," he said, the flutter of his lips brushing my neck. "For as long as it takes…"

"Perry, what do you mean?"

"…in the Ocean of Souls."
His head rolled onto my shoulder.
"No!" I cried. I laid my ear on his chest.
Two beats.
One beat.
Silence.

CHAPTER FORTY-EIGHT

I think Perry died on Friday. When Emma left my room earlier this morning, carrying a tray with my untouched breakfast, she'd frowned, and said this was the fifth day I hadn't eaten. She left the croissant behind, in case I changed my mind.

I remembered blue flashing lights, shouting. How, when we got back to the dock, the police prised my arms from around Perry. Yes, I remembered that. But I had no idea whether minutes or months had passed since my world collapsed.

They must have brought me back to my room. A doctor may have visited. I vaguely recall that Frank and Nancy spent many hours watching over me, holding me. I don't think I went outside—not even when Nancy begged me to share a sunset with her.

Dignified people, some in uniforms, others in suits, came, spoke quietly and left. Kris brought an Australian detective to my room who'd recently been posted here. I don't know if I helped with his questions. I do remember the next day Frank reading a document slowly to me, repeating the words "Take your time" and saying that if it was accurate, I could sign it. Someone emailed Malcolm to let him know what had happened. The detective asked if I minded staying at the resort until he'd completed his report, and that he'd return in a few days when I could concentrate.

And every time someone mentioned Perry, my heart ripped open.

Tangaroa, Morfil's driver, went on record saying two surly men in white naval uniforms had arrived to see Thurston Morfil the day after Perry died, and his boss had invited them in. Ten minutes later, Morfil had ordered Tangaroa to go to the market and buy a moray eel. When he'd returned, Morfil, in an unprecedented flurry of smiles and cash handouts, had dismissed his staff for twenty-four hours. Tangaroa didn't know when the sailors left, but the remains of the sautéed eel were found in a well-burned pan on his boss's stove. Morfil's body was recovered from his swimming pool. The police stated they were not treating the death as suspicious, and the coroner entered a verdict of suicide.

I hadn't checked my emails and when the phone rang, I ignored it. My world had been plunged into a vacuum from which every last ounce of energy and hope had been sucked.

I felt detached from the gaunt face in the mirror. The one with dark eyes, hollow cheeks. When the tears finally ended, I was launched from a terrible dream into a stark reality that did not—and would never again—include Perry. After three sleepless nights, Nancy gave me a blister pack of two sleeping pills. She encouraged, begged and bullied me to eat something. I refused the pills, but she left them on my night table by the bed, just in case.

For such a brief, while my soul had soared above the clouds, before it had been hurled to earth in flames. Every bone had broken; now my spirit hemorrhaged too. The one person I loved, in a way I'd never imagined possible, had been stolen from me in an act of unfathomable treachery—by a man I once thought I knew. A man who, despite his faults, I could never have imagined capable of such a thing.

Every moment of suffering I'd experienced in my life, every blow and bruise to body, mind and spirit was nothing. When I could think, I wondered if it would have been better if I'd never met Perry. Or taken that bullet myself.

Forget destiny, karma, life purpose, fate, or any idea that I might learn an important lesson from this. Only one thought kept returning: How would I ever get through the rest of my life?

I'd followed Lizzie's letters, watched for signs, opened myself to the universe and, finally found my best friend and my best me. I'd done everything I was supposed to do—and I'd still wound up alone, empty, devastated. I had been a small part in a complex sequence of events—why had it ended this way? What happened to good and bad, right and wrong?

A knock at the door. Emma stood there with Frank and Nancy, armed with fruit and mineral water. With strained smiles and hushed voices they tried to make conversation. Frank chuckled when Nancy said she'd always found Edward un-Bear-able but I couldn't laugh.

Later, Frank opened the door to the Australian detective who said Edward was behind bars, and they now had witness statements from the others. He emphasized how helpful and courteous Dragan had been. I shook my head when he described Edward shouting at the police, begging Dragan and Morfil to protect him. Apparently he'd dropped to his knees when Dragan had reiterated that he barely knew him.

The detective told me that while the police had been busy in the tender, the trawler had motored back to the purse seiner with the drums still onboard, and both had sailed. With no evidence of waste dumping, the survey vessel had been allowed to leave too. Apex Predator, with Dragan and his goons aboard, was due to sail this evening.

Frank sat beside me. He kept checking his watch. When the phone rang, he moved quickly.

"Yes, she's here. Just a moment, please."

"I don't want to talk to anyone. Not Malcolm, or Sammie, or—" But Frank thrust the phone in my hand. "Please Teal, take *this* call."

"Teal? Is that you?"

The voice sounded vaguely familiar. The uncertainty didn't.

"Who is this?"

"Basil. How are you, my dear? I apologize for bothering you, but I wanted to offer my sincere condolences."

"Sir Basil?" I said, as his face reconstructed in my mind.

"Yes. Basil Thane. I won't take up any more of your time than is absolutely necessary. That helpful fellow—Frank Butler—briefed me and of course, Malcolm's been updating me regularly too. I want you to know how impressed I am. You've done an incredible job."

When I didn't speak, he continued.

"Rumors have been circulating about Thurston Morfil for some time. Apparently he had serious financial problems. Spread himself too thin, owed money to the sort of people you don't want to owe money to. I'm very—Teal?"

"I'm listening."

"Grateful that you exposed him, but it's still a great shame he—"

"That story on the grapevine before the award ceremony...that all wasn't quite as it seemed at Musculus. Was that about Thurston Morfil?"

"I don't understand."

"You said you were only interested in expensive Bordeaux wines."

I waited for an answer.

He cleared his throat. "The point is...a fine example of Instinct—Intellect—Integrity. I'm impressed. It occurs to me you may have wondered if I even wanted the truth. Fact is—"

"That *did* cross my mind."

"I sent you because Malcolm said you were the best. Hungry to prove your worth, as well. Listen, I've just come off the phone to the Prime Minister down there. He's concerned on the impact this could have on tourism, and is in full support of the establishment of a marine sanctuary, with charitable status. I will be personally recommending it to the Musculus Employee Charity Scheme, as soon as the legals are taken care of. The Prime Minister's planning to nationalize the gold mining to finance the sanctuary. You'll never guess who rang him with that brilliant idea."

"You?"

"Dan Dragan. Suggested they name it the Dragan Marine Sanctuary."

"I don't know what to say." *You're kidding!*

"Whatever you think of that Dragan individual, he's smart. He reckoned he'd thrown money at the mines that he wouldn't recover, so he tried to salvage something. He knows that positive PR never hurt anyone."

"Did the Prime Minister fall for it?"

"Puleleiite's a wily old fox—sent the scoundrel packing! He seems very on-message—thinking about using any mining surplus to establish more sanctuaries in the region. Teal, you have my very deepest sympathy and gratitude regarding the, ah, personal matter. You must take as much time off as you need. By the way, a slot has opened at our investigations desk. You start first thing on Monday."

"Thank you, Sir Basil. That's...well, it's what I've always wanted, but—"

"But? Whatever are you butting for? I'm demonstrating how highly I value you. Of course, Thurston Morfil was a terrible shock. This whole unfortunate episode has been. For you, more than anyone. Anyway, as you know, my nephew's the team's high-flyer, he can show you—"

"I didn't know you had a nephew."

"Yes, Simon. You can get to know each other better..."

Simon? Who won the Musculus investigative journalism award...twice? "It's a kind offer, Sir Basil. I just can't get my head around big decisions right now.... I feel like...there's more I could do here. I'm not really ready to leave."

"Oh yes, of course. I understand. Too much, too soon. Well, my dear, if you want to stay there for a while, you can be our on-the-spot representative. Start first thing Monday.

"Here's an idea: Puleleiite asked if I knew anyone local who could take care of the social media, the press, write progress reports on the sanctuary—that sort of thing. I'm thinking of adding an environmental feature to some of my titles. If you don't want the investigative job, why not have a stab at that? See how it goes for a month, and we'll take it from there. I'll throw in a pay rise too."

"Thank you. I'll give it some serious thought."

"One more trivial matter. I still need a written report on Thurston. No rush, but this time tomorrow's fine. The very best to you, and if you need to talk, I'll leave instructions with Sigvard to have you put straight through, though I'm in China from Friday for a week. Oh, one question. I heard how remote the island is—how did the police get to you so quickly?"

"No idea."

"Is the resort owner there? Kristopher Davies, isn't it?"

"The co-owner's right here." I said goodbye and passed the phone to Emma.

"Yo, this is Emma."

I watched the rise and fall of her brow, the smile that stretched her chartreuse lips.

She spoke in a rush. "Perry always called Kris 'chum', and Kris always called him 'mate'—but Perry reversed it in a radio message from the boat, so Kris knew something was up, and he radioed the police boat. For some weird reason, they thought Kris's voice was Morfil's, and they responded super-fast."

Emma winked at me as I played back her words in my mind: *For some weird reason, the police thought it was Morfil on the radio.* For the first time that day, I smiled as I remembered Kris's impersonation of Morfil's pompous voice the morning of my interview.

After a pause, eyes wide, she said, "That's ace karma, Bazza! Thanks, bro! Respect!" She replaced the phone and turned to face us.

"Dragan has surrendered the lease, and Mr. Prime Minister wants us to stay on and run the place as an education center! And sir boss-man said he'd throw a pile of cash at it for modernization. Wait till Kris hears," she said, skipping out.

Nancy took my hand. "One day Angel, I pray you'll be able to see the good that's come from all this."

I looked blankly back at her. "Has Bob been consulted about the sanctuary idea?"

"He's given his full blessing. It's what Perry wanted too," Frank said gently.

"How are you, Angel? Would you like a little sun? The ocean looks so sparkly and beautiful today," Nancy said.

"Malcolm, Rob, Sammie and a whole bunch of your colleagues send their love. There's an e-card from them, when you're in the mood," said Frank.

*   *   *

Later that afternoon, Emma joined me, pulling a beach chair next to mine as I gazed out at the ocean. As Nancy had promised, it was beginning to sparkle a bit. Just at the corners.

"Sorry I'm late, honey. Mother-daughter yoga class. What's hanging?"

Everything was still taking a while to come into focus though. I looked at her, watching the sun gleam on the sand, backlighting her.

"Emma, I wanted to ask about your thesis. You said something about 'if only an outsider could experience one of their legends.' Would it be helpful if I described what happened to us?"

"You *serious*, Teal-baby?"

"Give me a few days—we'll talk while it's still fresh."

She hugged me. "Love you! And you know what? If I write it up, and win the Templeton Prize, the money goes to the sanctuary. Oh! Here comes Bob."

Bob had visited but, eyes downcast, he'd hardly spoken, spending much of his energy drawing lines in the sand with his feet. We'd walked along the beach, then sat side by side until the fireflies came out. Finally, tears in his eyes, he'd said goodbye and trudged off. It was exactly what I'd needed that evening.

He leaned close to Emma now, and spoke in low tones. I heard something about how little time was left and Solomon wanting to see us again.

"My grandmother heard him too," I said, seeing Emma's kind but disbelieving look. "He called with music. His special whale song."

I lifted my beach bag, and pulled out Grandma's letters, which now accompanied me wherever I went. "She didn't know who, or what was making the music. His voice was always distorted, and there were never words. Just feelings. I've heard the music. So has Perry." I gulped saying Perry's name.

"There is little time," Bob said, shifting his weight from foot to foot. "Kris and the Butlers are waiting in Coconut."

"Isn't it out of action?" I asked.

We hurried towards the dock, my arm through Emma's, the letters safe in my bag.

"The deck's a bit charred, but one engine's running fine," Kris said, after greeting us.

Soon we churned seaward.

Solomon waited in the swell beyond the reef. When he blew, I flinched at the pink that tinged the vapor. It wasn't the deep, chambered resonance I'd grown used to, but brief and shallow. It caught mid-blow, as if the old whale had been lanced by pain.

"Dear Solomon!" A sob choked in my throat.

"He wanted to say goodbye," Bob said, his voice cracking. "And thank you."

I looked into the old man's face. Tears followed the wrinkles of his cheeks.

Solomon drifted close to the boat. Bob climbed over the transom onto the swim platform and crouched, the whale wallowing with its head beside him. His great body leaned over, and a fin fanned an over-correction. Solomon blew again, and when I looked into his eye, I saw the mist that had settled there.

Together, we drifted beyond Wailing Rock, into the deeper waters of the channel. Six humans and one vast, gentle, dying whale, united by grief.

There were no words—we were only here for this magnificent, extraordinary creature. Bob reached out and touched his old friend. Solomon trembled.

The gulls circled lower, and the first gray shapes ghosted beneath the waves. A shark, double my height, snaked past.

"Tiger shark," Kris said softly.

"Isn't there something—" Nancy began.

"I'm afraid there's nothing we can do—we must let nature take its course," Kris answered. "If I kept a rifle, we could have deterred the sharks for a bit and bought some time. But even then..."

Bob was speaking in the language he'd used at the wallet ceremony. He repeated a phrase over and over, his words growing faster, his pitch rising. His arms were raised when the tiger shark rammed into Solomon.

"No!" I shouted as the water foamed behind the whale's head. A sickle tail beat the surface as the shark drove its jaws deeper. Solomon's fin flapped gently, as he failed to swat his tormentor. Then, the tiger shark broke free, trailing blubber from its jaws. As he swept past, concentric rainbows blossomed around the wound, calming the ocean surface.

"Oil," Kris explained as we stared at the jagged hole in Solomon's flank.

The whale lay still as other sharks butted his side. They rolled, twisted, thrashed, in search of grip. Solomon blew a great shower of scarlet that hung there, staining the cotton bud clouds. The blow ended in a deep moan that lingered with the bloody vapor.

I wiped my eyes. Bob's words came faster now.

Solomon shook, great spasms wracking his body. His tail rose high above the water. The gunshot-like tail-slap scattered the sharks. Then slowly, slowly, his body rolled over until his pale belly faced the sky.

The sharks slid back, circling, probing. It was as if they knew their moment had come—the first blunt-snouted brute charged, clamped on, shook, tore. Others soon followed in the building frenzy. Gulls cackled and dived; more flocked in. As they gnawed on the lifeless Solomon, I knew his mortal remains would be consumed, his minerals and proteins reclaimed, in the great cycle of nature. I also knew that no shark, no gull...could eat his soul.

Bob whispered a new phrase. Then he turned to face us, tears dried. "His next journey has begun."

"Good bye, Solomon." I prayed that he would find peace in the Ocean of Souls.

Emma helped Bob back into the cockpit. We drifted another mile, everyone quiet with their own thoughts. When the time felt right, I pulled Grandma's letters from my bag, and the ribbon fell away.

I read slowly—as much to myself as to the others.

"My very dearest Teal,

If you are reading this letter, then you must be at the end of the search. I am so proud of you because it means you have discovered the secret of the music. I am not surprised—I knew you could do it. You're the smartest, most resourceful girl ever. Who it was, why he tried to contact me though—well, I'll never know. But it's amazing that you figured it out. Thank you and congratulations, dearest."

When I had collected my thoughts, I said, "Grandma's family were once whalers. They grew quite wealthy on it, and the fortune was passed down through several generations. She adored my grandfather, who wouldn't go into her family's business. He was a marine artist. Her favorite picture, "The Last Wave", hung beside her writing desk. But he wasn't the son-in-law her parents envisaged for their only daughter, so they were cut off. When he got pneumonia, they had no money for medication. He died in his forties."

"Any idea why *she* heard the music?" Nancy asked.

"She was wonderful with animals. Had this gift that she could understand what an animal thought, felt. Called it 'anpathy'. Maybe that was why."

Bob cleared his throat. "A few of us are born with the gift, others develop it. Be still around whales. If you listen, you will hear."

I waited a moment before returning to the letter.

"I'm sure you don't remember, but when you were young, you asked me why I stared at the ocean. I explained it was a gestalt (I bet you know the meaning of that word now!) and that I felt it, or someone, stared back at me. I still get that feeling, more now than ever. I wonder whether you ever do, Teal. Or maybe, with your busy life in New York, you don't get to see the water much. I'm not sure I could live somewhere without a view of the ocean."

Nancy smiled. "I'd have liked to have met your grandmother."

"Thank you, Nancy."

I took a deep breath and continued:

I apologize if I am rambling, dearest. The important thing is I have attached a second piece of paper. An apology. Please would you fill in the name of the person or people I have offended, and if you'd like to sign it, or know anyone else who would, you must all do so.

Now for some good news: I rescued the seal pup! It was stranded on a rock and I paddled over, wrapped it in a towel (my judo black

belt came in handy as it wriggled like Dooby Scoo the first time we
tried to bath him) and I took it back to the colony. You should have
seen how happy the other seals were!! Had a little tumble on the rocks
when I dragged the kayak out, but it's not much of a headache.
Maybe I'll go to the doctor tomorrow.
   Grandma Lizzie xox
   P.S. Carmilla is getting braver—on Monday she fed a dead
mouse to Monty Python, but she still won't try my garlic chilli chicken!
   P.P.S. I've left space on the bottom of the second sheet for you to
add anything you think important."

"She died that night of bleeding on the brain," I said quietly. Nancy's
hand settled on my shoulder.
"Oh, Angel. I'm so sorry. Take your time."
I lifted the second sheet.

"To........................
   I feel I know you. And I fear I have offended and harmed you
deeply. It may be because of a deliberate act on my part, it may be
because of my stupidity or ignorance. Maybe I have turned a blind eye
to something that's happening all around me, or I have taken—
perhaps without knowing—what isn't mine. Or sat back and allowed
others to. One can be just as culpable through action as inaction.
   For whatever has happened to hurt you, I am truly sorry. I ask for
your forgiveness and the understanding and courage to mend my ways.
My signature below is my commitment to change. To start anew."

Kris asked who the letter should be dedicated to.
"Solomon?" suggested Frank.
Bob shook his head. "The whole ocean. Solomon came from the
ocean, but his calling us was not about him. He wanted us to know two
things: The first is the great harm we bring to his world."
"And the second?" Nancy asked.
"Love. He never hated anyone, even those who damaged his world."
A minute passed before I managed to speak. "P—Perry dreamed of
marine sanctuaries. Not just here, but in vulnerable places in all the oceans.
To give the ocean a chance to recover."
I took the pen and wrote on the bottom of the paper.
"Would you mind reading it out, Frank?"
"Of course. It says:

Perry wanted the United Nations and the world's governments to
understand how strongly he felt about the desperate need for a network

of marine sanctuaries. The time has come for the UN and all governments to work together, to listen to the scientists, to the informed, to those who care about the future and not to those who place financial gain before all else. We must make these sanctuaries a reality, before it is too late."

Frank returned the paper to me and when I trusted my voice, I asked, "If we are agreed?" before writing "The Ocean" at the top of the page. Then I passed it to Frank. When everyone had signed it, it was returned to me.

"Bob, you should decide what happens to this."

"It must go back to the ocean for the apology to be heard…and to let the magic happen, so that Perry's wish comes true."

He climbed over the boat's transom again, onto the swim platform, and placed the paper by the edge. His hand went into his pocket, and he sprinkled purple petals over the letter of apology. He bowed his head, and spoke in his language. When his voice reached a crescendo, a wave reached over, and dragged the paper away. It drifted on the surface, swirling a little deeper as it became waterlogged. Then we watched its descent into the depths, each of us alone with our hopes and our prayers.

CHAPTER FORTY-NINE

We had said our farewells, hugged and promised things would begin to change. I walked back to my room, but as I slipped the key in the lock, I wondered what exactly I'd meant by that.

Trying to get comfortable on the veranda's bamboo chair, I sighed when my thoughts turned to Edward, who had decayed inch by inch since I'd met him, culminating in Perry's cold-blooded murder. At first, I'd thought he'd pulled the trigger out of jealousy. I'd reasoned he was envious of Perry's vitality, looks, charm.... But over the past few sleepless nights, I had come to wonder whether Edward was capable of such comparisons.

Finally, I decided he'd been motivated by one thing and one thing only: He'd lost a million dollars. In that barbaric act, he'd shown that he'd aligned himself irrevocably with Dragan. Edward, pitiable in his under-achievements, was a murderer who lacked Dragan's...subtleties.

Grandma used to say that it was better to have loved and lost than to have never have loved at all. As I sat alone—completely, desperately alone—a part of me wondered if I agreed. With a sickening thud, I wondered yet again if it would have been better if Edward had shot me too.

A giggling child ran past, dwarfed by the psychedelic beach ball she was kicking. It rolled towards me and she stopped. I pushed it back to her. Laughing, she swung her foot at it, missed. A second kick was more successful.

"What sort of world will be left for you?" I asked her retreating back.

I had always wanted to be investigative, to expose evil, greed, destruction—because that struck me as a way of making a difference. It was easy to dress Dragan, Morfil and Edward in the black hats. The rest of us in white. Sometimes life was that clearly defined. The problem was that Dragan had sailed away, unpunished and undeterred. Soon he'd find another Developing Country short of cash and long on crooks where he'd negotiate to dump waste. What happens next time? A few days of public outrage followed by false promises, and life would go on.

I reminded myself Frank and Nancy would continue pressuring wayward corporations, and Horseshoe would now become a marine sanctuary. But I had no idea what tomorrow or the next day would bring for *me*. My life felt like I was caught in a whirlpool. For all I knew the emptiness that dragged at the pit of my stomach, despite Nancy's kind reassurances, might even *get worse*.

What would happen if I did nothing? The ocean would continue as a giant garbage can, its dwindling resources plundered. Would it heal itself or slip into a death spiral? A few weeks ago I wouldn't have asked myself the question. If I had, I'd have played the optimist, while focusing on my stagnating career. Maybe on my love life too.

I had learned so much here. What had I written on the bottom of the note? That the UN and governments must listen to the informed. The informed? Now that sort of included—me. To walk away would betray not only Solomon and Bob, but the whole ocean. Perry too. And myself.

How many companies had the crusading Frank and Nancy bought a share in? How many more did they not know about, or lacked the resources to pursue? That Der Spiegel report on Annobon Island had mentioned American and British companies. Exactly how widespread was this problem? Clearly, the planet wasn't going to get better by itself.

For the first time in days, a sense of calm settled on me. Exposing evil might help in some—or even many ways. But another realization was pushing through. It came back to that conversation I'd had with Perry about righting wrongs and writing about them.

I couldn't walk away—I had to get involved, be proactive at the front line, if I really wanted to make a difference. And I did. I realized I wanted to stay here, help establish the sanctuary, perform the role the Prime Minister had mentioned, represent Musculus, accept Sir Basil's job offer. The problem was I also knew I didn't have the energy or courage right now to do it.

What I wanted so desperately to know, my conscious, sensible, professional mind reminded me could never be answered. But I spoke the question aloud anyway. "Is...Perry...alright?"

The sun broke from behind a cloud, and the ocean teased me with a new shade of indigo. People swam, sunbathed; a Frisbee floated by. From their laughter, I guessed they knew nothing of what had happened here. A sunburned man shouted at a beach boy, pointing at the jet skis pulled way up the sand. Emma and Kris had decided the jet skis should be decommissioned, and the first holidaymaker had been disappointed. Would it affect their business—or ultimately help it? We would all have to make sacrifices. It looked like the first steps towards change had already begun.

But how could I face the future without knowing Perry was safe? He had said thousands of charlatans had grown rich on the desperation of the bereaved. I'd treated the Amazing Anastasia as a joke, but everything she'd predicted had come true. Maybe she could help? What a shame I'd thrown away her number. But I did have an alternative: the Legendary Lizzie.

I went back inside the A-frame and took her letters from my bag. I placed them on my lap, and looked around the room before closing my eyes. "Lizzie, I may be going crazy, but is there any way Perry can get a message to me to let me know he's safe? If I could just know that, I'd be able to start thinking, doing stuff...face the rest of my life. At least I could try. I know what I want to do now—stay here and help set up the sanctuary. But unless I know he's okay, I just don't think I have the strength..."

CHAPTER FIFTY

I rolled over to the edge of the bed, and opened the drawer of the night table. The two sleeping pills lay sealed in their blister pack. I lifted them. Lying now, eyes closed, I allowed myself a moment's stillness. Earlier today I had walked for ages along the beach with Nancy, broken down as I shown her Perry's gym, and had meditated with Emma. For the first time in days I felt drowsy. Did I really need these pills?

When I woke, I found myself in the stillest part of the night, a smoky light drifting through the windows. I frowned because the soft breeze on my face meant the front door was open. As I walked over to close it, a noise, more like a distant humming, filled my senses. The beach front spread before me, its details softened by mist. Ten feet from my door, Bob stood silently. But instead of the shorts and faded T-shirt, he wore a grass skirt; white paint adorned his bare torso and a shell and shark tooth necklace hung from his neck. He was waiting. Just waiting.

Beyond Bob, a great war canoe rested in the shallows. A motionless line of warriors lined its double decks, paddles raised. Beside them stood another powerfully built man in a grass skirt and bowler hat. Age had sagged his shoulders and whitened his hair, in which feathers were woven and shells bound. He waved at me—in a slow semi-circle. I trembled because I'd seen him before: the ghostly figure on Wailing Rock.

Bob motioned to me, and together we walked towards the canoe. I gazed at its detailed paintwork, intricate carvings, shell inlays. Twin prows reached for the night sky. Behind them stood two thrones.

There was no color, only countless hues of silver. The sinewy warriors wore grass cloths about their loins. White zig-zags and chevrons adorned their skin, curved bone ornaments hung from their necks.

The Chief gestured for Bob and me to climb aboard. The warriors let me pass: I walked to the bow, unsure what I would do there. Bob indicated I should sit, so I settled on one of the thrones, feeling presumptuous, out of place. The Chief pointed his cane at the horizon and the warriors began to paddle. Everyone stared unwaveringly ahead as the canoe slipped along in a series of fast-slows.

We passed through the reef and soon left the rock far behind. Here and there, a star contrived to flicker from between the gaps in the cloud.

"Where are we going?" I asked Bob.

"Watch for the moon," he replied.

The warriors held their pace. I looked around, but Horseshoe had been swallowed in the blackness. It was as if they were aiming for the darkest, most remote part of the ocean.

Then ahead, slowly, ever so slowly, the moon broke free.

At first its light parted the clouds. As more moon revealed itself, it cast a beam onto the water, onto a familiar shape.

The sailboat drifted in a pool of phosphorescence. *What's Falcon doing out here?* I pinched my wrist and pressed my elbow against the throne until it ached. I turned to Bob, "If this is a dream, I've never had one anything like—"

"I told you on the rock: Life is but death's dreamtime."

The canoe advanced on the becalmed sailboat—and then I saw him, sitting quite still in the cockpit. He turned slowly; the familiar smile lit his perfect features. As we drew alongside, I thrilled to touch him again. He took my hand, climbed aboard the canoe, and wrapped me in his arms. I squeezed back, breathing into his chest, absorbing his essence. Then he kissed my forehead and settled on the throne beside me. With a wave of the Chief's stick, the warriors began to paddle again. I massaged Perry's warm hand, reveling in its firmness.

He turned to me. "I was waiting for you."

"I missed you," I said, my soul dancing.

The canoe cut left in time with the warrior's metronomic grunting. I tried to work out where we were heading, but this time I knew.

We sliced through the rebellious chop, and as the breeze cradled me in its warmth, I looked at Perry. He smiled back, his face etched in slate against the sky. The paddling ceased, and the canoe slowed. Somehow, I knew we were above the seafloor trench.

Bob tapped Perry on the shoulder. We both stood and Bob spoke, "Now Teal…the Final Truth."

Perry tightened his grip on my hand, and we moved to the edge of the canoe. Without looking back, we dived in.

Lazily, the bubbles climbed away. Then we swam, hand in hand, drawn deep into the midnight blue. Ahead, a vast, flickering ball dominated my vision. It extended as a giant globe, from seafloor to surface. A trunk of sparkling silver tethered the sphere to the trench. The tether flexed and turned like a swaying serpent. As we approached, I marveled at the interlocking animals and people, plants and insects, patterning the globe's surface. From the gaps between them, a light beamed its brilliance through us to infinity.

Ahead, the wall of souls rose, hand clasping leaf, fin wrapped around branch, fingers grasping fur. Twitching movements, adjustments, tremors, until the join was secure—then melded calm before new arrivals drifted in and the process repeated. As he pulled ahead of me, I realized Perry was going to join them.

He turned. "Teal, I must do this."

We would find our spot in the globe—wrapped in our love and in the universal love around us—to be bound together for eternity. At last it made sense. I had my answer. A stream of childhood images flashed through my mind. Mother's tight face, red, close—shouting. Grandma's soothing tones and cuddles. Carly, as we giggled at a long forgotten game. Edward came, but I willed him away. Finally, Perry was mine. Forever.

Perry wrapped me in his arms, and I held him tightly. But was there a subtle change as he pulled back to look into my eyes? Why was his brow creased? Then he kissed me again, the way he always did.

We stopped just beyond the globe's surface, and I watched the shuffling of energy as a horse and polar bear separated to create a space— our space. Perry watched me unblinkingly as he spoke.

"Teal, you can stay with me, or you can go back."

Even here, his eyes sparkled. I cried out, "Don't make me choose!"

"I want you to do what's best. Best for you, Teal."

"I—"

"What are years when measured against eternity?"

We embraced and his energy soaked into me. In that instant I made my decision, and a force began pushing us apart.

Releasing him, I whispered, "I'll do it. Because it's right for me. You want it. And I want to, too."

"I love you, Teal."

"I'll always love you, Perry."

I watched him as I drifted away, our eyes locked together. A silver thread paid out, heart to heart. Then he was absorbed into the globe by the primordial vibration. And he was smiling. He adjusted there, merging into the ball's sparkling surface. Perry had fulfilled this chapter of his destiny, but mine still had a long way to run.

Awash with love, hope, strength, though fighting off waves of sadness, I kicked for the surface. As I swam, I twisted to confirm the silver thread still joined us—it did. I whispered again his last mortal words, "Teal, I'll wait for you, for as long as it takes…in the Ocean of Souls."

A wave splashed over me, and I rubbed salt from my smarting eyes. Another wave tickled my calves. I lifted my head—I lay stretched out on the beach. How had I gotten here? Where was the war canoe, the old Chief, the warriors? Falcon lay quite still at its mooring, glowing warm beneath a climbing sun. Violet swooped low and landed beside me. She strutted back and forth, tilting her head, staring.

"Good morning," I said, climbing to my feet, brushing off sand. "I'll bet you're hungry."

*　　　*　　　*

I stayed under the shower's rusty water, thinking, adjusting. *Thank you, Grandma Lizzie, thank you. Now I know he's safe.* Then a pang of regret ripped through me—it would have been so easy to stay.

A few weeks ago, I had arrived here determined to renew my life with the wrong man, and ended up eternally bonded to the right one. Now, only weeks later, everything I'd believed about love, life and death, had been cast aside. A profound emptiness still gnawed at my soul, but it had been joined by a spark of hope. And by a sense of privilege that a great secret had been shared with me. That somehow, *I* had been worthy. Just when it made sense, I had made a decision. One I would have to live with for the rest of my life.

I had accepted my minute role in the universe, and learned how crucial each of us is to the survival of the whole. I remembered Fonu, the young man who had fought for what he had believed in, for his representation of the greatest secret with his extraordinary carved globe. And Solomon, the magnificent humpback whale—a Jesus-Gandhi with flukes—whose life-long struggle pitted his wisdom against the constant folly of human entitlement.

"Strange," I said, walking to the bedside table. I lifted the empty blister pack. "I don't remember taking those."

There was a knock at the door.

"Bob!" I said, as he smiled at me. Just like last night, he wore a grass skirt. He was naked above the waist and feather bracelets circled his biceps.

"I came to check on you."

"I'm a bit better," I said carefully. "I'm still trying to make sense of everything. But just knowing he's…."

I stepped past Bob onto the beach, and found myself staring at Falcon. I was struck with a need to be close to where Perry had lived, his beautiful yacht. Maybe alone there, I'd feel close to him too.

"Would you mind paddling me?" I asked.

Bob looked up at the threatening clouds. "Quickly, then."

I wrapped my teal-colored sarong around me, and we walked down to the surf.

The paddle dipped and twisted with Bob's thrusts. We closed on Falcon with Violet hovering behind us.

When we were close, he shipped the paddle, letting the canoe drift, and checked the sky. "You chose not to stay there. You could have."

"I know."

Bob spoke so softly, I had to ask him to repeat what he'd said.

"Many years ago, I too had to make the same decision."

"It took me some time to work it out. But I know you did. May I?" I asked.

I leaned forward, and parted the feathers at the top of his arm. A birthmark, almost a jagged scar, was unmistakable.

"Hello, Fonu," I said quietly. "It's a great honor."

"I never liked 'Firefly Bob'," he said.

"I began wondering who you were when you told me the end of your story. I noticed you used 'I' once, instead of 'he'. It was when you were describing Fonu falling in love with Losa."

The smile spread slowly. "You noticed the fireflies?"

"I did wonder about them."

"They came after she died. It was her way of telling me she was watching over me." He sighed. "It was so long ago. It's taken until now to believe I made the right choice."

"You deserve to enjoy—if that's the right word—this moment." Then a thought came to me. "Fonu, as rightful Chief, you should live on the island. Do you want to?"

"Yes."

"Perhaps, with Morfil out of the way, if we wrote to the Prime Minister...?"

He spoke softly again. I had to lean in to hear him. "Yesterday, I was contacted by a government official. After so long, he said they finally believe me." His eyes misted, "I have waited seventy-two years for this."

Fonu's voice thinned to a whisper as he stared at the ocean. "Yes, dearest Losa, you were right."

"Your story is incredible, Fonu. May I ask about that man Jackson? What happened to him after the war?"

"He came back, set up the fishing camp. I named Black Jack after him, because he devoured anyone who got in his way."

Suddenly Perry felt so far away, and the tears came. Despite them, I said, "I know what I'm going to do to help."

Fonu dropped his hand on my shoulder. "Solomon told me he saw those spirit globes in other oceans."

"Every ocean, throughout the world? A soul link with the heart of the planet?" I wiped my eyes. "Is it okay if I tell Emma?"

He resumed paddling. "Tell whoever needs to know, because we must quickly become many of body, but one of mind."

The canoe stopped by Falcon, and after steadying his craft alongside, Fonu turned to me again.

"This world has changed so much in my lifetime. Most of those changes have come from your people who have no understanding of the ways of the past, or the future that awaits us all if we don't take care of our planet. We must not forget about sand."

"You mentioned this before."

"Sand is time's way of reminding rock who is boss."

He waited as I climbed aboard Falcon. Then, with a small nod, he paddled away.

I moved carefully, butterflies in my stomach, as I crouched to climb inside the yacht.

Walking around the cabin, I willed Perry to materialize, knowing he wouldn't. His whale map was spread across the chart table. A calculator, a fishing weight, a book and the swell box held its corners down.

"To think it all started because of that box," I said, smiling at the fish scales stuck to the chart table's varnished surface.

My mind returned to our first dinner on Falcon—perhaps the most perfect evening of my life. Here again, surrounded by Perry's possessions, I expected to hear his voice, as deadpan, he delivered a joke or, full of passion, shared an ocean fact. Tears tumbled down my cheeks. I let them. Finally, I looked around, the hairs on the back of my neck lifting. "P— Perry?" I whispered.

I wiped my face, but was soon sobbing, emptiness billowing inside. Then a voice—Grandma's—told me to be strong. I closed my eyes, and stared into the swirling black behind my eyelids. Then I remembered what I'd asked Lizzie for—the chance to know that Perry was safe—and all I'd learned last night.

Looking around the empty cabin, I said, "You are alright, Perry. And one day we'll be together again. Forever. Until then, I know what I must do. I will stay here, I will help set up the marine sanctuary. I will do everything in my power to make it work. And this sanctuary will be followed by others."

The first drops of rain were tapping Falcon. I rubbed Lizzie's ring for strength as my gaze fell on the swell box again. *I guess now I'll never know why he carved my name on it.* Didn't he say he'd try and leave a clue? Sadly, time had moved too fast and if there was a clue, I'd never find it.

He'd said the box captured "a prayer and a dream". His concern— his passion—was about saving the oceans. He'd said he had a way to stop people destroying the planet—that he had thought about it a lot.

I picked up the box and a corner of the map curled up to reveal sheets of paper stapled together. I was turning away when I caught my breath. *What* did the typed heading say? I looked back and with trembling fingers, lifted the sheets and stared at the title.

Then I began to read.

A POEM FOR TEAL (as promised)

1.

The Tower—rich misted Dreamtime,
In an ocean's inverted waves,
Where I stumbled on my Teal-child,
Who unchained me from my slaves.
I was hauled through clouded meanings,
Sleet-salt, whipped and tied,
Gifted hope from desperation,
When the hero in me died.

2.

Frigid waters topped iceberg'd currents,
Through tropics of breathless heat,
Bequeathed a toxic present—
Help truth's vibration speak.
Accept no mind-farmed explanations,
Whaling mourn, wailing morn,
Or the liar's glib-spat promise of
The new day's fairer dawn.

3.

Greed fuels the final crisis,
The offal vulture thieves,
In lipogasmic worship
As our tortured planet grieves.
That Predator prowls in twilight,
A spurting life-force bled,
While men led by their shadows
Compose anthems to the dead.

4.

One legend's timely lesson,
Their fabricated charm,
An abyssal guardian's wisdom,
The humpback's selfless calm.
Love locked in swirling eddies,

The seafloor trench now sighs,
As countless spirits mingle to
Forgive…apologize.

5.

You wrenched me from the gallows,
Bemused and wracked by pain.
You soothed my broken spirit,
In thought and deed and name.
Will friends like blue-foot Vio-
Let Solomon us guide,
To the symbiotic maxim
The guileful strive to hide?

6.

The Universe binds forever,
The souls of beast and man,
Though self-serving ignorami
Fulfill Night's envenomed plan.
Right and left, hearts open fully,
In humbleness rejoice,
My ally, friend and lover
We revere the silent voice.

7.

A shift of power has started,
The temple columns downed,
The thronging meek are rising to
Displace the barking clowns.
All fear the fractured icons,
As the Closed Ones meet their Sendings,
While we, who've breathed in starlight,
Pay homage never ending.

Epilogueogueogue

Where fireflies pulse in moonbeams,
And the faintest echoes chime,
You're more than mortals dream of,
Strolling meadows in my mind.
Wrongs cannot quench our secret,
Laughed tears in wake and sleep.
The eternal thread that binds us

As we're rolling in the deep.

My lucent Teal-eyed flame,
Enough my lonely life.
I ask on bended knee,
Will you become my.........?*

*I'm still trying to find a word that rhymes here!

Now and always, your adoring Perry xxx

P.S. If you look closely at the poem, you'll see I'm
thinking eschatologically about love!

*   *   *

Maybe ten minutes after my third reading, I put the poem down. I had savored every image, every rhyme—but in the back of my mind, something felt wrong. In my career, I'd proofread a thousand articles and whatever it was, it was deflecting my attention from the poem's message. *Think Teal!* I picked the sheets up again, and read each line back to front, as I'd been taught at journalism school.

I began with verse one and paused on the first letter of the fifth line. I held the paper closer to my face. Was there something a little different about the first word of that line—the capital *I*? Was it a little smaller than the one three lines above it? And was it a different font? There wasn't a printer on Falcon, so it was likely Perry had used the old Epson in the business center. Hadn't Kris said it was unreliable? I read on.

I stopped again in the second verse. This time it was more obvious: The word *Accept* had clearly been typed fractionally smaller and there was that different font again. When I checked word's position, I noticed that again, it was the first word of the fifth line. So, I skipped to verse three and to the same position, where the word *That* was different too. I scanned down the sheets, and confirmed that a single word was printed differently in the same location of every eight-line verse. I'd never heard of a printer, old or otherwise, making so consistent a change to a document.

Could this be the clue Perry had mentioned?

I joined the words together, and spoke the encoded sentence aloud. "I...accept...that...love...will...right...all...wrongs."

It was cleverly disguised, beautiful, poignant. But thinking about it, did it in fact get me any closer to deciphering the meaning of the letters on the swell box?

The rain had stopped drumming on Falcon, so I wiped my eyes, rose

309

and climbed the ladder out of the cabin to Falcon's cockpit. I left the poem on the chart table, so it wouldn't get wet. I'm not sure why I slipped the swell box into my hand before I climbed the ladder.

The cockpit was soaked and the last drops felt curiously opulent, pleasantly warm. Mist lifted from the deserted beach where the clumps and riffles in the sand lay smooth like brushed velvet. The clouds had slowed their skudding; a few opened, and shafts of light probed tentatively through. Blues, greens and golds seeped back. Then the sky split and the storm curled away.

I traced my finger along the letters carved in the box, as if doing so would reveal its secret.

"You *can* solve it," I whispered, "Perry wanted you to."

I rearranged the order of the letters in my head. The only anagram I found was *late*—which I dismissed because I couldn't find any relevance of that word to…well, anything. If it wasn't an anagram, or a name…maybe it was an acronym, I thought, as I remembered Perry's J—O—K—E story about the tourist attacked by a sea monster. I rubbed my face. What could the 'T' stand for? *Today? Tomorrow? Time?*

"Think, Teal!" I said. Wait a minute—Perry certainly was a *thinker*— and he thought a lot about…*eschatology.*

I looked around the boat, my eyes taking in a bronze cleat warming in the sun and a magnolia rope, coiled like a resting snake. The mast towered above me; the furled sail brought back memories of our sailing trips. I breathed in deeply, filling my lungs with the salty air, and returned my attention to the box.

A familiar squawk made me look up as Violet landed on the deck. She folded her wings and stared at me.

"I'm so sorry, Violet. He isn't coming back. But I'll take care of you. Promise."

She tilted her head as if trying to understand me.

"You loved him too? I know you feel hunger. Fear. And Perry said you enjoyed foot massages. So why shouldn't you feel love too?" I asked.

She waddled closer, and settled on the deck.

I was about to return to the cabin to read the poem one more time when I remembered the P.S. beneath it. My thoughts focused on the last four words. Violet jumped when I clapped my hand over my mouth. I hadn't checked what *font* they'd been typed in, but…I *knew* I was right.

"Of course," I said, as Violet rose into the air with a squawk. "*That's* what 'TEAL' stands for!"

When my breathing calmed down, I lifted the box: *Thinking eschatologically about love.*

So, Perry thought love of humans for each other, love for animals, for plants, for all living things—for non-living things too, like the water and air, the soil and the hills—for *everything*—was the answer. The only way we could turn this situation around and save our precious planet. The big idea he had been too shy to tell me because people had laughed at him. So, he had carved it as an acronym on the box, said a prayer and placed his special pearl inside it.

I shook the box gently; the pearl tapped the sides. But what could be so special about this pearl?

I sensed a movement in my hand, and uncurled my fingers. The seams of the swell box now dissected it in a series of cracks. Did a segment just twitch?

With fiddling, an end came free. Then the top slid off to reveal a small compartment, and for several seconds, I just stared—I'd never seen a pearl like this. I lifted it, marveling at its cool, smooth texture, absorbing its extraordinary proportions. The double-pearl, whose color mirrored the perfect cream of the passing clouds, comprised two shiny oblongs fused in an eternal embrace.

I turned towards the distant islands. Violet was now no more than a spec on the horizon. As my blue-green sarong fluttered in the breeze, I looked out over the fragile infinity of the ocean, and smiled.

And I had the strangest feeling that Perry was smiling back.

A NOTE FROM BEN

I'd love to hear your thoughts on this book or any of the topics it explores, comments, suggestions for future work, or corrections—do drop me a line at benstarlingauthor@gmail.com. I look forward to hearing from you.

Writing this story has been a rewarding labor of love. And there are several more stories to be told. Reader reviews make all the difference, and your review would be invaluable to me as I continue to write. If you feel strongly about this story and would like to post a review, please visit my *Something in the Water* page at Amazon and/or Goodreads.

If you believe your friends would enjoy this book, I'd be very grateful if you would share it with them on Facebook and Twitter.

With best wishes from,

Ben

London, England
September 21, 2015

ACKNOWLEDGEMENTS

This book could not have been written without the kind help of some very special people. Napier Marten's generous support and encouragement made *Something in the Water* possible. Napier is the founder of Mirthquake, a multimedia organization dedicated to raising awareness of the special relationship between humans and cetaceans, a key theme in my novel. It was Napier who challenged me to write this book, and I am enormously grateful to him. I hope that this story will help highlight the plight of our fragile oceans, and the role that I believe love will play in making our world whole.

A heartfelt thank you also goes to Robin Alcott, Linda Alton, Marc Rogoff of Marc Rogoff Photography, Julian Smart of Jutoh, Diane Layton, Margaret McGaffey Fisk, Edington the Great Dane (who ate my first manuscript), and all my kind beta readers, blog tour hosts and interviewers. And of course, Melisa....

Read an extract from a short story in the same series…

Something
in the
Air

BEN STARLING

EDINGTON
PRESS

Something in the Air is the first short story in this soul-stirring series by Ben Starling. *Something on the Fly* coming soon. Continue the journey begun...

California, May, 1973

With her hip thrust to the side and her hand resting there, she stood like she always had. The exact same pose as in the photo I'd carried in my wallet that the bullet tore through.

"Daniel?"

The river before me and the leaves on the gentling trees had frozen as the word rang in my head. It had come from behind me but it wasn't the sound of my name that had sucked the strength from my legs–it was the voice that had spoken it. I willed my shoulders to relax and still with my back to her, exhaled slowly.

"Happy birthday," I said.

"You remembered…!" said the voice from behind me.

"But you…left…town," I said, still staring ahead at–but not seeing– the river, the factory, the town's future.

"I came back."

My fingertips traced my clammy palms. I swallowed. Then, like a condemned man facing a firing squad, I finally turned.

And there she was. Dimples, shining, athletic. Buoyant and serene. Somehow all at the same time. With her hip thrust to the side and her hand resting on it.

"Hello, Willow," (I think) I said. I took her in, piece by piece before assembling the whole. Bittersweet memories. Memories I had tried to control with denial in the few private moments I had had during my endless deployment at Quang Tri. But a day, an hour hadn't passed when she hadn't slipped into my thoughts.

"It's been a while." She held my gaze with those green eyes. Her hand twirled a strand of hair. "Nearly three years."

"I know, Willow."

"You never wrote."

"You knew I wouldn't…I couldn't. It was too–"

She shifted her gaze to the shiny new factory on the far side of the river. The top of its chimney stack was level with the roadside viewpoint where we stood a quarter mile away. The tilt of her head, the half-smile that accompanied everything she said, were unchanged. But the plaits were gone, replaced with business-like, tied back hair. Instead of tatty bell-bottoms, she wore a crisp safari suit.

"You won't have seen that place before," she said. "Well, not operational."

"The guy at the gas station told me about it. That chimney must be a hundred feet high."

"Never seen it smoking though," she said.

"They must use it–the top's sooty."

"That place employs half the town's young men. Let's hope it can take more–now they're coming home." Her voice lowered. "Bobby Saxon gone. Geoff Rogers burned, lost both hands. Blue Walters? You remember Blue?" she asked.

"Captured. Still missing."

"He deserved better. You all did. I thought you'd head for the bright lights a soon as you'd received your honorable discharge and ticker tape parade. Well," she faltered, "there *should* have been a parade. "And Daniel– I'm so proud of you. I heard about the medal…"

"It was…nothing."

She shifted her weight from foot to foot, then looked down. "So…why have you come home?"

"I have some last respects to pay and a house to sort out. I guess old boats and gas engines don't mix."

"Everyone went to the funeral. Even Sam and Curly Collins."

Her eyes tensed and for a moment she looked about to speak.

"Willow?"

"Your uncle was under a lot of pressure–one man against a powerful corporation. That must explain the witness statements."

"Pressure or not, he was no drinker. No way he'd go to sea drunk. But how could I get a proper investigation started from seven thousand miles away? I'm sorry–I raised my voice."

"I know how close you were. With him gone, there was no one to oppose that factory. It's here now, whether we like it or not. I guess we better learn to love it."

I studied the spaghetti pipework that joined the stainless storage tanks to the sprawling buildings. "You're probably right."

"So…what are your plans, Daniel?"

"Not sure. I have to decide what to do with Steve's house. Apparently it needs rewiring, there's a hole in the roof, some rotten floorboards…"

"And when you've decided?"

"Head for the Big Apple. Charlie Macklin's old man says he'll see me, give me some tips, make some introductions. It would be dumb to not show up."

"They say you saved Charlie's life."

"The M16's a remarkable weapon until it jams."

"His dad's the guy with the Wall Street firm, right? When you make that million, don't you dare forget us, Daniel Dragan."

"You can take the boy out of San Prospero et cetera, et cetera. I just want to see the city, meet up with some buddies, hang out. Don't know if I could ever work there–as Uncle Steve says–said–it's better to be clean poor than filthy rich."

She took a few steps towards my VW camper. Looked inside. I caught her frown in the window reflection.

"Been living in it," I explained.

She turned slowly. "'Fraid I have to get back."

"Willow, did you ever complete your studies?"

She coughed before answering. With that raspy edge, it sounded like a smoker's cough. Surely she hadn't started–

"I'm qualified now. Working at Meredith Tucker's practice on the corner of Main and Hoover. Specialize in small animals. But around here our definition of small is pretty big…"

"Is Meredith still saving souls for the Salvation Army in her spare time?"

"Who has spare time? Plus I have an animal sanctuary to run. Jonah Bellows rents me some land on his farm. A few cats, chickens, ducks, abandoned Christmas presents. And Ray-Me, who's responsible for me starting the place. She's been with me three years now. Never thought she'd live."

"I'm guessing she's a doe?"

She nodded.

"She made it because you're good at what you do," I said.

"It was Meredith who saved her. The poor animal died on the operating table but she got her heart started again."

"As modest as ever. I bet you helped."

"I may have a fancy certificate on my wall but you know what? It's L-O-V-E the animals respond to best of all. It was lucky that Humphrey joined us a few days later."

She saw my puzzled expression.

"Humphrey the donkey. He's blind and who wants a blind donkey? Ray-Me had just about given up on life when Humphrey came in. They adopted each other as soon as they met and became inseparable. Ray-Me was soon bounding around, looking after Humphrey. As donkeys are very sociable animals, it did wonders for him too."

"So Ray-Me became his seeing eye deer? Sounds like a great *eye-dea* to me."

She smiled. "Still the comedian, I see. Point is, never underestimate the power of love. Afraid I gotta scoot–Amy Fletcher's finally bringing Joe Frazier in for neutering. His tally this month includes four car tyres and a ripped off bus fender."

I resisted the temptation to ask if a dose of L-O-V-E could remove the Rottweiler's testicles.

She opened the door of her '65 Dodge and I traveled back to that thundery August 1970 morning. We'd hugged then, broke apart, cried, hugged again. Her sobs had followed me inside the army barracks and on into the unknown when I shipped out with my platoon the next day.

The Dodge looked as if it had been through a war too. "Did you replace the radiator?"

"No–your gum's still blocking up the hole, just fine."

She swung one long leg, then the other in and wriggled her bottom to get comfortable. A bottom I'd first admired on the sports track as she broke the school hurdling record for the third time. Pretty soon I'd become a regular at the track too as I stretched, sprinted and jumped my way to zero victories.

She wound down the window.

"Willow? Look I'm around for a few days. I'll be at Steve's place. Maybe we could–"

She gunned the engine before letting it idle.

"You'll never guess who moved in across the street from your uncle."

~~~

Available now FREE at www.ben-starling.com

and FREE on Kobo.

Also available on Amazon.

Something in the Air is a short story in the same series as the novel, *Something in the Water*.

CONNECT WITH BEN

Twitter.com/benstarlingauth
Facebook.com/authorbenstarling
Goodreads.com/benstarling
Pinterest.com/benstarlingauth

www.ben-starling.com

Sign up at www.ben-starling.com to be notified of key events and new releases from Ben. He looks forward to hearing from you!

WORKS BY BEN STARLING

Something in the Water

Something in the Air

Something on the Fly (coming soon)

Printed in Great Britain
by Amazon